CW01638166

Other CULLEN books by Mark Farrer (in chronological order)

Dirty Barry

Where Seagulls Dare

(Woof Justice)

Bronchial Billy

A Fistful Of Collars

Pale Ale Rider

The Good The Bad & The Rugby

The Shed Pool

LAY MISTY FOR ME

mark farrer

funny business press

LAY MISTY FOR ME

ISBN: 978-1-9164892-7-1

Published by Funny Business Press

To Maisie
For knowing that thinking is so important.

This is a work of fiction.
Names, characters, places and incidents either are products of the author's imagination or are used fictitiously.
Any resemblance to actual events or locales or persons, living or dead, is entirely coincidental.
Except for Big Paul.

Here is the bird that never flew.

CONTENTS

ONE
TWO
THREE
FOUR
FIVE
SIX
SEVEN
EIGHT
NINE
TEN
ELEVEN
TWELVE
THIRTEEN
FOURTEEN
FIFTEEN
SIXTEEN
SEVENTEEN
EIGHTEEN
NINETEEN
TWENTY
TWENTY-ONE
TWENTY-TWO

POSTSCRIPT

AUTHOR'S NOTE

ONE

Malcolm Baxter had a face like a badly dislocated knee. It was an unpleasant arrangement of oddly-placed puffiness and bulging outrage choked beneath a mass of wiry grey hair which bristled at his temples and around his large ears. Below it was a small collection of chins which looked like they had been picked from a gourmet cheese board: a soft one, a blue one and one covered in ash.

In times of consternation, frustration, irritation or agitation - the combined sum of which represented 90% of his resting state - his prominent features would swiftly rearrange themselves, like gullwing doors disappearing into the bodywork of an exotic sports car. All that remained was a wide, bulging glare with blue veins in his nose and cheeks and a vivid redness everywhere else.

Malcolm, when annoyed, was half man, half angry bruise.

Actually, *Sir* Malcolm to you. And, since his father had passed away, to everyone. Even his son. And it was his son who was bearing the brunt of his annoyance right now.

"Emergency landing! Emergency bloody landing! It's a blasted disgrace." Malcolm spluttered.

Roly waited as Storm Malcolm continued unabated in the forlorn hope that it would shortly blow itself out. It had made landfall in Arrivals, whirled through the carpark and raged along a pre-determined path on the journey from Edinburgh airport, verbal wreckage strewn left and right as his father had gazed absently out of the windows from the backseat, his invective hitting the back of Roly's headrest like an aural jackhammer. Roly gripped the steering wheel tightly and tried not to grimace at his father in the rear-view mirror.

"They're only doing their job, Sir."

"Doing their job!" Malcolm snorted. "Firstly, their job is to get their passengers - in this case me - safely and swiftly to their destination. An emergency landing at bloody Manchester is a diversion, a delay and completely unnecessary. How does that constitute doing their damned job?"

Roly sighed again, more quietly this time. "And secondly?"

"What?"

"Secondly?" He tilted his chin upwards as if prodding his father's memory with it.

"Oh, yes. Secondly, how is it a bloody emergency? I mean how?"

"A man died, you said."

"Yes. Past tense. Died." Malcolm fumed. "Chap's dead. Why not just continue on to Edinburgh and get his blasted body off when we arrive?"

Roly considered this for a moment. "Because you can't have a container with more than 100ml of liquid in the cabin?"

Malcolm looked at his son in beggared disbelief. "You, boy, have all the intelligence of a full nappy. More likely, they just decided to add two hours to my journey time. Two hours!"

"I don't suppose they took that particular course of action simply to inconvenience you, Sir." Roly clenched his teeth, inwardly wincing at both the *boy* and the required *Sir.*

"Chap was already dead." Malcolm repeated. "Diverting to Manchester isn't going to resuscitate him is it?"

"I imagine it's standard aviation procedure - if someone dies during the flight?"

"Standard aviation procedure? Stuff and nonsense!" Malcolm shook his head several times. When those around him did not come up to his standards he would glower, an angry cloud hovering over him. This was augmented by an aggressive swagger and twitchy eye for any flaw or shortcoming on which he could pounce to ridicule and pityingly wound its owner. His effortless superiority - proclaimed, assured and reinforced through repetition and volume - was further displayed by his wardrobe of ever-present suit of sagging Tweed, rubbed bare at the elbows and running thin at the knees, a pair of braces rather than a belt to keep his trousers up and a loud Baxter tartan waistcoat, the red, green and gold of it all contributing to the overall display of plump, shiny, self-entitlement.

Sir Malcolm Sholto Finlay Baxter looked like a gloating tweed puffin overstuffed with £50 notes.

"How was London?" Roly tried changing the subject.

"Waste of bloody time." Malcolm growled. "Bloody doctors. I went to school with him, you know. Always was a duffer. Harley Street is not what it was, boy, let me tell you. Bloody blood pressure? Bloody nonsense. Two days out of my week when I need it least."

He glanced at his wristwatch and then glared out of the window, silently fuming. For a mere moment. On reflection Roly might have chosen a better time to give his father the letter.

"What's this?"

"It's, um, a letter. From Tessa. Came while you were away." Tessa Hancock, was the Sales Director. The past tense here being *was.* Roly swallowed hard. "It's a resignation letter."

"What!" Malcolm exploded and tore open the letter. He rapidly scanned the contents and turned a shade more scarlet. "This is preposterous! She can't do this. It says here *effective immediately*!"

"Yes, Sir."

"She has to give me notice!"

"She has, Sir. It seems that she had a backlog of untaken annual leave so, when you factor that in…"

"This is nonsense!" Malcolm fumed. "She's supposed to be hosting Tesco in two days!"

"Three, Sir."

"This is her project. She's been on it for months. She can't pull out at the last minute!"

"She has, Sir."

"Well, blasted well get her back!"

"I can't, Sir."

Malcolm, stunned, returned to the wording in the letter. "The woman's mad! *Overbearing*, she says. Ha! One woman's overbearing is another man's management style. Whose blasted firm does she think this is? It's got my name on it, it's mine! Am I supposed to sit back and watch it burn?"

"I don't-"

"And *condescending*!" Malcolm scowled at Roly. "That means I talk down to people."

"I know, Sir, I-"

"And here: *Nitpicky!* She says I'm nitpicky. That

should be hyphenated by the way." He threw the letter onto the seat and glared out at the scenery. Roly drove on in silence. After a few minutes, Malcolm gave a deep growl.

"Tesco are still coming, I take it?"

"Yes, Sir. Cheryl texted earlier to confirm."

"I don't have time for this! This naffing… nonsense! *We* don't have time."

"Sir?"

"Well, you're going to have to take over from her now, aren't you?"

"Me?"

"Yes. Who else?" Malcolm glowered. "That's rhetorical by the way."

"Sir, I-"

"Never mind all that. We have a lot to do between now and Wednesday. Clean-up, signage, rehearsals, paperwork..."

"I know, Sir."

"Don't *I-know-sir* me! How in blue blazes did I ever allow that stupid woman… Never mind. Put your foot down."

Malcolm continued fuming while Roly attempted to govern the Bentley swiftly onwards. The road swooped down a long strait, scratchy hillside and heather to their left and right, as they powered towards a crossroads. Turning left at the junction they passed a sign saying *Welcome to the Scottish Borders* and then swept past a stand of fir trees before a long bend brought the familiar rolling landscape into view, hillocks and fields extended like a rumpled green duvet folding into the base of the Moorfoot Hills.

A large sign shaped like a rooster on the roadside bore

the postcode and displayed an arrow indicating a turning on the right up ahead. But between their car and it stood a group of a dozen protesters, lining the verge and the turning bay opposite the site entrance, placards being raised and waved. In the luscious interior of the Bentley, the shouts and jeers came through in an unruly muffle but Malcolm's eyes still popped out on outraged stalks.

"What the Dickens?"

"They've been here since Friday." Roly explained matter-of-factly. "Waste of time if you ask me. They're not achieving anything."

Malcolm turned to his son in disbelief. "Not achieving anything! Have you lost all your marbles?"

"They just stand there and shout when you drive past." Roly shrugged.

Malcolm tried a quick scan of the faces as the car turned in and drove up to the main entrance, an unmanned security barrier stretching across the width of the road with an empty booth next to it. All he caught was some flashes of hi-viz tabards and a head of pink hair. Pink!

"Get rid of them." Malcolm ordered, scarlet-faced.

"What?"

"Man that barrier, day and night. And get rid of them."

"But-"

"But what? Get rid of them."

"But… why?" Roly screwed up his face under his father's glare before adding: "Sir."

Malcolm looked back through the rear window to the group in the distance, their placards now down. He turned to his son, his face like a smacked arse. "What do you think Tesco will say if they see that lot? Do you think they'll be pleased?"

"I think-"

"Well, don't. Think, I mean. Leave that to me since, clearly, thinking is not your strong suit. If they're here when Tesco come, I swear to God…" By way of completing his sentence Malcolm reached into an inside jacket pocket and brought out a small pill bottle. He flipped the lid, took two small tablets from it and swallowed them with difficulty, his hands trembling as he did so. "Actually. Never mind. You focus on the prep-work - that's more in your line isn't it?"

"Sir?"

"Paper-clips, coffee cups, stationery - stuff that doesn't fight back? You do what you're good at, boy. I'll get Eddie to do this. He'll bloody get rid of them." Malcolm suddenly squinted at his son in the rear-view mirror. "Is that a moustache? On your top lip?"

"Yes." Roly bit his cheek.

"Why doesn't it look like one then?"

"Well, admittedly, it is at an early stage."

"What stage? Research and Development?" Malcolm scoffed. "Get rid of it."

"Sir?"

"You heard me. I don't want Tesco scared off by some offensive bum-fluff. You get rid of that; I'll tell Eddie to get rid of them."

Roly cast his eyes down. Silently he rolled down the window and punched in his PIN at the small control panel. The barrier swung slowly up and they drove beneath it and onto the premises known formally as Baxter Farms Limited.

"Oh, bloody hell!" Shirley exclaimed as the kitchen knife sliced through a fingertip. One of the problems with cooking in Paul's kitchen was that he had a terrible habit of sharpening his knives until you could shave with them. Being a woodworker he had a thing for keeping his tools in tip-top order: *you never know when you need a sharp edge*, he would say, despite the fact that he seemed much keener on sharpening his tools than actually using them. Doubly true for these knives. And it wouldn't have been so bad if she could get used to them, but she cooked in his kitchen so rarely that, whenever she did, she forgot. This was the result.

The sun had been out all day, the afternoon warm and mellow, and they were both looking forward to a cosy evening over beer and burgers. Paul was out on the decking readying the barbecue, while she was chopping and prepping. But now she was bleeding over the worktop.

"Lover!" She yelled through the closed window but he couldn't hear her - or was choosing not to. None of Paul's windows opened due to the fact that they had been acquired cheaply - actually freely - from the back of a double-glazing lorry. Installed in the winter, Paul had been pleased as punch. Come the spring he had tried to open them, only to find that they were fixed units.

"Bugger." She ran her finger under the cold tap for a minute or so and then grabbed at some kitchen roll and wrapped it round her finger. Then she reached under the sink for his First Aid Kit. No, she corrected herself, his Second Aid Kit. Paul's First Aid Kit, as he was fond of reminding her, was in his van along with most of his other prized possessions. Except his dogs, Ant and Dec, two energetic Jack Russell terriers who accompanied him everywhere and were, at this very minute, also out on the deck arguing between them over one of the spare pair of slippers she kept in his bedroom.

She opened the red box bearing a white cross and rooted down through a top layer of depleted paracetamol foils, empty boxes of plasters and other mostly used detritus. Her hand came to rest on a vac-pacced something and she pulled it out of the box and then flung it onto the floor in horror. It was a packet of bacon. A very old packet of bacon.

"Paul!" He heard this time.

"Shirl?" He poked his head around the kitchen door. "Everything alright?"

"No!" She waggled her bloody kitchen-roll-wrapped finger at him. "No, it bloody well is not. I've just cut my finger on your bloody samurai knives and, searching for a plaster, I found this." She pointed at the offending item on the floor.

"Oh, cool." Paul nodded appreciatively.

"Cool? Look at it. It's green!"

"Ah, it's alright. It's bacon. Bacon never goes off."

"What? Of course, it does. Look at it. I was just about to throw it out."

"Glad you didn't." Paul grinned. "See - you've literally saved my bacon."

Shirley wasn't amused. "I have not saved your bacon and I *am* throwing it out."

"Shirl!"

"Never mind *Shirl.* It's disgusting. What the hell is an old packet of bacon doing in your First, I mean Second, Aid Kit?"

"It's for emergencies."

"Emergencies? Like "In Emergency Break Glass"

emergencies?"

"Well, yeah."

"More like "In Emergency Get Food Poisoning" emergencies you mean."

"Look… imagine you've cut your finger."

"I have!" She waved the bloody digit at him.

"Right, obv. Soz. What could be nicer than having a nice bacon sarnie to cheer you up after?"

"After what? After I've puked everywhere from the smell?"

"It's shrink-wrapped."

"And that's how it's staying. Get it out of my house!"

"It's my house." Paul protested, not unreasonably.

"Well get it out of your house then! It's disgusting."

"Aw, Shirl. Come on. I'll wash it under the tap."

She brandished her damp finger again. "I've already done that."

"I meant the bacon."

"What?"

"I'll wash it under the tap. It'll be fine."

"Are you mental? You can't eat that."

"You can't throw away perfectly good bacon." Paul was appalled.

"No, but you can throw away desperately bad bacon. Which is what *that* is!"

"Shirl." Paul said calmly. "Be reasonable."

"Be reasonable?" She looked at him quizzically. "Are you an addict?"

"A what?"

"An addict? Are you addicted to bacon? Meat in general, in fact."

"No." Paul frowned. "Although you make it sound like that's a bad thing."

"It is a bad thing! Think about your gout. Bacon doesn't help does it? Bacon's one of the things you should be cutting down on. Or cutting out."

"What!" Spluttered Paul.

Paul had gout, or periodic bursts of it, and had been reluctant to admit it to her. Had hidden it from her, in fact, to the point where she had foolishly thought he'd been hiding… well, she didn't want to admit now what she had thought he'd been hiding.

"I think you're an addict." She put her hands on her hips and looked at him intently. "Let's look at the evidence, shall we? Exhibit A: mouldy bacon kept under the sink. That's what addicts do - they have secret stashes they don't want other people to find. Hide it from themselves so they can deny they're addicted."

"It's not hidden! It's there for emergencies."

"What other stashes have you got? Have you got some in your van?"

"That's my First Aid Kit!"

"Ha! Proof, if indeed proof were needed." She gloated. "Exhibit B: when did you last go a day without meat? Have you ever gone a day - not a week or anything, just a day - without eating meat?"

"Yes! No! I don't know!" Paul cried, feeling not unlike a witness under heavy cross-examination.

"You haven't, have you? Ever!" Shirley rested her case. "You're an addict."

"I'm not! I'm just…"

"In denial?"

"Normal!"

"Like I said, in denial."

"I'm not!" Paul folded his arms, harrumphing, and thought for a moment. "Look, Shirl, everyone eats meat.

It's normal. There's all these adverts on telly for yoghurt and cereal and shit but you never see adverts for beef! Or bacon! You know why? Because people love beef and bacon and buy it anyway. And they're never gonna stop buying it. Next you'll be saying that we're all addicted."

"You know what? You're right." Shirley nodded.

"See?" Paul beamed.

"We are all addicted. Society's addicted!"

"No, no, no." Paul put his head in his hands.

"I see it every day, standing behind that counter in Greggs. People coming in for their sausage rolls, pasties, Scotch pies. Someone has to make a difference. We have to start somewhere. We've started with our vegan sausage roll and people are buying it! People are waking up and seeing the light. We don't have to eat meat."

"Shirl."

"No. That's it." She picked up the Second Aid Kit once more. "First I'm going to put a plaster on my finger. There are plasters in here I take it?"

Paul shrugged.

"Then I'm going to scour this place and throw out any meat I can find."

"Shirl!"

"Then I'll do the same in your van."

"Shirl!"

"Then I'm gonna go home and do the same in my flat."

"This is ridiculous." Paul blinked.

"And then we - you and me - are going to adopt a low-meat diet. To start with."

"To start with?"

"Yes. Come on, lover." Shirley said brightly. "It'll be an education."

You're not wrong there, thought Paul. This has taught me a lesson.

"You there! Be gone now. Off with you!"

Elaine turned her head towards this outburst and tried to spot the man shouting. Between the placards and the jostling shoulders hoisting them, it was hard to see anything more than glimpses of a chunky khaki-clad figure striding towards them. This handful of people Jakki had managed to collect were clumping together rather than spreading out, trying to look more than they were. But he was brandishing a shiny staff, the polished wood gleaming in the afternoon sun, and barking in a strong Afrikaans accent.

That was the giveaway.

"Shit! Hide me." Elaine dodged quickly back into the gaggle of protesters from her position near the front and sheltered behind Jakki's broad back.

"What are you doing?" Jakki tried turning to keep Elaine in view but it was like a horse trying to look at its rider. The placard she was holding wasn't helping her manoeuvrability.

"It's Eddie. Sir Malcolm's security man. Don't let him see me!" Elaine hissed and hunkered down further, wishing there were more bodies here than there were. Such a small group was a bit dispiriting really, but it was early days - Jakki had been at pains to remind her. *What was needed was a little time for the word to spread, the seed to grow. Posting on Facebook and sharing on Twitter, you'll see.* Jakki was confidence itself - sometimes completely unjustifiably so, Elaine thought - but you had to admire her persistence and tenacity. Actually, Elaine admired it whether one had to or not. That was what Elaine did in relationships: admired.

"You heard me! Get! Before I call the police!"

The accosting figure of Eddie was now almost upon them and he was sweating substantially, maybe from the simple exertion of swaggering so intently up the drive towards them or the inconvenience of wearing a restricting uniform in this unseasonal warmth. Or both. His uniform clearly belonged to him - it looked like he had lived and slept it in for many years - stained and worn shiny in places, stretched and folded here, bulging there. The tatty weathered trousers had clearly seen plenty of chairs in their time, the shirt-front plenty of takeaways.

Elaine, still cowering, felt Jakki's absence as her partner pushed forward until she was standing at the head of the group. Everyone had stopped chanting and their placards stood motionless in the air, bobbing slightly like discarded wine corks on a flat pond. In the silence Elaine unfolded herself and peeked through the heads to watch.

"This is a peaceful protest!" Jakki cried, her voice ringing across the open space in front of them. "We're not breaking any laws or causing any trouble."

Eddie drew up to her and Elaine could see how mismatched they were: Jakki was short and stout, a rotund Rubik's cube of a woman, with a wide neck and thick arms bare beneath her *Lay Off The Clucking Hens* T-shirt. This puffed-up security man was a thick chunk of brawn, leaning forward in an aggressive stance like a bulldog straining at its leash. He was smacking the ball on the end of his cudgel repeatedly into the palm of one hand.

"Is that what this is?" He had a really strong accent, Elaine had always struggled to work out what he was saying, even once someone had told her it was South African. *Ees thit wut theeses?*

Jakki passed her placard to Elaine and put her hands on her hips, projecting sass and defiance up into his scowling sweaty face. "What does it look like to you?"

"I can't tell what it is. But I know what it isn't." *Ah kent till wut it ees bot Ah nur wut et eesnt.* He thrust his face into Jakki's. "It isn't welcome round here." *Et eesnt wilkum hrand hier.*

"Well, tough toenails, sweatband. We're here and we're going to be here for a while. Better get used to us."

Eddie scanned the faces of the small group and when his eyes flicked and rest on Elaine's she knew the game was up.

"You!" He spat. "I should've guessed." *Ah shidve gist.*

Jakki looked around to see Elaine's face and then turned back to the man, scowling.

"And what's so wrong about that? She doesn't work here anymore you know. It's not against the law to gather peacefully here." She waved her hand in front of her as if presenting a place setting. "This is a public thoroughfare."

"This is a private road. That sign there? Says Private." *Prahvit.*

"A sign saying *private* does not make it private."

"Look. Disperse or it'll be the worse for you. You're not attracting anyone's attention." He gestured around to the emptiness beneath the enormous sky. "You're just wasting your time."

"Well, let us waste it in peace then." Jakki snarked. "If we're not bothering anyone."

Elaine reluctantly sidled to the front and stood beside Jakki, feeling the need to lend her moral support now that she had been recognised. Her reluctance only partly came from having to stand in full view; there was also a very strong odour of winning enclosure emanating from this thug.

"Listen, man. Don't give me all this. I have enough on my plate right now." *Leesten men, dunt geev me thit. Ah hiv eneff un ma plyte brayt nur.*

"Oh, I'm sorry, officer. Oh wait! No, you're not an officer, are you? You're just some chunk of change in cheap polyester."

Elaine winced. Jakki was on a roll and, when she was on a roll, would often slip into uncalled-for sarcasm which usually didn't end too well. For her. Eddie, she knew, would not take kindly to this - Elaine imagined he got plenty of that from Sir Malcolm Baxter all day long.

"Listen Eddie." Elaine piped up. "We're not here to make a fuss. We're just…"

"What?" The security man bridled, his puffy eyes narrowing as he focussed now on her. "If you're not here to make a fuss then why are you here? Of course, you're here to make a fuss. Now I'm warning you-" He lunged suddenly, swinging his staff in an arc in front of them at waist height. As one the group stepped back, their eyes wide. Even Jakki.

"Right. Call the police then!" Jakki said. "Let's see what they make of your threatening behaviour."

"Move away." He continued waving his stick, sweeping left and right, minesweeping the road, driving them backwards like sheep. "Go on! There's a perfectly good layby just up there, on the main road. The public road."

Jakki inhaled sharply, threw back her chest and held an outstretched hand towards her partner. "Elaine? Hand me my box of wasps!"

Elaine looked at Eddie, bemused, and tugged on Jakki's arm. "Jaks? Come on. Let's just move like he says."

Jakki was glowering, her teeth set, but she still backed off slowly as Eddie advanced with menace.

"This here." He drew an invisible line on the road in front of him with his staff. "This is the line you do not cross." He nodded over to the large layby some distance up the road. "There. You want to gather? There's a good place for you."

He folded his arms and waited while the group stood in silence. Elaine kept her grip on Jakki's arm but could feel her resisting. "Come on Jaks. Let's regroup over there."

"And give in to this… bell-end!"

"Please, Jaks? For me?" Elaine pleaded.

"What?" Jakki snatched her glare from Eddie and, looking at the dismay on her partner's face, instantly softened.

Elaine lowered her voice to a whisper and spoke out of the side of her mouth. "You know I'm not supposed to be here. I think we're closer than the permitted hundred yards."

Jakki blew out a lungful of air.

"Please Jaks?" Elaine said. "Look - here the only people who can see us are people coming into the plant. People who have a reason to be here. We're not going to change their minds are we? But over there, hundreds of cars passing every hour, we can reach a wider audience. Get our message heard!"

“Yah. You listen to her.” Eddie nodded in agreement and then checked himself as if wondering if he had just made things worse.

“Please, Jaks?”

Jakki blinked slowly and let her breathing return to something approaching normal. Looking again at Elaine’s pleading face, she let her own head drop and took hold of Elaine’s hand giving it a silent squeeze. Together they trooped obediently across the busy road, the rest of the group trailing behind them, and trudged up the wide verge towards the distant layby, placards dragging in the grass. Eddie watched them go, his eyes following the leading pair, still holding hands.

TWO

"Did you get rid of them?"

Malcolm was wondering why the stupid mouse on his laptop wasn't working and was busy banging it against the desk when his Chief of Security waltzed in, a gloomy look splashed across his sweaty tanned face.

"Yes, Sir." Eddie nodded. "But I have some bad news."

"Did you injure one of them?"

"No, Sir."

"More than one?"

"Regrettably not, Sir." *Rigrittubly nutsa.*

Eddie Helpmann was the epitome of an out-of-condition South Afrikaner. When he introduced himself to others as a Boer, people didn't know whether he'd said *Boer*, *boar* or *bore.* Although it didn't really matter because he was, in fact, all three. Recruited by Sir Malcolm Baxter on the back of some bigoted remarks he had made at a trade show when he thought he was out of earshot, Malcolm had recognised him as one of his own: a man who said what he liked and liked what he bloody well said. A man of action and a man of decisiveness. If not all of his actions were successful, and not all of his decisions correct, you couldn't fault him for his directness. Route One was his default setting and he was not a man who was ever troubled by his conscience.

What he should have been troubled by - but again wasn't - was indigestion. He had a roving appetite for bizarre foodstuffs and regarded something thought inedible as nothing more than a challenge thrown down by an unthinking, naive nature which had never been confronted with a stomach and a constitution like his. Eddie had the constitution of a wildebeest - if he only he had the gainliness of one as well.

For Eddie was a physical mess and, for someone with the unthinking directness of an unreconstituted bigot, the thinnest of skins. In the tradition of the Veldt where tourists would fly in to spot the Big Five - lion, leopard, rhino, elephant and buffalo - from this pantheon of physical attributes, Eddie had acquired a collection of the shortest straws: he had the hide of a leopard, the halitosis of a lion, the fleetness of foot of an elephant and the grace of a rhino. And he sweated like a buffalo.

Malcolm scowled. "Why ever not?"

"It's Elaine, Sir. She's one of them. Actually, she's one of them as well as one of them." Eddie smiled at his own witticism.

Malcolm had difficulty with Eddie's accent at the best of times. He spoke as if someone had flattened his face with a triple-ply saucepan. One had to persevere through the first few sentences, beginning each conversation anew by encouraging your brain to detect recognisable sounds and syllables - like fine-tuning a delicately fussy radio dial or cracking a stubborn safe. His staccato delivery and the contorted vowel and consonants which clashed in his mouth as he spat them out were the verbal equivalent of a ransom note. When the words resolved into something that made no sense, like this collection, it seemed like a lot of wasted effort.

"You're making no sense, man! Explain yourself." Malcolm gave the mouse a final, pointless bang.

"It's her alright." Eddie said, his lips moving with all the mobility of a letterbox. "She's a lezzer." *Tsuhr alhryt. Shiza lizza.* As if this confirmed it beyond all doubt.

"What?"

"Lesbian. Has sex with other women." The leer on Eddie's face spoke volumes. "Her partner's a right chunky monkey. Looks like Morrissey's let himself go."

"Elaine…? Morrison…?"

Malcolm was completely lost - Eddie's words were now registering as English but they still weren't making any sense at all.

"Morrissey." Eddie sighed. "Doesn't matter. They're the ringleaders, clear as day."

"Lesbians?"

"That's right." *Thits hryt.*

"And you can tell that because…?"

"Trust me. You can tell." Eddie gloated.

"Maybe *you* can." Malcolm flicked the useless mouse across his desk and gave Eddie his full attention. "What are you talking about? *Who* are you talking about?"

"The protesters. The ringleaders are Elaine Dunwoody and her pal. Name of Jakki Banks."

"Elaine… Dunwoody…" In the misty distance a bell ran dully in Malcolm's head. His eyes grew large. "Isn't that-?"

"The very same. I recognised her straight away."

"She's not allowed to be here!"

Eddie nodded, offended. "None of them are really. That's a free country for you." He looked in vain for somewhere to spit.

"Well get rid of her!"

"I have. They have been…" Eddie searched for a *bon mot.* "Dispersed."

Malcolm snorted, his head shaking slightly from side-to-side, jowls wobbling in indignation. "*She* is not allowed to be here by virtue of the NDA and contract of employment *she* signed. The fact that her employment has been terminated does not invalidate those documents. She is in breach!"

Eddie gave a slow, fat blink. "What would you like me to do about it?"

Malcolm looked at the wall clock over Eddie's right shoulder, puffed out his not inconsiderable cheeks, and then glared at his Chief of Security. "Would it be too much to ask you to do your bloody job?"

Eddie straightened. "I have been, Sir. I have looked into Elaine's background, checked her social media posts and so on. This scissor sister of hers-"

"Scissor sister?"

"Lezza."

Malcolm shook his head, sorry he'd asked. "Maybe she's her actual sister?"

"Don't think so, Sir. Elaine is tiny. That one? Her eyes are as far apart as her gym sessions."

Malcolm gave an impatient sigh. "Is any of this relevant?"

"She's all over social media." Eddie continued. "Leads some kind of Animal Rights Activist Group called SLAAC."

"Slack?"

"SLAAC: Scottish Lesbians Against Animal Cruelty."

"Great." Malcolm spat. "That is exactly what we bloody need!"

"They're just a bunch of mouthy lezzers."

Malcolm rose to his feet and planted both hands on his desk, leaning into a growing anger like a ski-jumper on take-off. "Do I need to remind you that I am trying to close the biggest deal *ever* with this country's largest supermarket chain? Must it be restated that we must do everything we can - everything - to ensure we close this deal and that nothing - nothing - must get in the way. Can you perhaps see how this *bunch of mouthy lezzers* might represent a teeny-tiny obstacle to achieving this objective?"

Eddie stood to attention, tight-lipped. "Yes, Sir."

"So, I ask you again: would it be too much to ask you to do your bloody job?"

"No, Sir."

"Good. Glad to hear it." Malcolm took a deep breath and exhaled slowly, attempting to calm himself, his heart a red steam engine in his chest thumping in the silence. "Well?"

"Sir?"

"What do you intend to do?" He calmed, his voice dropping back to normal.

"Well." Eddie said, after a pause. "Unfortunately, they have broken no laws."

"Broken no-? Did I not just say that she is in breach of contract?"

"Yes, Sir. But you fired her, Sir."

"And?"

"Well, it's not really enforceable. I mean you could pursue it legally, take her to court. Lot of bother, cost, delay. It's more a clause inserted to dissuade-"

"I'm sorry." Malcolm glared. "Are you a lawyer now?"

"No, Sir."

"Or, maybe, my HR Director?"

"No, Sir. You fired her too."

Malcolm's jaw clenched. "Your point being?"

"Nothing, Sir." Eddie swallowed. "Just thought that, if you wanted to clinch this deal, then you want a... swifter resolution to the problem."

"Yes. I do. I do." Malcolm sighed and strode over to his large office window, his empire of dark green buildings and dotted copses rolling out in front of him, left and right, filling his view. "It's a good word: dissuade."

"Sir?"

"You said *dissuade*." Malcolm turned and locked eyes with Eddie. "Perhaps you could dissuade Elaine. Prevail upon her to see how persisting with these protests will adversely impact her… prospects."

"Of course. But supposing she is disinclined to do so?"

Malcolm grinned. "A man of your obvious talents?"

Eddie weighed the compliment up. "Maybe."

"Yes, well maybe she will need dissuading rather more forcefully - in which case I am sure you will be suitably imaginative." Eddie's hand crept unconsciously towards the wooden club hanging from his belt and Malcolm raised an admiring eyebrow. "Or maybe she will just acquiesce with enormous grace."

"Jakki, not Grace." *Jakki nut Gryse.* Eddie said. "Although, yeah, she is enormous."

"I'm Jakki. Two K's. The first one is silent." The rotund woman had a greying buzzcut and more metalwork in her ears than a portcullis. She bounced into the bar area from the toilets like a panda late for a gameshow and extended her hand enthusiastically. Elaine allowed her own to be swallowed by this chubby wrapper and engulfed in a pumping flesh hammer which had almost torn her arm from its socket. "First time at Bumpin' Doughnuts?"

"Um, yes."

"Welcome. Welcome." The smile on her face made her cheeks solidify and glow in the recessed spotlighting. "Do you like Marx?"

Elaine was thrown. "Well… their big knickers are hard-wearing."

"Karl Marx." The smile hadn't faded, even a touch. "Socialist Worker Party?" Jakki thumbed a lapel badge proudly.

"Ah. Not… really. No, sorry."

"Quite alright. No need for apologies. Recent convert myself actually. I think maybe that's why I am currently so enthusiastic about finding like-minded people." Jakki swivelled her head around the room. "I've checked out all of this lot - no takers. Like going door-to-door with a clipboard and spinach in your teeth. Saw you, fresh meat so to speak. No offence. Thought I'd give you a try."

Elaine marvelled at the unfiltered openness streaming from this fizzing bundle of energy. She could almost feel the heat from the woman's pulse and it was unsettling her thoughts. She wondered what to say in the brief silence and came up short.

"I'm Elaine." She managed.

"Great to meet you Elaine." Jakki's eyes shone with vitality and warmth. "Would you like a drink? First one for newbies is on the house."

"White wine please." Elaine pulled a tight smile. "Thank you."

"Chardonnay, Pinot Grigio or Sauvignon Blanc?"

"Um." Elaine froze while Jakki raised her eyebrows

enquiringly and waited. "Whichever's cheapest?" Elaine heard herself say and then wanted the ground to swallow her up. She blinked as Jakki accepted her answer like it was the most obvious thing in the world.

"Why not? Alcohol's poison isn't it? If you're going to piss in your tank, might as well save on the petrol." She whisked off towards the bar and Elaine stood, dizzy at the speed with which this tornado had swept her up in its path and made everything else shrink into a vanishing black dot. Under normal circumstances she would have been rooted to the spot, rigid with embarrassment at not knowing anyone or fitting in, feeling all eyes were on her, judging her, nudging each other, whispering criticisms and giggling. But here she was somehow anaesthetised, unbothered and numb, blinking at this Jakki's broad back at the bar wondering what on earth to say when she returned with the drinks. As Jakki marched back towards her, a wine glass in each hand, the shiny metal adornments on her brash boots winked in the recessed spotlights.

"You, um, have a lot of badges." Elaine accepted the glass of wine and indicated the extensive collection of enamel and tin decorating the lapels of Jakki's scuffed red leather jacket.

"I have lots of interests. Multiple and various." Jakki said, looking down at her chest. "Although I could do with culling some of these actually. Bit out of date a few of them." She looked up into Elaine's eyes, her face beaming and her eyes alive and round. "I have enormous amounts of energy. Very exothermic. Fast metabolism."

Elaine looked at her wondering how this accounted for her stature, but said nothing.

"Save The Whale. Save The Planet. Save …" Jakki

reeled off some of her badges.

"Isn't that a, well, a bit of a lost cause?"

"This? No! Nothing is impossible."

"Hmm." Elaine frowned, seeking a factual example to counter this claim that offended her sense of rationality. "Can you lick your own ear?"

Jakki paused for the briefest moment, unthrown, and considered this as if it was the most reasonable question she'd ever been asked. "Probs not." She concluded. "But if you try, I bet you get seats to yourself on the bus!"

Elaine smiled and gave a little shake of her head.

"Also." Jakki added as if finishing an interrupted conversation. "I'm vegan."

"Really?" Elaine was immediately intimidated. Not by the announcement - vegans usually announced their proclivities without invitation; she knew there was no such thing as an uncommitted vegan. She instantly heard a small alarm go off inside her. This, she felt, was one of those times in everyone's life where a crucial crossroads is presented in front of you, out of the blue, and you instinctively realise you need to make an executive decision and whichever way you go it will affect you for the rest of your life. Stick or twist, in or out, now or never. This woman, whom she barely knew, seemed like an untameable force of nature. A larger-than-life juggernaut with iffy brakes and a barely working Satnav - you either got on board or you got out of the way. There was no middle ground.

"Me too." Elaine heard herself say.

"Excellent!" Jakki said, beaming like a loon-eyed Brian Blessed. She put a weighty arm around Elaine's shoulder and steered her towards a booth.

Elaine craned her neck back towards the rest of the

chatting Doughnut Bumpers. "But I was supposed to meet Vicki and introduce myself."

"Don't worry. Vicki likes to think she's in charge but really…? More a figurehead than a leader you might say." Jakki reassured, her voice dropping slightly. "Plus… she's transitioning. It's a difficult time." Elaine's eyes widened and Jakki smiled. "I know right? One minute you're rooting through her knickers, then whoops - unexpected item in the bagging area!"

Jakki stopped suddenly and gave Elaine a meaningful look - although Elaine couldn't identify the specific meaning. "I like you." Jakki said. "I think we're going to get on like a house on fire."

And that was how it had started.

"It's a summons, Sir. For next Tuesday. You're being called as a witness."

"Is it? Bloody waste of time!" Malcolm's face was turning redder and redder as he puffed angrily on a fat cigar. Health and Hygiene regulations were very clear about the absence of smoking on any premises involving food production and Roly had tried many times to dissuade his father from this habit. But his father being what he was, and Roly being what he was, these attempts had usually involved unseen facial grimaces, unheard polite coughs or unacknowledged wafts of hands at real or imaginary smoke. Roly wrinkled his nose as the acrid smell enveloped him and stifled a cough.

"Is everything ok, Sir?"

"Damn it, you've got eyes, haven't you?" Malcolm's breathing faltered as he stood grasping the back of a chair bearing most of his weight and Roly swallowed hard.

"Are you sure you should be smoking, Sir? Did the doctors-"

"Damn the blasted doctors! If I listened to bloody doctors, I'd be in a blasted bath chair eating egg in a cup!"

Roly winced. "Would you like to sit down?"

"Sit down? Sit down? I've got work to do, boy! I'll sit down when I'm dead." Malcolm stubbed out his cigar and glared out of the boardroom window. "Critchleys, Critchleys, damned Critchleys. What do they think they're playing at? I am well within my rights to ask them to leave. This eviction - it's their own damned fault!"

"I don't quite see how-"

"I'm sure you don't. We've already established the paucity of your eyesight, boy." Malcolm sneered. "It is quite simple. I own the land. They are my tenants. I give them perfectly legal notice to quit. They refuse. I initiate eviction proceedings. They appeal against it. And here we are."

Malcolm snatched the letter from his son and threw it a scant look of disgust.

The desk phone rang and Roly waited for his father to pick it up but he seemed miles away. After five rings, Roly answered it.

"Sir? Jean says there's a call for Tessa. Shall I take-?"

"Leave it, boy!" The mention of the sacked Sales Director instantly rechannelled Malcolm's annoyance. "She's gone and good riddance. I'll handle this." His father snatched the receiver from him and punched Line Two. "Yes?"

"…"

"No, you can't speak to her."

"..."

"Because she's got my dick in her mouth, that's why!"

He slammed the phone down, a victorious smile on his face.

"Who, er, was it, Sir?" Roly asked.

"Who bloody cares!"

"Did they say a name?"

"Fanshaw, Kershaw, something like that." Malcolm started scanning the court letter again.

"Kilshaw?"

"That's it." Malcolm looked up.

Roly swallowed hard. "That's Cheryl Kilshaw, Sir. From Tesco."

Informally, and popularly, Baxter Farms Limited was known to everyone as *the chicken sheds*. Each was three hundred meters of green maximum-security prison for hens, and there were eighteen of them in total. Silent and brooding, these bottle green metal warehouses were each alive inside with tens of thousands of egg-layers. But it wasn't their size or their silence which struck you when you got close to one - it was the smell. Fetid, stinking, ripe - there were many words you could use to describe the air as you approached, but breathable wasn't one of them. Inhaling was like trying to swallow a hot, gangrenous scarf. The ammonia in the air stung your eyes, the sulphurous odour of the droppings gouged at your nostrils, stripping their lining. In summer, the thick, heavy stench pressed down on you and made you retch.

God knows how the chickens managed, although they had no choice in the matter. Inside each stuffed and stuffy warehouse were 60,000 animals drowning in the air, as thick as water, which filled your throat, choked every pore, corrupted every alveoli. Huge fans at one end of the shed fed fresh joyful air in, only for it to be stained and corrupted so that by the time it emerged, blinking into the daylight at the other end of the monstrosity, it was exhausted, drained and literally out of breath. The dust from feathers and dried droppings floated lazily in this alien atmosphere, kicked up by squabbles and fights between spiky residents, whereupon it descended slowly to coat every surface, lying thick and deep like stinking ash in some infernal litter tray.

And the noise! The host of birds squawking a piercing cacophony, the jagged sound scratching and clawing at your ears. Endless scrabbling and jostling, arguments and battles for territory, condensed into a compact and confined battlefield that none could escape or hide from. Bleeding and limping, wounded birds everywhere - eyes gouged, beaks destroyed, wings clipped, feet chewed or broken by overcrowding or getting caught in metal latticework and machinery which moved the conveyors bringing in feed and removing eggs.

Baxter Farms owned all the land that was visible in this glen where the Scottish Borders rubbed shoulders with its northern neighbour Midlothian, bounded by the impressive Moorfoot Hills to the east and Cloich Forest to the west. In this picturesque valley, ten of the sheds were clustered together near the main site entrance. Huddling up close to each other, arranged in rows and columns like some claustrophobic 3D spreadsheet. The remaining eight were scattered around the landscape, almost entirely hidden from view by woodland or the natural rolling topography. Accessible only by unmarked or B-roads, dropped in the middle of nowhere, they were surrounded by curated woodland screening them from rare passers-by. Here you might catch a glimpse of a roof gable, there a chimney, if you craned your neck at the right split-second as you zoomed past on the A703.

To the uninformed commuters racing daily from their Borders homes to their Edinburgh workplaces, the purpose of the sheds was not at all clear. There were no signs, no windows, no lighting or hoardings. Nothing to show that these buildings were even in use, unless you got up close - the smell often precluding that - and saw the huge fans on the outside of the building stirring in their enormous cases. A few 4x4 vehicles would occasionally come and go, never more than one at a time, never more than one man in the vehicle. Several times a day, a refrigerated juggernaut would pull up at the security barriers and trundle into the site. These unmarked behemoths anonymously came and went, delivering unbelievable quantities of feed or medicine, or carrying away newly-laid eggs.

Eggs. Hundreds of thousands of them. Baxter Farms were Scotland's largest egg supplier. Almost a million eggs, every single day, packed and delivered to stores and supermarkets, hotels and restaurants, up and down the country. To Sir Malcolm Baxter, it was a vision of loveliness - chicken sheds basking in the autumnal sun, winking in the light as it blessed the beautiful rolling countryside all around. To his son, Roly, it was an ugly, brutal money-making machine, powered by animals that were barely adults and who would never make it to full maturity. It had no heart, no compassion, no conscience. His father didn't care about the environment, climate change, animal welfare, employee satisfaction, food health or corporate social responsibility. Not unless any of those things contributed directly and swiftly to the bottom line. *It's a cut-throat business*, his father was fond of saying. *There are a host of competitors out there eager to steal my customers, slash at my profit margins, watch my life's work die. I have customers who want to squeeze me for every penny, bleed me dry at every point, ask for contributions to their branding, save themselves money on their supply chains, grant them priority delivery and guaranteed volumes whenever they are needed. Don't talk to me about bloody climate change or social responsibility. I'm a business not a charity. You want environmental sensitivity, animal rights? Try Oxfam!*

In the central cluster of buildings near the main entrance there were only two with windows. One was the original farmhouse, which had stood on this land when it had been a traditional farm so many years ago. A home once surrounded by beautiful views in all directions but which had been gradually fenced in, each successive shed constructed around it and encroaching upon it until the house itself was lost from view, its inhabitants cursed for ever to see only dark green corrugated metal beneath an ever-dwindling sky.

The other building with windows, all limited to the upper level, was the administrative annex - a series of six interconnected offices along a central spine, windows along an inner corridor looking across to each other, and a measly ration of one external window each giving views of the looming shed next door on one side (reserved for HR, Quality, Finance and IT) and on the other side with magnificent views of the rolling Moorfoots (reserved for management, Marketing and Sales). It was from here that Malcolm could look out and admire his domain, like Alexander without the weeping.

Roly stepped from a small side door to this annex.

Wearing faded blue, spattered overalls and white wellies he trudged over to his Landrover, struggling with an unruly armful of signs and a toolbag. He hated this sitework, entering the sheds, enduring the stench and trying to blot out the awful sounds. Few who ever plucked half a dozen eggs from a supermarket shelf, opened the box to check them and saw them nestling fresh and pristine in their delicate holders would ever imagine the conditions under which these marvels of protein, one of the most nutritious foodstuffs on the planet, were produced.

Starting to sweat already, he looked up into a cloudless blue sky, warm and filled with birdsong and the smell of cut grass; then down at the stubborn, dried manure on his white boots. He hated this world he had been born into, this business he might one day inherit, this parent who called him *boy*. To be approaching forty and feel his life was going to be forever *this?* It made him want to weep. Roly threw the stuff into his car, slammed the boot closed, and sped out of the main gate.

THREE

A few miles along the A703 from the Baxter chicken sheds lies Eddleston, a small speck of a village, quiet and uneventful, with a population so small that, according to locals, they had to kill someone to start a cemetery. The village has a pub, a bus stop and a *Slow Down* sign and nobody pays much attention to any of them. Not even the bus drivers.

Set back from the main road, tucked away behind a swathe of trees, is a secluded street: Station Road. This road with no pavements is unusually wide, owing to the fact here once was a railway station with several lines and a siding, all now no longer in existence. Along this broad strip of tarmac are arranged the former station house and ranks of cosy cottages which wouldn't look out of place on the cover of a Thomas Hardy paperback. In one of these cottages, the former Post Office, a white single-storey house which long ago may have been thatched and now isn't, live Jakki and her partner Elaine.

If Jakki and Elaine were woollens then Jakki was definitely on the chunky side of the knitwear catalogue. Short and stout, her curves were plentiful and widescreen - she liked to think she was all in proportion but her overall aspect ratio was a little off. Hair, greying at the temples, tufty on top and shorn at the sides to a badgerish barely-there bristle. Ears pierced to the point where there was little gristle left to hold the copious hoops and studs of metal in place. Loose T-shirts, slogan heavy, worn under a large battered lipstick-red leather jacket - itself also bedecked with studs, badges and patches which sent offensive messages out in all directions. And leggings, always black, which tucked into or ended above, heavy leather boots, calf-height in a variety of day-glo colours.

Jakki was a domineering presence physically and her dress style was really a uniform for her movement *du jour*. An extension and advertisement for it which was designed to be an in-your-face statement of intent - Jakki could be very in-your-face if you please. Or if you don't please, it was all the same to her.

And the exact nature of her movement *du jour*? Well, blink and you'd miss it, because she had an eternally mobile agenda - one that would mutate and transform, sometimes in front of your very eyes, like a living virus in a petri dish seeking to evaluate anything it came across, then envelope it, attack it, destroy it and then, in order to keep itself fed, move on. And the food for this ravenous virus was debate, the more aggressive and rancorous the better. Jakki attacked every argument with vigour, every combatant with glee, every rival with vengeance in her eyes. She had a mind like a sabre and a tongue like a bullwhip.

Her beliefs were strong and articulated with a confidence and panache that left you gasping - it was only after you had retreated to lick your wounds and bolster your pride that you would realise there had been a hole in her argument, some fatal flaw, which now you could see but then, in the white heat of battle, you had crucially missed. But now you grasped it, now you could go revisit it, ask for a rematch, win the battle after that painful first skirmish!

But alas for you, Jakki would have moved on. She had gorged on your poor, overwhelmed inarticulacy, disabled you with lightning wit and a formidable arsenal stuffed with armour-piercing data. You were a defeated enemy, a problem solved, and she no longer had interest in you. Cannon fodder, dispatched with cold aplomb, defeated by the brutal truth. And who could say which Jakki enjoyed more - the truth or the brutality?

Jakki had spent years latching onto credos and beliefs, fighting her battles, then moving on. Like the once well-used railway line that ran through Eddleston, she may have started her journey at Lesbian Central but had travelled by way of Vegetarian Halt, calling at Meat-Is-Murder Bay and Vegan Park West, before somewhat ironically changing trains at Transgender Junction in order to catch the last train to Animal Welfare End.

But then she had met Elaine. And now, near the end of the line, in this unspoilt backwater, how unexpected it was, how unbelievable, that this mousy, quiet, retiring bland slip of a girl would be her match, give her pause. It left Jakki staggered.

But it was true. Elaine was like some rare earth element - pure rationality. All Jakki's bluster and thrust just glanced off Elaine's impenetrable shell of equanimity and reason. Jakki had met her match and was undone and obsessed in equal measure by this modest, kind and unarguable force. Jakki's fabled adversary wasn't unbeatable because of superior weaponry or firepower; she was unbeatable because Jakki would never have the heart to attack her.

Elaine had disarmed her.

Elaine, in contrast to Jakki as chunky knitwear, was a lightweight lambswool cardigan. All pastel shades and delicate buttons, a light garment which kept you warm but was never, ever, going to pass for stylish. A sensible garment for a sensible person.

Sensible Elaine.

She lived her life like a permanently coiled spring; an overwound watch, wrapped far too tightly and hamstrung by her own embarrassment at her imagined shortcomings and internally scolding critic. Like an orgasm on a tightrope, Elaine wanted to explode but was afraid of losing control.

Everyone called her Sensible Elaine - even her mother, who had christened her simply Elaine. It wasn't as if the adjective was necessary: Elaine is a very sensible name and most owners of it are also, intrinsically, sensible. It is one of those names, like Janet or Maureen, which have very much had their day but were still occasionally dredged up from the lists of baby names when a Grandma or well-loved Great Aunt died shortly before the arrival of an infant.

But nominative determinism being what it is, Elaine had been born sensible, raised sensibly and grown into an adult whose sensibilities were bang in line with those of her generation. If she'd been a Cynthia, she would now be a senior flight attendant working long-haul Business Class cabins; if Jennifer, she'd be adorning the Clinique counter at John Lewis; if Mandy, draping over someone's nails at Chez Boutique; and if Chardonnay, picking someone's pubic hair out of her teeth before taking the money off the bedside table.

So, Sensible Elaine it was and Elaine, in short, was sensible. She couldn't deny it. But Sensible Elaine was such a boring, dull handle. A life lived with it would only ever be… unsatisfying. No-one was ever going to want to whip edible knickers off a girl called Sensible Elaine. No-one was ever going to dip her on the dance floor, take her in their arms and make her swoon, or whisk her off to a secret wedding on a beach in Tahiti. They were going to hand her a Haynes manual, buy her a foot-stool or ask her to work out the square root of 1369.

37, she knew, fuming at this useless, unbidden knowledge.

Her sensibility manifested itself as a calm consideration when a new idea was raised, and a rational contemplation of options in order to make a decision. Examining the pros and cons, giving weightings to the competing factors, considering the risks and alternatives - preferably using a spreadsheet - these were things which gave her joy, letting her lose herself in a feast of analysis, sifting through oceans of information for more relevant data and then incorporating into an ever-more sophisticated model.

But there was the rub. The analysis was the thing, not the resulting decision. She was Sensible Elaine, not Decisive Elaine. The more complex and intricate the issue, the more factors and aspects to be assessed, the more data to be weighed - just made any decision harder. Making decisions stressed her out. On those occasions in her life which had required a snap decision of her she had felt it in her chest. A thumping, red-hot, beating drum making her feel everyone was watching her, every little thing she now said or did would have a life-changing enormity about it. She would lock-up in fear and sweat hoping that time would elapse and the need for a decision would go away, or that she would be allowed the time to cool down and ponder further.

Or that someone else would sweep down, decide and take the decision out of her hands.

This was where Jakki came in.

With any new idea or scheme, Elaine's proclivities were to question it, validate it, weigh it up and then approach it proportionally. As far as Jakki was concerned this was just delay, analysis paralysis, procrastination. Jakki never gave her time, she couldn't even catch her breath. Jakki would swoop Elaine up in her enthusiasm and verve like a whirlwind gathering force. And, perhaps, embracing others like Elaine was actually a necessary thing in order for Jakki to follow through - because it would have been the most natural thing in the world for Jakki to blow herself out before making landfall but, with passengers onboard, that extra heft and responsibility gave her just enough momentum to cross the finishing line. Whereupon she immediately surveyed the damage, found it wanting, and looked for something else to move onto.

Elaine was just swept up in it all, unable to do anything other than admire, adore and venerate this force of nature which was Jakki. Like a saffron-clad monk lighting incense at the foot of a gigantic golden Buddha, her role was to worship, contemplate and follow stoically, calmly, patiently.

She knew full-well that to the outside observer, their relationship must look odd, unlikely or doomed to failure. Elaine with her straitlaced, vanilla mindset and stunningly plodding rationality; Jakki with her explosive randomness and energy which sparked and flew in all directions and often set fire to things. But here they were, living together and somewhat joined at the hip, and she literally could not imagine life without her fantastic and fantastical, outrageous partner. Elaine had expected to find herself knocked off-balance by the sheer kinetic extravagance of the woman - but she hadn't. In fact, it was almost the opposite. Like some kind of spinning top, a whirling gyroscope, Jakki's constant movement had imparted balance and certainty to their relationship - something Elaine not only needed but depended upon.

It had been something of a whirlwind romance after their meeting at Bumpin' Doughnuts. To Elaine's amazement, the whirlwind had never really abated once their courtship had stabilised - Jakki had kept going, twisting and turning in all directions, always on the move. A new obsession here, a novel interest there. Manically latching onto some amazing idea or unlikely scheme before surpassing it with another - Jakki's tastes were always for the edgy, the provocative, the outre. Elaine on the other hand was solid, steadfast, reliable. She didn't binge on anything, was never tempted, never frivolous, spontaneous or, whisper it, fun.

Just Sensible.

So, like two wobbly pillars leaning against each other for support, each bolstered and stabilised the other, creating a fortified solid mass from two unstable components.

The village of Eddleston, however, was still in shock. Having a same-sex couple in Eddleston was like finding a rattlesnake in your daughter's pushchair - fear and disgust mingled with disbelief which could easily turn to confusion and anger in these parts of the Scottish Borders. How had it got here and how on earth did you get rid of it?

Someone had dropped a twenty-first century culture

bomb through an open Austen window and without it even detonating there was now unpleasantness spattered over the walls. And, attired in the form of Jakki, it was neon Pollock shock-value. What did one do? In Eddleston, you left well alone. Kept yourself to yourself, tried to forget that you had seen some fabled, twin-headed mythical creature making its nest in your cosy village, drew your curtains closed, and your children closer, and went about your business hoping not to disturb it lest it vomit out even viler poison.

Shirley bustled in, the Borders rain dripping off her damp coat and onto her kitchen lino. She plonked her two heavy bags-for-life onto the floor and shook the cramp from her fingers. Standing straight she looked Paul perkily in the eye and grinned.

"Okay, so here's the challenge. We're going to make a meal completely vegetarian."

Paul sat back in his seat, smiling in bewilderment. A foregone conclusion not worthy of more thought. He folded his arms, making him look not unlike Aladdin's genie - all olive skin, black goatee, beaming grin and bulging biceps. A gentle giant. "Can't be done."

"Of course, it can, silly!"

"Bless you, love. But you see, you need meat to survive."

"You really don't."

"Ha! No, actually you do!"

"Paul? Lover? You don't. Do you know what our number one bestseller is right now?"

"Sausage rolls. Always is."

"Nuh-uh! It's our vegan sausage roll! We're selling

billions!"

"What's that then? The same pink slimy stuff tubed into carrots or summat?"

"No pink slimy stuff. That's the meat."

"Aw, bless. I mean, I'm no vegan- "

"I've noticed."

"But even I'm not exactly sure what that pink slimy stuff is."

"Probably meat-derived."

"Aye, let's call it that."

"Do you know how they create that pink slimey stuff? It's called MRM - mechanically recovered meat?"

Paul held up a beefy hand. "Love, can I stop you there? I am happy to eat meat - I don't want to grow it, kill it, or deal with it in living form. Not my bailiwick. There's a reason why the name for the meat from an animal is not the same as the animal itself."

Shirley put her hands on her hips and cocked her head at her lover. "Explain?"

"Well, beef is called beef, not cow. Pork is called pork, not pig."

"And chicken?"

"Oh. Well, the exception that proves the rule."

"And lamb?"

"Ah, well no-one really eats lamb you know. Bit of a PR job truth be told. Too fiddly, fatty and just doesn't taste enough like beef or pork to get a look in."

"Lamb is a real thing, you know."

"Nah, first rung on the vegetarian ladder innit? After duck."

"Duck?"

"Aye. Well ducks live near water, on water. Almost fish, aren't they?"

Shirley sighed. "Can we go back to the vegetarian meal thing?"

"Ah, God Bless you, of course we can."

"So. You do realise there are vegetarian restaurants?"

"Aye."

"Well what do you think they serve?"

"Vegetarians."

"Bingo."

"Aye, but even vegetarians have to eat meat."

"What? Look." Shirley smiled at Paul, amused by his ignorance rather than impressed with it. "Lover. Some people don't eat bacon. Do you know how they do it?"

Paul shook his head, his partner clearly a lost cause. He prevailed upon her one last time. "Shirl, bacon is the water of life. The *joie de vivre*. The *sine qua non*."

"The what?"

"Read it in the Peeblesshire!" Paul nodded, impressed that he had read the local paper, remembered something from it AND found a way to shoehorn it into a sentence.

"Cine kwa non?"

"Aye. It means something you can't do without."

"Like bacon?"

"Correct."

"You may be surprised to know that there are millions of people around the world who don't like bacon. Who manage to avoid eating it every day. With ease."

Paul scoffed. "Millions? I don't think so, babe."

"No, really. Muslims won't eat pork and there's hundreds of millions of them. Maybe billions."

"But it's tasty." Paul objected. "And it smells…" He inhaled through his nostrils as if the actual act of smelling would somehow generate the very odour he was trying to describe. “Divine. There’s something primeval about it. It stirs something deep down, gets your saliva glands going at the drop of a wossname. You can’t resist the smell of bacon, Shirl. Can’t be done.” Paul unfurled a mighty fist into a clutch of massive digits and started tolling them off, one at a time. “Bacon is one of your basic food groups. You’ve got your bacon, your beer, your chips/pasta/pizza-stuff - carbs, that’s it. Dairy and then, obv, veg.”

“You are a marvel. Do you know that?”

“Aye.” Paul grinned at the imagined compliment. “You see, love, it’s genetic. One of the main differences on the X-Y chrome… erm, thing.”

“Okay. This I have to hear.” Shirley took a seat, rested her chin on her hands and looked rapt into Paul’s face waiting for him to elaborate.

“Oh. Well.” Suddenly he didn’t look so sure of his ground. “The human gnome-”

“Genome?”

“Yeah, the G-gnome, yeah. The human G-gnome is made of male and female parts and they’re different see? X and Y is what it is. One leg of a chromosome is missing so an X becomes a Y. And on the missing leg, see, is all the stuff that binds your body to meat. Now think. Have you ever - EVER - met a male vegetarian?”

Shirley thought for a moment and realised that, actually, she hadn’t. “You know-”

“See? There are none.”

“Well, we can’t say that for sure. I mean, I am hardly representative, am I? Most of the men I meet have come into Greggs. They’re hardly likely to be vegetarians, are they?”

“Thought you said your bestseller was a vegan sausage

roll?"

"Oh, aye." Shirley caught herself and wondered for a full second whether Paul might actually have a genuine point here. She tried to shoo the silly idea away but it wouldn't budge. She needed more ammo. "Go on."

"Right. So your X-Y thing, this dropped leg of a chromosome - that's prolly where all your tastebuds are."

"Oh, now you're being silly!"

"No, I don't mean your actual tastebuds - I know they're on your tongue! I mean the genes for your tastebuds. They must all be on this missing leg of the chromosome. Which is why blokes like the taste of meat and hate the taste of veg. Whereas you women…" Paul let the sentence hang in the air.

"Really? Is that it, then - gender stereotyping with some fallacious pseudo-science to back it up?" Shirley was irritated that Paul's case sounded like total bollocks, but she didn't have a counter-argument for it.

"'Snot pseudo-science, love. Google it - it's all there in black and white on the internet." Desperately in some last resort, Shirley did just that. She pulled her phone out from under the tea-cosy and scrolled for a minute. Paul waved away Shirley's research like a distant monarch riding jubilantly in an open-carriage of confidence, gaily tripping along the cobbles of disillusion, driven by six white horses of certainty. Only to arrive at the locked gates of the reality palace to find it protected by a baying mob of the better informed.

"A-ha!" Shirley waggled her phone screen at him, triumphant.

"Yes, my darling?" Paul smiled, still unaware that the tumbrils were en route.

"You. Are. Wrong."

"Really? I don't think you can argue with the science my love."

"I'm not arguing with the science. You're quite right that there is an X-Y chromosome difference between men and women." Paul nodded serenely while Shirley delivered the *coup de grace*. "Unfortunately, lover, it is the men who have the Y chromosome, the one with the tastebuds missing, not the women!"

Paul's shoulders slumped and Shirley's heart melted to see the dejection and deflation on his sunken face. "Oh babe, don't take it to heart." She slunk across to him and sat on his knee, draping her arms around his massive shoulders. "Why don't we cuddle up in bed? See if we can do some chromosome-mingling of our own, hmm?" She stroked Paul's stubble and gave him a peck on the cheek.

Paul took one sideways glance at her, grinning. Then he picked her up effortlessly and swung her into the bedroom.

Smoke was rising gently from a chimney into the lazy sky, the sun a pale, yellow stain behind the lifting mist as this fresh October morning started to stir the denizens of Station Road. Eddie parked his 4x4 and sat in it a while soaking up the scene. He overlaid it with a memory of a similar one from his South African homeland, a wide dusty road lined with mud huts and shacks, already baking in the early morning heat; a few people scuffing through the orange dirt stirring clouds of it up into the air as a couple of stray dogs rummaged in the ditch running down the side of the road. Mornings the world over were not so dissimilar - the only jarring difference here was a blue Nissan Micra parked opposite, its engine idling, a small gift of smoke puffing from its warming exhaust.

Eddie undid his seatbelt and climbed from his car, snatching his knopkierie from the passenger seat. This stout stick of polished hardwood with a large ball at one end had been a parting gift from his last employer in Durban before he had emigrated to Scotland. Originally Zulu in design, hefted in your hand it could be used as a throwing weapon or a club - although since the cessation of hostilities in the dark continent they had been used merely for ornamental or ceremonial purposes. Eddie's was used as a truncheon when required and as visual emphasis for speech when not. As he strode towards the front door, he slapped the ball into one hand while striking the stick up and down with the other. He was prepared for everything - except for Jakki opening the door when he rang the bell.

"Good Morn-!" The bright greeting was spoken before Jakki had caught sight of him on the step. Immediately she froze and her expression changed to a snarl. "You! What do you want?"

Eddie faltered for just a second. "Elaine?"

"Out." Jakki barked. "She's stage managing a production of Evita at the Eastgate - dress rehearsal. Not that that's any of your business."

Eddie paused and then realised that this was actually a better scenario than the one he had been envisioning. After all, this woman was clearly the ringleader - not feeble little Elaine. Jakki may be built like a refuelling tanker but she would no doubt be just as sensitive to pain or susceptible to menace. He gave a tight smile. "Perhaps I could have a word with you then? May I come in?"

Jakki looked at him as if he had lost his mind. "No, you bloody may not. I'd rather have my tits slammed in a car door."

"That can be arranged."

"Ugh. Eff off, knob-cheese!"

Eddie glanced up and down the deserted street and then leant into the doorway. "About your protests at the entrance to Baxter Farms? Sir Malcolm would like you to desist."

"Ha! I'm sure he would. Unlucky, sweat gland. This is a free country - not like the one you're from. Now hop it." Jakki started to close the door but Eddie was too quick for her. He threw his not inconsiderable bulk forward and bounced off the closing door into the hall, like some overly generous serving of mash which had missed the plate and found the tablecloth.

"Not so fast, Jakki Banks." Her face registered surprise and Eddie capitalised on it. "Yes. We know all about you. And Elaine."

"What do you mean by that?" There was a wobble in her voice. "What about Elaine?"

"You and her are… lovers." Eddie could barely keep the disgust out of his voice.

"And?" Jakki bristled. "It's not a crime you know! Not in this country anyway."

"It's not a crime in South Africa either. More's the pity." Eddie spat. "Damned Scissor Sisters."

"I'd rather be a Scissor Sister than a Dire Straight! Now, get out of my house, Nazi!"

Jakki tried to wrestle Eddie back towards the door but she couldn't make him budge, his solidity had him rooted to the spot.

"What is a crime though…" Eddie continued as if she wasn't straining every muscle to shift him. "Is posting defamatory claims on Social Media and making a nuisance of yourselves on your employer's premises-"

"Former employer!"

"And, as such, embarrassing or compromising the commercial interests of the business. Especially when your contract of employment expressly forbids such behaviour." He took a deep breath at the end of that sentence, relieved to have got it all out without error - he'd practised it several times in the car when he had first pulled up outside Elaine's house.

"Yeah? Well, she's no longer an employee so you can sod off!"

"I'm afraid not." *Am afred nut.* Eddie folded his arms, despite Jakki's onslaught. He stood in the hallway like some kind of uniformed statue - Saddam Hussein before the uprising - making sure he kept his voice as reasonable as possible. "The contract, and the terms contained within it, remain enforceable for twelve months after leaving the company's employ."

"Oh… bog off!" Jakki gave up pushing and stood back, digging in her pocket for her phone. "This is trespass. Get out. I've had just about enough of this!"

"You wouldn't say that if it came with medium fries and a medium coke." Eddie sneered.

Jakki flushed scarlet. "Are you saying I'm fat?"

Eddie smiled. "I'm saying I only know three fat people, and you're two of them."

"Funny, huh? Almost as funny as your weaponised body odour - not." Jakki scowled. "In this country you can't just go round calling people fat. That's as bad as the N-word."

"I don't think so. Not where I come from."

"Oh, I think so."

"No, it's not." Eddie said, still smiling. "If you're comparing two words and you can't even say one of them? Pretty sure that's the worst word."

Jakki had stopped listening, seeing no point in debating with a foul-smelling intruder. She punched in 999. When a voice came on the line, she put it on speaker and spoke loudly into it. "Police please." She gave Eddie a condescending smile.

"One moment please." Said the operator.

"I'm not bluffing." Jakki said, waggling the phone in her hand. "The police station's only in Peebles. Take them less than five minutes to get here."

Eddie grinned and reached for his knopkierie. "I better be quick then."

FOUR

Elaine was clutching several A4 binders to her chest while she wrestled with the key trying to open the front door. As she stepped inside some papers slipped from a folder and drifted to the floor. Stooping to pick them up she saw dark red stains on the welcome mat.

"Jaks?"

"In here!"

Elaine rattled in and her eyes widened when she saw Jakki, sitting at the kitchen table, bringing away a blood-stained flannel from her head.

"What's happened? Are you ok?" She rushed over and put her arm around Jakki, bobbing her head this way and that to get a good view of the injury.

"Baxter's security bloke came calling. Charm offensive. Emphasis more on the *offensive* than the *charm*. Left his visitor's card." Jakki pulled the flannel away and touched her temple gingerly with a testing finger. She winced and replaced her finger with the flannel.

"Eddie? Came here? What for?" Elaine slumped into a chair, her binders spilling out over the kitchen table. She put her head in her hands and closed her eyes. A teeming world of thoughts and fears crowded in on her and she lost herself to it for some moments before opening her eyes and shaking her head repeatedly. "Oh God. It doesn't matter. What do we do now? I told you this was a bad idea. Bad, bad, bad."

"It's okay. Nothing's broken." Jakki expelled a long

breath. "Apart from my sense of smell. Christ, he's got the halitosis of a diseased hippo."

"It is not okay." Elaine stared at her lover in amazement. "Look at you? How is this okay?"

Jakki wasn't listening. "And the body odour of… I don't know. Some large game animal. I bet you can tell what he had for breakfast by sifting for bones in his droppings."

Elaine sighed, determination written on her face. "We need to call the police."

"Already tried that."

Elaine, rummaging through her handbag for some paracetamol, recoiled. "Have they been?"

"Nope. Not coming by the looks of it, either."

"But… why?"

"Dunno. Maybe Baxter exerted some influence. Maybe crime in the Borders is such that me reporting a threatening individual isn't sufficient. Maybe they'll turn up tomorrow, just passing through, see if there's anything to it? Who knows? Who cares?"

"Who cares?" Elaine was horrified - this was not how things worked in her carefully structured and organised world. "Here take these. Look, this is assault! That's a crime!"

"You don't say?" Jakki gulped down the tablets with a mouthful of cold tea. "Lay, this is modern Britain. Look around you - we've got corrupt, self-interested, greedy bastards robbing normal people blind, the rich are getting richer and we're being fed shit, told we're all in it together and that the gig economy is liberating. Natural resources being exploited, climate being ruined and entitled public school knobs jostling each other to see whose head can get furthest into the trough. It's endemic, universal, tacitly condoned. And its getting worse every single day."

Elaine looked aghast at her partner. "What are you talking about?"

"This." Jakki prodded her head-wound and winced but her eyes were wild with excitement. "This is exhibit A. A small token example of what is going on all around us every single day. And we, blindly, continue to allow it to happen. All that is needed for evil to prosper is that good men do nothing. Said someone."

"I think maybe you've had a crack on the head."

"You think? Or do you think that it's a sharp reminder of the teeny-tiny difference we're making? That we're on the right track."

Elaine eyed her lover with concern. "What did he say?"

"Hmm?"

"Jaks, what did Eddie say?"

"Nothing."

"Jaks!"

Jakki glared at her and then gave a heavy sigh. "Something about breach of contract."

"What? Who?"

"You. Apparently, you're in breach of contract if you divulge any information about the business or go within a hundred yards of the premises."

"Oh! I told you that." Elaine cried. "I thought, maybe, since I don't work there anymore-"

"Doesn't matter, babe. The suits, the lawyers and those nice HR people? They've done you up like a kipper. Those smiling faces on the corporate brochures? It's a scam."

Elaine stared silently into empty space, the room

crushing in. Her chest felt tight. "I think it's time we stopped."

"What! That's exactly what they want!" Jakki exploded. "Exactly."

"Jaks. We live a good life. A happy life. We have everything we need, and we have each other. We have our health, a lovely home and plenty of years ahead of us. Can't that be enough?"

Jakki said nothing, her face hidden from Elaine's view.

"All we've done is stand outside, shout and wave placards. For just a few days." Elaine moaned. "And now you've got this as a reward."

Jakki shook her head in disappointment. "Head? Meet sand."

"But what's the point? I mean, we don't know that they mistreat *all* their birds, do we? I never got to see inside *all* of the sheds." Elaine shrugged. "I ran the numbers, saw that they didn't add up, made some assum..."

"Oh, come on!" Jakki's voice rose. "When you pointed this out to them, what did they do?"

"Fired me." Elaine said in a small voice.

"They fired you." Jakki snorted. "And when we protest with placards criticising them for animal abuse, what do they do? They come to our home and hit me over the head and tell us to stop protesting. Does that sound like we're on the right track? Or does that sound like we're wide of the mark loonies pointlessly waving placards?"

Elaine cast down her eyes and fiddled with her fingers. Jakki sighed and reached out to clasp Elaine's hands, to still their fearful fidgeting. "Lay?"

Elaine looked up at her, her eyes wet. "This isn't me, Jaks. I don't want this."

"What do you want?"

"I just want us to be happy."

"I thought you just said we were."

"I did." Elaine sniffed away a tear and tried to smile. "We are."

"I'm not."

The pair sat in silence for a while, each lost in their own thoughts, their own fears. Elaine broke it.

"Why not? Are you not happy with me?"

"No, no, no!" Jakki squeezed Elaine's hands, looking deep into her eyes. "I love you. I love us. But this? This… world. How can I be happy in this world with all this going on? I need to make a difference. Do what I can. I can't be happy just sitting on my hands."

"I love you too." Elaine said, shaking.

Jakki clasped tighter. "Well, then. Let's the two of us together make a difference! If we can be happy together now, just think how much happier we can be if we have - together - made the world a better place."

Elaine gave a rueful smile. "But I don't want either of us to get hurt."

"Neither do I." Jakki rubbed her temple and returned Elaine's smile. "So that's two things we need to do."

"Two?"

"Yes. One: we need to up our game. We're on the right line here - this is proof of that. But you're right, we're not going to get anywhere just waving placards at passing motorists. We need to go to the next level."

"The next level?"

"And two: we need to do it in such a way that you are not put in danger."

Elaine realised that her partner's words were only meant to reassure, but she didn't like the sound of that at all.

"Where the devil is she? We're run off our feet!"

Shirley was oscillating between the oven and the fryer, each beeping at her furiously while hot air was blasting from the one and boiling fat spitting from the other. She wiped one sleeve of her uniform across her forehead and it dragged against the perspiration on her brow. The air was heavy with the scent of burnt sugar and almonds.

"I'll call her again when the queue's gone down!" Traci yelled from the front of the shop and then smiled an apology at the customer at the head of the queue as she passed her a coffee and a covered doughnut. "Who's next please?"

The front of the line shuffled forward, the rest of it tailed out of the small Greggs shop front and down the street. The lunchtime rush was in full-swing, the usual litany of hungry mouths swollen by the addition of many kids swarming in from the High School.

Shirley battled on in frustration, her mouth a vivid slit across her face as she pulled out trays to cool, loaded new ones in, all the while whipping out one hand to press pre-programmed timers with an unseeing precision borne of years of experience. She spun to lift the basket full of yum-yums out of the fryer and tossed them onto a cooling rack before shoving a jug of icing into the microwave and reheating it ready to be poured.

The rush hour passed in a blur of heat and effort, her mouth praying for a drink of some kind to quench her thirst by the end of it. She leant against the coffee machine and surveyed the clear shop-front and emptying High Street through the plate-glass window. Traci was wiping the counter down and tidying unused stirrers and napkins. Shirley sighed deeply and took a long swig from a bottle of Snapple before slamming it down on the work surface and sighing again.

"It's not like her at all, is it?" She spoke more to herself than anyone, Traci still occupied with her back towards her. "Did she say anything to you yesterday?"

"Hmm?" Traci turned. "Elaine?" She thought for a moment, looking like someone trying to pick out details from a yesterday that had already vanished in her mental rear-view mirror. "No. Don't think so. Never really talks much does Elaine."

She talks to me, thought Shirley. Never bloody shuts up about her beloved Jaks at times. What's wrong with you that she doesn't chat, hmm? You work more closely with her than I do. But she just kept staring ahead out onto the High Street, thinking. Traci had been Shirley's second recruit after taking over as manager of Greggs; Elaine had been her first. And a Godsend at that.

Shirley had entered into the supervisory position with Greggs somewhat reluctantly when what-she-had-thought-of-as-her-career at Whim Hall Nursing Home was brought to a sudden end by her violent reaction to the proprietor flopping his shrivelled penis onto her shoulder during a shift on reception. It hadn't helped that one of the residents with mental health issues - a massive Russian who barked like a dog - had heard of the incident and decided to extract his own justice using his teeth. The proprietor was now said to be the owner of only a single testicle, giving his staff a further reason to refer to him as Hitler behind his back.

The opportunity at Greggs had come up and the Personnel Director who had hired her had taken a shine to her winning ways, convincing her that she was perfect for the job (and omitting to tell her, she later discovered, that the only other candidates had been an acne-scarred young man who looked like he'd never had a full meal in his life - hardly a walking advertisement for the company - and a bullshitting former accountant whose past as a thieving-from-her-employer par excellence had come thrillingly to the director's attention within ten seconds of his first reference phone call. Shirley was a shoo-in and, thusly, did he shoo her into the company's management training scheme).

She felt that her large frame had also been an advantage - being a bakery store manager and having to deter light-fingered customers from running off with the sausage rolls certainly benefitted from someone with the stature of a bouncer with a very firm grip. She also knew that her size had been a big factor in bringing her to the attention of her partner, Paul: big lass versus Greggs manager - which had held most sway with him? Her jury was still out.

But what had she known about running a bakery, managing a shop? Yes, Greggs provided training and there was whole shelf full of manuals, guides, processes and instructions on the back office and in her flat. She had studied and applied herself and got on with it - done a good job if she did say so herself. But she'd never felt in control, in her comfort zone. She'd been a nervous wreck, working into the wee small hours cribbing and learning by night and then sweating by day as she had to get to grips with customers and inventories and suppliers and recruitment.

But when she had seen Elaine's CV? It was like the clouds had parted, a huge hand swept down from the sky and presented her with a calm, rational, knowledgeable, experienced and business-focussed marvel. Someone who had spent years analysing business operations and explaining them, unpicking them and putting them back together to make them better, smoother, more efficient. And here she was - not just on a plate for Shirley, but gift-wrapped! She was available immediately, anxious to start and prepared to accept a drop in salary in order to simply fill what was becoming a yawning gap in her job history. Elaine had been somewhat reticent about the details behind her departure from Baxter Farms but Shirley remembered well the most remarkable letter of recommendation she had ever received on requesting a reference for Elaine:

Dear Ms Henderson

I am writing to provide a written reference, as per your request, for Elaine Dunwoody.

I am happy to say that Elaine is a former employee of Baxter Farms Ltd and, although she was only with us for a matter of months, leaving in March of this year, I can report that she was quickly fired with enthusiasm.

I really cannot say enough good things about her, suffice it to say that the quality of her work will astound you. In your shoes, I would waste no time in hiring her.

...

In closing, I would like to assure you that, in my view, no-one would be better for the job at Greggs than Elaine Dunwoody. You will be fortunate indeed if you get her to work for you.

Yours faithfully
Sir Malcolm Baxter

Elaine had also claimed that Sir Malcolm Baxter had put the word out to other businesses that she, Elaine, was not to be touched with a bargepole - let alone trusted. But Shirley didn't care. What could be more perfect for her? Everyone else's loss was her gain and she had acquired the treasured prize of Elaine for a steal and, from that point on, Shirley had been able to breathe an enormous sigh of relief and let her confidence grow to fill the uniform Greggs had provided for her. Elaine had been a stalwart and a rock, so much so that ironically Shirley had now grown to the point where she truly felt she had everything under control and would be able to accept the loss of Elaine on the day it would inevitably come. She was no longer afraid of managing alone but, HR aside, Elaine had not just been an invaluable employee - she had become a true friend.

So, where was she today? She hadn't come in for her shift at 11am and she hadn't called or messaged to say she was ill or running late or anything. *Something must be wrong*, Shirley concluded. And, when Shirley concluded something, it always meant that something would be done about it. Her conclusion in this case: she would pop around to Elaine's after work and find out what it was.

"I'm really sorry, Shirley. I don't know what came over me." Elaine was dabbing tears away with a tissue that Shirley had pulled from the breast pocket of her Greggs uniform.

"Hey, now." Shirley rested her hand on Elaine's knee

as they sat beside each other on the lumpy sofa, giving her a kindly smile. "This isn't very sensible is it?"

"No." Elaine grinned despite herself, sniffing back the tears. "I suppose not."

"No. So, tell me what's wrong. I'd like to know if - how - I can help."

"Well…" Elaine was still trembling and sniffing, her hair a matted rug where she had been twisting it and twirling it with tear-streaked hands. "He barged in and… and…"

"Who barged in?"

"Eddie… Helpmann." Elaine gulped, snatching at her breath. "He beat Jaks up! She called the police but they never came and she's…. she's…"

"What? Why?" Shirley asked but Elaine was wrapped up in her trauma.

"He has this stick… like a truncheon or something, with a ball on the end…"

"Did she go to hospital?"

"What? No." The question had shaken Elaine out of her recollection momentarily. Her eyes were swollen and her lip was trembling. Shirley reached out to hug her and Elaine collapsed into her chest, losing herself in the embrace. They both sat for a while, Shirley waiting for Elaine's breathing to steady and ease. After a few minutes she gently pulled Elaine up and clasped her hands on her lap.

"Now. Better?"

Elaine nodded and gave a little sniff. "Thank you."

"Is she okay? Jakki?"

Elaine gave another small nod and then burst into tears again.

"Right. So, who's this man and why did he attack

Jakki?"

"Eddie Helpmann. He's Head of Security at Baxters."

"Why was he here? You haven't worked there for months."

"No. I know." Elaine had her head down, shoulders pinched, staring at her lap. She started to shake. "It was about our demonstrations. He wants us to stop."

"What demonstrations?"

The question seemed to set Elaine off again. "I didn't know it was going to cause all this fuss."

"No?"

"Well…"

"Was this Jakki's idea?"

"Yes." Elaine sniffed.

Shirley sighed. Of course, it was. Shirley knew about Jakki - had met her a couple of times when Elaine had been in town and they had all bumped into each other - and even without Elaine's frequent tales of what the pair of them got up to, Shirley had had Jakki down as a firebrand and a troublemaker. And a woman who was never sated and quickly bored: issue followed issue in a bewildering whirl of protest marches, public meetings and demonstrations. A woman with the knack of rubbing people up the wrong way and proud of it, offending people with breath-taking ease and who would happily conduct a one-woman dirty protest if it would get her on the TV news. She was like a cross between Bernard Manning, Germaine Greer and Bobby Sands.

Elaine had once idly wondered if there might one day be any vacancies that would allow Jakki to work at Greggs; Shirley had made sympathetic noises whilst simultaneously disabusing her of the notion. Elaine's partner was *not* someone to project a positive impression of Greggs to customers - more like someone who would destroy their reputation whilst eating most of the stock.

"I see. So, stop doing them." Shirley suggested.

"The protests?" Elaine nodded, head still down.

"Yes."

"Jaks won't."

No, of course she wouldn't thought Shirley. Jakki was like a member of some paramilitary wing of the Animal Liberation Front. Buckling under pressure from some offensively wealthy businessman was about as likely as them promoting low-tar cigarettes for beagles.

"But Elaine… doesn't she care that she's being threatened? This Helpmann sounds like a dangerous man."

Elaine gulped in air, making wet choking noises. "But it wasn't her he was looking for! It was me."

"What?"

"It's me who's in danger. They want me!"

"Whatever for?"

"I used to work there. I'm the one with insider information." Elaine's breathing was ragged now, her sentences coming in bursts between gulps of air. "Eddie came to tell me to stop, not Jaks."

Shirley was appalled. "If you're in danger, surely Jakki will see that you are more important to her than… whatever issue this is?"

Elaine sighed, her shoulders raising up and then slumping. "She's told me… it's too important…"

"More important than you? Than your safety?"

Elaine sniffed again but stayed silent.

Shirley took a deep breath and blew out her cheeks while she considered the situation. "Well, then, go to the Police. This man can't threaten you like that. Or assault

Jakki. It's illegal."

"She doesn't care about the attack. Says it shows that we're on the right track."

"Oh, for heaven's sake. Well, you can report him!"

"That's the thing, though." Elaine lifted her head to face Shirley and started to cry again. "I'm breaking the law if I carry on protesting… in breach of my employment contract… and if I stop… I'm letting Jaks down."

"Oh, this is ridiculous!"

"I signed a contract of employment… which forbids me from doing something like that for twelve months after I leave… I checked... it says any such act will be prosecuted to the fullest extent."

"Well, then. Let them prosecute you - but that's not threatening to beat you up!"

"I'll go to jail!"

"I don't think so, honey." Shirley said. "In fact, I'd bet good money that if you stop, they'll just forget all about it. It's not worth it to them to prosecute. Legal costs, all that."

"Jaks won't stop… she wants to take our protests to… the next level."

"What does that mean?"

"I don't know!" Elaine wailed and buried her head in her hands.

"Look." Shirley tapped Elaine's knee and waited for her to look up. When she did, Shirley held her gaze. "Look Elaine. You've been threatened, okay? Is this the first time?" Elaine nodded obediently. "Okay. So, tell Jakki. Tell her how afraid and upset you are. Explain that you want her to stop - to protect you. Whatever level Jakki thinks she can go to, there's always some other way to achieve the same effect. She doesn't need any of this. Not really."

"And if she says No?" Elaine's brow creased, low self-esteem vivid on her face.

"You both love each other don't you? Why would she?"

"You don't know Jaks."

"You have to persuade her. Do you think you can do that?"

Elaine took a deep breath and exhaled slowly. She closed her eyes for a long moment before opening them again and looking at Shirley. "I can try. Might take a few days." She gave a wry smile. "Jaks doesn't convince easily."

"That's the spirit." Shirley smiled back and patted Elaine's knee again.

"But what if he comes back?" Elaine's eyes widened in terror, her imagination kicking in. "What if he comes back before I can convince Jaks to stop?"

"Well, then, you'll have to up your convincing game, won't you?"

"No! Oh No! No!" Elaine started breaking down again. "Please Shirley, help me!"

"I don't see how I can persuade Jakki if you can't." Shirley said. "I don't really have anything to bring to the argument, do I?"

Elaine shoulders shook and Shirley tried to think. "Look I'll tell you what. I'll ask Paul to be your bodyguard for a few days. Just until you can persuade Jakki. He'll hang around and if this Helpmann comes back, Paul will protect you. He's a big fella, he won't have a problem with some security guard with a stick!"

"He's much more than that" Elaine protested.

“So is my Paul.” Shirley smiled, reassuring her. “He’ll keep you safe, don’t you worry. And… his presence will show Jakki how scared you are. How real the threat is and how important it is for her to listen to you and stop this stupidity!”

Elaine pursed her lips together and gave a confirmatory nod.

“I get Paul to do this, you come back to work.” Shirley exclaimed. “Deal?”

Elaine let out a long, loud lungful of air. “Deal.”

FIVE

"Honey, we've had this conversation a thousand times. Your father's a dinosaur, you know he is. He's set in his ways, too old to change, too stubborn to change and unable to see the way the wind is blowing. How long before the business folds if he doesn't change his ways?"

Sally puffed out her cheeks and came to sit down next to her husband at the dining table. The farmhouse kitchen was cavernous and anciently equipped - an Aga, dark oak cabinets with tiled worktops and splashbacks, an ears-of-wheat toaster and a cream enamel bread tin which bore the long-scuffed legend *B EA* . She draped a tea-towel over her shoulder, sidled up to Roly and put a loving hand on his.

"I don't know." Roly hung his head and felt his shoulders sag. He sighed, long and slow. "He's fought every new policy or guideline brought in by Food Standards, found a way to cut every corner when it comes to meeting Freedom Food requirements. Organic is just another word for rip-off as far as he is concerned." He looked at his wife, sadly. "He'll no more willingly embrace animal welfare standards and ethical food principles than he will change his bloody Tweed suit!"

"And where will he be when every shopper insists on only organic or free-range eggs?"

"He'll be labelling and passing off our existing eggs as organic and free-range."

"That's illegal."

"Ha!" Roly cried. "Not if no-one knows about it…"

"It's still illegal."

"No-one gets killed. Nothing's on fire. Maah!" Roly mantra'd a well-worn saying of his father's, attempting and failing to emulate his lowland brogue in the process.

"And if someone does find out about it, what will happen then? What will become of you? And the business? And us? The business is our livelihood - if your father runs it into the ground, unintentionally or not, where does that leave us? You can see the writing on the wall. I can see the writing on the wall. The only person who can't is him!"

"And he's the only one who matters."

"No. We matter. You and I matter. Your customers matter, society matters. The law matters."

Roly cut a forlorn figure, collapsed in on himself at the old oak table. He was rail-thin with an apologetic apple-cheeked face, teeth slightly too far apart in a dark mouth that was never quite relaxed, like a letterbox awaiting the last post of the day. His brow was furrowed, his beetle eyebrows sad.

"I can see how we can pivot the business towards higher-end products!" Roly wailed. "Organic. Free-range. Speciality breeds. We'll increase our margins, improve our image. It's all clear to me."

"Really?" Sally's ears pricked up and she tightened her grip on her husband's hand.

"Yes. But it's irrelevant." He said, his voice dropping now to barely a whisper. "I hired a Business Analyst. Someone who could look at our operations, recommend changes, cost them out. Validate and put some meat on my ideas. We spent months doing it, together. I had it all worked out. Wrote a business strategy proposal and everything."

"May I read it?"

"If you like. Pointless though." Roly rooted in his portfolio and threw a sheaf of A4 pages on the table.

"Okay." Sally started to flick through the pages. "So what did he say about it?"

"Oh, he didn't read it!" Roly gave a sad laugh. "He asked me to summarise it - verbally - and then called it poppycock."

"Poppycock?"

"Well, that wasn't the actual word he used but… you get the idea."

"Oh, Honey."

"Then he fired her."

"The analyst?"

"Yes. Said she was a nosy-parker. Interfering. That I'd hired her behind his back."

"Did you?"

"I suppose." Roly exhaled slowly. "Couldn't really have hired her in front of his back, could I? Wouldn't have got past first base."

Sally gazed admiringly at her husband and jiggled his hand in hers. "This is really good, honey. This is you stepping up. Trying to make a difference. Being bold."

"Is it?" Roly gave the tiniest shake of his head, downcast and despondent.

"Yes!" Sally insisted. "And you have to push on. You have to convince him. Show him that change is the only way forward. Otherwise, we'll…"

"What?"

"Well, we won't have anything will we? We'll have this place - if he lets us keep it. But we won't have any income. Or prospects. And if he doesn't let us keep it…"

"Why would he kick us out?"

"Er, hello? What's he trying to do with his tenant farmers? Kick them out. Why would we be different?"

"Because we're not tenant farmers."

"In name only. This is his house, not ours. We may live in it rent-free but there's no law that says that can't change. And there's no law that says he can't kick us out if he so chooses."

"We have rights!"

"Do we?"

"Well, I hope so."

"I'm not so sure."

"But why would he do that to us?"

"Because he's a grasping, selfish bastard who thinks only of himself and his eponymous business. He has so much regard for you that he sent you away for most of your childhood to boarding schools-"

"As he was!"

"He employs you only because you will do the job more cheaply than someone unrelated to him."

"Not true. My salary is commensurate with my experience in this industry. I'm still learning the ropes remember?"

"You're trotting out his words, aren't you?"

Roly pursed his lips and said nothing. Sally continued. "He still calls you *boy*. Does he even remember your name?"

"I'm his son. His heir!"

"He constantly insults and belittles you."

Roly closed his eyes and sighed. "Sticks and stones."

"Yeah. Is that what he has for breakfast every day?"

"Sal! Look at our lovely home. Look at what we have, not what we don't."

"Lovely home!" Sally spluttered. "Yes, it is. Until you look out of the window or step outside. We're surrounded by these horrible chicken sheds, the stink wafting in through every crevice, every crack in these stupid old window frames. It's cold and it's draughty and it's-"

"Our home!" Roly interrupted. "Jemima's home."

Sally glared at him. He was used to this, a frequent litany of sins - rant even - that his wife directed at his father and Roly was torn. Torn between his love for his wife whom he adored and with whom he had a beautiful daughter, Jemima; and his love for his father. And he did love him - although he often wondered why, especially when Sally assailed him with these truths, for truths they were, at least of sorts. Roly wasn't stupid and he wasn't blind, but he was a coward.

His father was an ebullient, bellicose figure with determination, stamina, volume and velocity. Like some kind of comet hurtling earthwards, his father pushed aside any obstacle, plummeted through the foulest of atmospheres oblivious and caused panic in many of those who could only stand and watch. And quake. That was what Roly did. And he knew all of this because his therapist had helped him see it for what it was. Childhood trauma, built up over years - decades now - of ill-treatment, neglect and what was now regarded as psychological and verbal abuse. Never physical - his father had never hit him, but the threat of it was always there. Lingering in the air, a silent viper ready to strike, needing no preparation, no rearing-up time, no backlift - just a deadly blow which could happen instantly.

That was what Roly feared. And it was down to a smattering of childhood instances - usually when he had unwisely interrupted his father whilst he was doing... well, something important he would claim, but essentially anything. Children should be seen and not heard, they were an encumbrance and an inconvenience. Rory was quite convinced that he and his sister, Arabella, had only come into the world because their father didn't want their mother interrupting him, so he consented to two children to give her something to do. And when she died unexpectedly, he had no compunction just to send them both away to boarding school and hire a nanny during school holidays.

Roly had only wanted his father's attention, some affection and interest shown in his eldest off-spring. But none had been forthcoming and he had grown inward and reserved, adopting the strategy that if you don't ask you can't be denied, if you don't interact you can't be rebuffed. But this had left him cold, his therapist had shown him. And Sally - my God, he had learnt so much from her. She was a genuinely, warm, affectionate human who loved him and who had shown him, for the first time in his life, that he was worth something as he was.

He didn't need to try to impress his father - which, in spite of his unconsciously adopted withdrawal strategy, Roly now realised is what he had been trying to do. He had tried to make his way in the world in a way that would make his father proud - but he had failed at all of them. Started his own events management company which went into administration. Worked at a stud farm with a view to learning the business and one day running a stud farm of his own - only to discover that horses brought him out in hives and gave him asthma. Ran a brewery with an old school chum, producing artisan micro-ales for the Polo set. The chum had run off with a married woman, left the country and the business solely in Roly's hands. Roly had run it. Into the ground.

Even finding a wife as wonderful as Sally had been some kind of failure in his father's eyes, it seemed to Roly. Sally wasn't from gentry and the horsey set. She hadn't been to public school, her parents weren't professionals and her own education had been mediocre. When Jemima was born, his father had granted them the original Baxter farmhouse to use as their family home but somehow this gift had never turned into a transfer of ownership. Despite repeated reminders no paperwork had ever materialised, and their position had become *de facto* tenants, albeit at zero rent, in this house which had been Roly's childhood home-away-from-school. He was delighted to be able to live there, rent-free, and forever (in theory) since he could foresee no circumstances where his father would wish to take up residence in it himself. But that, perhaps, was Sally's entire point.

"Sal." He looked into his wife's eyes to talk her round.

"Rol. If you want me to live here, with you as my husband, of course I will. You and me and Jem, forever."

"Good." Roly smiled gratefully.

"But if you don't do something about… him! Well, there's not going to be a forever. We're not going to have a future and we're not going to have a home."

"But-"

"No but's. Do something. Please?"

"What?"

"I don't know. Something. Anything. Just..." She reached for him and held his face tightly in her hands, trying to will her determination into him through his eye sockets. "Please Roly, don't let him destroy us. For once in your life, don't just acquiesce. Don't let him walk all over you. Fight back. Be a man. Be a better man than he is. How hard can that be?"

She rose from her chair and walked from the kitchen, leaving Roly alone in the gathering dusk. He felt the forbidding dark kitchen units crowd in and he lowered his eyes to the scarred expanse of table in front of him, and the brightly-coloured pages of his business strategy document strewn across it.

The cold didn't bother Cullen anymore, neither did the wind - although it was gusty atop the Moorfoots right now and the outline of his path was lost in the darkness. He'd been stupid to push himself this hard and had been doing so for days now. He wasn't a young man and his body couldn't take what it used to.

He was strong and sinewed, the musculature of someone well-used to outdoor exercise and long walks. Normally he would move with an easy grace, arms swinging loosely as he pushed himself up a hill or through a forest. But it was getting harder, or he was getting slower. Bits of him would no longer do what they were told. He had trekking poles in his worn and trusty backpack, perhaps it was time he started using them?

They said that to survive on the Scottish hills you needed to be suitably dressed, knowledgeable and - most of all - know your own limits. Know when to turn back. Maybe you were too tired, or too cold, or too wet, or too hungry. If you pushed yourself too far you got too desperate, too scared. And you made unwise decisions. Decisions which could cost you your life. Especially if you were alone and no-one knew where you were.

But alone was the way Cullen liked it.

If he drilled back into his memory, he could remember his former life, his family, his career. But not his friends. Friends had never been his long suit. Or people. Either he didn't like them or they didn't like him - it was all one and the same to Cullen. They either slowed you down or let you down. He could count the people he could rely upon on the fingers of one hand. And the people he could still rely upon today were fewer still.

But being solitary had its price. Even if he hadn't been exhausted, he would never have seen the razor wire in the half-light, hidden in the gorse. It sliced through his left calf and he collapsed in the heather like a fallen chimney and looked up at the stars.

As they wheeled slowly above him and the wind ruffled the tops of the heather, buffeting his battered leather hat, he felt a warm, wetness on his leg and for a shameful second just lay there, reluctantly accepting that his body was shutting down, that this was the end of his search. The end of it all.

He was going to bleed to death up on this abandoned hillside.

He'd been foolish. Unwise. He'd made the wrong decision and now he was in trouble. He'd felt it but carried on anyway. His brain was tired - like an old trouser press, it wasn't switched on as often as it used to be and now gave him only the merest hint of an edge. Wheezing now and starting to shiver, he felt his eyelids aching to close and he struggled to keep his gaze focussed on the moon above as scudding cloud blew across it.

He tried to focus on his breathing. Slowly and deeply, in and out. Testing for pain or resistance, tightness or difficulty. He coughed awkwardly, a sudden spasm which caused him to sit up to get it out before he collapsed onto his back, his hat forgotten.

Then a dog licked his face and Cullen recoiled like a gazelle from a crocodile at a waterhole.

The dog persisted, slobbering on him as he tried and failed to keep it at bay. Realising that his strength was so low he couldn't fend the animal off, Cullen relaxed and let it snuggle in between his chest and one arm and counted off the seconds by the slow whump of its tail against his damp leg. The creature was attractively warm and as the minutes passed Cullen felt some spirit return to him. A clear thought took hold that the dog being here meant its owner was close by and, for a second, he really couldn't decide whether this was motivation to shout for help or flee from sight. Then his sanity prevailed and he opened his eyes and croaked a feeble "Hello?" which seemed to escape on the cold air and dissipate into the night.

He tried again, stronger and louder now, but there was no response. The dog pulled away from Cullen's cries and seemed to stand, wagging, waiting for him to rise. He hesitated and, as if understanding completely, the dog dipped its head and pulled Cullen's hat from its hiding place beside him. Cullen's eyes narrowed in the darkness but the dog stood its ground, tail wagging, its head jerking back as it struggled to keep the hat from dragging in the heather. A muted bark and another head jerk and the dog turned to bound through the gorse, bidding Cullen to follow on. Too exhausted to question anything, and too tired to chase the animal for his hat, Cullen rose unsteadily to his feet. He felt dizzy, probably from blood loss, and the pain in his left leg wasn't sharp and keeping him awake, it was warm and numbing and soporific. It was move or die.

Putting one shaking boot in front of the other, he followed the fast-disappearing animal down off the hills.

"Ellie, petal. Please don't cry. Scampi will be fine. Just you watch. He'll come bouncing in here any minute, right as rain!"

Rosie Critchley cradled her daughter's head in her hand and held the young girl to her bosom, hugging her and swaying her from side to side in an attempt at comfort.

Ellie was inconsolable. "But Mum - it's dark and cold and he's all alone. And he's been gone for hour and hours and hours."

"Look, young lady. It's one o'clock in the morning and you should be fast asleep." Rosie tried to be stern but she couldn't find it in herself, her own worry for their dog no longer at the back of her mind now that her daughter had woken her.

"I was in bed. And I couldn't sleep thinking about Scampi. And I looked out of my window and I watched and watched and he didn't come. I waited 'til I felled asleep on the windowsill and then I was cold so I woke up and he still wasn't there." Her words tumbled out like a babbling stream, lubricated by tears, as she sobbed into her mother's nightie. "Oh, where is he, Mum?"

Ellie had come nervously into her room and shaken her awake, teary-eyed, and Rosie's first thought had been to make sure Ewan wasn't woken too. She had shhh'ed her daughter, scooped herself into her slippers and then ushered Ellie back to her bedroom where she tucked her in and stroked her head, but Ellie had just sat up and resumed crying.

"Come on, now. Scampi knows those hills better than anyone. And he knows his way home well enough, doesn't he hmm? Remember that time he got stuck in a snowdrift up by the sheepfold? Dad came back to get a shovel to dig him out and by the time he had found one, Scampi was standing on the doorstep wagging snow all over the carpet!"

"Yes." Ellie smiled at the memory and gave her mother a hug. Rosie smoothed Ellie's hair with one hand and guided her down between the bedclothes with the other.

"So, don't worry sweetheart. If Scampi isn't wagging his tail in the kitchen by the time you come down for breakfast in the morning, we'll all go and look for him together. Okay?"

"Okay, Mum." Ellie gave a wet smile and allowed herself to snuggle into the pillow.

"Now, get some sleep. Okay?"

"Hmm-mm."

"Okay, then. 'Night 'night."

"'Night, Mum."

Rosie stayed sitting on the edge of the bed for a few minutes, watching Ellie slip into sleep, admiring her daughter's beautiful young face, no trace of a line or a care, as the Frozen bedside lamp played snowflakes lazily across it. She turned the light off and crept to the door, leaving it carefully ajar so that the hall light shed some illumination into her daughter's room. Ellie, like many a six-year-old, was not fond of the dark.

Standing in the hallway Rosie looked at the clock and wondered what had happened to Scampi. Perhaps she'd better check the back door was unlocked just in case the mad creature had managed to find its way home at this hour. She opened the kitchen door and turned the light on.

Scampi bounced into the kitchen, tail wagging cheerfully, a leather cowboy hat in his mouth. Behind him, leaning weakly against the doorframe was the fragile figure of a tall man in a green waterproof bearing a heavy pack. The lower half of his left trouser leg was stained wet and black with blood. She opened her mouth, unsure whether to be astonished or afraid, only to watch as the man slid slowly down the door-frame and fell unconscious into a heap on the kitchen floor.

"Ewan? Ewan?" Rosie leant over the bed and gently shook her husband by the shoulders. He was snuffling and half-snoring and showing no signs of stirring. She shoved harder and hissed. "Ewan?"

"Wha-? Hmm?" Her husband's brown hair was matted to one side of his face, a classic Ewan bed-head style, and he scrunched up his features in response to the bedside light she had turned on now that he was waking. "Aargh, turn it off!"

"Ewan, Scampi's back."

"Huh? Oh good." He didn't sound like he meant it. "What time is it?"

"Two o'clock."

"Two o'clock! You woke me up in the middle of the bloody night to tell me … what did you tell me?"

Her husband liked his sleep. A lot. Perhaps *liked* was too weak a word here. *Relished* was perhaps better, or *adored.* It was sometimes all she could do, once she had enticed him bedward for some conjugal activity, to keep him interested and stop him nodding off with enthusiasm. Being a farmer's wife was not, she knew, a bed of roses - and neither was being a farmer. The world might view you as a CAP-sucking, euro-subsidised landowner who got paid money for not growing anything and drove around in an array of shiny green farming machinery that cost six-figures a pop, bunging up the traffic as you trundled a smelly load from one empty field to another. But the reality was living hand-to-mouth, never having a family holiday, getting up at four and going to bed at eight, working in all weathers and then having to spend more on a couple of lamb chops in Tesco than you had been paid for the whole sheep they'd been butchered from. She counted to three, trying to let all this knowledge hold sway over his current irritation - and not wishing to count to ten lest he nod back off again in the additional time so granted.

"Scampi's back." She paused. "A man found him."

"Man? What man?"

"I don't know. Some man who was at death's door when he brought Scampi back. He collapsed in the kitchen, bleeding."

"What?"

"I put him in the spare room. Dressed his wound. Gave him a hot water bottle."

"You did what?" Now Ewan was wide awake. Springing out of bed he grabbed his shotgun from beneath the bed, shucked it and loaded it with two cartridges from a drawer in his bedside table.

"What are you doing?" Rosie cried.

"Do you know who he is?"

"Well, no."

"And you've just put him up in the spare room?"

"He passed out. He's weak!"

"Is he? Or could he be one of Baxter's men?"

"Oh, Ewan. Really."

"What do you mean, really? Do you not think he'd stoop to this?"

"What? Rescue our dog?"

"Or perhaps he stole Scampi so that he could deliberately bring him back, pretend he'd rescued him, and worm his way-"

"Worm his way where?" Rosie put her hands on her hips, incredulous. "Oh, you're being ridiculous darling! Paranoid! I mean, really."

"It's possible."

"It's ridiculous." She heaved a massive sigh. "Fine. Ok, by all means go and check on him. He's not going anywhere. But please, put the gun down. If Baxter did send him - and I don't for a moment think he did - he shouldn't have. The man could barely stand."

Her husband looked at her concerned face and let out a deep breath. He handed her the gun and she held it gingerly at arms-length, as if at any minute it could turn into an enormous turd. Ewan padded out of the room wearing only his pyjama bottoms.

For all her reasoning and intuition, standing there holding this gun with her half-naked husband about to encounter a stranger in their house, unarmed, the hairs on her neck stood while she strained to listen in the silence and hoped to God she was right.

Two minutes later her husband reappeared.

"He was asleep. Snoring." Ewan slotted himself back into bed. "I checked his pack."

"Ewan?" Rosie was appalled. "He's a guest!"

"We don't know what he is." Ewan scratched his stubble and squinted, looking at the blank bedroom wall as if some secret was held there. "There was nothing in his pack that told me anything. Although it looks like it contained all his wordly goods. I'm not surprised he could barely walk, I could hardly lift the thing."

Rosie replaced the gun under the bed and snuggled back next to her husband. "Maybe he was on a long-distance hike? Camping en route?"

Ewan shook his head. "No tent. No food either."

"He did look a bit thin. And frail."

"Looks strong enough to me."

"Well, he looked very weak to me." Rosie said, firmly. "He's probably lost a lot of blood."

Ewan rolled his eyes, but with affection. "Once a nurse, always a nurse."

Rosie stroked his shoulder and waited until he turned to look at her. His face, usually a placid, smiling oval framed with unruly curls was lined with concern. His normally twinkling eyes, those green eyes which had so attracted her to him, were bloodshot and lifeless. He looked tired and worried.

"Get some sleep, love."

"He can't stay here, Rosie. You should call an ambulance."

"He's sleeping. I'll check on him in the morning. If he needs to go to hospital then I'll call an ambulance."

Ewan looked disconsolately at the clock. "Gone 2am. Might as well get up, get stuff done."

"Go back to sleep, love."

"Nah, I'm wide awake now. Intruder in my house? Maybe a Baxter thug? Not to mention-"

"Shhh." Rosie said. "Come on, try and relax."

"How? It's our home we're talking about! He has no right to evict us and no Sheriff is going to side with him. It's nonsense!"

"Well, then, there's no reason not to relax is there? It can't happen. It won't happen. So, there's nothing to worry about. See?" She smiled her gentlest smile at him, willing him to perk up. Ewan wasn't in the mood.

"See yourself. Case shouldn't even have made it to court." Ewan glared at her. "The law's an ass. So, there's always a risk. Rich man with influence, knight of the realm. Big landowner, local employer. And us, serfs like some vestige from the feudal system. Tenants on his land. No rights, no money, no support. We're just his bloody chattels. His property to do with as he likes. Wouldn't surprise me if it turns out he has *droit de seigneur*."

"What?"

"*Droit de seigneur.* You know, the right to-"

"Ewan! Stop this at once, please." Rosie wrung her hands. "It's all I've been able to do to keep this from Ellie and you're so wrapped up in all this. I'm a nervous wreck - trying to keep you calm, trying to keep her calm. Who's keeping me calm? No-one." She hung her head and sniffed.

"Honey!" Ewan's voice softened and he reached to put an arm around her. He could feel her shaking quietly and he tried to think of what best to say. "I'm sorry. You're right. I'm all eaten up by this, stretched so thin, pulled so tight. I feel like I'm going to snap. Come on. Let me hold you."

She turned into him and let his arms hold her to him, burying her face in his broad, bare chest. She reached up with her fingers and teased the greying curls at his throat.

"Please let this end. Please let this end with us all still here."

"It will." Ewan shhh'ed and gently rocked her. "It will." But he looked up at the ceiling, closed his eyes and prayed.

SIX

"Welcome to Baxter Farms, Cheryl." Malcolm had risen from his seat when Roly had led her into the boardroom and now he extended his hand and she shook it. "I appreciate you overlooking the slight, er, communication problem over the phone." He smiled thinly, his chins glistening in the striplight glare. "A disgruntled employee, it seems. I have dealt with him."

"Hmm." Cheryl mused. "It sounded awfully like you."

"Yes, indeed. Quite the mimic I understand. Quite the mimic." Malcolm wrung his hands. "Still we're all good now I take it?"

"Do you have many? Disgruntled employees, I mean?"

"Not at all, not at all." Malcolm purred. "Very low staff turnover. Very low. One big happy family here, isn't that right Roland?" He ploughed on, not waiting for his son to answer. "I'd show you the files if-" He bit his lip before he could finish with *I hadn't fired the HR Director* and then waved his hand in front of her. "Can I lead you this way, Cheryl?"

"It's Cheryl, actually Malcolm." Cheryl bridled. "Cheryl. With a *ch*, not a *sh*."

"And I'm Malcolm. With a Sir." He beamed. "Please, take a seat."

Thirty minutes later, with his Powerpoint presentation rolling interminably onwards, Cheryl couldn't stop checking her phone under the lip of the boardroom table. Sir Malcolm Baxter certainly liked the sound of his own voice and loved, loved, loved the story of his progression from "penniless" millionaire farmer to egg-moghul-to-the-masses. He deserved his knighthood, had earnt his knighthood, and here were sixty-four hagiographic slides polishing the halo of Sir Lord Malcolm of Eggshire ramming home the point. All that was missing was a video montage of him doing good works - missing for the excellent reason that she (correctly) assumed no such footage existed. She prodded her phone, glancing occasionally upwards as St Francis of Eggsisi continued to brown-nose himself.

"Any questions?"

Cheryl blinked and tried not to appear startled. Malcolm was looking at her, eyebrows raised expectantly. She flicked over two pages and laid her fountain pen on top. Her eyes ran down the list of bullet points she had drawn up on the drive over that morning.

"Your projections for the next five years show a significant growth in organic and free-range eggs-"

"Indeed, they do." Malcolm beamed, interrupting her flow.

"Do you expect this to come at the expense of a reduction in barn eggs and other-"

"On the contrary. We are eggs-panding our production and eggs-pecting - ha! Just a little yolk there! Here is our nutritional data." Malcolm pulled up a different slide. "Shown here per egg grade and production type. We have over 800,000 Free Range birds and a further 120,000 Organic birds, all housed in the highest welfare facilities available."

"I see."

"Any other questions?"

"Yes." Cheryl said. "Would you mind if I used your toilet?"

Cheryl Kilshaw was the Senior Product Executive, Eggs & Dairy, for Tesco in Scotland. Newly promoted from Breads & Pastries she realised she had much to learn about this market but she was nevertheless aware that she had drawn the short straw with this supplier. Her company's strategic goals for the year involved deepening their supply chain in Eggs & Dairy, thus giving more leverage in any upcoming discount wars with their competitors - discount wars which always came - and providing more protection from market disrupters, such as the avian flu outbreak the previous year which had reduced bird numbers and consequently increased prices. All this she understood and was fully on board with.

Baxter Farms were the big beast in the Scottish egg production and you couldn't ignore them. She wasn't really sure why Tesco's had never had dealings with them before - but now she had up close and personal experience of Sir Malcolm, she mused as she reached for the toilet roll, perhaps she had her answer. The man was unbearable, but he was getting on. No doubt he was grooming his son to take over the business reins so perhaps his retirement was looming? That would put a different complexion on things. She made a mental note to check this out more thoroughly later.

Malcolm was standing at the lectern, silent, on her return.

"You are out of toilet roll in the Ladies." Cheryl pointed out, gently, as she resumed her seat.

"Again?" Sir Malcolm blustered to the room as a whole. "What is it with women? When a man takes toilet paper off the roll, he does it like he's cracking a safe. Women do it like they're pulling another woman's knickers from your bloody glove compartment!" He turned to his son. "See to it please."

Cheryl gazed, slack-jawed, in amazement.

Ellie cracked open the door as quietly as she could and crept into the spare room. It was dark inside, the curtains still drawn even though it was mid-morning. The old man in the bed was snoring softly with his face towards her. She watched him for a moment and then moved over to the chair beside the foot of the bed and sat down. Clinging to her soft toy, Molly, she started singing a song in a very quiet voice. She studied his face while he slept. It was lined and creased, deep canyons carved around his eyes and into his forehead, and his skin was leathery and brown like her Mum's purse. His hair was curly, like hers, but it was mostly grey and it looked like it needed to be cut. Her Mum was always telling her that she should brush her hair every day to keep it shiny and healthy but it didn't look like this man had ever brushed his hair. Or washed it. She wrinkled up her nose, conscious for the first time of a stale smell in the room.

After a couple of minutes, she thought she could see the man open his eyes and look at her. She stopped singing and clutched Molly tightly.

"Hello." The man's voice was hoarse and croaky, as if he hadn't used it in a long time.

"Hello. This is Molly. Molly the Moo Cow. She's my special toy. She loves me and I keep her with me all the time so we can be best friends. Do you have a best friend?"

"No."

"I think everyone should have a best friend. Molly's not really my best friend. My best friend's called Jemima. She's going to help me do a Brownie badge. I'm new. I've been in Rainbows for ever so long but I'm going to be seven soon and they have space so my Mum says I can move up to Brownies. Were you ever in the Brownies?" The man seemed distracted and Ellie stopped talking as he wasn't answering any of her questions. Ellie cocked her head to one side. "What's your name?"

"Cullen."

"Cullen? That's a funny name. Do you have a middle name? My middle name is Charlotte. I think that's a pretty name, I like it. My Mum doesn't have a middle name at all - isn't that funny? My Dad has two - he says that's one for him and one for Mum. I think that's nice." Ellie paused for breath. "Do you like vegdibbles Cullen? I don't. My Mum says I should eat them up but they're so yucky. Are you okay? Shall I fetch my Mum?"

The man had a strange expression on his face that Ellie couldn't translate, although she could see he was in some kind of pain. She looked anxiously at the open bedroom door and wondered whether her mother would be angry at her for coming in and waking the man up. She faltered briefly, looking first at him and then at the door ajar. The man let out a groan and Ellie made a decision.

"I'll go and get her. Maybe she can make you some nice soup? Soup is nurishing, that's what she says. She makes a lot of soup. It's usually tasty but sometimes she cheats and makes vegdibble soup. That's not nurishing.

It's green with bits in." She glanced at him one more time. "I'll go and ask Mum to bring you some soup. I'll tell her to make sure it's not vegdibble."

And with that, she had nipped through the door into the backlit hall and was gone.

"I'd like to thank you, on behalf of Chris and myself, for meeting with ourselves on this occasion. We at Tesco like to be at the forefront of delivering ever-improving value and quality to our customer base and we are delighted to have this opportunity today to go through with yourselves some of the key drivers from our five-year strategic plan which, we believe, will keep ourselves ahead of the chasing pack in the race for the consumer spending trends we can see developing in the months and years forthcoming."

Jesus Christ, this woman was a windbag!

Malcolm caught himself puffing out his cheeks and quickly turned this into an exaggerated facial exercise of bulging one cheek then the other - better for her to think him a bit odd than enormously bored and unimpressed with her corporate gobbledygook. What he wouldn't give now for a nice cigar.

"I'd like to share, with yourselves, our supplier qualification process today - at a high overview level - so that it is clear and transparent as to the steps Chris and myself, will be taking throughout this ongoing, um, process. There will be subsequent visits required from ourselves for such purposes as, for example, assessments by our quality assurance team, led by Marcus, as well as conversations and discussions on aspects such as logistics, packaging, traceability, contract volume and, of course, um, price."

Malcolm's ears finally pricked up. This was the chase she seemed to have difficulty cutting to but, at the end of the day, in his long experience these supermarket chains were all about price. Lots of guff about everything else but ultimately it all ended up in a view of the bottom line and how they could squeeze fractions of a penny from suppliers and add it to their own margins.

Cheryl was struggling with her fancy handheld clicker which seemed to have decided it was going to advance the slides when it wanted to and not when she clicked it. Malcolm did his best not to concentrate on the beads of sweat on her upper lip or the rapidly growing pit-stains on her aquamarine bolero jacket. It was unseasonably hot in here and he made a mental note to catch Eddie on the way down to the sheds and have him give Shed Twelve a quick blast with the air-coolers - not normally something he would waste on mere livestock but today he wanted Cheryl and her team to leave with the best possible impression of his business and its facilities.

"Our customer surveys have shown that freshness and provenance are key factors in any purchasing decision and we at Tesco believe the key to market share is reducing time from lay to factory gate to supermarket shelf down to as little as possible, and projecting a brand which depicts the highest standards of animal welfare and product quality."

Malcolm couldn't help but smile inwardly at this: she had just confirmed his on-off, long-running argument with his son over price versus quality. He could hear that damned boy whining now, as Cheryl droned on:

"See, Sir? It is just as I've been telling you - they want the highest animal welfare standards from their suppliers.

Provenance and sustainability are key. Her very words!"

"Poppycock! You're not listening closely, you just hear what you want to hear. Verbs, boy! It's all about the verbs. She said they want a brand that *depicts* animal welfare and quality. Not epitomises, or embodies or exemplifies - *depicts.* I don't know who taught you business, boy, -"

"You did, Sir."

"Brand depiction is purely marketing, plain and simple. Nothing to do with manufacture or production - put any old eggs in a box, make the box look likes the dog's bollocks, tell 'em it's produced by the happiest, best-fed hens on the bloody planet and people'll think it's top-grade organic gold. They'll crawl over piles of birdcack to get their hands on it!"

"That's hardly ethical, Sir."

"Ethical! This is business, boy, not philosophy."

"But every business has to have an overarching philosophy. Something it stands for. That's what the brand does."

"Pah! There you go, using the wrong verbs again. It's what the brand projects, not what the business stands for. Look at washing powder manufacturers. Or cereal manufacturers. All these products made by the same company, perhaps even on the same production line. Different brand names, same old shit in the packet. Advertise the crap out of it and there's a stampede in aisle nine!"

"But, Sir, we're not talking about washing powder. We're talking about eggs! Living animals which can harbour and transmit disease! Fresh produce which can go bad - can even kill you if it's not treated properly. It's not just product quality-"

"An illusion."

"Or provenance-"

"Ditto."

"It's public health. Reputation. Trustworthiness-"

"Which is where the brands come in"

"If we cut corners which result in some virus or bacteria which gets into the food chain, we're done for. It won't be just our eggs which are shunned and the business going bust - we'll be up on criminal charges of public endangerment. Or worse!"

"Which is why the branding is key. And you know how much I hate that bloody word!"

"Key?"

"Yes. The bloody English language is going to hell in a handcart and it's the likes of this woman driving the tumbrils."

And, just like that, Malcolm was back in the room, listening to the warm waves of verbal diarrhoea that Cheryl continued to spoon out. For the next forty-five minutes.

Ellie stood and twirled in her new Brownie uniform, a vision of blonde curls dressed in brown and yellow. Her eyes sparkled with glee. "Look. I'm a Brownie too, now!"

Jemima cast a critical eye over Ellie's new uniform. "You'll need some badges. To go on your sash. I've got lots of badges."

"Do you? How many?"

"Ooh, lots. I've got one for Baking, one for Collecting, one for Dancing and I'm going to get one for Performing!" Jemima pirouetted and finished off with a little curtsy. Ellie's eyes sparkled at her friend's display.

"Performing!"

"Yes. I'm on Grade Two piano so I'm going to play something and my Mum's going to video it and put in on Youtube." Jemima said. "I want to be on X Factor."

Ellie was little deflated. "I might do a badge of growing vegdibbles."

"It's not vegdibbles." Jemima corrected. "It's vegetables."

"Veg-debals." Ellie tried, tentatively.

"Eat. Your. Vegetables."

"Eat your vegdibbles." Ellie repeated.

"Never mind." Jemima sighed.

Ellie wrinkled up her button nose. "I don't like vegdibbles." She was quite clear on this issue, nodding to reinforce her young but stout opinion on the matter.

"Oh, I do. I l-o-o-o-ve vegetables." Jemima boasted, showing a large gappy-toothed smile.

"All of them?"

"Most of them." Jemima waggled her head from side to side, weighing up a list. "Broccoli. Carrots. Carrots are my favourite. Specially carrot cake-"

"Carrot cake!" Ellie interrupted. "Yuk."

"It's lovely. Not vegetables at all really."

"Could I have carrot cake with my roast potatoes?"

"No, silly! It's a pudding." Jemima laughed and Ellie felt foolish. She clung to Molly The Moo Cow a bit more tightly but Jemima gave her a look, her eyes narrowing so Ellie forced herself to relax her grip. Jemima continued with her list: "Also I like sparragas, arctic-chokes… and peas!"

"What's sparragas?"

"Sparragas? Don't you know?"

Ellie hung her head and asked quietly. "No. What is

it?"

"It's like tiny green spears." Jemima's eyes grew large. "It makes your wee-wee smell funny!"

Ellie burst out laughing and the pair of them giggled, nudging each other on the hay bales as they did so. The two girls were sitting in the barn, high up where they could look down on anyone passing in the farmyard out front. Earlier that morning they had spent an hour dragging and heaving the bales like slaves assembling the pyramids, these giant Weetabix blocks being rearranged into a den of sorts, albeit a roofless one.

"I might eat tiny green spears." Reckoned Ellie. "They sound cool!"

"We have them all the time at school. Every week."

"Maybe I could grow sparragas for my Brownie badge?"

Jemima gave a little snooty pout. "You could I suppose. Sparragas is expensive though, so growing it would be good. Maybe you could sell it?"

"Why is it spensive?"

"I don't know. But my Mum says it's a good job Grandpa pays the school fees, otherwise I'd be home and then I'd never get sparragas."

Ellie considered this new nugget of information for a while. "Do you have to pay for school then? When you're a grownup?"

"Oh, only good schools. Normal school is free." Jemima declared. "Do your parents pay for your school?"

"I don't think so."

"Maybe your Grandpa does?"

"I don't have a Grandpa." Ellie sniffed and hugged Molly once more, regardless of whether Jemima gave her a disapproving look or not.

"Why not?"

"I don't know." Ellie screwed up her young brow in thought. "Maybe we can't afford one?"

"Oh, you don't need to pay for Grandpas! It's Grandpas that pay for you!"

"Really?"

"Sure!"

"Huh. I wish I had a Grandpa." Ellie said. "Maybe he'd be able to buy me some sparragas to grow for my badge."

"My Grandpa could buy a whole field of sparragas!" Jemima exclaimed.

"Is he very rich, your Grandpa?"

"Oh yes. He's an egg millionaire!"

"I don't know what that means." Ellie admitted.

"It means he owns millions and billions of eggs."

"Is that a lot?"

"Yes, duh! He owns the most eggs in Scotland."

"Wow. Where did he get them from?"

Jemima scoffed. "From hens, silly! Where else do eggs come from?"

"Does he own the hens too?"

"Of course. He has these great big buildings stuffed full of lovely hens and they lay eggs for him every day and he gathers them up into baskets and they put the baskets onto lorries and the lorries go to the shops and the shops sell the eggs and give Grandpa the money! He's very rich."

"Just from selling eggs?"

"Yes! I told you, gazillions of eggs."

"Gazillions!" Ellie liked the way the word sounded. "Gazillions and gazillions and gazillions!"

"Gazillions of eggs and gazillions of hens!" Jemima joined in and the pair skipped around in a circle, chanting and laughing. "Gazillions! Gazillions!"

"I thought it would help. If you met some vegetarians." Shirley explained. "Widen your exposure to other types of diet. See that we don't all have to stay in the same rut." She plonked a pint glass down in front of him.

"I like my rut." Paul said despondently, looking around the lunchtime throng in the Lamb & Flag. "What's this?"

"Lime and Soda. Beer's bad for gout."

"Lime and Soda? It's gout, not scurvy."

"It'll help."

"Won't bloody help my mood." Paul scowled and pushed the glass away from him. "Can I have some pork scratchings?"

"No, you can't! Meat's off the menu for a while. As well you know."

"There's no meat on a pork scratching." Paul protested. "It's just the name. Could just call 'em scratchings. They're a superfood."

"No. They're. Not."

"Plus, they're only 40% fat."

"Really? What's the other 60% then?"

"Crunch."

"You do know that 100% of that is untrue?" Shirley was getting used to Paul's protests by now. This was Week Two after Day Zero - the name Paul had given to the start of their new regime since that was how he had measured his morale. "Where do you get all this rubbish from?"

"It's not rubbish."

"It's from Davy isn't it?" She looked around for the offending landlord but he was nowhere to be seen.

"Not all of it!"

"You spend too much time with Davy. Too much time in here."

"It's my local!"

"Only because you're always here."

Paul scowled and looked gloomily around at all the other patrons enjoying themselves. "Is there anything I can have which *isn't* bad for gout?" He whined.

Shirley met his eyes and threw him a wink. "Later, lover." She looked at her watch. "Right, they'll be here any minute. Now, best behaviour okay? I don't want you offending them or anything."

"Thanks." Paul pouted. "For the faith you put in me."

"I know what you're like." Shirley looked at her partner and sighed. "They're vegetarians *and* gay. You won't be able to stop yourself, will you?"

"It was your idea to have me meet Uncle Lez and her mate." Paul reminded her.

"Yes. And that's exactly the sort of language which will be… unhelpful." She remonstrated. "You do realise there are many different genders nowadays, and that gender equality is a thing?"

Paul sniffed. "There's not many genders. There's only, oh I don't know, five."

"Oh right. I didn't know you were an expert. Enlighten me then: what are the five true genders, Oh Wise One?"

"Well there's women and men, obv."

"Obv."

"Then lezzers and woofters. And weirdos."

"Charming." Shirley sniped. "And what categorises the *weirdo* gender then? I'm sure such people would be flattered by the terminology."

"Well, it's your people that don't fit in the other four, isn't it? Your BLTs and your She/He/They's. All them."

"I see you've got the taxonomy down. All very Linnean, I must say."

"Ha!" Paul claimed, triumphantly. "I know what that means! Have I ever mentioned the SH/IT: Swearword Hierarchy/Insult Taxonomy?"

"Not now." Shirley shook her head wearily, and then suddenly stood up out of her armchair and waved to a figure who had just entered the pub. "Here they are. Best behaviour, okay?"

"Sorry I'm late!" Elaine panted, shaking the raindrops off her umbrella. "I've just come from Evita."

"You don't look very brown." Paul said.

Elaine looked at him, uncertain. "Rehearsals?"

Shirley just rolled her eyes. "Elaine, this is Paul. Paul, Sensible Elaine."

"Sensible?"

"Yes." Elaine said primly as she scooped her coat beneath her and sat down next to Shirley. "Sensible by name, sensible by nature."

"Got it." Said Paul, nodding, as if nothing could be more normal.

"Where's Jakki?" asked Shirley, looking towards the door. "I thought you were bringing her with you?"

"Oh, she'll be here. Surprised she wasn't ahead of me. Not like her to be late." Elaine scoped the pub, craning her neck to check for her partner, seeming all on edge.

"Well, while we wait. Just to let you know that Paul

has agreed to be your minder." Paul beamed at Elaine and this seemed to make her more, rather than less, nervous.

"Are you sure this is necessary?"

"Dunno about necessary." Paul interjected, an energetic gleam in his eyes. "But it means I'll get improved meat rations. So there's that."

"Payment in kind, you might say." Shirley clarified for Elaine's benefit, jerking her head towards her partner. "Give him an incentive."

Paul's grin widened further.

"Well, if not necessary, then." Elaine persisted. "Is it… sensible?"

"It's just a precaution." Shirley reassured her. "A sensible precaution. If Baxter's thug comes round again, he'll think twice before messing with my Paul, won't he lover?"

"Aye. He won't want to mess with a gargantuan vegetarian like me."

"I thought you just said you were getting increased meat rations?" Elaine wrinkled her nose in confusion.

"'Sright." Agreed Paul. "But I'm still a vegetarian."

"Who eats meat?"

Paul leaned in as if imparting a nugget of incalculable wisdom. "I'm an apex vegetarian. I only eat animals which are vegetarian."

Shirley rolled her eyes again. "Ignore him, honey. He's an idiot."

Paul deadpanned. "A vegetarian idiot if you don't mind."

"Quite so." Shirley stood up. "Excuse me a moment while I go powder my nose."

Paul watched her disappear out of sight and turned to

Elaine. "So. Elaine isn't it?" She nodded. He lowered his voice. "Is there anything good about being a lesbian?"

Elaine blanched, unsure how to answer this question she'd never been asked before. "Well… you never have to touch a scrotum."

"Huh." Paul considered this morsel of information and then, nodding to himself, buried his face in his Lime & Soda.

SEVEN

"Am I to understand that your son plays an active senior role in the business?"

The presentations were at an end. Cheryl was standing, stirring her coffee in Malcolm's best china cup and saucer, as they stood together in the boardroom surveying the Baxter Farms estate from its windows.

Malcolm barked a laugh. "Ha! I should say not. I mean, he's not completely useless - he could always serve as a bad example - but in terms of experience in running the business. He has none."

"Yet?" Cheryl pressed. Malcolm looked askance at her and wondered if this woman could, unbelievably, consider Roland as some kind of linchpin in any deal they would reach. He rapidly reconsidered his response.

"Absolutely. Absolutely. I mean, he may be a little wet behind the ears but he's coming on in leaps and bounds. Chip off the old block, you see."

"Wet behind the ears?" Cheryl frowned. "How old is he, may I ask?"

"How old is he? Well, let's put it this way: he still says *basgetti*." Malcolm caught himself too late - the words were out of his mouth. "Ha-ha! Fatherly joke. Forgive me. He will. Roland is, erm, in his forties. Forty-six I think?"

"You think?"

"I know." He calculated quickly. "Forty-eight. And eminently capable of doing the right thing." *Only after he had exhausted all the other options*, he thought to himself.

"Are you grooming him as your successor? We at Tesco are very keen on succession planning. We believe it shows a long-term commitment to a business."

"Yes. Erm." Malcolm, seeking for some unobtainable positive statements, sought refuge in his trove of ambiguous employee references. "Well, you see, there really is nothing about business that you can teach him. You would, um, do well to observe him at work."

"Hmm." Cheryl pursed her lips. "Does he, perhaps, have a background in Public Relations?"

Malcolm furrowed his brow by way of a silent answer, uncertain where Cheryl was going.

"It is just that, I have to say, Sir Malcolm, that ourselves at Tesco are concerned. Public Relations, of all kinds, is a major - major - consideration for all our operations. We have a team who do nothing but social media all day. Watching, searching, checking, posting. You wouldn't believe the volume of tweets and Facebook posts that go up every day - from abandoned trolleys (as if there is anything we can do about that!) to bananas with spiders in them, tinned peaches containing bones or other unsavoury foreign objects. I'm sure you can imagine." Malcolm nodded in what he hoped appeared like empathy. "And we have to be scrupulous - absolutely scrupulous, and seen to be so - about our supply chain. Provenance, treatment of workers, animal welfare. This is all key for today's consumer."

There she went again, referring to plurals in the singular: consumer when she meant consumers. He wouldn't have been surprised to hear her say trouser or knicker, and then his mind immediately strayed to what knicker she might be wearing beneath her trouser. She was a fine-looking woman, all nails and hair and satin blouse stretched tautly over a shapely chest. Cheryl with a *ch*, not Cheryl with a *sh*. Stickler. He liked that. And she wasn't afraid to stand up to him. He liked that too. And she also had a head for business which came across in her every manner.

"I can assure you, Cheryl. As you will see when we show you around, animal welfare and the working conditions for our employees are paramount to us." Malcolm spread his palms open, smiling broadly if a little too strongly. "And as for provenance - Roland will be able to show you our records for sourcing, disease control, health records, the works! Baxter Farms has always prided itself on its quality."

"Yes." Cheryl pouted. "I was referring more to the reports about a current court case. With your tenant farmers?"

"Ah." Malcolm sighed.

"Ah? Is that all you have to say on the matter?"

"Not at all. A little local difficulty. A minor incident, unrelated to the business and our soon-to-be business with yourselves."

"Unrelated? They are your tenants are they not?"

"Yes, of course. But they are farmers. They are not employees here at Baxter, have never been so, and as far as I am concerned, never will be. We are in the process of expanding our business - and our meeting with you today is evidence of that expansion and desire for business growth - and these nuisances are obstructing our plans. The land they farm is ours and I would like it back."

"To build more sheds?"

"Perhaps. Certainly to extend our facilities and

increase volumes. Without…" Malcolm gave a greasy smile. "Without compromising quality."

"It is a court case. Which could go against you." Cheryl raised her eyebrows. "Could be bad publicity."

"All publicity is good publicity" Malcolm smarmed, quoting someone he couldn't recall.

"No, Sir Malcolm. It is not. In this day and age a business can be brought to its knees overnight by an adverse remark, a clumsy reaction to a complaint, a tin-eared Press Release. Let me assure you: there IS such a thing as bad publicity." She placed her empty cup and saucer on the boardroom table and folded her arms to conclude her point. "Ourselves at Tesco wish no connection to such bad publicity."

Malcolm's eye gimleted as he bit his lip and told himself to count to three. "Of course. It is a small matter. The court will find in our favour. I am confident it is something and nothing. And certainly, nothing to concern you or Tesco in regards to your business dealings with us. Now, if you would like to join me for a tour-"

"I'd like to thank you for meeting with ourselves today." Cheryl interrupted. "I think this dialogue has been highly constructive. I shall report back to Head Office and call you later this week with an update. Perhaps a tour could be arranged at that point?"

She swept her folder off the boardroom table into her bag and extended her hand towards him. It was clear to Sir Malcolm that the meeting had come to an end.

"Which badge do you think I should do first?" Ellie was sitting at the kitchen table clasping Molly The Moo

Cow and swinging her legs to and fro wondering how old she would be before she could reach the floor.

"Well, sweetheart. There's quite a lot to choose from isn't there?" Her mother was flicking through the My Badge Book which she had bought online from the Girlguiding Shop. An A5 spiral bound handbook in fluorescent yellow and brown - all part of the matching "starter pack" which also included a hoodie, T-shirt, skirt, leggings, badge sash, backpack and neckie. Rosie had drawn the line at the gilet. A hundred quid down and here she was skimming through this badge book while her daughter swung her legs like she hadn't a care in the world. Which, of course - bless her - she hadn't.

"Something to do with aminals?"

"Well, that would be a good choice wouldn't it, living on a farm. You'd probably have a head start on the other children."

"I don't want a head start Mum! I have to earn a badge fair and square - that's what Jemima says."

"Hmm, Jemima. She's a little girl with a lot to say for herself, isn't she?"

"What does that mean?"

"Never mind. There's a badge for growing things - plants and vegetables?"

"I don't like vegdibbles, do I? Jemima does, but I don't."

"No, sweetheart, you don't. Okay, what about pets? There's a pet badge." Rosie read through the accompanying blurb. "You need to learn about caring for a pet, how to feed them and keep them healthy and safe, make them feel loved."

"Ooh, yes. I can do that with Scampi!" Ellie's eyes widened in delight and she hugged Molly with a surge of pleasure.

"Ah, well Sweetheart. I don't think you can call Scampi a pet." Rosie saw her daughter's face drop and hurriedly tried to reword her sentiment. "I mean, Scampi is a working dog. On our farm. I know he seems like a pet to you but I'm not sure that Brown Owl would agree." Rosie knew that miserable woman, Jeanette, who shouted at the girls like she had permanent PMT - the only resemblance to an owl was that she screeched like one.

"I would like my own pet." Ellie pondered aloud, giving Molly an extra-strong hug and making the plush animal's eyes bulge alarmingly. Rosie made a mental note to check the stitching next time she stole the toy away for a wash. Ellie had had Molly since she was a baby and it was the devil's own job getting it out of her clutches for a refresh. The poor creature was saggy and grubby and almost bare in places where the plush had been rubbed raw. "I think I'd like a hen."

"What?" Rosie was shaken from her thoughts by this left-field statement from her daughter. "A hen! Whatever for?"

"Hens live on farms, don't they? Although we don't have any. And they lay eggs that we could eat. I like eggs." Ellie nodded, reminding herself. "I like eggs but I don't like vegdibbles."

"Well, they're not very cuddly though are they, hens? Not like a bunny rabbit or a kitten?"

"Oh, but the baby chicks!" Ellie squished her shoulders together and lowered her chin into her chest, giving herself an imaginary squeeze of joy. "Oh, they're so cute. All yellow and soft and fluffly. And they go *cheep, cheep, cheep*!"

"Yes, they do. You're right." Rosie wondered if it wasn't such a crazy idea after all. "And they don't eat much and they don't take up much space."

"And they're so cute!" Ellie repeated. "Oh, yes please Mum. Can I have a chick?"

"Well…" Rosie thought for a moment. "I don't actually know where you get them from? They don't have them in pet shops, do they? Or do they? Hmmm."

"Jemima says her Grandpa has millions and hundreds and gazillions of chicks! He keeps them in great big sheds and they lay squillions of eggs! He's like an egg millionaire, Jemima says."

"Yes. I'm well aware of Jemima's Grandpa and I am equally sure that he wouldn't give us a chick. And, more to the point, I wouldn't want one from him!"

"Why not?"

"Well, Sweetheart…" How can I express this without getting angry and upsetting my daughter with the truth, Rosie thought? Keeping a six-year-old innocent in these times was an ever-more impossible job but she was determined to let her daughter have the playful childhood that she herself had been denied. "The hens that Jemima's Grandpa has are a bit like Scampi, you see. They're not pets, they're working animals. I know it might be hard to understand but it's true."

"Oh." Ellie sighed and looked at her swinging feet again, her patent-leather school shoes gleaming on her white-stockinged feet. "Well, I don't mind where we find one. And I don't mind if it's a chick or a hen. If it's a chick it'll be fluffy and grow into a hen. If it's a hen it'll lay eggs and one will turn into a chick! Let's just find one!"

Rosie smiled to herself. Yes, it was as easy and as

simple as that to a child wasn't it: just find one!

"But why, Sir?"

"But why, Sir?" Malcolm mimicked cruelly. "Why always the questions? Why, why, why? Can you not just do?"

Roly closed his eyes. He knew what his father's disappointment looked like - he didn't want to confront it right now. Perhaps it was this submissive gesture that stirred something in his father, or perhaps it was coincidence, but Malcolm's tone softened slightly.

"Cheryl has pointed out to me - and, I believe, with some not insignificant glee - that she is aware of the appeal and consequent court case about our tenant farmer's eviction. And that this is not, and I quote, not acceptable, unquote. Such non-positive - her words - publicity can adversely affect their brand and image and it is not - I repeat not - a situation which can go unnoticed when considering initiating a key supplier contract. With ourselves. At this time." Malcolm exhaled loudly and gave a slight shiver. "I trust I have conveyed to you in suitably tortured English the way in which Cheryl chose to communicate the fact to me that-" He raised his voice in a stern blast. "We need to get the blasted Critchley's out!"

"Or win the case, Sir?" Roly offered.

"Win the case?" Malcolm clenched his jaw and gave a sneering shake of his head. "Court cases take time, boy. Time we don't have. I want this deal - I need this deal. With ourselves. At this time."

"So?"

"So, we need them to withdraw their appeal. Accept

this decision - this completely legal and rational decision - with good grace and move on!" Malcolm huffed. "See to it."

Roly stood and blinked.

"Off you go!"

"But… how, Sir?"

"Don't know. Don't care."

"Isn't this more, um, Eddie's line?" Roly suggested.

Malcolm slumped into his chair and then, seeing the look on his son's face, rolled his eyes. "Look. Are you familiar with the tale of the sun and the wind? They have a contest to see who is the strongest, who can get a man to remove his coat?"

"Um?"

Malcolm shook his head in disappointment. "The wind huffs and puffs and throws out icy blasts, trying to blow the coat off the man - but he just tightens his collar, leans into the wind and hugs the coat closer to him. The harder it blows the more the man hangs onto his coat. Whereas the sun, soothes and warms, all calm and confident. Turns the temperature up and, without any fuss, the man takes his coat off and walks along in his shirtsleeves, happy as can be."

"I see." Said Roly, not really seeing his father's point at all.

"In this analogy Eddie is the wind: cold but effective but all too likely to just make things worse. Whereas you, my boy, are gentle and kind." Roly was suddenly taken aback by the unexpected personal pronoun which his father had smuggled into his speech. His eyes widened. Briefly. "To a fault. Too willing to see the other side, too lily-livered to raise a fuss, too feeble to inflict any damage."

Roly blinked, temporarily lost in thought, only to hear his father revert back to his usual, impersonal, style.

"You, boy, have just the right degree of compassion and consideration for others which, in every other situation imaginable, would make you completely unsuitable for the task. However, these Critchley's-" He made their very surname seem like a criticism. "They too are gentle, genteel even, folk. They don't want a fuss, won't respond to threats. They need to be soothed, stroked, cajoled. Just your… cup of tea."

"That may be the nicest thing you've ever said to me."

"You're welcome." Malcolm wafted the thanks away, magnanimous and heartless in equal measure. "So, go visit them. Reason with them. Appeal to them. Offer them money if you must. Just get them out!"

"Yes, Sir. Thank you. I'll do my best."

"You'll have to do better than that, boy." Malcolm glared up at him and dismissed him with a wave.

Roly left and closed the door softly behind him, clutching on with all the positivity he could muster to that single small diamond of a personal pronoun he had found winking in the dirt.

"So, here's the plan." Jakki unfurled a sheet of A3 paper on the trestle table and secured the corners with small stones she had scooped up from the gravelled Beer Garden. Jakki had a foaming pint in front of her and Paul was admiring it enviously, unable to submit to buying himself one as he knew the pair would rat on him to Shirley and his misery would be compounded. Davy had smiled brightly at him when he had ordered his pint of Lime and Soda at the bar.

"I'm no more happy with it than you, mate." He'd said to Paul, not quite convincingly. "Sends all the wrong signals doesn't it? On the other hand, the profit margin on it is insane."

Paul had skulked off to the Beer Garden in the hope that none of the regulars, denizens of the darkest corners of the pub, would venture out into daylight and see him drinking a puff's drink.

"This is the A703." Jakki ran a pudgy finger down the blue ribbon which ran across the width of the paper. "The main entrance is here. And these are the groups of sheds: here, here and here." She was circling three groups of rectangles on the drawing: the largest clustered just off the main road; the other two smaller groups were situated several hundred meters away, one on the other side of the road, the other way off behind the main complex separated by a significant amount of woodland. "These…" She tapped the largest group for emphasis. "… are the ones we target."

"Why?" Paul asked.

"Why are we targetting them?" replied Jakki.

"No. Why those and not those?" Paul waved at the more distant clusters of sheds.

"Lay?" Jakki looked up at Elaine and smiled.

"Well, it would be easier if we targetted these other two groups, right enough. You can't tell from the map but they are almost entirely hidden from view and accessible only by this cinder track here. If you didn't know they were there..."

"But?" Jakki prompted, unhappy at the direction Elaine was taking.

"But I'm not sure if these more remote sheds are… what we want."

Paul furrowed his brow. "Why not?"

"Look." Jakki said, tight-lipped. "Has Shirley explained what's going on here?"

"Said I'm on improved meat rations!" Paul grinned.

"I mean what we're doing here? The *operation*?"

"It's an operation?"

"Yes." Jakki snapped. "It's got a name and everything!"

"What's it called, then?" asked Paul.

"Operation Shellshock." Elaine offered, brightly.

Paul considered this briefly. "I don't get it."

"Look." Jakki shot Paul a look and then, realising she had raised her voice, looked anxiously around the Beer Garden and then lowered her tone. "We are going to break-in to these sheds here." She tapped the diagram for emphasis. "Take video of the atrocious conditions the hens are kept under and release it onto social media."

Paul looked at Jakki, then Elaine, then back to Jakki. "Why?"

Jakki folded her arms. "Lay? Tell him about the sheds."

"Well-" Elaine started.

"They're hellholes." Jakki interrupted. "The hens are hemmed in, ten or twelve to a community cage. They're called community cages to make it sound like it's all friendly and sociable but these are stressed animals packed in tight. The weakest get trampled on or shoved out of the way for food, bullied and ostracised - I'm sure there are mental health issues for the birds. Plus, there are fights and injuries, maimed and bleeding hens lying around, jammed between bars or left to rot and die on the manure-strewn floor. Other hens just pecking around them. It's like a war zone."

Elaine lowered her head and added quietly. "Choking air, suffocating heat, feather-dust and powder-dry manure everywhere. In your lungs, on your clothes, in your hair." She gagged at the memory.

"You can't hear yourself think." Jakki took over again. "The constant din of 60,000 hens squawking and the thrum of the machinery which brings in food and medicine and takes away the eggs."

"You've been inside?" Paul asked.

Elaine nodded, her voice little more than a whisper. "If you try rescuing an injured one… well, it doesn't know you're rescuing it. You just end up with a flapping monster attacking you with a sharp beak while a thousand of its colleagues treat your wellies as breakfast. And the cacophony you cause when you move through the flock? Makes your ears bleed."

"So we want to highlight this animal cruelty. Stop this shocking abuse. Humiliate and punish Malcolm sodding Baxter and get these birds fair treatment. And all the other birds being farmed and treated this way." Jakki snorted. "Operation Shellshock."

Paul nodded. "Ok, I get it. And these other sheds?"

"We think they're different." Jakki pursed her lips. "Maybe they're actually housing well-cared for hens, kept humanely, properly treated and cared for. We're not sure."

"And some of these are new. This one is still being built. These two weren't there six months ago." Elaine looked up at Paul, her eyes moist. "I used to work there. Briefly."

"So that's why we target the ones in the main complex?" Paul nodded again.

"Correct." Said Jakki.

"Even though we might be seen getting in?" Paul tapped on the map. "There's only one way in and out, and it's on the main road."

"Let me worry about that." Jakki puffed her chest out. "I have a plan."

Paul looked at Elaine, who returned his gaze deadpan, and shrugged. He didn't need any incitement not to worry - worrying wasn't his department. And anyone who was called Sensible Elaine had to be, well, sensible. She probably had enough sense for all of them, even if it seemed that Jakki wore the trousers in their relationship. If she's willing to go along with this then that was good enough for him - thinking and planning weren't Paul's department either.

Everyone has strengths and weaknesses, and Paul, rather than dwelling on his weaknesses, preferred to focus on his strengths: persistence and ignorance. Persistence would get you there pretty much every time - if something didn't give, hit it; if it still didn't budge, hit it harder. The rare times this strategy failed was when you introduced wisdom into the equation and decided that perhaps there was a good reason why it wasn't working. This was where his second strength came in: ignorance. You didn't give up with your first strategy if you didn't know any better. You just kept on until reality gave in at your stubborn naivety. Some might call it stupidity rather than naivety, but not to Paul's face - six foot five tall got you a fair chunk of manners from most people. So, Paul's attitude was to leverage these twin strengths - which he liked to bundle together as a single superpower: dogged determination.

Let the Jakkis and Elaines of this world worry about complexities and nuances. In a world of smartbombs and surgical strikes, Paul was very much still the blunderbuss or trebuchet of weaponry. On the downside there tended to be a lot of collateral damage at the scene; on the upside it was a low-tech solution with not much to go wrong. No lasers to fail, no failure to ignite, no AI to interfere. Paul was very much fire-and-forget in human form.

"So, what do you need me to do?" He asked, now keenly awaiting his exciting brief.

"Nothing." Jakki patted his hand. "You're there to protect Elaine should anything go wrong."

"Nothing?" Paul scrunched up his face.

"You're our insurance policy. Safety net. Backup procedure." Elaine smiled, reassured by his mere physicality.

"Is that all? That's a bit… well, shit." He said despondently. It had gone against the grain to allow himself to be drafted into this *operation* - her word - but the tariff of meat payment-in-kind had been too tempting to pass up. He had allowed himself to dream of an opportunity to also nick a truckload of eggs. They were limited by Shirley as well and Paul had envisaged a fortnight or so of surreptitious cooked breakfasts as reward for his part in this scheme. Not now.

"Well, that's just how it is." Jakki confirmed. "I have planned this meticulously, made contingency plans for every, well, contingency I could think of. Which means it's going to be dull as ditchwater for you, I'm afraid. No chance of injury or getting caught. It's fool-proof and failsafe and I'm expecting it to go off without a hitch."

Paul sulked. This didn't sound exactly like stirring stuff. Operation Shellshock? More like Operation Runny Egg. He took a sip from his Lime & Soda, but that only made his mood worse.

“Okay. So, Operation Shellshock. Are we all clear?” Jakki folded up the sheet of A3 and stuffed it into her handbag.

Paul and Elaine nodded stiffly.

“Excellent. Tomorrow at 2100 hours, then.” Jakki announced. “Paul - bring your van.”

EIGHT

Rosie Critchley opened the door and her face instantly changed from a smile to a black glare. Roly took a startled step back.

"What do you want?"

"Good morning!" He tried bright and breezy and flashed his best smile.

"Is it?" Her voice had real bite but also sounded like it was struggling to cope. Like someone trying to use a hole punch on a wad of paper that was too thick for it.

"Ah, well you see this is… well, rather awkward I'm afraid."

"Yes, I imagine it bloomin' well is!"

Roly still holding his smile, raised his eyebrows in expectation. "May I come in?"

"No. You may not."

"Ah." Roly nodded. "Right."

Bugger. He'd been thinking about this encounter since his father's instruction the previous day and, with his own wife's dismay still ringing in his ears, he had been weighing up precisely how to deal with the tenant farmers. This was a decisive step for him. His first mission, and he had chosen to accept it.

"Right." He repeated. "Well, I was hoping that perhaps I could just explain… erm, on your doorstep…"

"Why your father is trying to evict us from our family home?" Rosie demanded.

"Well-"

"And offer us nothing for a lifetime of my husband's efforts?"

"No, you see-"

"Not to mention his father's and his father's before him?"

"Yes, well I understand your position-"

"Well, I don't think you do!" Rosie glared. "I don't think you do at all!"

Blimey. Was this woman going to self-destruct in ten seconds? He took a deep breath.

"Look, Mrs Critchley. I don't want us to get off on the wrong foot. If perhaps-"

"Well, it's a little too late for that, isn't it *Mister* Baxter?" Rosie spat his name back at him. "And there's no perhaps about it."

"I am willing to, erm, talk terms."

"Are you?"

"Actually yes." Roly smiled his broadest smile. Rosie winced. "My father is not unreasonable."

"You could have fooled me!"

"Yes, well, he can come across as abrasive. At times."

"You mean when he's awake? Those sorts of times?"

"Look, Mrs Critchley. I am keen-"

"*You* are keen?"

"My father is keen." Again, Roly thought of his mission. He wished he was able to rip off some mask and expose a smooth, expert slickness capable of dealing with any obstacle. He stifled a whimper. "To avoid any unpleasantness. You and your husband are, as you have pointed out, long-standing tenants and, again as you have pointed out, have invested a significant amount in this farm business. That is not, erm, unappreciated."

"It seems pretty bloody unappreciative to me to force

us out and give us no option but resort to the courts to defend our rights!"

"Well, you see we maintain that, well... unfortunately... he is within his rights to terminate your lease on this estate-"

"Well, let's see what the courts have to say about that shall we?"

Roly took a moment to calm his nerves. Rosie was still scowling at him.

'Cajole. Persuade.' His father had said. 'Offer them money if you must.'

'Be a man.' His wife had said. 'A better man than him.'

"Perhaps we can avoid the courts?"

"I don't think so. My husband's with our solicitor right now." She sneered at him. "When he should be up on the hills doing his job."

"Well, perhaps we can bring this to a swifter conclusion? Nip this in the bud, so to speak."

Rosie appeared to move instantly from defiance to suspicion. "What do you mean?"

"I mean..." Roly cleared his throat. "Perhaps we can come to some mutually agreeable solution. Obviating the need for legal action. Maybe a financial solution?"

"You want to pay us off?"

"Not at all. We would like to look at ways in which we can reimburse you, and your husband, for the efforts and investment you have made to this estate over the years."

"Like I said, pay us off."

"Look. Mrs Critchley. Let me leave this with you." Roly slipped an envelope from his jacket pocket and extended it to her. She looked down at it then back at him, narrowing her eyes, but he pushed ahead. "Go on. Read it. Discuss it with your husband when he gets home. I'll come back tomorrow… if that's ok?"

Rosie reached out slowly and plucked at the envelope in his hand as if it was gelignite. As she hesitated, a small head of blonde curls appeared from behind her skirt.

"Hello, Mister Baxter!" Ellie beamed and sparkled up at Roly, dimples in her cheeks. "Have you brought me a hen?"

Rosie grabbed at the envelope and stuffed it into her pinnie, stooping slightly to take Ellie's hand. "Shush, honey. No, Mister Baxter is just here to talk to Mum and Dad about things. I'm afraid it's not about a hen." She tweaked Ellie's nose to try and get her daughter to chuckle, unsuccessfully.

"Is that right, Mister Baxter?" Ellie pouted.

Rosie turned back to him and glared, defiance sparking in her brown eyes, and a sudden bolt of lightning shot into Roly. It took him a split-second to recognise it for what it was: initiative.

"Actually, no." He heard himself say, attempting to smile goofily once more. "Are you looking for a hen? Because if you are, I know where there are thousands of them!"

"Ooh, yes! I want a hen! Can I have a hen! Do you have a hen just for me!" Ellie clapped her hands together, her eyes wide with delight. Rosie's eyes, the polar opposite, narrowed and held Roly's own. He looked frantically between mother and daughter Critchley, his mind a whirl. It was now or never.

"Well, yes Ellie, I believe I do!" Roly blurted. "Shall I bring her round the day after tomorrow?"

He eyed Rosie with a determined look and waited for

a response. Ellie gave a little cheer and hugged her mother but Rosie stood, white-faced.

Roly smiled one final smile. "Maybe I can come in next time?"

His first mission had been accomplished.

"Okay, so there's a guard." Paul shrugged.

"You said there wouldn't be one!" Jakki hissed at Elaine.

"There never used to be one when I worked there. Maybe our protests have tightened their security?"

"Huh." Jakki nodded. "So…"

"I could take him out." Paul offered helpfully.

"No!" Elaine protested. If her partner was intent on this project, so be it - but she was a reluctant follower. Elaine no more wanted to harm a security guard than she wanted to harm a chicken. This was to be a peaceful operation, no injuries, no damages, in and out and some video captured. Jakki had assured her that was the plan.

"Can you see what he looks like?" Jakki asked. They were sitting in Paul's van, lights off, parked in a turning-circle-cum-layby directly opposite the main site entrance to Baxter Farms. It was getting dark.

Paul looked through the viewfinder on his camera and squinted. "Too far away."

"Can't you zoom in?"

"Camera doesn't have a zoom."

"Doesn't have a zoom?"

"Nah. Don't really use it, you see. If I want to take a photo, I use my phone."

"Well why did you bring it then?" Jakki was already disappointed with Paul - and this was early days.

"Couldn't find my binoculars."

"You said you had some!" Jakki was indignant.

"I do. Just couldn't find 'em. Must have left them in my wossname."

"Great. Just great. Lay? Remind me to bring *my* phone next time."

"We could just move closer." Suggested Elaine. "If we can't bring the mountain to Mohammed..."

"Well, he's not wearing a turban." Paul said, still squinting but now looking to see if he could make out the man's skin colour.

"What? No. It's an expression." Elaine exchanged looks with Jakki. "I mean we're going to break in anyway - it's not like we can do it from here."

"Lay's right. Let's get closer." Jakki undid her seatbelt.

"He'll see us!" Elaine cried.

The three sat silently for a while, thinking.

"We could create a diversion!" Paul suggested.

"Like?"

"Well." He pondered. "You two could walk up closer to the shed and then come over all randy, start feeling each other up like, undressing each other. That'd get him interested and, while he's absorbed, I could sneak round the back of the trees there and see if there's a rear entrance."

"Certainly not!" Jakki was outraged. "Is that what you think us lesbians get up to, is it?"

"Well, all the ones I've seen, aye."

"Oh, I see. On the internet I take it?"

"Well, there's a lot of porn out there. It's not going to download itself."

"Disgusting." Jakki was flushed with indignation.

Paul tried to row back, not entirely successfully.

"Well, I mean, I don't know any muffdivers personally do I?" He put his hands out in front of him, quickly. "Present company excepted."

"Muff-? How dare you!" She snapped her neck around and glared out of the window.

Elaine looked at Paul impishly. "You can't be a muff-diver if there's no muff." She gave him a salacious wink. "Jakki likes a clean work surface."

Paul's eyes stood out on stalks while Elaine turned and slid her arm inside the crook of her partner's elbow, snuggling in. After a few moments silence, Jakki spoke up, mollified. "Let's go home. I need to consult my expert source about the best way to deal with on-site security."

"Expert source?" Paul furrowed his brow.

"Yes." Jakki snapped, clearly in no mood to expand on her statement. "Let's come back tomorrow night, same time."

Two girls were playing on the floor in his room. Each had a colourful horse with luxurious mane and tail and a Barbie-Doll rider. Manes and tails and accessories were multi-coloured with the predominant hue pink. The girls chatted animatedly, unaware he was watching. The memory of his daughter at their age played over the scene, flitting in and out of focus. He wondered why he had never sat down on the floor and played with his own daughter like these girls were playing now. His vision blurred further still.

"Are you alright Mister Cullen?" the familiar one asked, seeing him awake. "Are you sick? Shall I fetch my Mum?"

"I'm…" He cleared his throat, wiped his eyes and struggled to sit up in bed. "I'm okay." He ran his eyes over her face looking for similarities with his own daughter. He looked at her hands, and the dolls she was playing with.

"Would you like to play with us?" She asked. It sounded like she was toying with him, a question that was almost a threat.

Cullen knew it didn't make any sense. Playing with these two girls now wouldn't redress not having played with his daughter all those years ago. Wouldn't bring her back now either. But somehow, in his fevered imaginings, it made sense and needed to be done. From somewhere else he heard a voice say "Yes." It was his.

The girl sprung up and skipped out of the room only to return moments later with a brown horse, with no rider and a small brush intended, he presumed, to comb the horse's mane and tail. *His* horse's mane and tail. She laid the horse and brush on the duvet near his mottled hands and resumed her place on the floor next to her friend. The floor was scattered with other paraphernalia: fences, bushes and trees, some orange cones.

"We're going to have a gymkhana." Her friend announced.

"Yes!" The blonde girl said, eyes gleaming. "That's horse-jumps, Mister Cullen! Let's all give our horses names!"

"Good idea. I'll be Silver Sparkle Glory." Declared her friend. "You be Rainbow Fairy Fountain." She looked sadly over at Cullen cradling his brown horse. "And you can be… Plain."

"Girls! Girls! What are you doing? Come on, now. Please come out of there. The poor man needs rest."

Rosie bustled in and shooed the girls out, picking up their Barbie paraphernalia where they'd left it as they scurried out, squealing with a combination of protest and delight. She turned back to him, her eyes full of kind concern.

"Are you okay? Can I get you anything?"

"I'm fine." His voice was a croak but a stronger one than yesterday. She looked down and saw the horse in his hands.

"I'm sorry about this. I told them not to bother you but, well, I guess because you rescued Scampi..."

Cullen frowned.

"Our dog. Scampi? You found him."

His eyes creased. "I think maybe it was him that found me."

"Well, whatever. You brought him back and that's all the matters. And what matters now is that you get some rest and build your strength up." She went back to the door and picked up a tray she'd left on the floor. "I made you some soup."

Cullen looked at her, a faint trace of a smile in his eyes. "Is it vegdibble?"

"Eighty thousand pounds." Rosie proffered. "It's not be sniffed at."

"Are you serious?" Ewan was shaking his head and pacing their living room, shaking and pacing, his hands manically alternating between being clasped behind his back, stuffed into his trouser pockets and then being wrung in front of him. He looked like nothing so much as a life-size automaton triggered by a clock striking twelve. "We can't buy anything with that."

"We wouldn't need to buy anywhere." Rosie reasoned. "We haven't bought here. But we could rent somewhere else. Pay off our debts, have money in the bank?" She rolled her tongue around her teeth, tasting the amusing novelty of being in the black.

"And three generations of my family's sweat and investment adds up to this... pittance. Is that it?" Shake and pace.

"No, Ewan. If you look at it like that then it's not a good deal, I grant you." Rosie gave a tight little smile. "But that's all sunk cost, isn't it? Spent. Gone. We would never have got that money back if we'd stayed here, would we?"

"What are you trying to say?" Ewan stopped pacing and looked at her, his face stern and lined with worry.

"Look. Imagine if Baxter had never terminated our lease."

"He's not going to!" Ewan's nostrils flared. "I'll bloody see about that!"

"Yes, but imagine. Please." Rosie let out a long, soft breath and lowered her tone. "Suppose he had never had the idea and we had continued working and living here. At some point, maybe when Ellie was grown, or maybe when you decided you'd had enough of farming-"

"Never!"

"Ewan? Honey, be reasonable. One day retirement, or infirmity, or both would come along. For whatever reason, a time would come when we would be thinking about leaving here. What then?"

Rosie looked at her husband, his eyes now cast down onto the carpet, his fingers rapidly interlacing between the hands behind his back. He was silent, brooding, thinking. She knew he was listening so she continued with her train of thought.

"If that day came, we'd have to walk away from here with nothing. Nothing! We'd have no income, few possessions and perhaps only our old age pensions to keep us. It could happen!" Rosie's mind raced. She was really playing devil's advocate in order to engage her husband in some discussion about the Baxter's proposal so he didn't just dismiss it out of hand. She might not have thought this through, but the more she spoke the more she wondered if she might be onto something. Maybe they could salvage something from this wreck of a situation which was wearing them both thin. "If we take this money-"

Ewan interrupted her with a non-verbal snort but she took heart by the lack of words and ploughed on.

"*If* we take it. The court case evaporates. Our stress levels return to normal. We pay off our loan and our credit cards. We have plenty left and we could start again. Start afresh. We're still young, still have time." She warmed further to her theme. "Maybe we could even live a normal life like other people - have holidays, lie-ins. Evenings to ourselves. Weekend trips with Ellie!"

Rosie stopped talking and realised she had become animated during her little speech, her hands and eyes wandering. She looked across at her husband who was staring vacantly out of the window at the Moorfoots beyond. Rosie walked over to him and gave him a hug from behind. He clasped her hands at his waist and gave them a squeeze.

"This is Critchley land. Not Baxter land."

"You know that's not true, honey." She said softly. "It's Baxter land that's been developed and nurtured and farmed by Critchleys. But it was always going to have to be handed back one day. Do you think Ellie is going to want to take over this place when we're too old to manage it on our own?"

"I don't intend to ever be too old."

"Honey, come on." Rosie gave him the hardest squeeze she could and nuzzled the back of his neck. "I'm not saying definitely let's take it. I'm saying let's think about it, not write it off. Maybe we could ask for more? Maybe we could say, no thanks, but if you make it a hundred thousand…"

She could feel his muscles and strength even through the thick shirt he was wearing, smell the effort of the day on him, the fresh air in his hair, the dirt on his hands. Rosie loved this man and hated to see him torn and worn and beaten and defeated. She released a hand from his grip and ran it gently through his thick curls on top of his head, turning him slowly to face her.

"Will you think about it, hmm?"

His eyes were moist and his face wore a softened expression. He didn't look like he wanted to talk about this anymore and she didn't want to cause him further pain. Rosie felt his chest heave and heard him let out a large sigh.

It was 9.30pm and Jakki tapped on the dashboard. "Right. This time we sit here and just monitor the guy on shift, okay?"

"Okay." Elaine sat with a notepad on her knee, scrunched up uncomfortably in the back of Paul's van on a pile of smelly dog blankets. "Can we do this quickly? It's a bit whiffy back here."

"Are you complaining about my pets?" Paul was

wounded.

"No." Elaine explained. "Their blankets. I think they could do with a bit of a freshen up. How often do you wash them?"

"Wash 'em?" Paul frowned at this weird idea. He was sitting in the driving seat, Jakki next to him training her own binoculars on their surveillance target bathed in the sodium light of a tall lamppost right next to the security booth. He hoped no police came past and told him to move along, or worse arrested him for suspected dogging. Two lesbians in his van - Blimey, that was a plot for a porn film and a half. Shame it was these two. One looking like kd lang with a thyroid condition and the other like Laura Kuenssberg with an extra pole up her arse.

He grumped. "What do you want me to do?"

"Just sit there." Jakki nipped. "Can you do that?"

"I'm good at sitting." Paul confirmed.

"Yes. Why am I not surprised at that?" Jakki returned to her binoculars. "If you can keep a note of the time, Lay? I'll call out when something happens."

Elaine sighed, trying not to inhale through her nose, but when she breathed through her mouth, she could almost taste dog hair. "If the barrier is manned 24/7, aren't we just wasting our time?"

"Not at all." Jakki said. "Firstly, my expert source makes very clear that surveillance and timing of security procedures is crucial to a plan's success. Secondly, even if it is manned 24/7 - and we won't know that's the case without undertaking this surveillance…" She waggled her head the tiniest amount. "But if it is, well, there have to be shift changes, toilet breaks, stuff like that. If we can establish a pattern then we can identify a window of opportunity."

"Yeah." Said Paul, thoughtfully. "You mentioned this expert source before. Who is it?"

"It doesn't matter who it is. What's important is that they have provided me with copious and detailed notes appropriate for successfully executing a clandestine operation like this. I have studied them carefully and used them to construct our plan."

"Where did you get it?"

"Never mind where I got it." Said Jakki, peevishly. "Just trust me. You're in good hands. Now look - the bloke's leaving the booth. What's the time?"

"9.40."

"Ok, let's see where he goes and how long before he comes back."

She watched as the guard checked his watch and then ambled away from the main gate to the nearest chicken shed before disappearing through a green door built almost invisibly into the side of the building. She waited patiently for his return, almost holding her breath.

"He's back." Jakki said eventually. "Time?"

"9.50."

"Ten minutes. Hmm, ok. Do we think it was a toilet break? Or a check of the premises?"

"How can we know?" Elaine asked hopelessly.

"By seeing when he does it again. If it happens at the same time in the next hour, say, then we know it's not a toilet break. Unless he's incredibly anal about timekeeping."

"Or got a very weak bladder."

"Well, if he disappears again at 10.40 for ten minutes we can be sure it's a routine. That means we can come back again tomorrow ready to enter!" Jakki was delighted, Elaine sank into silence. Paul piped up.

"I need a slash."

"No more soup, I'm afraid… oh, sorry."

Rosie had walked in without knocking, carrying a cup of tea and some toast on a tray, to find the man was up and trying to dress himself. She had bustled in to be greeted by his pale, hairy arse as he struggled to pull his pants up with his back to the door.

He whirled and lost his balance in the process, falling onto the bed, trousers around his calves. Unable to stop herself, Rosie snorted and then blushed with embarrassment. "I'll, er, leave you to it, then shall I?" She scurried away without waiting for an answer.

A few minutes later, he limped into the kitchen, fully dressed. He was tall and sinewy, looking like he would normally move with a smooth easy gait but right now he seemed halted and stiff.

"I was undressed. In bed."

"Yes. I, er. Well, I thought…"

"You did it - undressed me?"

"Yes. I, er. Yes. Sorry." Rosie blushed, almost crimson.

"And my leg?"

"Yes. I cleaned it and put a dressing on. I used to be a nurse." She said by way of explanation. "I'll need to take another look at it, see if it needs re-dressing."

"That won't be necessary." He eyed the makeshift breakfast she had made him, sitting on its tray now on the kitchen table. "Is that for me?"

"Yes. Yes, please. Go ahead." She pushed the tray towards him and he reached for a piece of toast, still standing. "I didn't know whether… I mean I thought you might be… please, have a seat."

He continued devouring the toast but stayed standing. "Thank you. I'd rather stand."

"You weren't saying that the other night!" Rosie blurted, smiling. "Sorry. Please sit down. You have a bad cut on your leg and you might be-"

"Tired." He interrupted. "I was tired. Now I'm… not."

"You collapsed on the floor." Rosie said, doubt written on her face. "More than tired, I'd say. And hungry." She nodded at the fast-disappearing plate of toast.

"Yes. Thank you. Sort of lost track of time."

He pulled up a chair and Rosie sat in silence, sipping her own tea, while he cleared his plate. Eventually she spoke.

"Thank you for finding Scampi."

"I told you: he found me."

"Up on the hills?"

Cullen nodded.

"Well, it's easily done. Getting lost up there." She said brightly. "Done it myself enough times. Ewan's always telling me-"

"Ewan?"

"My husband. We're farmers. He spends most days up there, tending the sheep, fences, so on." She looked up, unconsciously, at the hills out of the kitchen window. "Your cut - did you walk into some razor wire?"

"I guess."

"I thought so. That bastard!" Rosie's face flushed and she clenched her jaw. "Ewan's done that to himself before now. And we've lost a few sheep that way over the years."

"Who's the bastard?"

"Sir Malcolm Baxter. Landowner and arsehole-extraordinaire. Owns all the land around here, puts up razor-wire to protect his precious grouse shoots, and now he's trying to evict us!"

He looked at her, his lined face suddenly alive with intelligence and interest.

"I'm Rosie. You are…?"

"Cullen." He gave a terse nod.

"Is that your first name or last name?"

"Only."

"Oh."

The little blonde girl appeared in the doorway, clutching Molly, her eyes wide gazing at Cullen. She looked from him to Rosie and then ran towards her mother, making a wide arc to keep well away from him in order to get to her mother's side. Rosie scooped her up and sat the girl on her lap. The child buried her face in her mother's breast and clung to her tightly.

"Did you wash your hands and face?" Rosie asked.

"And brushed my teeth!" Ellie lifted her face, beaming, and then spying Cullen looking at her, buried it again.

"It's okay, honey. This is the nice man who found Scampi!"

"I know." Her daughter replied. "Mister Cullen."

Rosie looked up at Cullen and smiled, but his eyes were locked onto her daughter. "This is my daughter, Ellie."

"Eilidh?" He intoned, his voice an echo from somewhere left behind long ago.

"No, Ellie."

But Cullen wasn't listening. Now he couldn't take his eyes off this girl. She, in turn, at her mother's words started to pull herself away and turn to face him. Her eyes were liquid and curious, scared and confused. They stared at each other for a moment and he felt the hairs on the back of his neck rise. Suddenly, he felt extremely cold.

"Say hello, Ellie. Say thank you to Cullen for finding Scampi." But Cullen was gone, lost in his past. His own daughter's face gazing back at him beneath the golden curls of this little girl.

"Thank you, Daddy." He heard and he felt his eyes well up. She smiled and his vision blurred. He felt himself shiver and he shook his head to try and dispel the image, steal back into the present. His own Eilidh was looking at him, head cocked to one side, examining him like a new toy. "Are you crying Daddy?" She stole from her mother's lap and ran across to him and reached out to give him a hug. Cullen shot up from the chair, knocking it over, and stepped back away from his daughter. This wasn't real. This wasn't her. He blinked away tears and turned towards the door, a searing pain shooting up his calf.

"I have to go."

"Don't go Daddy! Don't go."

But it was too late. Cullen was out of the door, shaking. Half-running, half-limping across the pasture towards the hills, flight his only thought. All hunger, exhaustion and pain dismissed by the desperate need to flee from his daughter's words ringing in his ears. He clapped both hands to the side of his head, trying to push the sound of her voice away but it wouldn't leave him. Panting, sweating and shivering in the sunlit morning, he stumbled and tripped as he crossed a small footbridge and disappeared into the hills.

NINE

The following evening, they pulled up into the layby at 9:30 and Jakki gave final instructions.

"Now, remember. Ten minutes, is all we have to get in. Once we're in we'll have an hour before we need to get out again - plenty of time for what we need."

"Will there be any need for me to run at all?" This was Paul.

"Hope not. Why?"

"Just this jumper's really rather tight and I'm not sure how much movement it's giving me." He tugged at the restrictive neck of his black army jumper which was already leaving a red mark at his throat.

"Didn't you have anything bigger?" Jakki sighed.

"Yeah, this. Seems to have shrunk since I last wore it."

"I'm sure that, should running be required, the tightness of your jumper will be your least concern. Now, let's just double-check we have everything. Lay, the list please."

Elaine obediently rattled through the piece of paper Jakki had given her before they left home.

"Video camera?"

"Check." Said Jakki, patting the small case strapped over her shoulder.

"Torch."

"Check." Said Paul, hefting an enormous Maglite.

"Wow. Big enough?"

"Big Paul by name… of course, it's not the size that matters, it's what you do with it." Paul ogled. "Although not that you ladies-"

Elaine cut him off. "Stills camera?"

"Check." Said Paul, again, holding up his phone.

"Synchronised watches?"

"It is 9.34… now."

"How do I-?" Paul fiddled with his phone looking for how to adjust the time.

"Never mind that now. Let's get outside the van, ready for when he makes his move."

The trio bundled out and hunkered down, peeking around the rear of the van to watch the guard. True to form he was looking at his watch. Then he pulled up his trousers by the belt and emerged from the booth, trotting up the lane.

"Right. We go on *three.*" Jakki instructed.

"Wait!" said Paul with a furrowed brow. "Do you mean *one-two-THREE?* Or *one-two-three-GO?*"

"Wouldn't it be better if we counted down - to avoid the confusion?" Offered Elaine. "If you said *three-two-one* no-one's going to go on *one* are they? They'd wait for *Go.*"

Paul nodded appreciatively. "That's very… sensible."

"Thank you."

"You're welcome."

"Fine." Spat Jakki, all her attention focussed on the receding guard. "Three-two-one-GO!"

Together they plunged across the deserted road into the shadows of the tall hedge which ran alongside the lane leading up to the barrier. The guard disappeared inside the chicken shed and they scurried forward, towards the glowing pool of light thrown from the lamppost. High up on the post, Paul thought he could make out a distinctive shape and he threw both arms wide to stop the two women from proceeding further.

"Look up there." He nodded to a spot about halfway up the post.

"Oh great." Cried Elaine. "How are we supposed to get past a security camera?"

Roly was standing on their doorstep brandishing a pet carrier inside which Rosie could make out a bundle of speckled feathers.

"She's a rescue hen." He smiled a gormless, gap-toothed smile. "Is that a problem?"

"Well... no, I don't expect so." Rosie managed before Ewan appeared at her side and thrust his face and chest forwards. Roly took a step back, alarmed.

"Tell your father the money's an insult!" Ewan stormed. A flash of terror flew across Roly's face and for a brief moment Rosie thought he looked like a small child about to be slippered for some minor misdemeanour - a bewildered infant unaware of the reason for impending punishment.

"Ewan!" Rosie admonished her husband but Ewan just threw her a scowl and retreated back into the hallway, his participation in negotiations over.

"I'm sorry." Rosie grimaced to Roly. "My husband is very upset by your offer. His family have been here for generations you know."

"I understand, Mrs Critchley." Roly was slowly recovering himself but his face was white and flappy, like someone waving a small piece of tripe.

"Please, call me Rosie." Rosie's lips were a tight, thin

line. "Roland isn't it? Would you like a cup of tea?"

Roly's eyes grew and some colour returned to his cheeks. He followed her into the kitchen and looked for somewhere to put the pet carrier down. Rosie, embarrassed, started scooping books and sewing paraphernalia off the table and chairs and dumping them on the tatty sofa on the far side of the aga. He gratefully placed the pet carrier on the table and sat with his hands in his lap, waiting for something. Rosie felt a need to keep it light.

"You know, I'm not even sure Ellie believes having a hen as a pet is possible. Children at their age - full of fanciful ideas that last a micro-second before their imagination whisks them onto the next one. I'm sure Jemima's just the same."

She smiled at him and, for an instant, something about the sunlight gleaming off the bonnet of his shiny Range Rover through the window and his clean, pressed pink trousers made her step outside herself and look at them both, side-by-side. It wasn't a flattering comparison.

Here she was, a drab tenant farmer's wife working long hours, struggling to make ends meet and spending her days baking and cleaning, mending and caring for Ellie, then her evenings cooking and bathing and trying to grab some time with her husband before he fell asleep by the unlit fire, weary and worn before retiring to bed in order to be up for 4am the next day. And the next. And the next. No weekends, no days off, no holidays. The seasons turned and the fields needed tending, the sheep shearing, the machinery cleaned and the silage removed. The drudging reality of subsistence farming thrown into sharp relief by this moneyed, soft-skinned and educated man, a daughter the same age as hers with a future her own daughter would probably never know. She tried to conjure up the beauty and loveliness of her life with Ewan, the connection with nature, the wholesomeness and timelessness of it all - and couldn't. Standing there in her holed jumper, amateurishly self-darned at the elbows, her tired, muddy wellies and her dirty hands and rough fingernails, she felt small, poor and inadequate.

"I'm not sure I know exactly what a rescue hen is?" Rosie said as she put the kettle on.

"Well, it's pretty much what it sounds like really. It's a hen that's been rescued… from the factory-farm system." Roly caught himself. "Well, you don't need to know how hens are kept for egg production but, well, she's a bit dilapidated I'm afraid."

Rosie crouched down to look into the large caged pet carrier. Nestled uncomfortably on a thin layer of straw was a bedraggled looking chicken, white, grey and speckled, some patches of feather-rot on its wings. Its eyes were closed and its breathing was fast and ragged. Was this how chickens slept?

"I'm sure it'll be fine." She looked up at Roly and smiled thinly again. "Ellie will be thrilled."

"I've brought a small sack of feed. I don't know if you know anything about keeping hens at all?"

"Not really." Rosie rolled her eyes. "Not at all actually. Not impressive is it, for a farmer's wife! I guess I'll have to read up pretty quickly."

"Well, I've also brought a wee booklet. Tells you everything you need to know about feeding, care and so forth." He pulled a pamphlet from his jacket pocket and handed it to her. "What I can tell you is that she's not diseased or carrying anything. She may not look in great shape but we do make sure all our animals are infection-free and they get regular medicines added to their water supply."

"Thank-you."

"She might be a bit stressed and show some odd behaviour to start with." Roly assured her. "But she'll settle down after a few days. It's odd to think about it but she's just a baby herself really. Probably only just over a year old. Imagine that!"

They sat chit-chatting over tea for a while, Rosie surprised to find herself warming to this mild-mannered man but thinking that perhaps this was always the way when parents with daughters of a similar age started talking. But all the while she was aware of the elephant in the room. It was Roly who brought it up first.

"I'm sorry your husband is unimpressed with our offer, Rosie. I believe it is really quite generous."

Rosie's face darkened. "You must understand, Roland. This farm's been in Ewan's family for generations! He feels this connection with the place that I can't obviously, but I can completely empathise with his fury - I'd be furious too if someone tried to take away not just my livelihood but my inheritance and family legacy. He has worked himself into such a state over this court case. Even if we do win, I don't think Ewan or I will ever be able to look out at those hills and see the view in the same way ever again. Things'll never be back to normal - and the shadow of it happening again will hang over us." She looked up, eyes wet with tears, and gazed at this same view through her kitchen window. Heather-clad hills dappled by shadow which flickered across the landscape with the scudding clouds. "What you once thought was solid and permanent turns to dust in your hands, makes you realise the fragility of life and… everything. Makes me worry about Ellie and her future. What does tomorrow hold for our children in a world where rich men can do as they like?"

"Look." Roly lowered his head and looked up into Rosie's tear-stained face. "I understand. You need more time to talk it over. Perhaps your husband will come round?"

"Not for eighty thousand pounds he won't."

"A hundred thousand, then? Would that make a difference?" Roly raised his eyebrows and waited.

The corners of Rosie's mouth turned up at the edges by the tiniest amount and she gave a thoughtful nod. "I think it might."

"Great." Roland's eyes were newly alight. "Please, talk to your husband. And let me know how Ellie likes the hen. Have you told her about…?"

"Good God, no!" Rosie wiped her nose roughly on her jumper sleeve and then caught herself, realising too late what he might think of this uncouth action. She sniffed away the last of her tears, determination swooping in to replace self-pity. "She's six years old. She'll see the world for what it is soon enough. For now, she still believes in Santa and the Tooth Fairy and the Easter Bunny. If I can give her a few more years of wonder and delight at the beauty of it all, before the cruelty and injustice start to appear… well, I blooming well shall. God knows there's not much else I can do. Other than pray. But I can do that!"

"Well, look then. Sally and I are happy to have Ellie at ours any day over the holidays to play with Jemima. If that will give you some time on your own, with Ewan, to talk this through and come to a decision?"

Rosie sniffed and nodded. "Thank you. Although we're both so busy during the day and-"

"A sleepover then?" Roland urged. "Just call me or Sally and we'll pick Ellie up and have her over one evening - the girls can have a nice sleepover, hmm?"

"Thank you, yes. That would be a real help. I'll speak to Ewan." Rosie stood and then pointed to the pet carrier. "And thanks for coming over with this. I am sure Ellie will be delighted with it. Her."

"My pleasure." Roly gave a final floppy grin. "And… if I could get something in writing, from your solicitor maybe?"

"I'll speak to Ewan."

"Thank you." He extended his hand, Rosie shook it, then he picked up his car keys and she walked him to the door. She watched as he climbed into his shiny car and reversed smoothly out of the farmyard and bobbled down the track in the noonday sunshine.

"Spray paint?" Elaine screwed up her features into a ball of doubt.

"Black spray paint." Paul said.

"For a CCTV camera halfway up a lamppost?"

"Black spray paint, on a stick." Paul beamed waving his home-made contraption at her. It looked just like a paint gun gaffer-taped to a broom handle with a cord tied to the trigger of the paint gun - because that's exactly what it was.

"High tech." Elaine nipped. "Are we in an old episode of the A-Team?"

"Look, Lay, it'll do the trick okay?" Jakki reassured

her. "We're not looking to over-complicate things."

"I can see that." Elaine said and then started exhaling in short, sharp bursts, psyching herself up for the task ahead. "Okay. Okay. Okay."

"Right. Everyone ready? It's 9.39. Go!"

The three shadowy figures sprinted across the road and then sidled along the hedge until close to the perimeter of the circle of light from the lamp-post. Paul hesitated.

"Go on, then." Hissed Jakki. "Time's against us."

Paul gave his contraption a practice squeeze and, gratified to find a blast of paint spurt from the gun, he jogged over to the lamppost and looked up for the camera. The glare from the light dazzled him and he couldn't see a thing. The paint gun swayed at the end of his stick.

"Spray it!" Jakki ordered in a loud stage whisper.

Blindly, Paul waved his stick under the light, pulling on the cord to hold down the trigger like a tail-gunner in a dogfight. Paint shot everywhere, but enough must have found the camera because the next thing Paul knew Jakki and Elaine were right beside him, tapping him on the arm to stop.

"Great job. Come on!"

The pair ducked beneath the security barrier and sprinted off into the dark. Paul found himself blinded by the afterimage from the light. He threw down his stick and walked slowly forwards, arms extended, groping for the barrier which hit him in the midriff. He went down with an *oof* and then emitted another one when he picked himself up off the tarmac and cracked his head on the barrier. He sat rubbing his head, trying to blink away the orange spot filling his vision. It was just dwindling when he felt Jakki's arm on him again.

"It's no good. There's a padlock on the door."

"Oh." Paul wasn't entirely unhappy to hear that their adventure for tonight was at an end.

"We'll have to come back again tomorrow." Jakki observed.

"We can't do that!" Said Elaine. "We've left paint everywhere. Do you not think they'll notice?"

"Right… Well… Er… Look we don't have time for this now. He'll be back in a couple of minutes. We need to get home and regroup. Come on!"

Paul grabbed his stick and the trio fled back along the hedge, dashed across the road and hid behind the van just as the security man came out of the building, whistling softly in the quiet night air.

"Just think, for a moment, of the intelligence of the average shopper." Malcolm was drumming his fingers on his desk, annoyed that he even needed to be having this conversation.

"Okay." Said his son.

"They're stupid, yes? Sheep."

"Well…"

"Now, because they're the average, realise that half of all shoppers are more stupid than that!"

"Well..."

"Roly, That's two *well*s. Where are you going with the *well*s?"

"Well…"

"Three."

"That's not how averages work, Sir." Roly grasped the nettle.

"Don't lecture me, boy, on averages. I've been in business since before you were born."

"Yes, sir. But perhaps I could illustrate with a different scenario?"

"Really?" Malcolm pursed his lips. "Proceed. With care."

"Okay." Roly took a deep breath. "Do you realise that the average number of legs for someone in the UK is less than two?"

His father scoffed. "Let me just stop you there."

"No, really. The average number of legs is less than two."

"Nonsense!"

"Well, obviously, most people have two legs." Roly persisted. "Probably 99.99% of the population. But some, maybe several thousand, have only one. And perhaps a few hundred have none. Add all the legs up, divide by the number of people and the average will be ever-so-slightly less than two. 1.99999…."

"Ah, yes, I see. Clearly." His father brushed this explanation aside as one he'd understood all along.

"But it does not follow then, that half of all the people have less than 1.999 legs. As you suggest. Because obviously most people have two. What you are thinking of is the median, not the mean. The median is the middle figure in any set of numbers, where half the data set is higher and half lower."

Malcolm was silent, a resentful look on his face. Roly continued: "So if the median figure for legs was 1.9999 then, and only then, would half the population have less than 1.99999 legs."

"Fewer." Malcolm thrust his chin out and stood.

"Sorry?"

"It's fewer, not less. Fewer legs, not less legs."

"Yes, but I said less than 1.9999."

"Ah, but it's not the number that's important - it's the object of the sentence. Its the divisibility of the object. If we were discussing traffic density and said traffic density is less than 1.99 that would be correct. But if we said there were less than 1.99 cars on the road, that would be wrong. It would be fewer than 1.99 cars. Do you see?"

Roly sighed and let his shoulders sag. Today's lesson was over. "Yes, Sir."

"Excellent." Malcolm rubbed his hands together, satisfied in a job well done and another issue discharged. "Then we shall say no more about it."

"About what, sir?" Roly said, confused.

"Ha! That's the spirit. Now, where's that bloody Eddie?"

As if summoned by his very name, Eddie bundled in through the half-open door.

"Where the hell have you been?" Malcolm glared at Eddie who stood at ease, feet splayed apart in traditional military manner, hands clasped behind his back.

He was wearing his usual tight-fitting khaki uniform as if he had just been drop-shipped from the set of a Mexican drug cartel, the uniform he had arrived in the UK wearing and which Malcolm, idiosyncratically, had allowed him to retain. The uniform had actually grown on Malcolm - although not as much as it had actually grown on Eddie. His uniform seemed bonded to his skin at the molecular level so that skin and uniform were perhaps now one and the same. They certainly shared the same aroma, like stink on sprouts, although this odour was undetectable as far as Malcolm was concerned - the absence of a sense of smell being one of the more vital attributes of a successful business owner who spent much of their time in or around enormous metal barns stuffed with thousands of shitting chickens.

"Investigating, Sir." Eddie said through thin lips. "We have had intruders."

"What?" Malcolm exploded, his eyes enlarged and he cast a scowl at Roly before turning his full attention back to his Security Chief. "Where? When?"

"Last night at the front gate, Sir. Spray-painted the security camera, no other signs of entry."

"No other-" Malcolm fumed. "Did they get in?"

"We don't know, Sir."

Malcolm stormed to his feet. "You don't know? This is the sort of half-cocked competence I would expect of him-" Malcolm jerked a thumb towards his son, who stood with his eyes cast down, and then pointed a menacing finger at Eddie. "Not you."

"We're looking into it, Sir. None of the padlocks have been disturbed. But… kind of difficult with no camera footage to-"

"Don't look into it."

"Sir?" Eddie was bemused.

"Don't look into it. Deal with it." Malcolm puffed out an enormous breath and sat down again.

"Would you like me to-"

"Do your bloody job? Yes, I would." Malcolm sneered. "Far be it from me to tell you how to do said bloody job, but at the very minimum I think it only prudent now to-"

"Install more cameras?" Eddie interjected and immediately regretted it.

"Bollocks to your cameras! If they can disarm one with spray-paint, they can disarm them all. And…"

Malcolm added with a sarcastic flourish. "It's not as if we need to identify the intruders is it?"

"Sir?"

"It's them isn't it? The protesters? I thought you'd dealt with them?"

"Well, I-"

"I expected better from you, Eddie. Much better."

"I am sorry, Sir."

"Don't be sorry." Malcolm snapped. "Just don't do it again."

"No, Sir."

Malcolm gave a heavy sigh and looked up at his office ceiling. "I suggest you replace the locks. If they can disarm a camera, I'm guessing they can overcome a padlock."

"Yes, Sir."

"And make sure your team are on full alert." Malcolm gave Eddie a thoughtful look. "Perhaps you should take a nightshift or two yourself?"

"I'll brief my team, Sir. I'm sure there's no need for me to-"

"I'm not."

"Sir?"

"Sure. I'm not." Malcolm smirked. "Take a shift."

"I already get less hours sleep than I need, Sir."

"Fewer. Not less, fewer."

"Yes, Sir." Eddie sulked and dismissed himself from the room.

"Have you never seen those wine programmes? They say things like: "I'm getting leather. And willow. Cork. And sweat."

"That's cricket." Said Paul.

"No! It's what they do when they taste wine. They smell the wine." Shirley wafted her hands in front of her face, conjuring djinns from the air, waving them towards her nostrils. "Inhale it. Savour it." She sniffed deeply. "Give it a go."

"This isn't wine."

"I know."

"It's veg."

"So?"

"Not wine."

"As I said: so?"

"Very not wine." Paul complained. "No alcohol in it at all, actually."

"Of course not! It's veg!"

Paul sniffed tentatively, his face hovering over the plate when he'd rather have been hoovering over it. "Smells like wet dog."

"Wet dog?"

"Aye."

Shirley contemplated her lover. His big, sad eyes made him look not unlike a wet dog just now but she refused to be bowed. "Ok. That'll have to do for the smell test. Now taste it."

Paul curled his bottom lip, an overlarge schoolboy on the verge of tears. "Can I have some bacon with it?"

"No!"

He looked down at the beige thing on the plate. "Have you got it in a meatier colour?"

"Paul! Lover. I've made this as easy as I can for you. You're apprehensive. It's your first time. I get it. That's why we're starting you off with something that looks like meat."

"It doesn't look like meat."

"It looks like what it is." Shirley said. "A sausage roll. A roll with vegan meat in it."

"We both know that the pink stuff in sausage rolls probably doesn't fully fall under the meat category."

"Doesn't stop you eating them!"

Paul screwed up his nose, appreciating that he was at risk of arguing against himself.

"Paul, it's veg." Shirley persisted. "You've eaten veg before."

"Not on its own!" Paul whined. "It's all kinda lonely here on the plate. Missin' somethin'"

"You'll be missin' somethin' if you don't get it down you, you big Jessie!"

Paul nibbled gingerly at the unsavoury offering in front of him. Chewing with an audience was not his idea of a spectator sport but he knew better than to rile Shirley while she stood over him, metaphorically or physically.

"Well?"

"It's like greasy sponge."

"Sponge? Like cake?" Shirley said, hopefully.

"No sponge. A real sponge made of actual sponge." Paul added, unnecessarily: "The greasy I'm fine with."

"Is that it? Is that all the lyricism you can manage. With the enormous lexicon that the English language has bequeathed us-"

"Bequeathed you."

"Bequeathed us." Shirley didn't even break stride. "All you've got in your puddin' head is sponge?"

Paul breathed out, heavily. "It's like a sponge that's been soaked in angry wasp spit, hung out to dry on a mouldy clothesline on a damp Tuesday and then tumbled until it's tinder-dry, whereupon it has been chemically castrated, mixed with the pus from a lanced boil and smoked over sustainable charcoal. Organically."

Shirley put her hands on her hips, drew herself up to her full height and gave him her twelve-out-of-ten customer hard stare. Paul returned her gaze, twinkling, and withstood. Shirley grabbed his T-shirt by what would have to pass for a lapel.

"You are a complete monster!" And then, to his complete surprise and bewilderment, she pulled him into a massive snog. "And I love you. Come to bed."

"Mmm." Paul struggled to make a sound beneath Shirley's insistent lip pressure. "Can we not just now? I think I've eaten something that disagrees with me."

TEN

The big man in the back of his patrol car was being thrown around on the unmade road as Jenkins gritted his teeth over every pothole and mound. Marvellous. His day was going as well as his week and his week had been bad. And it was still only Wednesday.

"You sure this is the way?" His passenger protested, looking out the window for some respite.

"Let's agree on a division of responsibilities right now, shall we? I get us there and you sit quiet. How about that?" He scowled into his rear-view mirror.

"Just sayin'"

"Well don't, okay? Roadworks isn't it? Always bleeding roadworks." Jenkins looked at the satnav screen which was absolutely zero help. Never follow the bloody things: that was his attitude. So why had he done so now? Because he was annoyed that's why. Annoyed and not thinking clearly. Dogsbody for Her Magnificence - again - and now, oh the very charm and joy of it, in uniform. In fucking uniform! He was still mentally shaking his head in disbelief even while wincing at the stiffness of his new shirt collar and the tightness of his old trousers. She'd outdone herself this time. Found some new way to shower him with indignity and scorn. She was sorry, she said. Had good reasons, she said. It was only because they were so short-staffed, she said. Temporary arrangement only. No reflection on him.

Bollocks. He was a Detective Sergeant! No reflection

on him, his arse.

"You goin' to tell me what I've done wrong?" The big man on the backseat again.

"This time?"

The man squinted back at Jenkins' reflection in the mirror. "Do I know you?"

"No. But I know you. Or your sort anyway." Jenkins scanned the road ahead looking for an end to the rollercoaster misery. "I bet this is not your first ride in a police car, is it?"

His passenger pursed his lips and stared gloomily out of the window.

Good, thought Jenkins. That's shut him up. He puffed out a long breath and checked the satnav again. He'd always hated being in uniform. Spent five years in it and hated every bloody unending second. Passing his sergeant exams and being assigned to She Who Must Be Obeyed had been a godsend. Back then. Oh, if he'd known then what he knew now. Okay, she could be considerate and amenable - but too often she was cold and unyielding and just… hard work. Always focussed on results, always pushing forward. And up. Guess that's why she'd made it all the way to Detective Chief Superintendent. That was good going - for a woman.

"Are we nearly there yet?"

Jenkins closed his eyes briefly. "What are you, seven?"

"I'm just not feeling too great."

Jenkins looked up in the mirror. His passenger's olive skin was far from pale but his face did appear to be registering some discomfort.

Good. Serves him right, whatever it was he'd done. See, there was another example of how Her Majesty conducted herself - sending him out as a bloody taxi service without telling him what for. *Just bring him in*, she'd said. *I want to speak to him.*

"What did I say about division of responsibilities?" He reminded his passenger.

The man turned away and Jenkins muttered to himself and looked back at the road. An enormous pothole loomed in front of him and there was a car coming in the other direction. He slammed on the brakes but the offside front tyre ba-zoomed into the hole and there was the awful crunch of metal as the car regained its footing on the road surface.

Bollocks. That'd be the suspension knackered then. Great. What else could go wrong?

He glanced back up at the rear-view mirror just in time to catch sight of his passenger projectile vomiting across the headrests between them.

Detective Chief Superintendent Kate Lorimer smiled broadly at Big Paul as Jenkins led him into her office and then dismissed himself. "We meet again, Mr McInnes. What a pleasant and unexpected-" She wrinkled her nose in distaste. "What's with the unusual perfume?"

Paul rolled his eyes. "The latest from Gregg's - vegan sausage roll. It's their bestseller. Apparently."

"Yes, well I guess you're supposed to eat it, not wear it."

"Did both. One then the other." Paul sniffed sadly. "Think I'm allergic."

"Yes, well perhaps we could clean you up?" She yelled through the glass door. "Jenkins!"

Her sergeant appeared carrying a bottle of spray cleaner and a cloth. "Ma'am?"

"See if you can clean Mr McInnes up, would you?"

"I was just going to do my backseat, Ma'am. Stuff's everywhere."

"Yes, well, clean him up first, could you? Somewhere out of range?"

"Ma'am." Said Jenkins glumly and he started to lead Paul out of her office.

"Oh, and take this while you're at it." She handed him a piece of A4.

"Ma'am?"

"It's a BOLO. Take some copies and circulate please. I want this man found ASAP." She nodded at Paul. "And don't forget to bring him back?"

"Yes. Ma'am." Jenkins scowled and tugged at Paul's arm, dragging him out and slamming her door.

"Nothing like someone who enjoys their work." Kate said, shaking her head and returning to her paperwork.

When Jenkins returned Paul to her office, the T-shirt spanning his broad chest bore a large wet stain. His face was newly washed but it wore a look of suspicion on it.

"I've done nothing." He said. "Unless…"

"Unless? Unless what?"

Paul's face contorted in horror. "Is eating meat a crime now?"

"No." She narrowed her eyes, confused.

"So why am I under arrest?"

"You're not under arrest."

"Oh."

"It can be arranged though." Kate chirped happily, but Paul remained glum. "I need your help actually. A favour."

"Huh?" His face brightened. "Always willing to do my bit. Been called for jury duty and everything."

Kate smiled. He was referring to a court case last year at Selkirk Sheriffs Court where she had testified and he was supposed to have been on the jury. Only he hadn't been. In pursuit of Cullen she had met Paul McInnes who, it seemed, had been a friend also looking for him. "Yes. About that: failure to attend for jury service after receiving a summons to do so, unless you have valid reason for exemption, is an offence."

Paul's face fell. "How did you know about that?"

"Imagine my surprise when I found Cullen sitting in the jury. Former police officers are exempt from serving on a jury. Did you not know?"

"Ah."

"No need for anyone to know or prosecute though, really. No harm was done. But, you know, technically anyone ignoring a jury summons can expect to receive a significant fine."

"A fine?"

"£1000 maximum."

Paul gulped. "A favour you say?"

"Yes. I'm looking for him."

"Cullen?"

Kate nodded. "I would like you to bring him to me." She saw Paul's face register severe doubt about the viability of her request. "Or at least give him a message. Ask him to come and see me."

"Why can't you find him yourself?"

Kate cleared her throat. "That BOLO I gave my sergeant?"

Paul looked non-plussed.

"Be On The Look Out." She explained. "A notice for all officers to keep an eye out for a specific individual. In this case, Cullen."

"Well you don't need me then."

"If only." Kate's eyebrows gathered. "He doesn't like being found. You know that."

"Yeah, but you're the police. You've got… resources."

"So has he. And he's had a lot of practice. Turns out he's very good at not being found."

Paul nodded, understanding.

"So, I need all the help I can get."

"I can do that." Paul nodded. "If I see him."

"I need you to see him. I'm in a hurry."

"Why?"

Kate sighed. "How much do you know about Cullen's past?"

"What do you think?"

"Well, last time we spoke you didn't even know about his daughter so… I'm thinking not much. Unless you asked him about her - as I suggested?"

Paul shook his head. "Nah. Never seemed to be the right wossname."

"Wossname?"

"Well, it just never, you know, came up."

"Well it's come up now." Kate tapped a thick folder on the top of her intray. "Tell him I need to see him. About his daughter."

"And if he ignores me?"

Kate looked at him coolly. "He won't." She rose and went to her door, calling for Jenkins as she opened it. He appeared in the doorway still clutching a bottle of spray disinfectant and a bunch of wipes, a look of distaste on his face.

"Ma'am?"

"Could you take Mr McInnes back now, please?"

"Ma'am?"

"Take him back."

"But I've just done my car, ma'am."

"Excellent. So, you can take him then?"

A muscle in Jenkins' jaw spasmed. "It's all slippy. On the backseat, ma'am. Probably not safe until it dries out properly."

Kate pursed her lips. "Then sit him up front."

As Jenkins led him out of the room, scowling, she nodded to Paul. "And you? Don't get into any trouble now, you hear?"

The night air was still and cool and the main road off the layby completely deserted. Paul turned his van engine off and opened the door. There was no sound other than the hum of insects and a faint background hiss of distant traffic from somewhere miles away.

"Well, this is nice I must say." Paul took a deep gulp of fresh air.

"Yes, well let's not get carried away just yet, hmm?" Jakki said. "'Til we've got through the locked door?"

"No worries." Paul reached into his canvas tool bag.

"What've you got?" Elaine asked.

"Bolt cutters." Paul grinned. "Open Sesame!"

"What are we waiting for?" Jakki lifted her eyebrows and her eyes gleamed.

Once the security guard had done his usual disappearing trick, the trio bolted from the van and scurried safely beneath the barrier, jogging steadily towards the first shed. They turned the corner to find some new additions to the entrance. Next to the door was a foot-bath, a security notice and a clipboard on a string with a biro and a flapping sheet of paper clipped to it. The single entry on the paper had yesterday's date on it.

Jakki smiled and then her face froze as she turned to look more closely at the windowless door itself. Above the simple lever handle was a ten-digit brushed-steel punch panel.

"Oh bollocks!" She moaned. "So much for Open Sesame."

Paul pursed his lips together at this latest setback. "You know, it would have been easier if we'd set out on a ring quest."

"Don't suppose you know the code, Lay?" Jakki raised her eyebrows expectantly at her partner.

"Didn't have PIN codes when I worked here." Elaine said sadly. "Plus, this is obviously brand new. Wasn't here yesterday. Which means someone is beefing up security. Told you we shouldn't have left the spray paint on the camera."

"Look, it's too late to worry about that now." Jakki bristled and pointed to the keypad. "What do we do about this?"

"You could try 1-2-3-4." Paul offered.

"Really? Why?" Jakki sneered. "Negate the whole point of the security by using a code any numpty could guess?"

The corners of Paul's mouth turned down. "'Swhat I'd use." He stepped forward to try it.

"Why am I not surprised? You know I'm wondering if he's a jinx." Jakki turned to Elaine. "I mean nothing's gone right on this operation since he came on board has it? Think about it. So far-. What?"

She turned to see what Elaine was gaping at and saw

Paul standing in the open doorway, a huge grin on his face. "Ta-da!"

Jakki shook her head, smiling despite herself. "I don't believe it."

"Trust the soup." Paul said, waggling his eyebrows.

"The what?"

"The soup."

"What are you on about?"

"Chicken soup?" volunteered Elaine.

"Nah. *The* soup. The soup that's all around us, that we're all part of. We're all connected to everything in unknowable ways and, every so often, usually when you least expect it but most need it, the soup reveals itself and a solution drops into your lap. Ha ha - Open Sesame!" He bellowed, delighted.

Jakki pushed past him, still shaking her head as she entered the building. "You know, your mouth is uttering total bollocks. You might want to have that looked at."

She led them through a large empty ante-room, the floor swept clean with bare walls freshly painted. Off to the right and left were two identical doors. Jakki chose the left and it opened onto a vast space which stretched away into the darkness beyond the reach of her torch.

It was completely empty.

Jakki shone the torch on her face and shook it, as if believing that the torch was at fault for showing her an empty shed. She splayed it over the cavernous space again but with the same effect.

"Maybe the other door?" Elaine suggested and they all scurried off to the other side of the shed.

That too was empty.

"What do you think the chances are that all the sheds have the same stupid PIN code?" Jakki scratched her head, exasperation rising in her voice.

"Thank you for agreeing to see me, Mister Baxter."

Kate had been incongruously ushered in by a sweaty security guard dressed like some kind of Bolivian customs official, all sweat-stained khaki and epaulettes. She approached the man himself who had stood behind a large blotter-topped desk and had extended his hand.

"Sir. Sir Malcolm Baxter. I think titles are so important don't you Superintendent?" Malcolm gave a cold but sincere smile as they shook hands. Kate took an instant dislike to him.

"Chief Superintendent. Detective Chief Superintendent actually."

"I stand corrected." Malcolm waved his hand to indicate Kate could take a seat, invoking one of the many ways he had of deflecting his errors without the need to actually say the S-word: sorry. "Would you like some tea? Coffee?"

"No thank-you." She wrinkled her nose in displeasure - not at the offer but at the strange and unappealing odour that seemed to have insinuated itself into the room - but sat down anyway.

"I have to say, Chief Superintendent." Malcolm over-emphasised her title, making it all too clear that he neither appreciated the difference nor being corrected. "I commend Police Scotland's speedy response and its acknowledgement of my position."

Kate looked puzzled. "I am afraid I don't follow?"

"If I may be candid." Kate figured he always was. "It is nice to see my standing recognised - I report a problem and they send a Chief Superintendent-" There was the emphasis again. "And not some oily constable. And so promptly too."

Kate saw they were clearly at cross purposes here but decided to see if it could be played to her advantage. For some reason Baxter seemed to think he had summoned her.

"Perhaps you would be so kind as to elaborate on your problem?"

"Ah. I see." Baxter gave a bitter smile. "Yes, well I imagine communication is always a problem in a public sector organisation which clings to outdated notions like chain of command. Chinese whispers, isn't it?"

"Quite." Kate was tight-lipped at the condescension dripping from his every syllable.

"Well, it's quite simple really. First, they protested - right at my very gates! Then, unhappy with that perhaps, they decided to attempt to break-in to these premises."

"Protesters?"

"Exactly."

"I didn't see any-"

"Well, they're not there now!" He snorted. "Got rid of them. Damned homo's and unwashed eco-warriors at the entrance to my-"

"Public entrance." Kate interjected. Baxter ignored her.

"Their blasted presence was bad enough, waving slanderous placards-"

"Libellous, rather than slanderous I would say."

"Damned lies, is what I would say!" Baxter steamed. "But, as I say, that was not enough, so they have taken to breaking in, at night. Or trying to at any rate."

"Ah." Kate sighed. Baxter's accusations at last straying into potential criminal territory.

"*Ah* indeed. You might well say *Ah*, Chief Superintendent. But saying *Ah* in my book is neither a sufficient nor proportionate response to these events."

"You filed a complaint I take it?"

"I did no such thing!" Baxter scoffed. "If I want to file a complaint, I would ask Eddie to do it. I have far more weighty matters on my mind right now to spend them embroiled in -"

"Eddie?"

"My Head of Security." Baxter bristled. Her constant interruptions were clearly riling him and Kate smiled inwardly as she sat ramrod straight in his chair waiting for him to blow himself out. "Embroiled, as I say, in endless bureaucracy. No. I rang the Chief Constable. Went to school with my son, knew his father. Gordonstoun, you know. Good sort."

"I see."

"And he at least had the good sense to send you down here pronto! So - what's to be done?" Baxter put his hands on his hips and glared at Kate, awaiting a response.

"How do you know they are gay?"

"What?" He was momentarily flummoxed.

"You said '*homo's and eco-warriors*'? How do you know they are gay?"

"'*Unwashed* eco-warriors' I believe I said." He corrected her, his voice rich with scorn. "And they're all gay, aren't they? This is just Greenham Common all over again. Hairy, pinko, dog-on-a-string wimmin who go crazy-eyed when they see someone eating a steak."

"None of those things are a crime, Sir Malcolm."

"Breaking and Entering is not a crime these days? Have we travelled so far down the politically-correct spectrum that it is now permissible to-?"

"No."

"Oh good. For a minute there I thought you were telling me I was in the wrong!"

"Only in so far as expecting to obtain any kind of redress through the use of personal contacts to bypass established police procedure."

"What?"

"Otherwise known as: filing a report."

Baxter took his hands from his hips and leant forward onto his desk, his face scarlet with disbelief. "Let me get this straight. Are you telling me that you are not prepared to do anything about these damned nuisances unless I fill out some bloody forms?"

"Yes. And No." She remained coolness itself, unmoved at this threatening display as he loomed over her while she was still seated. "*Yes,* in the sense that an official response requires someone - doesn't have to be yourself - to officially file a complaint so that we can take action. And *No*, in the sense that that is not actually why I am here today."

"What the bloody hell are you talking about woman?" He spluttered.

"I am talking about a cold criminal case: that is, a case which has been lying inactive for a considerable time but which was never formally closed. A serious - very serious in fact - criminal case for which new evidence has recently come to light."

"I completely fail to see-"

"Which involves your father."

To say the wind was taken from Baxter's sails by this one word was an understatement. This flagship man'o'war, cannons primed, which had been gloriously thrusting forward, fully-rigged with all sails billowing was suddenly arrested, its stately progress captured by an ice sheet which had appeared from nowhere. The very figurehead on the prow which had been assaulted by salt spray was now frozen mid-air, its countenance stunned and able only to silently blink and wonder what vengeful act of the Gods had brought this about.

For several seconds Baxter stood, gaping airlessly like some newly landed fish, until his brain caught up with his face and he slumped into his chair and reached frantically for something in his jacket pocket.

Kate sat, inscrutable, watching him snatch a pill and swallow it with a glass of water.

"Cold case you say?" This came out as a casual remark but Kate could see some worry in those rheumy eyes spying suspiciously out beneath his bushy grey eyebrows.

"Yes. Concerning your father."

"My father?"

"Yes. Lord Westloch."

"Baron Baxter of Westloch." Malcolm corrected her once more. "My father was a stickler for correct forms of address."

"A tendency I see you have inherited." Kate smiled thinly and then proceeded to ignore his correction. "Yes, Lord Westloch has been linked to some new evidence recently connected to an old case and I wondered if you could perhaps shed some light on this."

Malcolm's eyes had narrowed when she had intentionally used his father's title incorrectly again and then widened when he forced his words out. "Well, if I can possibly help of course I shall."

Kate watched as he stood and paced, hands fluttering

behind his back, over to the large window overlooking the rolling fields and the Moorfoot hills in the distance. His body language flat-out contradicted his words but she simply observed in silence. Pacing was good. "So…?"

She waited until he had turned around to face her again. The most important part of this meeting was here - his reaction to what she was about to say would tell her everything she needed to know.

"It concerns your father's relationship with a man called Iain McKenna. Are you familiar with that name?"

There was a pause, accompanied by a pained re-enactment of someone trying to remember, before a reluctant "No. No I'm afraid I'm not." A sad shake of the head completed the performance and Kate drank it all in.

"That's a pity." She looked away, herself enacting the role of someone chasing a lost cause and about to throw one final last hope onto the fire. "I don't suppose your father left any personal effects? Or records perhaps - of business meetings, contacts, that sort of thing?"

"Well, he did, naturally. Lots of them in fact. I remember going through stuff after his death but - well, that was a long time ago. I don't remember how much of it was useful at the time but whatever there was I kept, the rest I disposed of." Malcolm gave a heavy sigh. "If anything of his has survived it has long since become subsumed into my own records and so forth. And I certainly have no recollection or knowledge of anyone named McKenna."

"You seem very sure."

Malcolm yawned. "McKenna is not a name that the sort of people I deal with would have."

Kate smiled inwardly. The man could not have invested more condescending superiority into his voice if he had tried. That wasn't part of some act.

"No." She stood to leave. "I imagine there is no such thing as a Baron McKenna of Milngavie."

"No!" He barked an appreciative laugh at this ludicrous invention. "Although I do know a Lord Macfarlane of Kirkcaldy."

Kate furrowed her brow. "I'm sure you do. By all means, give him my regards."

Malcolm shook her hand as he showed her out in a manner which clearly told her that he had no absolutely no intention of doing any such thing.

Malcolm stood at the window, watching, until the Superintendent's - sorry, *Chief Superintendent,* he corrected himself in irritation - car had gone beneath the security barrier and left the compound. He strode back to his desk and sat down, drumming his fingers loudly for several minutes.

Whilst she had given him very little in terms of detail, what she had said had set off all sorts of memories and emotions within him - feelings he had made huge efforts to conceal, from her today and from himself up to this point. Sitting now in silence, the recollections came flooding back, scenes playing in his mind's eye as he felt the hairs rise on the back of his neck.

Malcolm had never been troubled with feelings of love or even tenderness towards his own father. A man who epitomised the ideal of Victorian fatherhood, who believed stiff upper lips, brutal discipline and emotional deprivation were the hallmarks of a good upbringing and would make a man of his son. But despite this coolness, he had been unable to deny that his father was his progenitor, that he loved him in his own way and that he deserved respect and obedience not just from his son but from those around him. His father had been a self-made man and climbed the social ladder to its very top rung - the House of Lords - and, as such, his memory was not to be besmirched or traduced.

In his lifetime, his father had demanded (and received) respect and, in his death, Malcolm was not inclined to do anything except ensure his father's legacy endured. And, in the process, protect himself from any collateral damage that might incriminate him personally. His father had been an inveterate letter-writer and journal-keeper, documenting the smallest things assiduously. The records Malcolm discovered in his father's strongbox after his death - a cache of photos, letters and detailed diaries - had been a potential bombshell which could have brought down not just his father but a huge section of high society.

But years had passed and Malcolm had buried the memories deep. It seemed almost impossible to dredge any of it back up, packed tightly and inaccessibly as it was underground - diamonds gleaming in a black coal seam. But with a single name this woman had appeared and the ground had collapsed under him. The diamonds now glittered in the sunshine, blinding him with the recollection of his own deeds and his knowledge of the deeds of others.

McKenna.

Malcolm had known of his father's sexual proclivities and the services McKenna had provided - had even availed himself of those same services on occasion - so the extent of his father's depravity revealed in the strongbox had not come as a surprise. But he had been shocked by the level of detail with which his father had documented these events, and the potential damage his records could do if they had fallen into the wrong hands.

He recalled spending days trawling through this sordid trove of memoirs and dates, destroying everything that might incriminate his father, his friends. And Malcolm himself.

From this mountain of paper, he had kept only one thing: a single diary. It wasn't from a particularly interesting year, or any especially significant event - it was just one of more than twenty years-worth of recollections his father had noted down in slashes of black ink cursive. As such it did a good job of illustrating the awful mundanity and ubiquity of the misdeeds, sprinkled in with the quotidian and trivial matters of every day. But that wasn't why Malcolm had kept this one and burnt the rest. In amongst the dense foliage of his father's records, receipts and impersonal notes were scattered musings and passing reflections on life - tiny blossoms of insight into the man himself. And in this one diary, on this one day - Saturday July 19th 1958, Malcolm had it etched on his memory - lost in the scrawl on a completely unremarkable page, was a single comment:

Saturday. Sports Day. Asked to present prizes by Headmaster. M won boys 60 yd dash and I presented him with trophy. So very proud.

Malcolm unlocked the top drawer of his desk and removed the diary from a cotton slipcover. He brushed his fingers across the cover as if tracing the memory of its contents one last time. With a lump in his throat, he dropped it into his wastebasket and followed it with a lighted match.

When the smoke alarm went off Eddie came rushing in, but by that time Malcolm was standing by the open window, looking out onto the Moorfoots with the bin in flames behind him and his eyes full of tears, smoke gathering up at the ceiling and drifting in clouds towards the open window.

"*Wit heppand?*"

"Blasted bin caught fire." Malcolm didn't take his eyes off the hills in front of him, letting Eddie talk to his back. "Put it out, would you? Damned nuisance."

Eddie frowned but, looking around the room and seeing nothing else untoward, grabbed a fire extinguisher from the hall outside the door and doused the flames.

ELEVEN

"Look, sweetheart. You have a present!" Rosie had covered the pet carrier in wrapping paper and made a large bow from some old ribbon she had found in her sewing box. The hen had remained asleep the entire time and she was now crossing her fingers that the reassurance Roly had given her about the bird's health was reliable.

Ellie rushed in from the car, Ewan looking over her at Rosie to catch her eye, wondering what was going on. Rosie beckoned him in and watched as Ellie skipped to the door, obediently removed her muddy shoes and struggled to put on her Frozen slippers as she trembled with excitement.

"What is it, Mum? What is it?"

"It's a surprise, silly! You have to open it." Ewan came in and gave her a kiss on the cheek as he smiled at this cosy family scene. They both looked on as Ellie tore at the wrapping paper and then jumped back in alarm. The hen was trembling in its container and moving its head stiffly from side to side, jerky movements as it eyed her daughter up with first one eye, then the other.

"It's a hen! Is it for me?" Ellie clasped her hands together under her chin, beaming adorably.

"Of course, sweetheart! Jemima's Dad brought it. It's your new pet." Rosie corrected herself. "She's your new pet. She's a girl."

"Ooh, can I get her out?"

The hen was now strutting around its confines with some alarm and making slightly scary clucking noises. Rosie wasn't sure now was a good time. At all. Now that it was on the move, she could see that one of its eyes was all grey and milky. Rosie wasn't sure whether it could see out of it or not - the way it was moving she just couldn't tell.

"Not right now, honey. You see she's very nervous, can you see? She doesn't quite know where she is or who we are. I think she probably needs to get used to us for a wee while before we let her out."

"Oh." Ellie couldn't hide her disappointment. She squatted down on her haunches and reached out a finger to poke through the cage.

"Don't do that, honey. It might peck you!"

"You said it was a she."

"*She* might peck you then. We need to let her settle into her new surroundings and not scare her."

"I only want to pet her."

"I know honey - but she doesn't know that. You're poking into her house and you're a lot bigger than her. Imagine if some huge finger came poking through our window right now - how would that feel?"

Ellie's eyes widened in alarm. "Ugh, that would be so scary!" She scanned the windows, front and back, with concern in case some such enormous digit should appear. Then she knelt down and just stroked the carrier, saying softly. "It's okay… Oh! What's her name? What do I call her?"

"Well, she's your pet. You get to name her."

Ellie was thrilled. "Oh. Oh. Oh. I could call her Elsa!"

Rosie sighed. "Does everything have to be about Frozen, sweetheart?"

"No." He daughter admitted, matter-of-factly. "But it is a nice name, isn't it?"

"Yes, it is."

"What's wrong with Elsa's eye, Mum?"

"I don't know, sweetheart. I think maybe she has cataracts or something."

"What's catacats?"

"Cataracts? They're things which can grow in your eye and make things difficult to see. They make your vision go all… misty."

"Can she see out of that eye then?"

"Well, I don't know. Perhaps she can see a little bit? We'll have to find out. There's a lot to read about looking after hens." Rosie said. "But then, isn't that all part of earning your Brownie badge - finding out how to care for Elsa?"

"Oh no, we can't call her Elsa now. Elsa's magical and powerful and… perfect."

"We can still call her Elsa though, sweetheart." Rosie bent down to stroke her daughter's hair. "Maybe she is magical and we don't know it yet?"

"I don't think so, Mum." Ellie rose to her feet. "She's just a hen with catacats. We'll have to give her a different name."

"Such as?"

"Misty!"

Roly Baxter stood and let his father's words wash over him like coloured jet streams in an angry wind tunnel. His father liked the sound of his own voice and never seemed to tire of it but Roly had heard enough. The summer sun sparkled through the large window behind his father's chair, bathing his head in some kind of corona of authority - a beatified Saint in a stained-glass window. Although, unlike a church in which such a window might command attention, this office was not cool; far from it. The sun had been shining all afternoon and now, as 6pm approached, the metal box in which he stood while his father sat, was a suffocating oven served inadequately by a decrepit air-conditioning unit up on one wall which farted and dripped and created the merest draft by barely moving the hot air around the room. His father neither noticed nor cared - just sat there in a tweed three-piece suit, glistening, like a sleek, well-fed sea-lion used to bathing in audience applause for his party tricks.

Roly waited for a pause in his father's diatribe and seized upon it.

"Can I ask a silly question, Sir?"

Sir Malcolm scowled at the interruption. "Like nobody else I know."

"Does the money for the Critchley's really matter? I mean, in the grand scheme of things?"

"I said eighty, not one hundred. Eighty."

"But they weren't going to accept eighty, Sir."

His father scoffed, barely able to conceal his disdain. "What's this business called?"

"Baxter, Sir." Roly said, bemused.

"That's right, boy. It's called Baxter. Singular. Not Baxter's possessive or Baxters plural. Baxter declarative. It is me and I am it. Baxter is my name and the name of my business. It starts with me and it ends with me. Not you, me. And it's just as bloody well that it is mine because with your head for business, this business wouldn't last five minutes. Of course, the bloody money matters! Give me strength."

"But..." Roly dropped his voice and swallowed hard. Here was the sort of point in a conversation where Sally would advise him to put his best foot forward, make his case for a future where his father retired, or died, or decided he'd had enough - the first and last ones were, as far as Roly was concerned, never going to happen. And the middle one, as far as Sally was concerned, was never going to happen. Roly felt himself flush as he cleared his throat and said: "But one day, Sir, surely you will expect me to run the business." He fumbled as he fell into the sentence and reached for support, which only came out as a negation of the sentence's intended purpose. "On your behalf, of course." He finished, pointlessly.

"Over my dead body!" His father blurted, eyes bulging in protest. "On my behalf? What do you think, that'll I just get bored one day and throw all this away?" He gestured dramatically with both hands, widening them out as if distributing bounty to an assembled throng. "My life's work?"

"But, one day, Sir. When you're gone?"

"Gone? Gone? I'm going nowhere, boy. Look at me! Fit as a fiddle. I'm in my prime with zero - zero, I say - intention of stepping down, passing on, or anything else for that matter. The only thing likely to have me keel over is if we don't win this blasted Tesco deal." Malcolm looked at his watch. "And, on that note, give me a sit rep. Pronto. We've still got plenty of hours left, let's not waste it if there's stuff outstanding."

"Well, it's gone six, Sir. The only people left here are you and me, so-"

"What!"

"It's gone six, Sir." Roly repeated, lowering his voice warily.

"I don't care if it's gone midnight! We've got Tesco's coming here tomorrow morning and I need to know that all the signage is up and that everyone has been appropriately briefed for the tour. One false move, one wrong note and we'll be done for!"

"The signage is up, Sir. I have been over and checked the three decoy sheds, inside and out."

"Demonstration." His father grunted. "Not decoy."

"Yes, Sir. Everything looks good."

"Humph. Let's go through the protocol once more, shall we?"

"Yes, Sir." Roly reluctantly drew a notepad from out of his leather portfolio and opened it. "11am tomorrow. Tour of the premises - all *demonstration* premises - to be visited by Tesco."

"Which are?"

"Only those signed as such."

His father nodded. "Go on."

"To be checked beforehand: signage, site clearance, packaging, cleaning, staff attendance, re-briefing. Dress rehearsal if required."

His father nodded. "Let's do one anyway, required or not. Belt and braces, all that."

"Right." Roly made a note and continued. "After that we come back up here and go through the three P's: pricing, promos, paperwork. Emma from Quality to be on hand and fully briefed ready for Cheryl's arrival."

"Good."

Roly swallowed hard. "And the Critchley's money, Sir? Bearing in mind that the whole point of this is to remove the court case for the sake of Tesco."

"I know what the bloody point is, boy!" Malcolm slammed his fist down on the desk, rattling the phone and desk tidy contents. The thud echoed around the claustrophobic metal walls. "They'll accept a hundred thousand, you say?"

"Yes, Sir."

"Okay. Just don't expect me to pay it." Malcolm jabbed a thick finger in Roly's direction.

"Sir?"

"Eighty's what I said - reluctantly I might add - and eighty's all I'll pay."

"But-"

"And get them to withdraw their appeal."

"But if you're not going to pay…?"

"You've agreed one hundred. They withdraw their appeal." Malcolm spread his hands, smiling malevolently. "Tesco sign. All bets are off. We pay 'em eighty. They can take it, or re-raise their appeal. At that point, I really won't care."

"But, Sir!"

"You heard me." Malcolm fumed.

And with that Roly backed out of the room and closed the door softly behind him.

"Mum, how did you know Misty was a girl?"

"Because she lays eggs sweetheart. Only girl animals lay eggs." Rosie smiled as she watched her daughter stroke Misty on her lap. Over the past few days, the stricken animal had calmed and become less agitated. Ewan had got busy building a small coop for it, a one-metre cube of plywood and chicken wire filled with straw. Rosie had freed up some space in the utility room to put the coop in there for the time being, but Ellie had pitched a fit until it was placed in her bedroom, at the foot of her bed. Once Misty had become used to it, Rosie had opened the door to the coop so that Ellie could go in and sit and stroke her. The two had already become fast friends.

"Do all girl animals lay eggs?"

"I think so yes. That's how babies are born."

A cloud of a frown drifted across her daughter's beautiful face. "Was I an egg?"

Uh, oh thought Rosie. I've got myself into a birds-and-bees type of conversation somewhat sooner than I expected. Being a parent was like that - there would be key times in the life of your child where you had to do your job and help them over an obstacle - whether it was admitting that Santa didn't exist, or their first day at school, or talking to them about contraception or watching them leave home. All landmark moments you knew would come. The sad truth was that, however much you thought about them in advance, you were never ever ready for them.

Here was one now.

"Well, yes, sweetheart. You were. A tiny, tiny egg in my tummy that grew into you!"

"And did you lay me in a nest?"

"Um, no. Well kind of. But that's not how people do it, honey. Different types of animals do different things. Birds lay eggs in nests. Mammals - like cats and dogs and cows and sheep - the eggs grows inside the Mummy and a live baby comes out."

"Am I a mammal?" Ellie's face was crunched up in concentration, or confusion.

"Yes, sweetheart. We all are - all people, I mean."

"So why don't birds have live babies instead of eggs?"

Now it was Rosie's turn to frown. "I don't know,

actually. That's a very good question! Maybe you could find the answer and use that for your Brownie badge write-up?"

"Okay." Ellie said, and that was the matter simply dealt with. Rosie breathed a sigh of relief.

Prematurely.

"What makes the egg turn into a baby?"

"Um, well that's where the Daddy comes in. The Daddy fertilises the egg and starts the process of it becoming a baby!"

"Fertisizes?"

"Fer-til-is-es."

"Fer-til-is-es?"

"That's it!"

"How does a Daddy do that?"

Aargh. "Well, again you see sweetheart - it's different for different types of animals."

This seemed enough to finesse the subject, for now.

"So, do we need a Daddy to turn Misty's eggs into babies?"

"Well, yes. If we wanted them to turn into baby chicks, we would need a Daddy hen."

"Can we get a Daddy hen!" Ellie was suddenly alive with excitement again. "What does a Daddy hen look like?"

"A Daddy hen? A Daddy hen is a cock-a-doodle-do, sweetheart. Although the proper name is a rooster, I think. No, a cockerel."

"Can we have a cock-a-doodle-do?"

"Well, we'll have to see how things go with Misty first won't we? Would you want to be woken up every morning at dawn by a loud cock-a-doodle-do?"

"Um, no." Ellie idly pulled at a thread dangling from

Molly while she watched Misty strut about her coop. "When will Misty lay eggs, Mum?"

"Well I don't know the answer to that, sweetheart." Rosie thought, maybe she won't. She regretted not asking Roly for more information. "We'll just have to wait and see won't we? It will be quite exciting. You can go and check every morning and see if she's laid an egg!"

"Yes!" Ellie clapped her hands in anticipation. "And then we can get a cock-a-doodle-do and fertisize the egg and then we'll have lots of little chickies!"

Rosie was just about to say "Well, I think the cock-a-doodle-do has to fertilise the egg before Misty lays it." And then realised where that might lead so instead said: "Well, let's see if Misty lays any eggs at all first, shall we? You know there's a saying?"

"A saying?"

"Yes, a thing people say sometimes. It's don't count your chickens before they've hatched."

"What does it mean?"

"Well, it means just because you have, say, five eggs it doesn't mean they're going to turn into five chickies. You can't tell if any egg is fertilised from the outside. You have to wait and see."

Ellie considered this wisdom for a moment. "Can you tell if it's a boy chickie or a girl chickie?"

"Not until they hatch. And even then, I think it's very difficult to tell the difference between boys and girls because the chicks are so tiny. I think you'd have to wait until they'd grown a wee bit."

Phew, thought Rosie, I think I'm out of the woods here.

Ellie sat watching her pet, tilting her head this way and that and trying to imitate the stiff neck movements of the bird as she pecked around her coop. After a while her daughter piped up again.

"I'm glad Misty's a girl. Aren't you?"

"Yes." Rosie thought. I have early enough starts in the morning as it is. "Girls are nicer than boys, aren't they?"

"When I was just an egg, did you want a girl or a boy?"

"A girl, sweetheart. Obviously." And she reached down and gave her daughter a cuddle, all the time thinking: *Well, actually, I just wanted a backrub - but that's your father for you.*

"Look what I've got!" Jakki opened the package delightedly. "Found it online."

"What is it?" Elaine asked. Two days had elapsed since their last evening excursion on Operation Shellshock while Jakki had been awaiting delivery for this new device she now brandished.

"It's a keypad-bypass device. You hold it next to a coded keypad and it works out the code and opens it!"

"How does it do that?"

"Absolutely no idea. Magic? Do we care or do we just want to open the doors?"

"Both?"

"Okay, well maybe you do. I just want to open the doors."

"There you go again: doors, plural." Elaine said. "Why plural?"

"In case." Jakki smiled. "They obviously know something's up, been improving their security. Maybe they've cleared out more sheds. Maybe they're moving stuff around to catch us out. We might need to try several sheds until we find a *right* one."

"They can't move thousands of hens around just like that!" Elaine demurred. "Not only is it a big job but they would never do it during the laying season. It's too problematic. The only time they clear barns out is when the flock is all laid out and they clear out the entire place, and deep-clean it ready for the next batch."

"Well, I don't know." Jakki bowed to her partner's greater expertise. "But I do know we are now equipped to open as many shed doors as we need. Tonight, we finally break in!"

"If Big Paul's available." Elaine pointed out.

"Ach, he'll be available." Jakki snorted. "When's he not available? Bloke's a poor excuse for a man - never working, never earning. Dresses like a slob most of the time. Always smelling of beer or dogs."

"I like him." Elaine admitted. "He's kinda funny."

"Funny peculiar, right enough." Jakki raised her eyebrows pointedly at her partner. "See, me and you? We don't need men. Don't want men. And right there is every indication of what a wise and sensible decision that is!"

"Well, it's not really a decision as such, is it? I mean, I didn't decide my sexuality. I just recognised and accepted it."

"No, you embraced it!" Jakki smiled. "Yes, okay. Not a decision. But you know what I mean. If it had been a decision, it's men like him that would vindicate us."

"I still like him."

"Fine. Each to their own. So, give him a call and let's arrange our hopefully final visit to the damned chicken sheds!"

Paul arrived late, as usual, with his dogs playing chase at his feet as he rang the doorbell. Elaine answered it and, seeing his dogs, her face fell. "Oh. Er…"

"Wotcha." Paul beamed and then checked himself. "Is there a problem?"

"Well, er, you see Jakki won't allow dogs in the house."

"Doesn't she like dogs? Ant and Dec are house-trained you know. Aren't you fellas?" He reached down to scruff them with his enormous hands and the pair frolicked and growled, competing for his attention.

"No, it's not that." She leant into Paul to confide in a whisper. "It's one of her little peccadilloes."

"Ah, don't worry." Paul breezed. "They won't attack it."

"What?"

"Her peccadillo. My boys are good as gold."

"No, no, no. I mean it's one of her … things. Idiosyncracies? She won't have pets in the house. Cats, dogs, anything. She won't even let me have tropical fish."

"Oh, right." Paul hmm'ed. "Ok, well I'll just pop 'em back in the van. Just wanted to give 'em a bit of a stretch. She's a bit of a funny one, ain't she?"

"We all have our little foibles." Elained shrugged. "I mean, don't tell her - because I'm supposed to be veggie too - but I'm a sucker for beef stew and dumplings."

"Well okay." Nodded Paul as he scooshed his dogs back into the van. "But I don't think you should probably call her that."

"Right. We all set?" Jakki asked, as they sat once again in the layby outside Baxter Farms.

"Yup." Paul waggled her phone in one meaty hand. "Camera, ready!"

"Lay?"

"Yes, I'm ready." Elaine said quietly, the immediate prospect of revisiting the inside of one of these hellholes suddenly crashing down on her.

"You okay?" Jakki put a gentle hand on her partners shoulder, her face clouded with concern.

"I guess. It's just... well, I know what these places are like inside. It's not going to be nice."

"I know, Lay. But that's why we're here. We go in, take some video, release it online. Voila! Public outrage, news headlines. No more mistreated chickens!"

"Aw, how bad can it be?" Paul said. "I mean, they're gonna die anyway, aren't they? When they've laid all their eggs 'n' that."

"Oh, you're all concern, aren't you? Typical man!" Jakki stormed. "Does animal welfare mean nothing to you?"

"Well I look after my dogs! I'm concerned about *their* welfare." Paul replied, feathers slightly ruffled. "But that lot are going to get eaten at the end of the day. Can't really bring myself to give a toss about some hens in a shed. I mean, maybe laying eggs hurts. It's like childbirth, innit? Maybe they'd rather be dead."

"What nonsense!" Jakki tried to shake his words from her head. "Come on, Lay. Let's do this."

When they reached the door of the second shed along, Jakki wielded her keypad device. "Here we go! Open Sesame!" She held it up next to the keypad and waited for some sound or something to happen. When nothing did, she tried the door handle. Nothing.

"Hmm. Are you supposed to key in a code or

something?" Elaine frowned.

"Well, that would kind of defeat the point of it wouldn't it? It's supposed to open this without me knowing the code."

"What do the instructions say?"

"I didn't bring them with me. But the advert online just implied you hold it next to the pad and then voila!"

"Can I try?" Paul asked. Jakki handed him the device and moved away from the door to let him near. Paul waved it around the keypad and placed it on all sides, all the while bending his head next to the panel, listening intently. After a minute or so he straightened up and inspected the device. Hefting it in his hand he flipped it over. frowning, and then opened the back cover.

"Here's your problem." He said, waving the empty battery compartment at Jakki.

TWELVE

Chicken Shed #8 was cavernous and scrupulously clean. It even had a pristine, shiny new Tesco sign mounted on the outside wall as she entered. Despite herself, Cheryl was impressed. And there was more inside.

She entered into some kind of anteroom where a complex web of machinery was being assembled by workmen in bright white overalls. Two conveyor belts, gleaming chrome, ribboned down from high up in the left and right walls like enormous, wide bicycle chains. The conveyors curved lazily around and down to about three feet off the ground where they joined together, flattening into a smooth shallow-gradient river of metal teeth.

"This is our egg delivery and packing equipment." Roly explained. "I can show you one in Shed #12 which is in operation but I thought we'd best start with one of your own dedicated sheds."

"Should we decide to do business with you." Cheryl reminded, but couldn't help but see the notices up on the large board to her right, next to an extensive control panel and LED display, which were all on what looked awfully like Tesco-headed paper.

"Of course." Roly smiled at her. "But I think you'll find, as I take you around, that any concerns or questions you may have will be amply addressed."

"We do supply other large supermarket chains with

eggs, you know." Malcolm chimed in, hands clasped behind his back. "Our processes and facilities reflect our experience in that regard."

"I am sure, Sir Malcolm." Cheryl bit her words out. "I am also sure that ourselves at Tesco take pride in providing premium quality at value prices."

"As do we, Cheryl. Very much so." Malcolm smarmed.

"The eggs laid in each of the main enclosures, left and right of this room, feed through on these conveyors." Roly continued, pointing out the various components being assembled. "Individual eggs nestle in these spaces where the chain links meet. They gently bump up against each other and then drain down into this funnel and pass beneath these mechanical arms. Each arm swings on an axis, here, picking up eggs by a sucker and depositing them into corrugated cardboard sheets, 10 x 10 eggs in area. Like these." He picked up the top brown layer from a huge pile stacked on a bouncing platform, like hot plates at the end of a self-serve buffet line.

"All the birds on our farm are Scottish-reared and bred entirely to our own specifications. This ensures quality of pullet which helps give consistency. Our Scottish-reared birds lay Scottish eggs so we feel it's important to employ only Scottish packers to give a 100% genuinely Scottish egg."

A nice touch, thought Cheryl.

"Over here..." Roly walked over to two plastic containers attached to tubes and taps which disappeared into the wall behind. "We have the feed and water which are fed through into the colonies. Any medicines like antibiotics are applied via a dosimeter into the water supply so that every hen receives a dose."

"What do they eat?"

"Bloody expensive feed I'll have you know!" Malcolm grumbled. "Specially designed, and consequently, especially expensive."

"It's enriched." Roly interjected. "Vitamins, nutrients and so forth. And colouring, such as paprika, which enhances yolk colour."

"Ah yes. I'd like to see your yolk swatches, at some point, if I may?" Cheryl explained. "Yolk colour is a key quality metric in our kitchens. Where we use eggs in preparing our own-brand Ready Meals and so forth. I'm under strict instructions to report back on that."

"Of course." Roly replied smoothly. "And if you require any… custom colouring… we are happy to work with you and our feed suppliers to get the yolks just the right shade!"

Cheryl nodded appreciatively while Malcolm glowered silently behind her.

"What about traceability?" She asked.

"All eggs that leave our farm are individually stamped for full traceability. The stamping code will be something like SC10827: SC says the eggs are Scottish; the first number indicates production method, 1 is Free Range; the 08 is our shed number and 27 is the flock identifier."

"Flock identifier?"

"Yes. All hens in a given shed are from the same flock, raised in the same space by our pullet breeder and kept apart from other flocks. They are all brought in at the same time - 8,000 per lorry load - and taken away at the same time when the hens are laid out. Keeping all the pullets from the same flock and supplier not only maximise egg consistency but also minimises the risk of bio-hazard, cross-contamination and so on. Our suppliers also have their own traceability systems in place, so if there was ever - god forbid - any outbreak or infection, not only could we trace it back to an individual shed but our supplier can then trace it back to an individual batch of eggs from which the pullets were raised."

There was an echoing clang as a section of the conveyor being assembled slipped from one of the workmen's grasp. There was swiftest, almost invisible, exchange of worried looks between the man and Sir Malcolm, but Cheryl spotted it.

"What about your staff?"

"All our staff have had extensive training on bird welfare and best practices. Not just in-house training but also from the relevant certification bodies. Their personnel files record the training received and dates, so that when any refreshers are needed, we can forecast them and schedule them as required." Roly answered smoothly. "All on-site employees do the government and Freedom Foods and Food Hygiene accreditation - whether they come into contact with the birds or not. And we have a continuous programme of health and safety training for everyone, and First Aid for nominated staff."

"It would be good to have a look at some of your training records." Cheryl asked but felt confident that they would bear out what Roland was saying. Compared to his father, the son was a very composed and impressive individual.

"Of course. Now, if we go through to one of the enclosures..."

"Mum! Come and look! Come and see what I have made for Misty."

Ellie was beaming with pride, her little cheeks stretched to the limit by a face-wide grin. Rosie smiled at her daughter and wiped her hands on the tea towel; the dishes could wait. Her little girl wanted to show off something to her Mum and Rosie wasn't going to let her down.

"Okay. Show me then!" And followed her daughter down the hallway to Ellie's room.

"Close your eyes."

Rosie scrunched her eyes up tightly and let herself be led by the hand unsteadily into the room. She could hear soft clucking over by the window.

"Open them." Ellie said and Rosie did so, her face dropping suddenly at the sight before her.

"Ellie, what have you done!"

"It's for my badge." Her daughter recited. "Caring for your pet. Making it comfortable and safe."

"Sweetheart, that's Mister Cullen's hat. You can't use that for a nest, you'll have to give it back."

"But he won't mind." Ellie declared. "He's a nice man. He rescued Scampi. Mister Cullen loves animals." She nodded to herself, confident in her logic.

"Yes, but-"

"And Misty loves it. See?"

It did appear as if the hen had happily made herself at home. Inside its cage, Ellie had put the hat on top of a blanket in Scampi's old dog basket, perched Cullen's battered hat on top of that, and filled it with straw. Misty was clucking contentedly atop her new nest.

"Yes, sweetheart. But-"

"Jemima helped me build it." Her daughter chimed,

oblivious to her mother's concern. "But it was my idea!"

Rosie looked at her daughter's happy face and tried to smile. "Well, it's a lovely nest, darling, but I do think we need to respect Mister Cullen's property." She approached the nest with caution, stalking forward like a heron in the water. "Perhaps we could find a different hat for Misty…"

She reached out a hand into the open cage door and the bird made a darting movement with its head. Rosie thought she saw the hen's eyes bulge, its cherished home under threat. Suddenly a nasty peck from this mangy bird seemed a very real possibility. She stepped back.

"Umm. Maybe I could find an old straw hat under the stairs and we - you - could swap it for this one. And then we could give Mister Cullen his hat back."

"I don't think so, Mum." Ellie folded her arms in serious contemplation. "Misty really likes it. I think she's made her mind up. This is where she wants to lay her eggs."

"Yes, but sweetheart." Rosie thought for a moment. This bird had as much chance of laying an egg as she did. Ellie interrupted her mother's train of thought.

"And when Misty lays an egg, I will take a photo and put it in my badge book!" She scooped up her Brownie Badge handbook and clutched it to her.

"Yes, darling. That'll be wonderful." Rosie replied. "But you can't just take someone's property and use it without their permission. That's not right."

"But Mister Cullen won't mind!" Ellie protested.

"Well, there's only way to find out isn't there?"

Ellie cocked her head at her mother in a confused manner.

"Ask him." Rosie said. "Go and find Mister Cullen,

take his hat, and ask him if he wants it back or if you can keep it as a nest for Misty."

Her daughter gave a sad pout and put her head down. "But Mum-"

"Ask him." Rosie repeated and left her daughter to extract the leather hat from her recalcitrant pet.

Inside the right-hand enclosure of Shed #12 Cheryl could hardly hear herself think, never mind hear Roly's commentary. The enormous fans at the far end made a fair racket, but even they could not compete with the constantly heckling birds, scratching and squabbling, sending dust and feathers into the air. It was all a tremendous contrast to the cool quiet of the packing anteroom in the shed they had just come from, where the only sounds had been the gentle whirr of the motorised arms and the quiet clinking of the conveyor as it looped the eggs down to be stacked in layers.

She gestured to him that she couldn't hear what he was saying so he smiled and led her out through another door and around the back of the building into the fenced outdoor area where hens were pecking happily.

"Sorry about that." Roland was all apologetic smiles. "You get used to it and forget how loud it actually is."

"Is it always like that?"

"Pretty much. Except when they're asleep - or outdoors, as here. So you will have noticed that we have two high-rise housing units running the length of each enclosure, three storeys high. On each level there are nestboxes with covers which close on a timer-basis to give the birds privacy and improved sleep. The eggs are laid in the nestboxes and fall through onto the conveyor below which carries them to the packing room."

"And their, um, poo?"

"The dung falls through onto large trays which are scraped clean every two weeks - gets a bit pongy otherwise." Roland wrinkled his nose up and Cheryl smiled at this boyish gesture. "Then we sell it! Its high in salt so really good for arable farm land, apparently."

He turned away from her and waved his hand over the pastoral scene in front of them. "We are Freedom Foods certified and registered with the British Egg Industry Council. And the Scottish Organic Producers Association, who insist on the highest level of bird welfare and organic standards in Europe. And we are independently audited several times a year to ensure our premises and processes are maintained to these high standards."

"Which means?"

"Well, for example, Free Range standards stipulate maximum densities under which hens can be kept. In a 36,000 square meter enclosure like that one it means no more than 70,000 hens allowed. The densities increase as you drop through the quality levels. So, for barn eggs or caged eggs you are able to cram more birds into the space. Obviously to the detriment of the animals' welfare so that is not something we do."

"Never been tempted?" Cheryl probed.

"No." Roland replied smoothly. "Obviously, before Free Range was a thing and EU regulations about animal welfare were a glint in anyone's eye, all UK eggs were from caged birds. But that was made illegal many years ago. In my father's day, of course…"

He left his sentence unfinished and Cheryl wondered what response his father would have given if he had been conducting this section of the tour. Malcolm had left her with Roland after being summoned by his Security Chief for some minor issue or other.

Roland led her through into the outdoor enclosure and Cheryl watched as she followed him down the back wall and up along the front, Roland pointing out the salient points as they walked.

"Similarly, the standards define the size and requirements for outdoor spaces such as these." Roland continued. "As you can see there are trees and shrubs for cover, crates and other arranged objects for interest. An *enriched* environment."

"And can the hens go outside whenever they want?"

"Pretty much. They need ten-plus hours of light a day in order to lay. It doesn't have to be sunlight, of course, and the sheds have indoor lights as you have seen. But the light source has to be bright enough to read a paper in to qualify - although why hens should want to read a newspaper…!"

She smiled and made a note in her book.

"What happens if they don't get enough light?"

"They go into moult." Roland paused and leant back on the fence watching the birds scratch around in the sunshine. "That is to say, they stop laying. It would happen naturally in the winter months when there is insufficient daylight - they'd come out of moult as the spring arrived. We work around this by giving the hens more indoor light when the weather is bad over winter."

"So, when do they actually stop laying?"

"Well." Roly looked up to his left as he recalled. "The pullets are usually brought in at sixteen weeks old and kept for sixty weeks. That's when we consider them spent. We allow a couple of weeks at the start for them to settle in before laying and then we'll get somewhere between 300-350 eggs per hen. There is some variability because egg production peaks during, say, weeks twenty-five to forty, then starts to tail off. But usually around seventy-six weeks old that's when they're considered done."

"And then?"

"They get taken away." Roly shrugged.

"How?" Cheryl laughed. "How do you round up, 64,000 chickens?"

"Very carefully." Roly grinned. "Actually, it's a very specialised job. We don't do it ourselves. I think it'd be a disaster if we did! No, we employ a firm who come in at 3am when the hens are all docile or asleep - they come in wearing head torches and creep around; looks really weird! They scoop them up into crates, one or two at a time, and… take them away."

Cheryl winced, smiling. "Not a job I'd want."

"Me neither. Anyway, once they're gone, we remove the last of the manure and get professional cleaners in to steam clean the whole place so we can get it ready for the next flock. Each shed is fallow, if you like, for about three weeks between generation restocks."

Cheryl closed her notebook with an appreciative nod. "So, what's a top tip you could give me - as an egg consumer?"

"As an egg producer, I'd say: buy medium eggs. Not large. Medium eggs come from younger birds so are better. Stresses the birds out less too. Larger eggs come from birds as they get closer to being laid-out. So, buy medium!"

"Well, thank-you, Roland." She reached to shake his hand. "I suppose we should head back and conclude our meeting with Sir Malcolm before we go on our way?"

"Of course." Roland led her out through a gate and they strolled back to the boardroom in the afternoon sunshine, chatting animatedly.

"I don't like him." Cheryl declared as Chris drove the car under the security gate and swept out onto the A703. "Never trust a rich man who brags."

"Why?"

"No-one gets rich by themselves. Maybe he inherited it, maybe he stole it, whatever. There were people on the way who helped him, or were fleeced or fooled or trampled by him. If he tells you he's self-made, it's a crock. Look at Trump."

Chris nodded to himself but said nothing. Cheryl was his boss and she liked the sound of her own voice, often not requiring or desiring a response to what she said. Sometimes, all she wanted was an audience. Besides, Chris had learnt a lot from her about the business, about sales negotiations and reading people. She could be a right royal pain in the arse when she wanted to be, Chris felt, but she certainly knew her stuff.

"Yeah!" Chris joked. "And he can't be that rich, can he? I mean, if he was that rich, he'd have people to brag for him!"

Cheryl ignored him and gazed out at the pastures and moorland as the car flew onwards to the city bypass. "It's a big operation he's got here. I can see that. And I can't complain about his pricing."

"But you're going to?"

"No." She smiled. "But I am going to haggle him down hard. Don't give them an inch, Christopher.

They'll always, always, take it." She alone called him Christopher, her crystal clipped tones making him sound like royalty when she said it and he had decided long ago that he very much liked it. "What are your thoughts on it?"

His eyes bulged involuntarily and he made a huge effort to keep staring straight ahead so that Cheryl couldn't see it. She was asking his opinion? What the actual…? He wrestled with the desire to look at her in the rear-view mirror as he mentally scrambled to work out what was going on.

"On Sir Malcolm do you mean?" He finally responded. "Or the whole deal."

"Both." Cheryl said. "Go for it."

"Well, he's certainly full of himself. Never met him before, having only dealt with Tessa."

"Yes, well there's your first alarm bell." He could hear Cheryl chomping her teeth together in thought. "Key personnel vanishing during the contract setup process. Not good."

"And he treats his son like dirt - although his son does seem like a bit of a wuss. Seemed to know his stuff, though, didn't he?"

"Yes." Cheryl agreed, biting her lip. "Didn't he just? He was impressive."

"Is that an alarm bell?"

"Hardly! I expect an experienced businessman to know his onions and a gifted salesman to be smooth and persuasive. So, between them…" She rested her head on the window and exhaled slowly. "There's just something bothering me. A gut feeling."

"The tenant farmers court case?"

"No." Cheryl sighed. "Sir Malcolm, and Roland, both

confirmed they're just waiting on paperwork to confirm the appeal is being dropped."

"His pricing, then? You said it's keen."

"No reason to not haggle." Cheryl looked up, smiling, to catch his eye in the rear-view mirror. "Never leave any money on the table, Christopher."

"Even if we're not going to sign?"

"Who said we wouldn't sign?"

"Well… you're saying you have a bad feeling - in your gut - about this." Chris frowned. "Aren't you?"

"I don't know what I'm saying." She sighed once more. "I'm saying it looks like a good deal. A very, very good deal."

"Maybe too good?"

"Maybe." She turned back to stare out of the window. "Maybe."

Up on the Pentlands a few souls were tracing lazy routes down the dry ski slope in the sunshine.

It had decided to rain. Jakki, Elaine and Paul scurried from the van into the lee offered by the second shed and grouped in a huddle around the main door one more time.

"Please God." Pleaded Elaine. "Make this the last time we have to come to this forsaken place."

"Amen to that." Agreed Paul. "Mileage I'm doing is ridiculous. My van's not cut out for all this to-ing and fro-ing."

"Team, team, team." Jakki played both hands palms down, as if she was patting a full duvet. "Relax. Here we go."

She placed the device next to the keypad and there

was an immediate beeping noise and a small light flashed amber on one edge. Jakki held her breath and waited. After about thirty seconds the beeping stopped and the light turned green. Looking in wonder at her two accomplices she gingerly tried the handle. The door swung open lazily and banged against the wall of the corridor beyond.

"Bloody hell! How easy was that?" Jakki beamed in delight. "Nothing can go wrong now!" And into the dark interior she stepped.

The alarm for Shed #18 went off on the control panel and woke Eddie up. These day and night shift combos were playing havoc with his sleep patterns and he would quite happily have been warmly ensconced in his own stinking pit if he could rely on his team to do the job required of them, and of Sir Malcolm to forgive him if his team screwed up. But he couldn't count on either. If you needed a job done properly…

Snatching his knopkierie off the table he scrambled to his feet and started for the stairs.

The shed door was, indeed, ajar. *Amateurs*, Eddie spat. He used his knopkierie to prod the door open and stepped inside the silent packing area. The egg machinery and gleaming conveyors sat silent and still, but the stench of ammonia and decay hit him straight in the face. The foul odour seemed to permeate everything, its tendrils wrapping themselves around him as he stepped further into the shed.

As he approached the left-hand door at the back of the packing area, he could hear a female voice:

"… in these appalling conditions. Despite EU and

UK legislation on animal welfare and the so-called rigour of SSPCA and SEPA assessments, you can see what the reality actually is. Are you happy that your eggs and your chickens are reared in hell-holes like this? Broken and demented creatures living out their brutish, short lives in a way which should shame us all?"

"Heeyar! Whut's yoor gyme?"

Jakki, who had been speaking to camera, jumped out of her skin and Elaine who had been recording on Jakki's phone gave a startled cry. "You can't just come waltzing in here! This is private property AND a carefully controlled food production environment maintained in order to prevent the transmission of disease and infection into the food chain."

"Don't make me laugh!" Jakki snorted. "Look at this place!"

Eddie raised his knopkierie to shoulder height. "Let's see if this'll make you la-"

An invisible sledgehammer hit him in the face and he collapsed like a badly folded shit. Paul stepped out from behind the door and motioned to the women.

"Come on! We need to get out now. Before anyone else arrives."

Jakki and Elaine didn't need prompting. The pair raced out of the caged area and into the central space, panting as they ran. Paul looked down to check Eddie only to receive a whip-fast crack across his shin from the fallen figure splayed on the ground. He cried out and kicked out with all his might, landing a vicious blow to Eddie's midriff and there was the distinct sound of bone snapping.

Paul didn't wait. He limped as fast as he could out through the shed and into the rain, wincing every time he had to put any weight on his left leg. Up ahead he saw Jakki in his driving seat, starting the engine.

"Wait!" He cried and saw Jakki's startled face, look first at him, then up and down the deserted road. She rolled down his window.

"We need to go!" she shouted.

"Wait for me." Paul panted. "I'm almost there."

"Come on!" Jakki gunned the engine and, from the rear, Elaine slammed open the side panel door and held out her hand. As the van started kicking up gravel, Paul made it to the door, threw himself in almost obliterating the tiny figure of Elaine in the process. The vehicle fishtailed out of the layby and down the road, its side door still open. Paul and Elaine gasped in the back, while Jakki, white-knuckled, gripped onto the steering wheel as they sped south through the driving rain.

Sir Malcolm inhaled deeply, held it and then exhaled at length, noisily and unfettered. "Aaaahh. Do you smell that?"

His father had a habit of taking an early morning stroll around the main site and it was indeed a beautiful morning. When he had suggested - ha! What was Roly thinking? Ordered - Roly to accompany him this morning, Roly had adopted his usual stance: frozen midway between devotion and disgust. He was repelled by and attracted to his father in equal measure and, in this case as in all others, found himself torn between wanting to be wanted by his father and wanting to run a million miles away from this immoral bully.

And, as usual, filial devotion won out.

Roly wrinkled his own nose, imagining a world where

this awful ammonia smell didn't exist - an endeavour in which, since he was not a very imaginative man, he failed.

"I love the smell of egg farm in the morning!" Malcolm lifted his head in wonder, marvelling at the extent of his glorious domain, glowing in the unravelling light. "Smells like… victory."

Roly eyebrows shot up. "Cheryl has agreed terms then?"

"Good God, no! She's a canny one. She'll play hard to get for a while." His father raised his eyes to the sky. "But she will. I can feel it. God's in His Heaven and all is right with the world."

"Really?"

Sir Malcolm scowled and peered at his son. "How could she fail to be impressed by the setup here? That was a slick job we did yesterday, boy. S-L-I-C-K. And by we I mean, of course, me. Although I am grateful for your assistance."

Roly sighed, but his father continued to wax lyrical about the current state of events.

"The protesters are no more. The Critchley's will withdraw their appeal. Cheryl's going to sign.

"And then?"

"Ah, well. At the risk of getting ahead of ourselves…" Malcolm clasped his hands behind his back and mused, looking down at the prints his wellingtons were making in the thin mud. "We can demolish the Critchley place and erect another cluster of sheds - that should give us more than enough capacity to satisfy Tesco. Then-"

"How you can say that?" Roly asked. "I simply can't conceive-"

"If only your mother had been able to say the same."

Malcolm sniped. "But, as any mother will tell you: conceiving is easy; it's delivering that's hard. We're not out of the woods yet, boy. Still plenty of work to be done."

"But you just said God was in his heaven and all was the right with the world!"

"I also just said: let's not get ahead of ourselves! Good Lord, were you dropped on your head as a child?" His father halted at this ridiculous notion. "No, wait, that would suppose you were ever held."

THIRTEEN

"My Dad took me into one of the sheds when I was little." Jemima boasted. "It was huge and shiny and... echoey."

Ellie was envious. "Wow! Can I have a look inside one?"

"No, no. It is not allowed." Jemima said authoritatively, shaking her curls.

"But your Dad let you see inside!"

"Yes, but that was when it was first built. It was all nice and clean. But there were no chickens in it. Once there's chickens in it you can't go in."

"Why not?"

"They have to keep the birds healthy so that they lay lots and lots of nice eggs. Germs and nasties can be transmitted to the birds."

"I don't have germs and nasties on me!" Ellie cast her eyes down at her hands and dress, checking to make sure there weren't hundreds of black things swarming all over her.

"We all do." Jemima said sadly. "You can't see them, but they're still there."

"But this is for my badge!" Ellie cried. "Just a quick look? Then I can describe it in my book."

The girls were sitting atop a farm gate, the metal poles warm in the sunshine. Ellie was contemplating the massive shed in front of them. On her lap was the battered leather cowboy hat which she twirled by its thin leather strap

"No. It is forbidden. And anyway, you need clearance."

"What's clearance?" Ellie asked.

"Permission. And you need to wear special welly-boots. White ones. And a hat."

"I have a hat!" Ellie twirled Cullen's hat again.

"No, a safety hat."

"Oh. Why?"

"Wellies so you don't step in chicken poo!" Jemima giggled. "And a hat so eggs don't drop on your head."

"Wow." Ellie exclaimed, wide-eyed in wonder.

"And." Jemima was warming to her theme, attracted by her friend's interest and her own ability to expand on the nuggets which she had gleaned from her father's brief guided tour a few years earlier. "They're very dangerous - the hens. If you disturb them. They can peck you."

"Aren't they in cages."

"Nuh-uh. They run around and can go anywhere. They have these little wooden windows and they get lifted on a timer and all the hens shoot out and run everywhere. They've even got little see-saws and shelters and slides and things. It's like a giant play park!"

"Wow."

Ellie fell silent as she contemplated the marvellous vision in her head of this magical playground for chickens, wondering whether Misty would like such a thing and if her Dad could build one - she reckoned he could. Jemima watched her friend in silence for a while and then nudged her.

"Why have you got Mister Cullen's hat?"

"I have to give it him back. My Mum says." Ellie was

downcast and she gave the hat another twirl as if in protest.

"Why?"

"Because it's his property and I can't just take it and use it as a nest for Misty." Ellie recited her mother's words as close as she could remember them. "Not without asking him."

"Are you going to ask him if you can keep it?"

"Yes."

"Oh." Jemima examined the hat in her friend's hands. It was battered and weathered, the leather brim fraying and splitting in places, some stitching loose. "I wouldn't. It's not a very nice hat."

Ellie looked at it more closely. "It makes a nice nest. I hope Mister Cullen lets me keep it."

"Well, why don't we go and ask him then?"

"I don't know where he is." Ellie was downcast at the thought. "He ran away."

"Why?"

"I don't know. Mum said maybe he forgot something."

"Well he did." Jemima declared. "He forgot his hat!"

"Yes." Ellie rolled the hat in her hands. "Do you know where he is?"

"No." Jemima wrinkled her nose. "And I'm not sure I want to. I think he's a bit smelly. So's his hat."

"Well I don't." Said Ellie, smarting at her friend's distaste. "I don't think Mister Cullen smells and I think it's a very nice hat. For a nest."

"Yes. For a nest." Jemima jumped down off the gate. "Shall we go and play in the barn again?"

"I don't want to. I want to find Mister Cullen."

"Maybe… he's in the barn? Smelly people like to live

in smelly places."

"He's not smelly!" Ellie pouted but Jemima just poked her tongue out and made Ellie laugh.

"Come on! Let's see if we can find him." Jemima sped off before Ellie had time to think and she bundled the hat under her arm, jumped down off the gate and charged off after her friend, the two girls laughing in the sunshine.

"Good God, man! You look like a Swiss Flag that lost a fight with a lawnmower."

Eddie's face was bright red and he had patched up his mashed nose up with some huge dressing, a massive white padded square covering half his face and taped in place by four pieces of strapping which splayed out from it like warpaint. He also suspected he had one or two broken ribs which he had heavily strapped beneath his already bursting uniform. Plus, he wasn't entirely sure his head was clear - all the meds he'd randomly self-administered.

"Thank you, Sir." Eddie winced.

"So then, tell me - Mister Head Of Security - how did these master criminals bypass your new locks?"

"I don't know, Sir." Eddie wrinkled his brow. "Only the three of us know the codes. I don't understand it."

"Pathetic." Malcolm shook his head.

"It's them, though." Eddie seethed. "Those bastards at the gates. When I get my-"

"Ah, Roland." Malcolm interrupted as his son slid in through the door and snicked it shut. He stood beside Eddie, visibly shaking, a newspaper in his hand. "So pleased you could join us, Roland. We're having so much fun here, aren't we Eddie?"

Eddie declined to respond.

"Have you seen this?" Malcolm stormed. "This… abomination!"

"Sir?" Roly's voice was a mere Dolby hiss.

Malcolm spun his laptop to face his son. "Look at it!" he roared.

Roly blanched as the shaky video played out on screen. Panning around the brightly-lit, horrific interior of a chicken shed in high-definition glory, the laptop speakers shrieking with the echoing din from the tormented animals inside.

Malcolm slammed the laptop closed long before the clip was due to end. "This is all over the internet! Isn't that right, Eddie?"

Eddie nodded sagely, aware that his boss's understanding of the online world was extremely limited.

"This is all your fault!" Malcolm was foaming spittle. Roly flinched, and Eddie hung back, ineffectively hiding a snide grin. He had no idea why his boss even kept Roly alive, never mind on the payroll - he presumed it was only because he was in possession of a kidney donor card.

"How is it my fault, Sir?"

"You hired her. This Elaine." The scorn dripped from his father's tone. "You and your big ideas about a business strategy. Poking her nose in is all she did."

"She was a Business Analyst, Sir. It was her job to understand our business processes and see how they could be improved."

"Understand our business processes." Malcolm mimicked, a man searching in vain for a will-to-live machine that he could plug himself into. "Understand them so she could infiltrate and then expose us you mean? Like some undercover reporter? She had an axe to grind. And now she's grinding it."

"She wouldn't have had anything to grind if she hadn't been fired." Roly heard himself say and then snapped awake as if slapped in the face. He'd used the passive tense rather than accuse his father outright but this was no consolation; the damage had been done. "Sir." He added much, much too late and far, far too weakly.

"Get it taken down." Malcolm ordered.

Roly swallowed hard before replying. "I'm sorry, Sir. It can't be done."

"Don't give me *can't*. There's no such thing as *can't*." Malcolm brought his fist down on his desk.

"I'm afraid there is, Sir. In this case anyway."

"Look. There must be a way. I'm no computer expert but surely if someone can put a video on the internet, someone can take it off?"

"Only the person who uploaded it can do that. Or the hosting service - in this case Twitter."

"Well, tell Twitter to remove it then!"

"They won't do that, Sir, unless the video is offensive or an incitement or some such."

"Oh, but it IS offensive!" Malcolm fumed. "Damned offensive."

"To us, Sir, yes. But generally? It's just another video amongst millions. Which-" Roly saw an opportunity to calm his father down. "If you think about it, there are thousands of videos uploaded every day. It's just as likely to get lost in the noise as it is to attract attention. Making a fuss will just-"

"Making a fuss!" Malcolm slammed his fist down

again. "This could destroy my business, you stupid cretin!"

Roly gritted his teeth. "If we draw attention to it, it will only-"

"Shut up!" Malcolm rose from behind his desk and stormed over to his son. "Shut up this minute! I want this video deleted or removed or whatever the hell the right word is. Do you understand me? Suppose Cheryl sees it, what then?"

Roly had no answer, but Malcolm simply thrust his face right into his and growled. "Either that video goes, or you do."

Eddie, feeling the need to return the focus to his personal persecutors, jumped in.

"The protesters, Sir?"

"Oh yes, them!" Malcolm spun and strode over to the window, looking down at the gaggle of placard-wielders gathered by the main gate once more. "So nice to have them back, don't you think? I think I quite missed them whilst they've been gone."

Eddie, teeth clenched, felt the pulse in his face more keenly but said nothing. Suddenly, Malcolm banged on the window and the whole room seemed to rattle.

"Get rid of them! How many times must I repeat myself? Damaging my property. Breaking and Entering! Making this video! Ruining my business!" He wheeled to glare at Eddie. "Smashing your nose! What more motivation do you need?"

"None, Sir."

Malcolm pointed a warning finger at his security chief. "Get cracking. Get down there and crack some heads with that... stick of yours."

"It's a *knopkierie*." Eddie countered, adding a

reluctant. "Sir."

"Don't care what it's called, son. Just care what you can do with it."

Roly's mouth fell open. His father had just called Eddie *son* - the one word he had never used with him, his actual son. It was unbelievable, as if his father's specialist subject was slashing at open wounds. The room shrank to a point and then winked out of existence, leaving Roly staring forlornly at the entrance to his old boarding school, a Rolls kicking up gravel as it sped out through the gates. He remembered how it felt to spend summer holidays with a parent who barely recognised him, let alone interacted with him - the missed opportunities it represented and the empty feeling of loss in his heart. The school had represented relief and sanctuary from pain - an alien but friendly outpost which, for months at a time, played home to the only people he enjoyed spending time with and who, it seemed, enjoyed spending time with him. Home: a word which promised so much but meant so little. He heard a soft cry - some small, bleak laugh - and realised it was him.

"What's wrong, boy?"

Roly blinked to find his father had turned to him and was waiting for some response.

"Nothing, Sir." He gulped.

"Frightened of delivering a little reminder to the proles, is that it?"

Roly remained silent. His father was having none of it.

"It is these very proles at my gates who will benefit from this deal with Tesco when it comes off. And, mark my words, *when* not *if.* They are the sort who shop at these places, whose only criteria for the food they buy is price. Quality be damned! So I am damning it. Give 'em what they want, that's success in business, boy! They want cheap stuff to shove in their gobs - and these are the sort of words they use to refer to eating, trust me. Note: no thought of deriving pleasure from the process. And God forbid they should have to cook something themselves! Pre-packaged, microwaveable, E-numbered, disgusting crap - that's what they like. Guess I should be bloody lucky they're happy to eat my eggs - probably the only fresh thing they put in their mouths on any given day."

Roly could barely speak but knew he had to. He swallowed down the distasteful lump of the misused *son* and struggled to clear his throat. Either his father found out the new bad news from him or from someone else - and Roly knew he would definitely come off worse if it was the latter.

"No, Sir. It's not the… proles." He handed his father a copy of the Peeblesshire News. "It's this."

Ewan Critchley was on the front page. Standing outside Selkirk Sheriff Court talking into a microphone, whilst behind him a small group holding up home-made banners: *Justice For Tenant Farmers, End This Modern-day Slavery, Free Our Farmers.* The headline read: *Baxter Tenant Farmer Appeals Unfair Eviction.*

Malcolm stared at it for a long while. In a reversal of their usual protocol, it was now Roly who was waiting for a response, watching his father, while the older man sat head down, eyes averted, silent.

Over the years, Roly had witnessed only a handful of truly gargantuan rages from his father - rages which stood head-and-shoulders above the persistent, latent levels of anger he maintained without breaking a sweat; as if the tectonic plates underpinning Malcolm's personality were continually irritating themselves as much as he irritated others. But these eruptions had been so terrifying, so nerve-shreddingly unbearable, that they were seared on his memory, and he knew the signs, feared them. And here they were again.

Sir Malcolm Baxter was about to blow.

First the ambient temperature plummeted, like some superheated body instantly sucking all the heat from the room, and with it all sound. Despite the sudden cold, Roly felt himself flushing and could see beads of sweat on Eddie's face as the pair of them exchanged a pregnant glance.

From somewhere came a rumble: the faintest, embryonic stirrings; the almost-indetectible jitters which would soon transform into frantic scribbles on a seismometer. It was the warning to get to a minimum safe distance - one that Roly wished he could take advantage of, rather than being rooted to the spot.

This led to initial venting: Malcolm would wordlessly fume and storm and project his immense mood into the atmosphere, indiscriminately unloading itself in all directions regardless of role or relevance. Blackening the sky and leaving everything choked under burning ash.

Then came dome build-up: the internal pressure and white heat of molten rage became too much for Malcolm's body to contain. He would inflate, his neck and face swelling up redder and hotter, his eyes popping, his chest heaving. There would be a tremendous boom to presage…

The magma explosion: sounds and fury would erupt - insults, expletives, and profanities would be ejected left and right, turning to superheated lava as they met the surrounding air, engulfing you and searing you alive.

And finally, when the explosion had subsided, came the pyroclastic flow of blame. You couldn't outrun it or escape it. Unfair and even vile accusations, finger-pointing and retribution for mistakes flew out from him at the speed of light, flattening everything in their path and permanently scarring the landscape.

Roly waited. His father, shaking under the tremendous internal pressure, was literally throwing a pill into his mouth, trembling so hard he almost missed. Gulping a glass of water, the silence seemed to last an eternity, the air rushing away from Roly, leaving him standing in an icy vacuum.

But there was no explosion, no transfer of blame, no unforgettable, awesome disaster. Malcolm's dome seemed to collapse, as if the internal pressures had suddenly found a weaker fault-line instead - one through which the anger could seep away into some underground reservoir, perhaps storing its energy for another, far greater explosion in future.

Malcolm's colour and breathing returned to something approaching normal and the room immediately warmed back up. Roly blinked, bemused, to see his father's transformation reversed. In the blink of an eye, he was back to his default, background radiation level of cynicism and vindictiveness.

Malcolm turned to Eddie. The sound of the protesters outside drifted in through the office window.

"Why are you still here? Get your big sweaty backside down there. Now!"

"Would you care to accompany me, Sir?" Eddie asked, finding his voice. "Watch me give them their dues?"

"Good God, no!" Malcolm gave a shudder. "I don't

want to get any on me. I'd get an infection!"

Eddie gave a curt nod and almost clicked his heels in salute before wheeling about to leave.

Malcolm let out a long, slow breath and spoke to the room. "Get up close to the great unwashed? I'll end up wanting to pierce my ears and wear a leather bracelet! No, I have other fish to fry."

He turned to Roly. "Mind the fort here. Give Eddie some time to crack some heads and then call the police. Actually, scratch that. Call them now. We're on solid ground. Evidence of crime all over the bloody internet!"

"Yes, Sir."

"And make sure to mention my name, hmm?"

"Yes, Sir." Roly nodded. "And may I ask - where will you be?"

"Off to see those damned Critchley's, boy. Do the job you should've done." Malcolm threw the newspaper into the waste basket. "And get rid of that blasted video!"

Roly winced but waited until his father had left before letting out a massive sigh.

The gaggle of protesters was a little larger than before, but not much. Two small terriers were loitering on the verge to one side, as if awaiting instruction. Today there was no sign of the diminutive Elaine - the group had the uber-lezzer Jakki at the helm, alongside that enormous bulldozer with the black goatee who had smashed him in the face. Despite the fact that Eddie had got a good shot at his shins, he was keen on a re-match now that the element of surprise was not a factor.

Eddie tightened his grip on his knopkierie and quickened his stride. He had enlisted the services of his two patrol guards Clive and Max who usually split the day shifts between them. The slightly dishevelled pair, unexpectedly assembled, would be no use against the big bloke - but he was Eddie's anyway - but up against all these other wimmin? Eddie reckoned it should be about even.

"I told you last time!" *Ar terld yu larst tyme.* "This is a private road. If you don't disperse, I'll call the police."

"Oh hello, again, sweat gland. Nice mask." Jakki stood, arms folded, a purple bruise on her forehead. She seemed emboldened by the presence of the giant who towered over her. For a moment he felt apprehensive. "Yeah, about that. See we looked that up and - guess what? Turns out you're wrong. Although I imagine you're used to that sensation. But, this is not a private road at all. We have as much right to stand here as you do."

Eddie arrived right in front of Jakki and the giant and held his knopkierie up between his face and theirs.

"See this? This doesn't care about your rights." *Yuur hraats.* "This only cares about me doing my job."

Jakki's face showed a flicker of fear - she was familiar with this weapon and her bruise seemed to glow in recognition of it - like the Hobbit's Elvish knife when Orcs were around. But the reassurance of the giant beside her seemed just enough to overcome it. She forced a smile.

"See this?" She jerked a thumb in the giant's direction. "He doesn't care about your job."

"We'll see about that." *Wheel si abaht thet.*

"We have every right to be here and you can't move us."

"Do you have every right to break into these

premises, take an illegal video and then upload it?" Eddie spat. "I think not."

Glancing to his left, Clive threw one end of a rope to Max and the three men formed a small cordon with Eddie at its centre, knopkierie aloft. Together they muscled forward, dragging the rope tightly across the gaggle of women pulling them back, like fish being hauled into a net. The giant reached out with both arms but he was pinned at his biceps and Eddie squirmed out of reach. Jakki was now being spun slowly around by the movement of the cordon and found herself with her back to the action as Eddie and the giant tried to face-off. Elaine appeared suddenly from behind this man mountain only to emit a shriek as the big man stumbled back and trod on her foot.

Eddie lashed out with his knopkierie and struck the giant on the left shoulder. The big man instinctively grabbed the site of this fresh pain with his enormous right hand, pulling the rope more tightly across his chest and getting a rope burn for his troubles. Eddie smiled in triumph as he raised his knopkierie once more to strike the man's other shoulder when three things happened:

A placard came out of nowhere, round-housing him, and smashed into his face, splattering his strapped-up nose anew.

Through the blood-red double-vision came the sound of a siren and tyres scrubbing to a halt on gravel.

Then everything went black.

Roly stood off to one side, some way back from the melee and watched as two uniformed officers sprung out of their vehicle. One scurried to the figure of Eddie lying bleeding on the ground, the other to the group of protesters who were stood suddenly muted and obedient, roped up against the hedge like outlaws caught by a posse. A large man towered over the rest of this small group, all of whom seemed to be women.

"You again!" The officer glared at the giant and took out a pair of handcuffs, shaking his head. "Un-fucking-believable."

"Who is in authority here?" The younger officer asked.

"Erm, I am." Roly volunteered, presenting all the authority of a "do not tumble dry" label.

"Mister Baxter is it?" The younger officer knelt over Eddie looked up towards Roly.

"Yes, that's right." Roly shuffled forwards apprehensively.

"We need to get him to a hospital. This is a very badly broken nose. And he's smacked the back of his head when he fell. Can you get a cushion or something to support him?"

"Um… yes, of course." Roly blinked.

"Someone get those bloody dogs off me!" The other officer was shouting and lashing out with his feet at the two Jack Russells who were harrying him as he led the handcuffed giant towards the car.

"Did you see what happened?" The younger officer asked Roly from his kneeling position.

"No, not really. It all happened rather quickly I'm afraid."

The officer nodded and turned to watch, amused, as his colleague bundled the man into the back of the patrol car, like trying to force a single fitted-sheet over a king-size mattress while being attacked by angry crabs. When the troublesome job was done and the giant was penned onto the backseat, he slammed the door and strode towards Roly, the dogs still grouching at his legs, jumping up and trying to bite his shoes.

"Will you fuck OFF!" He flung one leg up with a mighty swing and the animal attached to it went flying into the hedge. The other dog suddenly abandoned his own attack and yelped off after his mate.

"Mister Baxter?"

"Yes. Roland Baxter."

"We'll need to take a statement, if that's okay." It was actually a question but it sounded like an instruction.

"Well…" Roly sensed danger. A formal police report with possible arrests was not going to be easy to keep out of the papers - especially not after yesterday's headline. "I'm not sure I can help much, though. Didn't see anything personally, you understand." He bent into the officer and lowered his voice. "I… that is to say, we, are um… not too keen on pressing charges."

"You what? This man needs an ambulance." The officer frowned, and then shouted over his shoulder to his colleague. "Appleton? Call an ambulance!"

The officer was breathing heavily and took his helmet off to wipe sweat from his brow with a handkerchief. He stuffed it back into his pocket, replaced his helmet and strode back to the car. The giant in the back was squashed in like an exploded bouncy castle, his nose pressed up against the window. The policeman kicked the rear door as he passed.

"If you chuck up in my fucking car again you're a dead man!"

FOURTEEN

Malcolm swept his Bentley onto the farm track and charged along it until he pulled up right outside the farmhouse. A battered Volvo estate that was once white was parked over by the fence. Malcolm sighed, gritted his teeth and climbed out.

The boot of his car opened smoothly to reveal a two-level walnut gunbox, reinforced with carbon fibre. This sleek piece of furniture fitted exquisitely into the back of the car, its top two drawers were lovingly lined with inserts snugly holding bottles of champagne and Scotch, crystal flutes and shot glasses; the larger lower drawer contained the stock and barrel of his father's old shotgun, both polished and gleaming, and a tray of varying types of cartridges. Swiftly he assembled the weapon and cast his eyes over the selection of shot in the drawer and made his selection. He loaded the shotgun, snicked the breech closed and strode around the side of the farmhouse, intent etched into his features.

The weather was warm and blustery and he wasn't surprised to find a full line of washing snapping in the breeze. But he was surprised to find a small child come shooting out of the back door, straight into his knees.

"Grandpa, Grandpa!" Malcolm's eyes extended on stalks as his granddaughter Jemima threw her arms out and hugged his legs. Malcolm struggled to plaster a happy smile on his mood and the end result was some perverse, cold, stifled expression - like a constipated penguin trying to enjoy doing his tax return.

"Jemima? What in heaven's name…?"

"Hi Grandpa!" Jemima looked up at him, her face full of smiling delight.

"What're you doing here? Is your Mum here?" He looked around for Sally, certain not to waste his time looking for Roly.

"No, silly! I'm playing with Ellie. We're going to do a Brownie badge."

"Are you?" Malcolm crouched down and gave his grand-daughter a chuck under the chin, his mood lightening by the second. This little girl could lift his heart and wipe any unsmiling expression off his face in an instant. How she had emanated from his miserable, useless son he could not imagine but there it was. Perhaps talent and affection skipped a generation? "And which badge have you chosen?"

Jemima scrunched her cheery face up into a ball of cute concern and concentration. "Well… I would like to do performance but Ellie wants to do pets."

With that simple summary, she skipped happily off and disappeared behind the billowing wall of washing drying on the line. Malcolm shook his head, a genuine smile starting to smear itself across his face, when he remembered himself: while he might be delighted to see his grand-daughter, he was not at all delighted to find her fraternising with the enemy. Another topic of conversation to be had with Roly later. He set his face back to scowl, marched to the open back door and rapped loudly on one of its glass panes.

"Critchley!"

Rosie went to the back door, wiping wet hands on her apron. Her face dropped when she saw who it was.

"Sir Malcolm." She gave a slight nod. It was always tempting to want to bow to him as if he was some feudal overlord and she was some insignificant serf which, in a way, she thought she was.

"Still here I see?" Malcolm had never been one for conversational niceties.

"Rightfully and legally so, Sir Malcolm. As I'm sure you're aware." She said, looking nervously at the gleaming shotgun cradled casually in the crook of his arm.

"Not for much longer, my dear." Bitterness dripped from his voice. "Your husband not around? Perhaps too busy spreading libellous and malicious disinformation to the press?"

Rosie stiffened and dropped her veneer of neighbourliness. "He's up on the hills. Doing his job."

"As I said: not for much longer."

Rosie folded her arms, bristling. "What do you want here?"

Malcolm forced a thin smile which suddenly made his face seem colder. His eyes flared. "There is still time. Just. Time for you and your husband to see sense, call off this court action. I thought we had come to an amenable arrangement."

"My husband is still considering your proposal."

The distaste shone from his puffy, cold eyes as he tut-tutted. "I am afraid your husband's mouth has shortened my patience somewhat." He peered over her shoulder and moved forwards as if to push past her. "Are you sure he isn't here?"

Rosie drew herself up as tall as she could and stood

her ground as he breathed over her. "You can't come barging in here - this is our home!"

"Barging? This is *my* land, Rosemary." He gave her name a leering emphasis she really did not care for. "I am just paying a respectful visit."

"If you don't leave now, I shall call the police." Rosie gritted her teeth, partly to stave off the tears she could feel burning her eyes and partly to stop herself from spitting in Malcolm's face. She pulled her phone out from her apron pocket.

His smile broadened and he stepped back, spreading his arms magnanimously. "Police? To remove me from my own property?"

"You can't just come here and start threatening me in our home! We have rights!" She punched in 999 and waited for the connection.

"Rights, rights, rights. It's the terrible march of the snowflakes, isn't it? In today's society everyone has rights and everyone has the right to have their rights respected. But it's just not possible is it? We all have rights Rosemary. Every one of us. But not all rights are compatible, are they? Sometimes one man's rights impinge on another's. Then someone must decide which rights prevail. Isn't that so?"

"Quite." Rosie met his gleaming teeth with a steely glare. "And that is the job for the courts. They will decide. My husband is just doing what he can to make sure justice is done." The phone connected. "Hello? Police please."

"Talk to your husband. Consider my offer Rosemary. It is the last one I will make. And one more thing, before I go." He leant in closely, close enough that Rosie could make out the pores on his cheeks, the hair in his nostrils and taste the sourness of stale cigar tobacco. "If I ever find my grand-daughter here again. Or learn that she is fraternising with your child…"

"What?" Rosie's hackles rose. Her field of view shrank instantly into a tight funnel, all her senses zooming in on his face. All else was black. It was one thing to threaten their home, but their daughter! "What will you do?"

Malcolm looked at her, a silent smiling menace.

A voice came on the line and Rosie stammered into her phone. "Gladhouse Farm. There's a man here … threatening me with a shotgun!"

"I am not. Although, clearly, I am holding a shotgun." He admitted. "Only as I am about to go for a stroll up onto *my* hills. To check on *my* grouse."

"Watch out for that razor wire." Said a new voice behind him.

"Is it always like this, Sarge?" PC Appleton had taken off his hat and was scratching his head as he waited for the ambulance to arrive. Over on the far verge, the protesters were chatting to themselves and packing up.

"Oh aye. Always have to deal with chicken protesters on a Wednesday."

"Really?"

"I don't fucking know!" Jenkins complained. "I'm not normally in uniform, am I? This is most definitely not my thing."

"Only asking." Appleton sulked. He wasn't impressed either, this pairing of him with a detective. Whose idea was this? He'd rather be fooling with his normal patrol partner Nicki than taking grumpy lessons with Jenkins.

The radio at his lapel squawked and he tilted his head to listen.

A large woman from the group of protesters strode over and button-holed Jenkins before he could get into his car. "This was a peaceful demonstration. Perfectly legal and above board. There was no need for a police presence."

"Miladdo there wasn't so peaceful now, was he?"

"If you hadn't turned up, none of this would have happened." The woman was jabbing a finger with a bitten nail perilously close to his chest "We are all women, here. No danger is there?"

"This fella…" Jenkins jerked a thumb towards his imprisoned passenger. "He's not a woman. And he was embroiled when we got here."

"Embroiled?"

"I'm thinking assault, disorderly conduct." Jenkins sniffed. "Possibly resisting arrest."

"Resisting arrest?" The woman's eyes bulged. "If that man is arrested, I will personally come down to the police station and file a complaint."

"Up to you, love."

"Don't call me love, you chauvinist-"

"Sarge!" Appleton interrupted. "There's an incident over at Gladhouse Farm apparently. You're to stop by."

"Christ on a bike." Jenkins growled, glared at the woman and then looked over at the giant stuffed in the back seat. "What sort of incident? Am I going to have to take someone else in? It's a patrol car you know, not the fucking Tardis."

Appleton raised his eyebrows in an attempt at appeasement. "I'm just taking the orders."

"My nose! My nose!" Jenkins turned to see the injured

man on the ground trying to lift himself into a sitting position, one hand over the bloody pulp in the middle of his face.

"Oh, don't you start. Fuck sake." Jenkins pinched the bridge of his own nose and sighed. "There's an ambulance on its way. Just stay on the ground, hold your nose if you have to."

"I don't have a nose to hold!" The khaki guy whined, his accent fractured and guttural.

"It's not that bad." Jenkins said without even looking. "Paramedics will sort you out when they get here. They can work wonders that lot."

He turned to the angry woman. "Mrs…?"

"Banks. Ms."

"Well, Ms Banks. Why don't you and your pals toddle off, hmm? It's lovely sunny day."

"Don't you patronise me!"

"I'm not patronising you, Ms Banks." Jenkins sighed. "Look. Go protest somewhere else if you must, alright? Just. Not. Here."

He climbed into the patrol car, slamming the driver's door on what he hoped would be the last bit of madness for the day.

Malcolm whirled round, indignant. "And you are?"

"Unexpected." Cullen said. "And you are?"

"Sir Malcolm Baxter." He bristled. "Landowner."

"Ah yes, Owner of The Land of Razor Wire." Cullen mused. "Pulled tight across the moors up there so as to endanger others."

"Trespassers. Endanger trespassers." Malcolm narrowed his eyes. "Trespassers like you, perhaps?"

“Mister Cullen is not a trespasser!” Rosie interjected, her resolve strengthened by the knowledge that the police were on the way and that Cullen was now here. “And neither is my husband, or our dog. They have been wounded by your vicious… booby-traps. It’s unsafe and illegal. We’re not meant to run the risk of injury earning our livelihood.”

“They’re my grouse on my land. I shall protect them how I see fit. Just do your job and mind your own… sheep.”

“We will. If you will leave us in peace to do it!”

Malcolm chose his words carefully. “Farming. Shooting. They’ve always been in conflict. A delicate balancing act when the land round here can be used to raise sheep and home grouse. It always pays to take care. There is no need for your sheep to be grazing so high up the hills.”

“We can’t stop them!” Rosie’s face was dark. “Why can’t you put up bloody fences to keep the areas separate?”

“Cost, my dear. Cost.” Malcolm oozed. “And customers driving up to the shoots can’t drive through fences so we need gates or cattle grids. More cost.”

The sound of a car approaching drifted over from the front of the farmhouse and Cullen, glancing rather sheepishly at Rosie, said “Just came back for my hat.”

He stood there, looking expectantly at her and something suddenly came over her - the fright from Malcolm’s surprise visit, the shock of his threat to her daughter, the intense vulnerability she’d felt until Cullen had appeared from nowhere.

“He threatened Ellie.” She blurted, tears immediately misting her vision. “He threatened our daughter.”

Through this unfocussed veil she saw Cullen reach for the shotgun and Malcolm adamantly resist, the pair of them wrestling back and forth over the gleaming gun. Cullen was taller and would, presumably, have been much the stronger but he was still weak and Malcolm's bulk seemed to more than compensate for the difference in age and height.

From behind her she was aware of the sound of a car door slamming shut.

Then the gun went off.

When Jenkins heard the gunshot, he snatched his helmet off and pelted down the gravel drive towards the farmhouse. When he turned the corner, he was faced with the back of one man holding a smouldering double-barrelled shotgun in his hands, another man lying prone on the grass and a woman fussing over him and crying "What have you done?" over and over.

"Police!" Jenkins shouted as he slowed and then stepped carefully towards the man with his arms out. "Put down your weapon please, sir."

The shooter turned to face him, the shotgun wheeling with him, and Jenkins found himself looking down the barrel at a ruddy-faced old man wearing a bursting Tweed suit over a pair of Hunter wellies.

"Put it down, sir." Jenkins repeated.

The man eyed him cautiously, lowered his gun and then threw it on the ground.

"Sir? What's your name?" Jenkins demanded.

"Sir Malcolm Baxter." The man declared. "And this man was trespassing on my property."

"Sir Malcolm Baxter, you are under arrest." Jenkins

strode over, bringing his handcuffs off his belt.

"Don't be ridiculous!" Malcolm cried. "You can't arrest me!"

"I can and I am."

"Nonsense! This is my land." He gestured around him and then pointed at the man on the ground who had rolled over and pushed himself up into a sitting position, blinking hard. "And this man was trespassing on my property."

"Trespass doesn't give you the right to unload a shotgun at someone. You do have a license for this firearm I take it?"

"Of bloody course I do! What do you take me for?"

A trigger-happy landowner who thinks the law doesn't apply to them, Jenkins wanted to say, but instead he simply stared at the man on the grass who was puffing out a series of long breaths.

"Are you okay?" Jenkins called over to him.

The woman helped him to his feet and the man gave a short nod.

"Get off me!" Malcolm protested as Jenkins moved to grab a hand to cuff it.

"Would you care to add resisting arrest to grievous bodily harm?"

"Grievous… I didn't shoot him! The gun just went off! Look at him - he's uninjured!"

Jenkins stole a glance back at the victim and sighed. "Okay, well maybe we'll just settle on possession of a firearm with intent to endanger life?"

"He's trespassing!"

"Don't care." He snapped the handcuffs on Malcolm and then turned back, squinting at the victim. He pulled from his pocket the photo that Her Ladyship had given him and studied it again.

"Un-fucking-believable." He said under his breath, then, to the cuffed Malcolm. "Wait there a moment."

Jenkins strolled over away from the scene and lifted the radio handset from his belt. It was a very short conversation. When he trudged back to the group there was something defeated in his gait.

"You're free to go." Jenkins said.

"I should think so too." Malcolm snorted, raising his hands for Jenkins to release the cuffs.

Jenkins looked over at the man in the BOLO. "Cullen? You're coming with us."

Cullen, didn't move and Jenkins walked over to him

"He's a bloody trespasser! Make sure you throw the book at him." Malcolm cried, shaking a righteous fist.

"Sir Malcolm? I suggest you return to your own business premises." Jenkins said by way of a farewell. "Been a bit of activity there today."

"What do you mean?" Malcolm was caught wrong-footed by this casual remark.

"You'll see." Jenkins said over his shoulder as he led Cullen round the farmhouse to the waiting car.

Paul sat glumly in the back of the patrol car. Bent at the neck to fit on the backseat, the top of his head was pressed into the roof padding and the handcuffs on his wrists behind his back rubbed and dug into his skin. They only came in one size, apparently. He'd asked.

He looked out of the window at the beautiful scenery before him. He knew this area well: Gladhouse reservoir and the Moorfoot hills. Had spent, in fact, many a happy afternoon sitting by the reservoir fishing. The bright sun shone down casting late afternoon shadows on the trees around the reservoir and the single track which led around the lake to the various farms and remote dwellings scattered at the base of the purple heathered hills.

Paul had brought Shirley fishing here on a kind of third date, some years ago. She said she'd been keen to try it herself, having never fished before, so Paul had borrowed a spare rod, bundled all his kit into his van and the pair, along with Ant and Dec, had trundled up to the off-road parking at the perimeter of the reservoir.

He had led the way, throwing an old towel over the No Fishing sign and picking a path through the trees down to the shore.

"What was that?" Shirley had nodded to the towel-covered sign.

"Fisherman's code." Paul tapped the side of his nose. "Someone else comes up here, sees that? They know to go fish elsewhere. There's only so many fish to go round you know!"

"Oh." Shirley nodded in naive approval at this fiction.

The weather had been sunny and warm, just like today, and they had passed a lovely afternoon lying on a tartan rug eating picnic snacks he'd hurriedly grabbed from Sainsbury's and drinking cider, the two fishing rods in their stands at the water's edge showing no sign of attracting any catch whatsoever. Paul hadn't cared - this woman had a dirty laugh and a twinkle in her eye that held a promise of fun and good times - and they'd even enjoyed a kiss and a fumble, rolling around on the rug like two teenagers until Paul had landed on top of the last of the pork pie which had soured his mood somewhat.

"Cheer up!" Shirley had said, picking the smushed

pieces off the rug and throwing them to his dogs. "It's only pork pie!"

Paul had done a double-take and hastily revised downwards his opinion of the potential of this pairing. He'd kept his counsel but remembered thinking to himself: *she'll learn.* Oh, what he'd give for a pork pie now. His stomach rumbled in empathy.

He smiled at this memory. Maybe he should bring her back up here as a kind of anniversary surprise or something? Wait, when was their anniversary again? Bollocks.

The car door opened and disturbed him from his reverie.

"Budge up inside there, pal." The policeman called, holding the door open, his face invisible from where Paul sat. What Paul could see was the bottom half of a lime-green waterproof over a pair of dirty camo pants worn by a man being coaxed into the police car. Paul screwed up his face and then shook his head. Nah, couldn't be.

"No talking now, gents. Not far to the station."

A handcuffed figure folded himself onto the seat next to him and Paul's eyes stood out on stalks. It was Cullen. Hatless. His look said it all.

The policeman bent down to peer into the backseat and immediately saw the look on Paul's face. He stared at Cullen and then back at Paul. "You two know each other then?"

A beat. "No, no. God Bless You." Paul said and waited for the door to be slammed shut.

He exchanged disbelieving looks with Cullen in silence who sat, ramrod stiff, next to him as they jostled along the track away from the farmhouse.

FIFTEEN

"Well, well, well. Isn't this interesting?" Kate could not have made her smile broader if she'd had it pried apart with forceps. Jenkins had led Cullen and Paul into her office and here they stood, side by side, in front of her. "Wasn't quite what I had in mind, Mr McInnes, when I asked you to bring him in but I guess I should have expected the unconventional from you."

On hearing this, Cullen turned to Paul at his side and gave him a killer look. Paul raised his eyebrows and pulled a "Who Me?" face.

"Cullen, ma'am." Offered Jenkins. "Causing an affray. Landowner threatening to prosecute for civil trespass."

Kate couldn't resist a small smile and looked at her captive as he stood, impassive but gaunt. Unshaven and dirty, anyone unfamiliar with him would take him for a vagrant which, thinking about it, is actually what he was.

"Nice." She looked over her glasses at Cullen but he didn't look at her, staring at the wall behind her as if he was alone in the room. "Thank you, Jenkins. But there was no need to bring Mr McInnes back again."

"That's what I said!" Paul piped up.

"Under arrest, ma'am. Separate incident. Assault."

Kate looked at Paul with renewed interest. "Really? After I'd said for you to stay out of trouble?"

She nodded for Jenkins to take Paul away and waited until he had closed the door behind them.

"Causing an affray?" Kate smirked. "Bored, were

you?"

Cullen looked at her - Christ he looked rough, she thought. A sudden fear shot through her and the smile left her face. "Are you okay?"

"I'll survive."

She inhaled deeply and let her breath out noisily and slowly. "Right. I remember. No small talk."

"Can I go now?"

"Oh no. I've been looking for you."

His eyes betrayed him. He tried to remain impassive but those steel-grey eyes, once so clear and now dull and weary, flashed briefly. She saw it and knew he was intrigued. Good.

"I won't beat about the bush - I know you appreciate… directness." She knitted her hands together in front of her. "I need the photo."

She had him now. His face couldn't hide his surprise and guilt, but he kept silent.

"The Polaroid?" She prodded.

"What Polaroid?" Cullen stonewalled.

"*The* Polaroid. From your daughter's file." Kate stood and walked around her desk to stand in front of him. She leant back and scrutinised his face. "Where is it?"

"No idea."

"Huh. Want to play, do we?" She walked back behind her desk, sat down and opened the manila folder in front of her. "Okay, would you like me to tell you a story?"

"You're going to anyway I'm guessing."

"Cullen? It's me. Little old me, remember?"

"I remember."

"We go back a long way. Used to be… friends? Colleagues certainly."

"Friends." A rare confirmation from him. She was

surprised by how much she was pleased to hear it.

"I want to help. Really."

"I don't need your help."

"You sure?"

He didn't reply for a while, eventually settling on: "Tell me your story."

"Okay." She sighed briefly and then clapped her hands together. "Last month there was a fire down at some allotments in Walkerburn. Lots of fires, actually. Don't suppose you'd know anything about that?"

He was just staring at the wall behind her, so she continued.

"A number of allotment sheds, all burnt to the ground. In the ruins of one of them we found two old tins. Buried under the floorboards."

"Not interested in archaeology."

"Oh, they weren't that old. Few years maybe. Scorched badly but their contents were intact."

Cullen shrugged.

"The shed in question had been previously owned by a certain Iain McKenna. Iain Nesbit McKenna. Interested now?"

His eyes peeled away from the wall and he looked directly at her. *Yes*, was the silent answer.

"Inside one of the tins we found these." She picked up a pack of evidence bags from the folder and held them in front of her face. Each one contained a Polaroid photo. She handed them to Cullen. "Dusted for prints. McKenna's all over them."

Each of the photos showed a young woman or girl, tied up and gagged. Cowering in fear in the back of a white van, the camera flash reflecting the terror in their eyes. Cullen studied each one briefly and then handed them back. Kate waited but he didn't say anything.

"Look familiar?" She asked. "They looked familiar to me. Identical in fact. Identical to one I remember seeing in another young girl's file, long ago." She paused and scrutinised his face as she said the next word. "Eilidh's."

There it was, the flicker. The tell. He could bury many things but he couldn't keep this hidden. The wound was too deep. Unscarred because he hadn't been able to leave it alone, all these years. Picking at it and picking at it. Examining it every which way, desperate to fix it, heal it. Because it would never go away.

"So, I checked her file. Eilidh's." She said his daughter's name again, deliberately. Wanting to provoke him, stir him from this trance. "It's not there."

She held out her hand. "Give it to me."

"I don't have it."

"Liar. Give it to me."

"I don't have it."

"Cullen. I can charge you if you wish. And Gosh, so many to choose from! I mean, withholding evidence, tampering with evidence, theft, obstruction-"

She wasn't enjoying this and when she saw his eyes pricked with tears she stopped in her tracks and waited. There was a long pause.

"It's all I have left."

His face broke and Kate saw a memory from before - a man, a father and a husband who had been a dedicated police officer, a role model to her, and others. A man who had had his world shattered and everything precious torn from him and who stood before her now, empty, with nothing left but grief and rage and sadness.

"I'm sorry." Her heart melted as she looked into his eyes, her voice a whisper. "I need it."

"It's all I have."

A tear rolled down his cheek and Kate gritted her teeth. "Jenkins!" She shouted through the glass door as if trying to reach across the channel. When her sergeant appeared, she nodded cursorily at Cullen. "Put him in the cells for a while. He needs to think."

Cullen blinked away the tear and looked down at her. She saw a plea but what she wanted to see was comprehension. She would wait as long as it took. "Take him." And she watched as Cullen obediently followed Jenkins out of her office and down to the cells.

"Perhaps you can start by telling me what you were doing at Baxter Farms in the first place?" Jenkins asked, bored already.

"Bodyguarding." Said Paul.

"Bodyguarding?"

"Aye. Being a bodyguard."

"For whom?"

"Sensible Elaine."

"Sensible Elaine?" Jenkins waggled a finger in one ear.

"Don't know her full name. Everyone calls her Sensible Elaine." Paul shrugged. "Elaine's her first name." He added helpfully.

"I imagine. And why does she need a bodyguard?"

"She's a whistleblower. For Baxters. And he's not happy about it." Paul confided then, wondering if this was too provocative, qualified it with an "Allegedly."

"He being…?"

"Sir Malcolm Baxter. The owner."

Jenkins nodded. "And what in particular has she blown the whistle about?"

"Erm. Working practices? I think." Paul cast his mind back to conversations partially listened to. "No! Animal welfare, that's it! Not treating chickens properly. Or summat."

"Hmm." Jenkins made a note. "And who has she blown the whistle to?"

"Er…" Paul considered this. "Don't know actually. My girlfriend?"

"Your girlfriend? Does she work for the SSPCA?"

"No."

"DEFRA?"

"No."

"Is she, by any chance, an undercover journalist?"

"No! She works for Greggs."

"Greggs?"

"You know. The place that sells vegan sausage rolls that I'm allergic to?" Paul said wearily. "She's the manager. In Peebles."

"Do they buy chickens from Baxter's?"

"Baxter's don't sell chickens, they sell eggs."

Jenkins sighed. "Does she buy eggs from Baxter's?"

"No."

"Look, Mr McInnes. There are only so many hours in the day and I have only so much patience. If we carry on like this, we're going to run out of both." Jenkins scratched his forehead, a dull pain starting to form between his eyes. "Let's come at this from a different angle. Why did you assault Mr…" He checked his notebook. "Helpmann?"

"I didn't."

"His nose says you did."

"I didn't assault him. I was protecting my client."

"Your client. Sensible Elaine?"

"Correct."

"Are you, perhaps, a professional bodyguard, Mr McInnes?"

"No." Paul admitted. "Joiner."

"Have you had any special training which would justify calling yourself a bodyguard?"

Paul thought for a moment. "Erm, no."

"And were you being paid for your bodyguard services by your client?"

"Erm, no. I was doin' it for Shirl."

"Shirl?"

"My girlfriend. The manager of Gregg's?"

"Right. Was *she* paying you?"

"Only in kind." Paul grinned broadly and then instantly regretted it.

"So." Jenkins closed his notebook and slapped it on the desk in front of him. He looked at his mug of tea which had gone cold. "You were - are, in fact - just a big bloke using your size to help protect your girlfriend's pal. Correct?"

"'Swhat I said!" Paul held both hands out, palms up and looked skywards, delighted that the penny had finally dropped.

"Mr McInnes. You cannot go around assaulting other law-abiding citizens and call it bodyguarding. Assault is a crime."

"It was self-defence."

"You said you were protecting your client. That is not self-defence. I don't imagine that Mr Helpmann, given the differences in your relative sizes - not to mention grasp of basic legalities - would actually attack someone of your stature. That would be foolhardy."

Paul remained silent for a while and, when Jenkins

didn't speak, said: "Was that a question?"

"Probably not." Jenkins sighed. "So, tell me in your own words what happened. How about that?"

"Okay." Paul took a deep breath and Jenkins felt his stomach drop, like a long shaggy dog story was about to unveil itself and soak up the rest of his afternoon. "I hit him with a placard."

"You hit him with a placard?"

Paul nodded. "In the face. Swatted him like."

"You swatted him with a placard?"

"He was coming towards us. Weaving through the crowd. I pushed him back but he kept coming so I grabbed a placard and batted him with it."

"Battered?"

"No. Batted. You know, like in cricket?"

"Oh. So, was this a cover drive maybe? Or straight over mid-wicket?"

"Unh." Paul puffed his cheeks out. "Wasn't a big whack. More like a reverse sweep. Or a leg-glance."

"I see. And what did Mr Helpmann do?"

"He fell down." Paul considered the cricketing analogy. "Like a silly mid-on."

"Ma'am?" Jenkins had poked his nose around her door. "Ma'am, we either charge him - Cullen - or we let him go. It's five o'clock."

"Oh, bugger. Already?" Maybe she was getting older and more tired, or maybe the job was wearing her out - either way the days were passing in a flash and she was getting nothing done in them. "Okay. I'll come down and talk to him. See if I can change his mind. Off you pop."

"Ma'am." Jenkins said gratefully, disappearing for the day.

"Ah, before you go Jenkins. Perhaps we could quickly compare notes?"

"Ma'am?"

"About Mr McInnes?"

"Ah." Jenkins sighed deeply. "We let him go."

Kate's eyebrows rose. "We?"

"Me. I did."

"Because?"

"Oh, there's nothing there, Ma'am. A scuffle, some protesters. Six o' one and half o' dozen o' the other. Not going to charge some big eejit just because a sweaty security guard got a face full of hardboard."

"I trust that's not what you put in your report?"

"No, Ma'am. I jazzed it up a bit. It's in your tray there."

"Thank you. That will be all."

"Right you are, Ma'am." Jenkins beamed a smile and started to close her door.

"Oh. How's the car?"

"Ma'am?"

"The smell?"

Jenkins cheery face fell. "Fading, ma'am. Nearly gone."

There were two reports from Jenkins in her tray, one for McInnes and one for Cullen, and she quickly cast her eyes over both. Then she picked up a third report and strode from her office.

Cullen was sitting stoically in the cell, rigid on the low bunk staring at the opposite wall. He looked up dully when she entered. He looked different without his hat on - older and thinner. She cast her eyes over him once more. Everything about him seemed tired: his boots, his clothes, his coat, his face, his hair. She remembered the energy and drive of this man long ago, back when he had been her mentor and a relentless searcher for truth and justice. Kate had been a wet-behind-the-ears Detective Constable, straight out of college, and he had been hard on her, pushed her hugely, assuming much that she didn't, couldn't, know but making her a better DC in the process and allowing her to grow so quickly. Looking back now was like viewing someone else's past, not hers; one she had cast off like a snake as she had slid smoothly up the hierarchy to Detective Chief Superintendent. He, on the other hand, was like the old skin she had shed - pale, mottled, grey, shrivelled up and dry. A husk of his former self. She looked in pity at the state he had reached and sat down next to him on the bunk. He flinched slightly but didn't move away. Progress.

"Cullen?" She examined his profile while he continued staring at the wall. "What's it to be?"

When he didn't respond she looked at her watch. "You have five minutes until I charge you."

He turned towards her, eyes dull and lifeless, and then turned back to face the wall in silence. Kate slapped the report on her knee, stood up and paced up and down. When she reached the cell door, she turned to face him again.

"Would you like to know what else we found in the tins under the shed?"

She saw him swallow and waited. In vain. She pressed on. "The tin containing the Polaroids - remember? Also in the tin was an old business card. The card belonged to Baron Baxter of Westloch. Portcullis on the card and everything."

Cullen still gave no response. Kate tried a more conversational approach.

"Fancy titles these Lords give themselves nowadays, huh? Get a life peerage, give yourself a fancy handle."

"You said Baron."

Kate smiled. Of all the things to get him talking again - a detail about the title of some obscure noble. "Baron. Lord. Same thing. I think. Baron this, Lord the other. They all get to set their own names. As grand as they like. And sit in the House of Lords. Or claim they do and take the money. Life peers." She shook her head, sadly. "Still - it's not that bit of the name that's interesting though, is it?"

"No?"

"No. It's the *Baxter* bit."

Cullen slowly turned to stare at her, meeting her eyes for the first time. "They're not-?"

"They are." Kate beamed and waved the reports. "Baron Baxter of Westloch is - well, was, he's dead now - the father of Sir Malcolm Baxter. The very man on whose land you were trespassing."

"Allegedly."

"Well I think we can drop the allegedly, don't you? You were on his land when we picked you up."

"With the tenant's permission."

"Says you."

"Ask her."

"I will." This sudden transition from silent curmudgeon to staccato combatant in a game of verbal tennis had taken her by surprise and she was at risk of losing her way towards her goal, which was to get him to give her the Polaroid. She took a deep breath and tried to tack back to where she wanted to go. "Isn't that interesting, though? The man you… met today, is the descendant of a man whose business card we found amongst a load of Polaroids which match the one in *your possession* of your own daughter."

She waited for a denial this time but it never came. Kate knew she was close now. She could see the tiniest muscle twitching in his jaw as he fought to keep silent.

"On the other side of this business card - the side that is usually blank - was a rough drawing done in biro, but quite skillful nonetheless, of a wizard. Underneath the drawing was the word *Merlin*."

Cullen's eyes ranged all over her face, as if searching her for some visual clue to explain what this meant. Failing to find one, he frowned as if to say *"And…?"*

"Yeah, well it didn't ring any bells with me either. But - and I guess they didn't have this in your day - but if you type some stuff into a police computer these days it does all sorts of crazy searching and pattern matching. Really quite remarkable. And very fast. Not like the old days, remember, when we were still using cards sometimes and -"

"Tell me."

His face was suddenly sharp and intent. Hooked. She had him.

"Several years back there was an investigation by the Metropolitan Police into a high-level ring of child prostitution and abuse amongst the rich and famous. Lots of high-ranking people incriminated or suspected at any rate - businessmen, government ministers, judges, clergy. Lords, even."

The muscle twitch had turned into a spasm and she watched as he also started clenching and unclenching his fists resting on his thighs.

"It never concluded. Reports went missing. Suspects died or disappeared. One government initiated a public enquiry which dragged on for years until the Chief Justice chairing it resigned and was never replaced. The whole thing was kicked into the long grass and forgotten about."

Cullen was shaking now, a terrible tremor which affected his whole body. She spoke her closing sentence in barely a whisper.

"It was called Operation Merlin."

Somehow his face was white but his eyes were black.

"Why didn't you tell me this earlier?"

"This is police business." Kate said. "Highly sensitive police business. You're not in the police anymore, remember? I shouldn't be telling it to you now."

"Then why are you?"

"Because I want you to give me the bloody Polaroid, you stupid bastard!" The words stung and God knew she was probably torturing him enough just telling him all this, dragging all this dirt into the open. But maybe - just, maybe - she thought, she might be giving him hope.

"We have all sorts of technology these days, Cullen. Stuff you'd only have heard of in sci-fi: DNA-matching, fingerprint-mosaicing, chromatography, PCR. Stuff that'll make your head spin. And it can be used on old evidence. This-" She slapped a report down on the bunk beside her. "This is a cold case, as cold as they come. The only person keeping it warm is you - and you're not, are you? You're just nursing it like some toddler clinging onto a damp rag. I don't know if you're grieving or seeking salvation or what, but this… this is a lead! A fucking lead! Remember them? And that Polaroid of your daughter? Along with these we have? And this business card. We could find something! We could find-"

"Eilidh?" His voice seemed to silence the room. She couldn't tell whether it was loaded with hope or fear but she could tell it was urgent and voracious.

"Maybe. I don't know." Kate took a deep breath and exhaled loudly and slowly, recomposing herself. "Cullen, I can't promise anything. I don't know what happened to her. I don't know if she's still alive. But neither do you."

Cullen hung his head and she could see him close his eyes.

"If you don't give me that Polaroid you'll never know."

"You can have it." He said, head down and eyes still closed.

"Thank you." She said softly and held out her hand.

"I don't have it on me." He lifted his head and looked at her. "It's in my pack. Back at the farm."

Kate sighed and stood to her feet. She smoothed out her skirt and picked up the folder. "Well, then. I guess you're not under arrest. Come on."

"I just thought we could do it together." Shirley said, disconsolately, as she unpacked her shopping onto the kitchen table.

"Sorry, my love. What did you say?" Paul appeared from behind his Peeblesshire News.

"Vegetarian diet!" Shirley exclaimed. "We could both do with losing a bit of weight. I had hoped you'd be more… willing."

"I am, my sweet."

She finished unpacking the last shopping bag. The table was covered in produce and Paul started to take an interest in some of the more exotic items.

"Almond milk?" He picked up another. "Coconut milk?"

"They're good for you." Shirley said.

"What's wrong with… beef milk?"

"Vegetarian, remember?"

"Milk's got no meat in it!" Paul argued, not unreasonably.

"Vegetarianism isn't just about avoiding meat."

"Isn't it?" Paul's face crumpled visibly.

"No! It's about avoiding animal-derived products." Shirley explained. "Like milk."

"And cheese?" Paul asked, suddenly alarmed.

"Yep!"

"Oh, come on! This is getting ridiculous."

"What's ridiculous about it?"

"No meat? No beer? No cheese?" Paul wailed, ticking off the fingers on one hand. "No bacon?"

"Bacon is meat, lover."

"What's left?"

"Vegetables!"

"And?"

"And… look!" Shirley pulled out a selection of lurid coloured things in string bags. "Forbidden fruit!"

Paul narrowed his eyes in suspicion. "What is it?"

"Well, I say forbidden fruit." Shirley admitted, ripping open one of the bags. "It's just fruit. This is Scotland after all." She threw him an apple. "Here! One of your five a day."

"Five!"

"A day." Shirley confirmed.

"Does my Lime and Soda not count in that total?"

"Nope." She finished putting all the food away and

sat down next to Paul, tapping him on his arm to make sure he was paying attention. "Listen, lover. I wanted to talk to you."

Paul's eyes grew in alarm. Shirley saying she wanted to talk was not a good sign. He did his best to remain calm.

"About what, my love?"

"Your arrest."

"Ah."

Shirley sat waiting for Paul to elaborate but he decided to sit it out. After half a minute of silence she relented.

"Meaning?"

"Well, it was your idea."

"To get arrested?"

"No." Paul accepted with a head waggle. "But it was your idea for me to keep by Elaine and make sure she didn't get hurt."

"And did I say to get arrested in the process?"

"No. But it was a protest. A crowd. Security guard muscling in. Couldn't be helped." Paul shrugged. "Being a bodyguard? This sort of thing's an occupational wossname."

"Hmm." Shirley sighed. "You see, the thing is… well, it's not going to impress my mother."

Paul was taken aback by this screeching conversational left-turn. "What's it got to do with your mother?"

"I've invited her for dinner on Sunday."

"But… but…" Paul spluttered.

"It's the tyranny of personal pronouns, you see." Shirley continued. "We are in a relationship. You are arrested. I am implicated."

"But… how will she know I was arrested?"

"She'll know."

"But how? She's never even met me?"

Shirley shook her head sadly. "It won't make any difference."

"Can you direct me?" Kate asked, snapping off auto-pilot. "I've just realised I don't know where we're going?"

"Right in about a mile." Cullen said and resumed gazing out of his window.

When they pulled up at the farmhouse Kate undid her seatbelt but before she could open the door Cullen opened his and said "Wait here."

She watched him stride around the rear of the building and out of sight. When he returned, Kate rolled down her window. He was holding out a small dirty envelope.

"Thanks." Kate said. She put on a pair of disposable gloves, took the envelope from him and dropped it into an evidence bag. "Do you have a phone?"

Cullen was immediately on guard. "Why?"

"You'll want to know what we turn up won't you? As soon as we have something?"

"Yes." He acknowledged, the thought stinging in his head.

"So give me your number."

She handed him a scrap of paper and a bitten biro but he appeared reluctant to take them.

"Cullen?" She pushed her offering forward and he took it, scrawled his number and handed it back.

"Charge it up, keep it on." She instructed. "And keep it charged."

He scowled at her but she could tell he would comply. He wanted to know too badly.

Cullen jerked his head at the envelope. "Can I have that back when you've finished with it?"

Kate looked at him with sad eyes. "You know I can't do that. It's evidence. I can only release it if…" She stopped herself from finishing the sentence and he nodded silently, not wanting to finish it for her.

"You said you found two tins underneath the burnt-out shed?" He said suddenly, as if he was continuing a conversation.

"That's right."

"The Polaroids and the business cards were in the same one?"

"Yes."

"What about the other one?"

"Nah, nothing." She pulled off the gloves and stuffed them into the door pocket. "Different prints, newer tin. Unrelated."

"But what was in it?" He pressed her and she looked up at him, wondering why.

"Just some rizlas and some gout tablets."

"Gout tablets?"

"Yeah. Allupurinol, keeps it at bay; and Diclofenac, an anti-inflammatory for treating it." Kate looked at Cullen's expression curiously. "Why?"

"No reason." Cullen said, but Kate could've sworn she detected the trace of a smile as he turned and disappeared back behind the farmhouse.

SIXTEEN

Rosie was sitting at the trestle table which lay on a slant at the front of the farmhouse, a mug of tea in her hands, as she surveyed the bright blustery morning. She closed her eyes and let the fresh breeze play across her face, stream through her hair. When she opened her eyes Cullen was standing in front of her and she started.

"I left you sleeping." Her eyes creased as she surveyed Cullen's face. "I was worried about you."

"No need to be. I'm fine."

She sipped from her mug while he just stood there in silence. "Didn't think you'd be back. Again."

"I left my hat." He said, his eyes not focussing on her face but on some point away over her shoulder. He still looked pale and tired, worn thin by … something. His clothes hung off him, and he was in need of a good wash, a haircut and a shave. She ruminated briefly on the parallel between this man and the rescue hen she had just acquired - both badly treated, dishevelled and pushed to the point of exhaustion. Who was going to rescue him?

"Would you like some tea?"

He shook his head but sat down at the trestle table anyway.

"Was that a no?" She smiled, amused, at this odd man's manner. It was almost as if he wasn't used to company, a solitary wolf forced into society with no tools to deal with people, no information to help him adapt to these new and perhaps scary circumstances.

"Sir Malcolm Baxter." He spoke out of nowhere and she raised her eyebrows, silently, unsure where he was going with the name. "Nasty piece of work."

"Yes."

"I take it your husband is going to see the eviction appeal through?"

Rosie barked a rueful laugh. "If he wasn't before, he will now." Then she started to tear up. "Ewan is beside himself over this. If he fails, we'll be without a roof and a livelihood. He's a proud man and this farm means everything to him. He came in the other day, an axe in his hand, and his face was black with fury. Black! And when I asked him what the matter was, he said: 'One minute you're chopping wood and the next minute you're wondering how much force it takes to split a human skull.' He meant Baxter's."

Cullen nodded. "Your daughter..." He left the sentence unfinished.

"Oh my God! When I tell Ewan that he's threatening Ellie…" She looked up at Cullen with defeat in her eyes. "What should I do? We have to take his money, to protect ourselves. Protect Ellie."

"She reminds me of someone."

Rosie saw sadness in his face, a man recalling bitter-sweet memories. He made her feel awkward and she had a sudden urge to fill the silence.

"She's a handful I can tell you." The little laugh she gave took a huge effort. "Full of energy and life! Such energy - always rushing here and there, never settling, always onto the next thing almost before the current thing is done!"

Cullen's face broke into an almost-smile and Rosie was taken aback by the difference it made, how the years fell away from him and the life returned to his eyes. "A life-force. That is what they have - children - until the world wears it out. Snatches it away." The sudden change in him vanished without a trace.

Rosie pictured Ellie, laughing and skipping across the farmyard, holding Molly the Moo Cow close. A fierce determination stole across her face. "We have a duty to protect them. Keep that energy, that life-force, strong within them for as long as we can. Parents, I mean."

Cullen nodded imperceptibly. "Duty."

"Do you have children?" She asked.

That look shot across him again and disappeared in a flash. He looked down at his boots, worn and scuffed, feathered laces bleeding mud. "Perhaps."

Perhaps? What did that mean? Did he not know? He didn't seem like any kind of Lothario, although there was some resemblance to *Fathers for Justice* about him.

Before she could ask him to elaborate, he added: "I too have a duty."

"What sort of duty?"

"Different to yours."

"Paternal as opposed to maternal do you mean?" She waited to see if this prod would clarify his previous ambiguous answer.

"I have a daughter. Or had a daughter." He looked up from his feet and locked his eyes on hers, a frightening determination on his face which instantly crumpled. "I don't know which. Your daughter-"

"Does she remind you of your own?"

He took a deep breath and turned away again, back to his boots. "She reminds me of my duty."

This man was all unspoken riddles, Rosie thought. "Which is?"

"To answer that question. And, depending on the answer, punish the guilty."

"I'm sorry, I don't understand. Do you think something happened to her?"

"I know something happened to her. I just don't know the outcome."

She looked at his face, lined and haggard, fifty or sixty years old, despair etched into every pore.

"You hope to find her?" Her voice was now barely a whisper.

He nodded. "Yes."

"If - *when* - you do. Well, there'll be nobody guilty to punish then, will there?"

"There will."

She gave a tiny shake of her head, mystified. "Who?"

He looked up at her, tears in his eyes. "Me."

"Funny isn't it? How many vegetarians are fat." Paul stuffed the last slice of black pudding into his mouth and placed his knife and fork daintily on the smeared empty plate, crossed in reverence for the breakfast he'd just enjoyed.

"Jaks isn't fat!" Elaine protested, wiping her egg-stained lips with the back of her hand.

"Isn't she?" Paul squinted, wondering whether Elaine's eyesight was all that it should be.

"No!" Elaine finished chewing and swallowed. "Okay, so she's not slim, either. But I don't mind." She smiled warmly at the memory of this morning's cuddle before Jakki had left for the day.

"Well that's okay. My Shirl's no Audrey Hepburn. Although, in your case, there's a big size er… difference though, isn't there?"

"Well I am diminutive, you might say." Elaine admitted. "Got it from my Mum. I'm a size eight, just a smidge over five foot, and my shoes are a size three."

"Three? Blimey. Can you walk in snow?"

Elaine ignored him. "Fat is a feminist issue."

"Is it? What does that mean?"

"I don't really know. But Jaks says it all the time. Something to do with the male gaze."

"And what's that?"

"That is the way men look at women." She leant over and lowered her voice. "Sexually."

"Huh. So, you being a lezzer an' all. No offence." Paul threw this in, the nagging voice of Shirley rising up in his recall.

"None taken." Elaine said, scowling.

"So, don't you look at other women… you know, sexually?"

"No! Well…" She pondered this for a moment. "I'm sure it's not the same."

They sat in silence for a while, each thinking their own thoughts. Eventually, Paul sighed a happy sigh and took a gigantic swig of tea from his tin mug. One of the perks of being a regular.

"They're not all fat - vegetarians. Not all of 'em." He said. "But a surprising number are. Weird innit?"

"No." Elaine retorted. "Do you have something against fat people?"

"No."

"Do you look down on fat people?"

"No." Paul contemplated. "Unless I'm on a seesaw with one."

Elaine gave him a dark look and then returned her

gaze to the mound on the plate in front of her. A pang of guilt turned her face upside down. She pursed her lips. "I shouldn't be doing this."

"What?"

"Eating this."

"You're alright. Hardly any meat on you. You could use a decent meal inside you."

"I'm not sure that's how I'd describe this fry-up."

"Well, I don't know about you but it's a damn sight better than anything I've been having to eat recently." Paul stabbed a fork into a square sausage on Elaine's plate and chewed it enthusiastically. "You know what I had to eat the other day? Skate wing."

"Skate wing?"

"Yeah. Fish. Apparently."

"I know it's fish."

"Well you wouldn't say that if you tried to eat one. It was like eating flippers. Only more rubbery."

"Never tried skate."

"My advice? Don't." Paul gestured with his fork. "I sneaked it under the table, gave it to my dogs. They chewed it for twenty minutes. Took it out their mouth, wasn't a mark on it."

Elaine looked despondently again at the contents of her plate. "If Jaks knew…"

"Aye, well. Same for me. If Shirl gets wind…" The pair sat in silence together, each contemplating their guilty secret and its ramifications.

"It's okay. Just our little secret." Paul tapped his nose. "Neither Shirl nor Jakki will ever know."

"Oh yes. Because it's just between us, isn't it?"

"Aye."

"And all the other patrons of this establishment? And

the staff? And anyone who sees us arriving or leaving?"

They were sitting in the corner of Tricia's Diner, a muggy din-filled establishment with net curtains at the windows, pine-clad walls and old linoleum flooring. To Elaine's dismay their booth was near the door.

"Ach." Paul swatted the empty air with a huge paw. "Who's going to tell? Who's going to pay any attention to us?"

"You never know." Elaine looked around the diner with a concerned frown. "I don't know any of these people… but they might know Jaks. Or Shirley."

"Nah." Paul said confidently. "I've been coming here years, man and boy. They do a great fry-up and I have never EVER seen anyone in here I know, let alone that Shirl might know."

"Coming here years? I thought you were supposed to be on a diet?"

"I am."

"But you've just eaten three sausages."

"Yeah, but I usually have four. Diet, see?

A scruffy herbert in overalls scrambled into the fug of the diner, shaking rain from his straggly blonde thatch. "Alright Beep!"

"Ey up, Mikey." Paul threw him a pal's upward nod and turned back to Elaine unfazed. Her eyes widened in terror and her voice dropped to a whisper.

"He knows you!"

"Oh, that's just Mikey. He doesn't count." Paul sniffed and frowned at her. "What are you doing?"

Elaine was hunkered down, hiding herself behind Paul's massive bulk. "I'm trying not to be seen." She looked around nervously. "Can we go now? Please?"

"Really?"

"Yes. Really." She grimaced and threw her eyes towards the door.

Paul puffed out his cheeks "I thought you wanted to talk about… the plan?"

"I did. I do." Elaine sighed heavily. "I'm not very good with things being left open, unfinished. I want closure. Tidiness." Paul squinted, trying to picture what this strange thing called tidiness might look like, but allowed Elaine to continue while he struggled. "I don't want to do any more protests. I want to go to work without needing a bodyguard or worrying about police knocking at the door."

"I kinda like this line of work." Paul admitted. "As a client, you're growing on me. Even as a lezzer."

"You're so sweet." Elaine fawned.

"Don't get me wrong, mind. All these night raids? Been a dog's breakfast. Your mate can't plan for shit."

"But that's the problem!" Elaine hissed, still half-crouching at their table. "She hasn't got a plan any more."

"Any more?"

"Okay. She's got this secret source. This great planning guru?"

"Yeah, well, from where I'm standing-"

"I know." Elaine insisted. "I know. But I think that's all there is. I mean, I think this secret source plan covered us breaking in and getting the video. Now… well we're just drifting. The plan seems to be: wait until the video goes viral, meanwhile keep protesting at the gates."

"And has it gone viral?"

"No! She's moaning about no-one seeing it. Says it's not making a splash. It's just… sitting there."

"So… we need a new plan."

"Yes." Elaine agreed. "But I don't want to hurt her feelings. And I certainly don't want to usurp her."

"Hmmm."

The pair sat in silence, contemplating Jakki's dissatisfaction and their own dissatisfaction with her planning abilities thus far demonstrated. By their absence.

"I know!" Paul brightened. "Look, we need a new plan, right? And hers isn't working." Paul extended a finger with each point he made. "And I'm no good at plans. And you don't want to usurp her." He looked down at his one remaining finger. "That only leaves us with one option."

"Which is?"

"Cullen!"

"Who?"

"Cullen. He's this, um, friend." Paul nodded, the mere mention of the name somehow making a solution appear closer.

"And is he good with plans?"

"He thinks he is."

"Do his plans always work?"

"Not all the time." Admitted Paul. "But when they don't, the soup is there to pick up the slack."

"The soup?" Elaine furrowed her brow. "You mentioned that the other night."

"Aye, well, trust me. It works."

"Well, if it works, maybe we don't need your friend Cullen?" Elaine raised one eyebrow.

Paul shook his head. "It's not, um, what you'd call reliable. The soup."

"Right. Is he?"

"Well he's certainly… unorthodox. But he does get things done."

"Hmm. So…?"

"Well, I need to find him first. Bumped into him yesterday actually. But…" Paul considered this for a second and then his face broke into a strange mixture of dawning realisation and delight. "I know where he'll be!"

"Well, good. Now, can we get out of here before anyone else sees us?"

From nowhere, a bustling matron appeared, a whirlwind of gingham check and excessive hairspray. She scooped up the empty plates and wiped the table with a smooth, practised motion. "Your secret's safe with me, honey. Ain't that right, Beep?"

"'Sright. Been coming here yonks." He winked at the waitress and then winked at Elaine. "Tricia runs a tight ship. We're all fugitives from justice in here."

Elaine looked up at the waitress and Tricia smiled a beaming smile. "He's only half-joking. My clientele:" Tricia nodded her head back to the packed seating and steamed windows of the diner. "You got one-third hungover blokes looking for a morning grease fix so they can be back in the boozer for lunch; one-third knackered truck drivers looking to load up on calories so they can make the dash down to Dover with their tampered tachographs; and one-third veggie-vegan fugitives desperately in need of some real umami. Everyone's hiding something - that's why my windows steam up! The very fabric of the building knows to be discrete."

Tricia expertly balanced their empty mugs on the plates in the crook of her arm and swerved away. Elaine leant forward across the table, her voice a whisper. "What's umami?"

Paul surveyed the laminated menu with a practised eye. "Dunno. It's not on here. Maybe I'll ask for it next time I'm in."

"Wow. That's really very kind of you." Paul accepted the gift from Rosie wide-eyed.

"If you're a friend of his, you're a friend of mine." Rosie smiled. "Besides, it's been in the utility room for ages. Neither of us drink it. Might as well go to a good home."

Paul eyed the four-pack of Guinness like a lioness surveying her cubs. "Any chance you could stick 'em in the fridge?"

"Sure."

"Ah. Not this one." Paul grabbed at one of the four and pulled it from the plastic ring. "I'll be needing this one. While I wait."

Rosie smiled and disappeared back into the farmhouse. Paul pressed the tab on the can and raised it in salute to Cullen who had been sat watching silently from the other side of the trestle table. "Cheers!"

Cullen nodded, silent.

"Nice place. For a convalescence home." Paul looked around this pleasant spot in the sunshine as he chugged on his can.

"I'm not convalescing."

"What are you doing here then?"

"I could ask you the same question."

"Just visiting a friend is all." Paul smiled. "And how cool is this? Lovely sunny day sitting outdoors. First beer for… Christ, can't remember actually. Seems like I've been on Lime and Soda since …."

"I always said you drank too much." Cullen said.

"You've never mentioned it!"

"I believe I did. I just don't think you heard me."

"Oh, don't you start. Shirl's always telling me I don't listen to her." Paul grumped. "Or something like that."

"Well, if I didn't say it, I always thought it."

"Hmm. You know, it only used to take one drink to get me drunk, actually."

"Really?"

"Yes really." Paul retorted.

"Which one was that then? The twelfth one?"

"Look. I have changed my ways, okay? Plus, when I drank, I only drank the right amount: sober enough to know what I was doing, drunk enough to enjoy doing it." Paul explained. "Tricky balance. Lots of practice required."

"Yeah well as far as practice goes - you certainly put the hours in. I'd hate to see the state of your liver."

"My liver's in great shape. It's done a lot of heavy lifting." Paul smiled. "I have the liver of a nineteen-year-old."

"You might have. One day. If you're not careful."

Paul contemplated his can of Guinness again, already half-empty. "Not right, you know. Having to drink Lime and Soda. Not natural."

"Diet's isn't it? Good for you, though."

"So why doesn't it feel like it, then? Why don't I feel better?"

Cullen shrugged. "Early days. Maybe your body needs to rid itself of all those toxins first. Maybe you should eat more vegetables?"

"Maybe you shouldn't jump to bloody stupid conclusions." Paul scowled.

"You're a big bloke. You could do with losing some weight." Cullen lifted a finger. "And I *have* told you that before."

"Ah well, you see… a few weeks ago I would've agreed with you. But now? Now I have a vested interest in keeping myself this size."

"Go on, enlighten me."

"Well, it's all to do with the fact that I am considering a new profession." Paul confided. "One where bulk is a positive advantage."

"Oh aye. What are you going to be, then? A boulder?"

Paul ignored the insult and stuck his chin in the air. "A bodyguard actually."

"A bodyguard?"

"Yep. Already doing it, as it goes. It's going really well." Paul sniffed. "Apart from the arrest."

"Right." Cullen nodded, sceptical. "Someone has appointed you as their bodyguard?"

"Well, Shirley appointed me. But that's, like, a personal reference isn't it?"

"You're Shirley's bodyguard? You sure you don't mean boyfriend?"

"No! I'm not guarding Shirl - one of her employees, Sensible Elaine."

"*Sensible* Elaine?"

Paul nodded.

Cullen scratched his stubble. "She doesn't sound that sensible to me - wanting you as her bodyguard."

"Hey! It's going really well."

"So you said. Apart from the arrest."

"Look. That wasn't my fault. It was a peaceful protest until flaming Baxter's thug came out, spouting the odds."

Paul felt a sudden temperature drop and looked

inquiringly at Cullen who now had a stone-cold look on his face. "Baxter?" Cullen asked. "Malcolm Baxter?"

"Sir Malcolm Baxter, apparently. Anyway, his security guard bloke gets all pumped up by his boss's rhetoric, starts pushing and shoving, grabbing placards. Pushing and shoving *my client!*"

"Sensible Elaine?"

"The very same. So, I did my job. Boldly inserted myself between her and him. Got myself arrested for my pains. Just doin' my job!"

"Maybe it was the *boldly* that did it?"

"Look, if you're gonna be a bodyguard you got to have presence. You can't be a wallflower. Prevention is… nine-tenths of the law? Or something." Paul puffed his substantial chest out. "You got to have body confidence."

"Hmm." Said Cullen, unconvinced. "I'm not sure that's body confidence. More like disregard."

"Well, if you mean for my own personal safety - then yeah! Us bodyguards have to be selfless."

"That's not what I meant." Cullen said. "So… why does your client need you as a bodyguard?"

"'Cause she blew the whistle on Baxter."

Cullen leant forward and held Paul's gaze. "Go on."

"She used to work there - at Baxter Farms - and there's some dodgy practices going on. We broke in and took some video, to highlight it 'n' that. But it's not working."

"What sort of practices?"

"Bad ones. You should watch the video."

"Hmm." Cullen said, non-committally.

"Anyway, look. That's why I'm here. We need your help."

"You and Sensible Elaine?"

"Yeah. We need a new plan."

"You had an old one?"

"Yeah, well Jakki - Sensible Elaine's, um, partner? She had a plan. Only it's turned out to be bollocks and we - me and my client - we're kinda looking for a better one."

"To get at Baxter?" There was an unhealthy gleam in Cullen's eyes.

"Aye. What do you say?"

Big Paul could swear that Cullen almost smiled. "Funny you should ask."

SEVENTEEN

The lazy afternoon had worn on and Paul was showing much of that wear. Rosie had brought Paul's cans back out in a small crate packed with ice and then made herself scarce. Unused to alcohol after his prolonged experimentation with Lime and Soda, Paul was half-dozing in the sunshine, his dogs snoozing in the farmhouse's shadow. Cullen was silent, thinking, watching a scruffy hen scratching in the dirt.

Woozily, Paul roused himself to take the top off his last can of Guinness.

"What did your lady friend want with you at the cop shop then?"

"She's not my lady friend. She's a Detective Chief Superintendent."

Paul snorted. "She looks at you like she's your lady friend. Kate innit?"

Cullen scowled, thoughtful, and then said: "It's a long story."

"Got nothin' but time!" Paul raised his drink in salute. "You first."

"Look, I already told you why I was arrested. Why were you arrested?"

"I wasn't arrested as such. She wanted to speak to me."

"'Swhat I said!"

Cullen's eyes narrowed. "Actually, that reminds me: what was all that about being asked to *bring me in*?"

"Ah." Paul took a long, delaying swig. "She pulled me in a few days ago - told me she wanted me to help find you and tell you she wanted to talk to you. About your daughter."

Cullen said nothing.

"Said she'd do me for avoiding jury duty if I didn't cooperate." Paul continued. "You being arrested kinda got me off the hook, there."

"I wasn't arrested."

"Whatever. Still got me off the hook."

"You're welcome."

"Cheers." Paul waggled his can in the air again. "If I thought you meant it. So, what about your daughter."

Cullen gave a heavy sigh and weighed up his friend. They had known each other for a number of years now, ever since they'd met outside the dentists when the police had arrived to deal with an unfortunate incident. Paul had proved extremely useful in the years since then and, loathe though Cullen was to admit it, in his own unreliable way he had shown himself to be trustworthy.

"I have a daughter." Cullen said slowly. "Maybe had. I don't know."

"You don't know?"

"She disappeared." Cullen was hunched over in his seat, talking at his boots. "Never been found."

"Jeez, Mungo." Paul's face was crumpled, his large brown eyes filled with concern. "So where does Kate come in? Have they found the-?"

"A new lead." Cullen jumped in. "In the ashes of the Walkerburn allotment fire."

Paul blinked in surprise. "Wow. Small world."

"Yeah." Cullen looked up and met his gaze. "How's the gout?"

"Huh?"

"The gout. How is it?"

Paul blew out a large breath. "How d'you know about that?"

"Used to be a detective, remember?"

"It's okay. At the moment." Paul nodded, ruefully. "So: this new lead?"

Cullen looked back down at his boots. "Polaroids. Lots of them. All alike. Same as the one we found for… Eilidh."

"That your daughter's name: Eilidh?" Paul squinted, pausing, a bell ringing somewhere in the distance. "The jewellery box thing, the one you asked me to mend! That was hers?"

Cullen nodded, silent.

"And the Polaroids?"

"They found McKenna's prints all over them."

"McKenna's shed!" Paul exclaimed and then nodded, understanding. It had been shed #19 on the Walkerburn allotment, a shed formerly owned by Iain McKenna, where Paul had stashed his gout medicine hoping to keep his ailment a secret. "Hence the gout."

"Funny place to hide your stuff." There was the faintest trace of a smile in Cullen's voice.

"Yeah, well you wouldn't let me hide them in your caravan, would you?"

Cullen sighed. "I thought-"

"Yeah. I know what you thought. And you were wrong, weren't you?"

"Sorry."

Paul snapped his head back at this unexpected utterance. The pair sat in silence for a while, Cullen's head still bowed. Then he spoke again.

"Also found with the Polaroids: one business card belonging to Sir Malcolm Baxter's father."

"Wow again!"

"Wow is right." Cullen looked up. "Small world indeed."

"Indeed." Cullen's voice was cold and empty, a grave unfilled.

"What's in the Polaroids?" Paul asked, as gently as he could, but Cullen just gazed out across the fields, his mind miles and years away. The silence lingered and Paul drowsed to the sound of insects buzzing in the lazy afternoon sunshine.

After a long time, Cullen found his voice, quiet and still, in the close heat.

"Young girls. Tied up. Gagged. Fear for their life in their eyes." His eyes misted over and he reached for his pocket before remembering his photo wasn't there anymore. "Posed almost. Like some grotesque portraits. Taken in the back of some unmarked van, most likely. Maybe their last moments…"

He sniffed back a tear and let out a long, deep breath to try and stifle the sensation of loss in his chest. Calm at last, he looked round at his friend, snoozing peacefully in the sunshine.

"Did you wash your hands?" Shirley's mother nodded down at Paul's fingernails tapping the new tablecloth uncomfortably. "Or don't they let you do that in prison?"

And so it had begun. Shirley clenched her teeth and cast a dejected glance at Paul. It didn't matter that Shirley had made a special effort for this first meeting between her lover and mother over Sunday Dinner; that she'd driven all the way over to Livingston to collect her mother so they could all eat together; and had coached Paul beforehand, lowering her own expectations in the process so as to avoid crushing disappointment.

She had expected it to be a little rocky, but it didn't help that the tanker that was Paul seemed to be fond of rocks. He had no qualms about steering for them, looking up to check they were still there, and then ploughing on regardless. His personal belief that something would turn up, all would be well, enshrined in his pithy phrase *"trust the soup"* meant that her warnings to him beforehand had made little impact.

But none of this mattered when her mother was prepared to find Paul wanting on first contact. And she had.

"Yes, mother." Shirley spoke for Paul from the kitchen cubby. "Working with wood leaves your fingers and nails looking a bit grubby sometimes. Varnish, woodstain, you know."

Paul pulled a tight smile and raised his eyebrows in silent acknowledgement.

"Well, they don't look clean to me."

"That's what I'm saying." Shirley brought in the nut roast, steaming from the oven and placed it on the mat in the centre of the table. "They may not look clean, but they are. Isn't that right, lover?"

"Aye." Paul managed, holding up the fingers of his left hand to examine them anew, picking at the quick on one with his enormous right thumb. "Bloody stuff is stubborn. Someone should invent summat that gets it off easy. They'd make a fortune."

"Why not do that then?" asked her mother.

Paul looked instantly under pressure. Shirley attempted a rescue again. "Paul's a joiner mum, not a chemist!"

Her mother pursed her lips together. "Why's that then? Did you not get the grades at school to be a chemist?"

Paul looked at Shirley in horror. The tiny insistent nod she gave told him he needed to answer; the glare she shot him told him it needed to be good.

"Didn't like chemistry at school." Paul passed over the fact that he had no grades in anything to speak of. "Woodworking, that was me. Always." He glanced up at Shirley, smiling happily at his answer, then foolishly over-reached. "And rugby."

With lips clamped further still, her mouth a tight red line across her stern face, her mother's eyes blazed icy disappointment. "Rugby!" She spat, the very word unpleasant on her tongue. She glanced at Shirley. "Your father never followed sport. He was a worker. A grafter. Always thinking how he could provide. Put food on the table. Not frittering away his time on idle pursuits."

Her mother's voice had this odd cadence, like a perpetually jamming stapler. It would spit and rattle then pause, before biting back at the rest of the sentence and gouging out another metallic nugget. Every word came with a painful cost: words - like money, time and food - were not to be wasted. Especially not on someone as clearly unimpressive as Paul. Shirley had grown so accustomed to that voice that it no longer registered. But she realised how bitter and resolute her mother sounded: she had found life wanting, drawn her own hard-won conclusions and was no longer willing to argue, or allow herself to be persuaded, that life was anything other than a joyless marathon involving putting one weary foot in front of the other until you looked down into the grave. And if you didn't recognise it yourself you needed to buck your ideas up and get a grip.

This demeanour showed in her carriage and the lines on her face. Slightly stooped and frail, but walking with a hardiness that spoke of resistance to whatever life would throw at her - the stoop like that of a living tree used to harsh winds which grew branches at weird and wonderful angles, the whole result showing an organism that endured its tough environment. Her face was hard and leathery, wrinkles etched deep and clear and plentiful, like a beginner's attempt at lino-cutting. Weary eyes, faded blue, looked out under hooded lids, suspicious and wary; thin, tight lips permanently poised ready to snap off any friendliness, levity, optimism or hope.

Her mother was, in short, a fun sponge. Shirley could walk into her mother's house full of life and wonder on a summer's day, a spring in her step and love in her heart, only to feel all the warmth and hope instantly sucked from the room, hoovered up by the gravitational pull of her mother's gloom and crushed into non-existence by its super-massive negativity. Not even light could escape, the very room darkening and cooling as you crossed the threshold; the ambient atmospheric temperature vanishing to match the likelihood of any joy surviving the encounter: absolute zero.

To his enormous credit, as the meal had worn on, Paul had withstood. He had beamed and winked and answered dutifully. Shirley had pinched herself. Did this man possess some kind of kryptonite to her mother's joylessness? A kind of force field which kept him immersed in a bliss bubble, impervious to judgement, cynicism or world-weary pessimism.

Or, he was just oblivious.

It could have been better. For instance, Paul kept referring to her mum, Ivy, as Number 4 - a jape which neither her nor her mother had understood until Paul had explained that IV were the roman numerals for 4. Ivy = IV = 4. Her mother had shaken her head sadly and looked at Shirley as if to ask *is this man suffering from brain damage, or am I having a stroke?*

Ivy was old-school, working-class aspiring to be middle-class, and for her, neither Paul nor Walkerburn would cut it. Walkerburn may once have been a thriving mill town along the Tweed but those days were long gone, and now it was just another down-trodden, charm-stripped assemblage of grey buildings you drove through to get somewhere nicer. Shirley had rented her flat in Walkerburn out of expediency, and - let's not be coy - cost. Pay in the care sector had never been handsome and Shirley was adamant that making ends meet and having a nice home (on the inside, if it couldn't be on the outside) was the way to live. An inherited maternal trait. Now on the management ladder at Greggs - well, perhaps she would be able to afford to move somewhere more *upmarket* (her mother's word uttered with a peerless sniff)

Not that Shirley's position at Greggs counted for her mother either. Well, actually it did count - against her. As far as her mother was concerned, Greggs was a low establishment frequented by people who were *common* (a sin second only to *hope* in her mother's eyes). Being in charge of the place almost made it worse: Shirley had no excuse such as working there only for the money, or until something better came along. Being manager, to her mother, was like wearing a neon sandwich board which read: *Look at me, everyone! I'm squandering my potential!*

Disappointment with her daughter shone from her mother's face and rained down on her over countless phone calls. And that was before she had met Paul. While he was ensconced in the kitchen washing up, Shirley decided to grasp the nettle.

"So, Mum, what do you think of Paul?"

Her mother's beady eyes blinked coldly, judgement passed. "I hate to use the word *loser*, Shirley, but he leaves me with little choice."

"Mum!"

"I just don't see what you see in him?"

Shirley heaved a disappointed sigh. "He has bags of-"

"Money?"

"Charm! Bags of charm."

"Not from where I'm sitting, Shirley."

"Oh Mum! Can't you just be happy for me?"

"I will be happy, Shirley. When you find the right man." Her mother leant forward, confidentially. "Your clock is ticking you know. Time is short."

"Suppose Paul is the right man?"

"Huh." Her mother snorted. "Does he have money?"

"No."

"Ambition?"

"No."

"Prospects?"

Shirley huffed. "Mum. Paul's future is as bright as he wants to make it. Everyone needs a joiner these days - fitted kitchens, bedroom makeovers, log cabins, garden studios - not to mention building companies putting up new homes left right and centre. Timber is the mainstay -

literally - of the housebuilding economy and men who could work it would never be out of a job."

"And how bright does he want to make it, his future?"

Paul, Shirley knew, wasn't really interested in working other than to put (just enough) food on the table. He didn't have ambition, drive or a vision. "He is strong, healthy, kind, self-employed." She managed.

Her mother's lips remained pursed. "Is he honest?"

Shirley hesitated only to realise, too late, that for her mother *she who hesitates is lost.*

"I see." Her mother said with a satisfied smile.

"No, mother, you don't see." Shirley fumed. "Paul is a decent, faithful, generous man who has a big heart and will do anything to help others."

"But can you trust him?"

The afternoon light was fading but not so quickly that it should have shrunk rapidly into this dusky ball which suddenly smothered Shirley and left her blinking in some brilliant spotlight. She gasped as the world around her dropped away to a whisper and all that remained was her mother, looking at her with unforgiving eyes, saying: *Final answer?*

"Yes." Shirley snapped the word out and folded her arms, she hoped in victory.

The doorbell rang and Elaine answered it.

"This is Cullen." Paul pointed to his friend.

Paul was standing on the step next to a gaunt, scruffy man with grey curly hair who looked distinctly uncomfortable - although not as uncomfortable as Elaine, who suddenly stood opening and closing her mouth wordlessly, like a ventriloquist's dummy.

"But… I'm not ready." Elaine managed, finding her voice.

Paul gave an apologetic smile. "No time like the present."

"But I haven't told her yet!"

"Ah." Paul hesitated as Elaine stood there in a daze. Seemingly impatient, the man Cullen stepped past her and into the house. The hallway was cool and dark after the bright sunshine. She instantly snapped to and scurried after him, the sensation of Paul heavy at her back.

Cullen strode into the living room and Jakki, with her back to him, whirled, her mouth a thin line, instantly on her guard at this stranger thrown in her house. She saw Elaine behind him, looking nervous, and her eyes automatically went to the table where a number of maps and sketches were laid out. Jakki glared at Paul, eyes flashing a warning.

"It's okay." Paul reassured her. "He's here to help."

"Help how?" Jakki asked, seemingly in need of further information in order to drop her guard.

"Er." Paul sought out Elaine, but she just bowed her head.

"What's this all about?" Jakki raised her voice, throwing some authority in with the embyronic outrage.

"Er…" Paul gulped, stalling. Elaine moved up to stand beside him, shamefaced, offering her silent support by way of apology for not fulfilling her part of their agreed deal - telling Jakki of their mutiny. The pair stood there looking like mismatched saucepans - one battered soup tureen and one shiny milk pan - the last two empty vessels on the discount shelf. The silence, and their awkwardness standing there in it, grew.

"Lay, what's going on?" Jakki focussed on her partner, glaring in confusion, waiting for an explanation.

"I meant to tell you, Jaks." Elaine was wringing her hands in front of her, like some errant schoolgirl up before the Deputy Head.

"Tell me what?"

"We… that is, Paul and I… we were wondering… if it might not be a good idea to…" She trailed off. Ignited by her efforts, Paul took to the plate.

"Thought, maybe, we could review the plan. Get a fresh pair of eyes on it. This man is the best planner I know." He smiled broadly, hoping to defuse Jakki's suspicion with boyish charm. It didn't work.

Jakki glanced at Cullen, unimpressed, and then glared back at Paul and Elaine.

"What's wrong with the plan we've got?"

"Nothing." Elaine mumbled. "It's just… well…"

"We've had a few setbacks." Paul said with an apologetic smile.

"Indeed." Jakki agreed, her jaw set. "And they were all overcome. Thanks to the plan from my expert source. The plan we agreed."

"See, Jaks. That's the thing you see…" Elaine bit her lip. "It's not you that we're questioning. It's this expert source. Do you see?"

"No."

"Well it's been a bit of a…"

"Dog's breakfast." Paul interjected. "No offence."

"None taken." Jakki said, her intonation conveying the exact opposite.

"We just wondered who this expert source was?" Paul looked sideways, down at Elaine, and they both shuffled their feet. Silence dragged for a while. It was Cullen who broke it again.

"Who is this expert source."

"You don't need to know that." Jakki retorted. "That is strictly on a need-to-know basis."

Cullen's eyes narrowed. "I need to know."

"No. You. Don't." Jakki surveyed the three people in her living room who all seemed to be opposing her right now and she didn't know why.

"Please Jaks." Elaine spoke up, although still muted. "We just want to be sure that we're doing the right thing and that we're going to be successful. If any one of us gets caught, we'll all suffer."

Jakki stared in silence at her partner, the muscles in her jaw flexing causing a vein in her temple to throb visibly. "Right! No problem." She strode over to her rucksack and rooted inside it. "You want to destroy the chain of command? You want to do the planning, hmm?"

"Jaks!" Elaine pleaded, her brow furrowing.

"No! It's fine. Here." She pulled out a pale blue A4 booklet from her rucksack and flung it onto the table. "Satisfied!"

No-one moved for a few seconds and then Cullen walked over and picked up the booklet *How To Rob A Bank: Lessons From A Master. By Lester J. McArthur.* He turned his gaze to Elaine and Paul. Paul shrugged and raised his eyebrows; Elaine was galvanised into action and scurried over to take the booklet from Cullen's hand.

"How to Rob a Bank?" She looked at Jakki, mystified. "But we're not robbing a bank!"

"The basic process is the same. Don't you see?" Jakki's eyes were glowing with excitement. "We observe, scope out, probe for weaknesses, gain entry, plan the operation, implement it and then make a getaway. It's just the same."

Elaine flicked through the thin booklet. "Where did you get this?"

"From Lester J. McArthur."

"Who is?"

"A bank robber!" Jakki almost squealed. Maybe she had been wrong to withhold her expert source from the others. Here was a chance to get them more on board, more energised. "A genuine bank robber!"

"Who wrote a book?"

"Yes! Containing all his tips and expertise." She paced over to Elaine and took the booklet from her, brandishing it to the three in the room. "This is all the information we needed to execute a perfect raid."

Elaine exchanged glances with Big Paul and they both made the same *who knew* face at each other. "Well… in that case…" She started but Cullen interrupted.

"How many banks did he rob?"

"What?" Jakki was caught off-guard by the question.

"How many banks did he rob?"

"I don't know."

Cullen walked up to her and took the booklet, looking at the back cover. "Don't you think it's odd? That a bank robber, selling a book outlining his exploits, wouldn't boast about how successful those exploits had been?" Cullen glanced across at Paul then back at Jakki.

"Well…"

"Come to that, did you not think it odd that a bank robber would write a book?"

"Maybe he just did it for the money?"

"For the money? How much was it?"

"A tenner."

"A tenner? What sort of bank robber finds it easier to make money from writing books that sell for a tenner than from robbing a bank?"

"Er..."

"A failed one." Cullen answered his own question.

"Yeah." Paul chimed in, finally pulling at the thread Cullen had loosened in his mind. "And who would write a book admitting they were bank robber anyway? The police would just go round and arrest them."

"Oh, he wasn't worried about that when he wrote it." Jakki said confidently.

"How do you know that?"

"He wrote it in prison."

Cullen looked at Paul, Paul looked at Elaine, Elaine looked at Jakki, Jakki turned back to Cullen.

"What?" Jakki said.

"You-" Cullen corrected himself. "We, need a new plan."

Elaine and Paul nodded and sighed, Jakki folded her arms. "Why?"

"Well, what's your next step?"

"Er…" Jakki felt she was suddenly on shaky ground

"You broke in, took some video, got away. Now what?"

Jakki took a deep breath. "We need to do more to promote our video. Get it seen!"

"How?"

"Er… Lester doesn't cover that."

"No. Because this is the ravings of a failed small-time crook." Cullen said, throwing the booklet onto the table. "You need to command attention. Make a scene. Get the world to sit up and take notice."

"Yes!" Jakki's eyes grew as she saw, for the first time, some similar light of evangelic fervour in his face.

"We need more ambition. We need to think big!"

Jakki was rapt. "Oh. Great!"

Paul looked down at his feet and sighed. "Oh. Shit."

EIGHTEEN

"Okay. We have one hour." Cullen said. "I'm guessing there's alarms and sensors all over the place that we'll trip or affect without even noticing it. Based on what you've told me I'm imagining more have been installed since your last… visit."

Jakki, Elaine and Paul all nodded ruefully, chastened, but Elaine was relieved now that someone else was in charge of proceedings. They had spent much of yesterday talking and discussing the plan and Cullen had been a model of quiet control.

"We'll take this side." Cullen nodded at Paul, gesturing to the buildings to the left of the main drive. "You two that side. Back here at …" He checked his watch. "2am. Sharp."

Jakki sped off and Elaine bustled behind her, heading for a gap between two sheds that led through to the most distant buildings in the complex.

"Why don't we start here?" Hissed Elaine.

"Because." Jakki said over her shoulder.

"What's wrong, Jaks?"

"Nothing." She stopped and heaved an alarmingly loud sigh.

"Jaks!" Elaine caught up and reached out for her partner's arm but Jakki shrugged it off and started off again only to stop after a few steps. Elaine reached out again. "Are you okay?"

Jakki stood stiffly, breathing through her nose in short

angry bursts like a horse with bronchitis. Her eyes were searching over Elaine's head but seemingly unfocussed on anything in particular. Eventually she lowered her gaze and locked eyes with her lover. "Yes. I'm sorry. He winds me up."

"Cullen?"

"Both of them, actually. Cullen - Mister I-have-a-plan-follow-me - and Paul…"

Elaine screwed up her face, mystified. "What are you talking about?"

"This was my operation. My design, my plan, my project." Jakki's face was distorted, crumpled, a determined adult on the verge of tears.

"It is! It still is!"

"Well, I'm going to make sure it is." Jakki clenched her jaw and Elaine saw the tendons in her neck flex in the moonlight. "Okay, there were a few setbacks. In the early days. But it's all about detail. Detail! Well, we'll see won't we?"

"Jaks, we're on the same side here. All of us."

"Yes. But what's in it for him, hmm? I'll bet you he's not interested in animal welfare - couldn't give a monkey's. What's his agenda?"

"I don't know."

"Well I'm not sure I trust him at all."

"Paul does."

"Paul!" Jakki snorted. "Don't talk to me about Paul."

"What's wrong with him? He protected me from that Nazi. Twice."

"What's wrong with him? He's a male chauvinist pig's what's wrong with him. Have you heard him? The names he calls us?"

Elaine tilted her head this way and that as she tried to

recall conversations with her nominated bodyguard. "He means well. He's just a big bear really."

"He's just another bloody sexist bloke." Jakki fumed. "Think's 'cos his van's a manual that it can only be driven by a man."

"He's got a good heart."

Jakki ignored her. "And he's not vegetarian!"

Elaine felt the hairs on the back of her neck bristle. It suddenly turned very cold and she shivered. "How do you know that?"

Jakki leant into Elaine's face, their noses almost touching, and sniffed loudly. "I can smell it. He reeks of bacon."

Elaine's eyes widened and she waited in fear for her lover's next statement. When one didn't come, she swallowed hard. "He's trying hard. On the road to becoming veggie. Won't be long before you can claim yourself another convert!"

Elaine gave a tight, nervous smile in what she hoped was encouragement. Perhaps in the darkness Jakki couldn't see it. Perhaps. The pair stood in silence for a few moments longer until Elaine was more confident that the dreaded accusation was not going to be uttered. She jumped in.

"So, what's the plan then Jaks? Why not start with this shed here?"

The question gave Jakki a chance to exert control and she recovered her poise and took it. "Because we don't want to be late and get stranded here. If we start furthest away and work our way back, if we run out of time at least we'll be close to the van to get away." She said, her voice already lifting with the confidence she felt in her own opinion. "And, the more sheds we open, the more birds will get out, the more noise there'll be. Don't want to be at the far reaches of this place when we wake everyone up."

"Will we wake everyone up?" Elaine grimaced.

"I think it's inevitable. I don't think half a million chickens will go wandering free on tiptoe."

"I suppose."

"And remember, I want everything captured on camera, okay?"

"Check that." Elaine brandished Jakki's phone in evidence. "Fully charged!"

Jakki gave her a peck on the cheek and Elaine's eyes moistened as she looked at her partner.

"If anything goes wrong, Jaks. I just wanted to say *I love you.*"

Jakki's eyes sparkled in the security lights. "I love you too, Lay. But nothing's going to go wrong. Trust me." She gave Elaine another peck, this time on the forehead. "Can't say the same for those two though!" Jakki pulled out the keycode unlocker from her pocket and waggled it at Elaine. "How're they going to get in if they don't have one of these?"

And together they sidled up to one of the sheds, hand in hand.

"The problem with these is you don't even know how many digits are in the code. Could be four, five." Cullen slumped with his back against the door to the chicken shed, defeated by the sight of the keypad where the lock should be.

"We could try 1-2-3-4." Paul suggested.

"Is that the level of security you would deploy?"

Paul shrugged. "It could be that."

"Yeah. Or it could be the digits from someone's National Insurance number."

"Try 1-2-3-4."

Cullen did, but the door remained shut. He looked askance at Paul.

"What's your National Insurance number?"

Paul looked at him blankly. "Eleven?"

"Eleven?"

"Uh, twelve? I don't know!"

Cullen blew out a long sigh. "You could have told me the doors had combination locks."

"Soz. Forgot." Paul didn't look apologetic, but rather upbeat. "See, the girls have got a device. Opens 'em like magic. But now that we've split up…"

"Great."

"Never mind. Stand aside. Let the dog see the rabbit." Paul gloated.

"What're you going to do?"

"Cometh the hour, cometh the wossname." He bent down and began rooting through his toolbag, picking things up, considering their suitability for the job in hand, and then discarding them.

"Hurry up." Cullen said, testily.

Paul looked up at him. "You got some place to be?"

"Yes. Inside this shed. Before someone sees us."

"Is this, perhaps, because you've come up against a problem you can't solve?" Paul's knowing smile shone brightly under the security light over the door.

"It's a locked door. Not the Rosetta stone."

"Doesn't matter." Paul leant up from his toolbag, a large screwdriver in his hand, and contemplated his friend. "See, this isn't just any old locked door is it?"

"Actually, it is. It's a locked door to a chicken shed."

"No, no, no." Paul shook his head with a wry smile. "It's a locked door that you can't open. Different. You thought you'd be able to just rock up here, whip out your picks and get us in. And you can't."

"And you can?"

"Oh yes." Paul hefted the screwdriver confidently. "And you don't like that, do you?"

"I am supremely indifferent to it."

Paul's teeth glimmered in the yellow light. He handed Cullen a small torch. "Course you are."

Standing, Paul attacked the screws on the top hinge of the door. "Up here, Mungo. I'm in my own light."

Cullen obediently nudged around and shone the torch on Paul's hands.

"Not budging. Hang on."

Paul bent down, there was a spraying sound and he came back up with a can of WD-40. He sprayed the top hinge liberally, dropped the can back into his toolbag, and then attacked the bottom hinge with his screwdriver. The screws gave smoothly. But not those in the top one. Paul smashed the hinge with the hammer and then addressed it with the screwdriver once more. This time they yielded and Paul smiled. "Percussive maintenance."

"Very high tech."

"The best tool for a job is the one you have." Paul quoted, airily. "If you have a hammer use it. It's a hinge, not the space shuttle."

"Are we in?" Cullen asked, checking behind them.

"Aye, just need a hand lifting this off."

The pair lifted the door smoothly off its hinges and leant it up against the side wall. Paul gathered up his stuff.

"Since you are now officially no use with doors, I will go and open the doors to the other sheds." Paul declared. "You stay here, empty this one and then go on to the next shed. By the time you get to it, I'll have the door off and be on to the next one. And so on."

Paul swept a congratulatory hand in front of him but Cullen remained stony-faced.

"See? I can have plans too you know!" Paul beamed.

"So I see. I, however, do not plan to go from shed to shed all night. I have other priorities. Can I have a look in your bag a minute?"

Paul frowned but handed his bag over. "So, these priorities. You gonna share them?"

Paul leant back against the wall in the darkness, arms folded, while Cullen attacked the large toolbag.

"Maybe." Cullen replied, pre-occupied.

"We've talked about this before, haven't we? Sharing? How sharing can increase the chances of a plan's success?"

"Baxter's going to need more than chance when I get hold of him."

"Why? What're you gonna do?"

"Not sure yet." Cullen said, rooting through the toolbag. "Would you happen to have a baseball bat and a bin bag?"

"No." Paul frowned.

"What sort of toolbag is this?"

Paul ignored him. "Look, I don't get it. I mean, I don't really get why Jakki and Elaine are doing this but I understand where they're coming from. But you? What's Baxter done that means so much to you? I didn't think you'd be bothered about a few chickens."

"I'm not. Although it's not a few, it's half a million."

He dropped Paul's bag on the floor and the tools within made a loud clang and thud. Paul glanced around in case anyone was in earshot or some light came on. None did. Cullen looked up. "You know, I explained all this to you already."

"You did? When?"

"When you came to get me at the farmhouse."

"Oh."

"Yeah. Guess you nodded off while I was telling you."

"Soz." Paul looked suitably shame-faced. "Can't you give me a quick recap now though?"

Cullen looked at his watch. "No. Let's just say he has some information I want."

And with that he ducked inside the shed leaving Paul alone to work out which shed door to attack next.

"Do you have any spare batteries?" The light from Ellie's torch was dimming badly under the duvet while Jemima's was as bright as the sun.

"Try banging it."

"I don't know what you mean."

"Look." Jemima took it from Ellie and smacked the torch down on the mattress. The light flickered briefly but then steadied, its brightness no better than it was before. "Hmmm. Shine this on me so I can see what I'm doing." She gave her own torch to Ellie who obediently shone it on her hands as Jemima screwed open the base of the torch and let the batteries slip out.

"Sometimes if you give them a rub, they work better." Jemima said, rolling each battery between her little fingers. "I seen my Dad do this with the zapper."

"What's a zapper."

"The thing for the TV." Jemima wrinkled her nose up.

"Oh, the buttons."

"Buttons?"

"That's what we call it. Pass me the buttons."

"Well, it's called the zapper. Not the buttons." Jemima finished reinserting the batteries and turned Ellie's torch back on. The light shone brightly once more.

"Wow! I'll have to tell my Mum that. For her toy."

Jemima snorted. "Grown-ups don't have toys! They're grown-ups."

"My Mum has one. I've seen it."

"Really?"

"Yes. In her bedside drawer." Ellie blushed at the memory of being caught rummaging where she shouldn't.

"Does it have batteries then?"

"Hmm-hmm."

Jemima gave an intrigued frown. "What does it look like?"

"Um. It's big. And black." Ellie enlarged her eyes, remembering. "She said it's her special toy. No-one else is allowed to play with it."

"Special?"

"Yes." Ellie nodded obediently. "No-one else is to know about it. Not even my Dad."

"Why not?"

"I don't know." Ellie pulled her mouth into a thoughtful moue. "She said she only plays with it when he's not there. Maybe she's worried that he might break it?"

"Huh." Jemima puzzled over this nugget of information.

"Does your Mum have a special toy?" Ellie asked.

"I don't know." Jemima considered for a moment and then, her interest in the subject apparently vanished as she shone her torch back onto the display of Barbie's they had arranged at the foot of the bed. The girls had constructed an Aladdin's cave using their combined duvets on Jemima's bed and strewn all their sweets, chocolates and biscuits for their midnight feast in plastic bowls and saucers from a doll's tea set. "Now, you say: *which of these treasures contains the genie?* And I say: *this one.* And then you say: *what is the secret codeword which will wake him?* And I say- What's that noise?"

"That's not the secret codeword!" Ellie protested. "It should be *abracadabra* or something."

"No." Hissed Jemima. "What was that noise?"

The two girls froze in place, holding their breath, listening intently. There was no sound but it was starting to get uncomfortably warm under the covers so Jemima threw back the duvet, took a gulp of cold air and sat up in the darkness listening again. Ellie sat up beside her, watching her in silence.

There was a sudden bang, very close, and Ellie's eyes widened. She felt the urge to grab hold of her friend and hold her but Jemima had shot out of bed and scrambled to the window.

"There's people outside!" She whispered, urgency and excitement in her voice.

Ellie crept cautiously to the window and peered out from one side, not wanting to be seen. "Where?"

Jemima had her nose pressed against the glass, eyes scanning left and right. The view of the sheds and the

Baxter compound was illuminated by lamp posts and small security lights attached to the corners of buildings. The night was clear and cloudless, the blackness a rich backdrop against which any slight movement stood out starkly. "There! And there!"

Ellie poked her head out from her hiding place and saw two figures dash across the open space between two sheds and disappear out of sight. In the foreground another shape emerged from shadow and walked carefully across to one of the sheds closest to them. Under the security light the shadows threw the man's profile into view.

"It's Mister Cullen!" Ellie's fear turned to amazement and then excitement. She instinctively turned to look at the spare bed in Jemima's room she'd been given for the night. At the foot of it, resting on the overnight bag her mum had packed for her, was Cullen's hat.

"He's going into the shed!" Jemima squealed as quietly as she could manage.

Ellie turned back and watched, breathless, as he disappeared inside. She waited for what seemed like hours but nothing else happened and no-one else appeared. Beside her Jemima was fidgeting. The excitement seemed over for the time being.

"What is he doing?" Ellie wondered out loud in a whisper.

"I don't know."

"Who are the other people?"

"I don't know."

"Shall we go down to see him?"

"What? No!" Jemima looked at Ellie in astonishment. "We're supposed to be asleep. And we're in our pyjamas. Mister Cullen isn't supposed to be in the shed." She frowned in consternation. "It's not allowed."

"But Mister Cullen is a nice person. He's not naughty. Maybe he is rescuing another hen!"

"What?"

"Like Misty." Ellie explained, pleased to be able to tell Jemima something she didn't know rather than the other way round. "My Mum said that Misty is a rescue hen. Because she was rescued from the sheds."

"Why would hens need to be rescued? Rescued from what?"

Ellie raised her eyebrows - this question hadn't occurred to her before. "I don't know."

"Huh." Jemima was unimpressed. "Usually when you're rescued it means you've been saved from something nasty. Like drowning. How can something nasty happen to hens laying eggs in these sheds?"

"Maybe there's been a accident?" Ellie's eyes grew large with an imagined wonder. "Maybe Mister Cullen has gone in to rescue lots of hens because there's a fire."

"There's no smoke. Or flames." Jemima scoured the scene in front of her for any signs of fire or other dangers she could think of. Nothing was moving anymore, the view from her bedroom window the same as it was any other night. Except for the door propped up against the wall of the shed that Cullen had vanished into.

Suddenly a riot of thoughts surged in her head, an intense sparking of different ideas and events colliding in her brain. She verbalised her conclusion, almost before she realised she'd made one. "Let's follow him!"

Ellie opened her mouth wordlessly, closed it again, and then said "That's what I said and you said *No.*"

"You said *let's go down there*. I'm saying *let's go into the shed.* You wanted to see inside, didn't you? Here's your chance."

"But it's dark. And cold."

"It'll be light and warm inside."

"I've got my PJs on."

"So have I - but we can change!" Jemima's eyes were gleaming in the reflected light from the compound. "Come on! You can give Mister Cullen his hat back!"

This last appeal to Ellie's obligation to her Mum did the trick. She heaved a reluctant little sigh and climbed down from the window. Jemima did the same and the girls stood by their beds and changed out of the pyjamas.

"Don't forget your torch." Jemima said, picking up her own.

"I thought you said it would be light and warm inside?"

"It will, I think. But it's dark outside. And we might need to signal to each other."

"Why would we signal to each other?"

"If we get split up."

"Why would we split up?" Ellie paused in putting on her trainers, a new fear in her voice.

"We won't." Jemima reassured her. "It's insurance."

"Insurance?"

"Yes. It means *in case.*"

"In case what?"

"In case we get split up." Jemima snapped, tired of all the questions. "Come on!" And the pair, armed with torches, fleeces and joggy bottoms, crept out of Jemima's room, down the stairs and out into the night.

Inside the shed Cullen found two doors built into the

green interior walls, left and right, at the back of the space. *Eeeny meeny miny mo.*

The door gave onto a dark hell-hole with an appropriately infernal stink. The air was thick with choking dust and the acrid tang of ammonia. He stood in a kind of atrium, separated from the hens by a floor-to-ceiling cage containing an embedded door. Beyond, in the dim light it looked like every surface was covered with dull, faded plumage - birds huddled, sleeping and grousing, on the floor, on steps, shelves and perches. Between the crush of animals all over the floor were scatterings of excrement, broken eggs, rotting carcasses. Towering above, left and right, were banks of cages, overstuffed like giant greying duvets which could no longer be crammed back into the covers.

Elaine had told him about the exit hatches which lined the walls of the sheds - these were what needed to be opened if the hens were to be released. On the other side of this cage. He covered his mouth and nose with one hand, opened the wire door into the main enclosure and waded through the hellish carpet of birds, the beaks from a few of the animals he disturbed pecking harmlessly at his stout leather walking boots. He shone his torch over the external wall for catches or release mechanisms to the hatches, seeing none. When he reached the far end of the cage, up on the wall he saw a gleaming control panel with a handful of large stopper buttons, red and green.

The buttons weren't labelled but Cullen didn't care.

NINETEEN

Malcolm leant back in his chair, removed his glasses and smashed the remains of a cigar into a large cut-glass ashtray on his desk. The characters on the laptop screen in front of him were just a muddy smear. He picked up the coffee cup on his desk but it contained only some dregs, so he pushed it away and looked up at the battered ceiling tiles in the dim light from his desk lamp. They needed replacing.

A quiet alarm beeped at him and he checked his watch. 2am. He stood and paced over to the long window which ran down the side of his office. Outside the night was clear, light from a decent moon and the starry spots from the various lampposts and security lights dotted around the complex gave off a cosy Christmassy feel. He stuffed his hands in his pockets and paced up and down next to the window, shaking his head as he considered his situation.

Tesco would sign tomorrow - he knew it. Cheryl had gone through all her contractual points several times, with him and his legal adviser Henry, an old school friend. Everything had been covered, everything was in order. Any qualms she may have had ultimately had just come down to price and he had squirmed and wriggled, delayed and debated with himself as to what he was prepared to accept and what would break him. The latter was a hard figure, he knew exactly what price he would break even at and what margins he would get above that;

what he kept changing his mind on was the value of the contract in volume terms, the uptick, the long-term prospects for growth. His solution to the price-gouging of these supermarket chain bullies was simple - it wasn't possible to sell below cost because then he would go out of business; and he had cut costs to the bone, always had, always would. But free-range rearing, and organic on top of that, was costly. Better feed, better conditions, more medication, more space, shorter laying ranges - all these things contributed to the bottom line and the position was, very simply, that it was not possible for him to sell organic, free-range eggs at the prices they wanted. And if it wasn't possible for him it wouldn't be possible for anyone.

But that was the genius of his solution - it meant that if he could sell at those prices there was no way his competitors could ever price match him - not long-term anyway - so he would be the *de facto* winner in this war. If he could sell at that price. And now he could. Because all it required was for him to pass off bog-standard, battery eggs as organic, free-range. If you crammed hens into cages, fed them rubbish and farmed them until they were laid out your cost base came right down. Right down. To the point where the profit more than compensated for the cost of deceptive signage, extra groomed space to show visiting customers, SSPCA and SEPA, veterinarian advisers and so forth. He had built a large complex within his own site which was no more than a Potemkin egg farm - a movie set which looked pristine but genuine, and would pass any accreditation survey with flying colours.

He had a second set of accounts, a fleet of separately liveried trailers for trucks which were never used and never deployed, except when major clients came to visit. An entire working operation producing, packaging and delivering eggs which did nothing of the sort and was just a, ahem, shell operation. Malcolm smiled. In a few short hours the deal would be signed. The only question now remaining was should he go home and try to get some sleep or just stay awake, stay here in the office, and see it through until morning? Maybe another cup of coffee would help.

He caught an unexpected flash out of the corner of his eye. Turning back to the window he scanned the grounds in front of him. There! A winking light. Two. Jiggling along in the shadows of Shed #8. He followed the lights as they skittered along the ground - pocket torches he thought - until they reached the corner and their bearers stepped into the light. It was Jemima and her friend!

What the blasted…?

And then he saw it. How had he missed it when he had scanned the grounds earlier? And the girls were heading straight for it. The back of Shed #6, tucked away in the corner almost out of sight from his window, its door not just open but seemingly taken off its hinges and resting against the shed wall. The gaping entrance to one of his secret sheds an open wound illuminated by the small security light above it.

Malcolm froze in disbelief, too shocked to move. But then adrenalin shot through him. His beautiful plan was in danger of being exposed, now, right at the death. He didn't know what was going on down there but he had to prevent his grand-daughter from going inside and he had to stop whoever or whatever was going on from ruining his longed-for plans. Rage building within him, he stormed out of his office and along the corridor to the stairwell. Outside, the cold night air hit him with a shock and it triggered an idea: he dashed over to his Bentley and opened the boot.

From the break of trees which ring-fenced the rear of the Baxter premises it was possible, in daylight, to see the full length of sheds four, five and six. Of course, you could only access this perimeter by entering the complex via the front entrance and travelling all the way through it and coming out of the back. Or, if you knew what you were doing, you could try and trace your way through the woods and thickets beyond, a crazy maze of conifers and brambles which tore at your clothes and lashed you across the face.

In the shrinking darkness, though, this view was softly illuminated by the moon and the scattered spotlights which dappled the grass of the enclosures attached to the sheds. Looking now from this unobtainable position, a notional observer would have been absorbed by the sight unveiling itself. In a slow-mo, synchronised display, a number of hatch doors started to open - hatches no taller than knee-height running the length of each shed, every hatch perhaps six or seven yards wide, their flaps lifted hydraulically into a horizontal position where they stopped and waited for an exodus of poultry to swarm into the countryside. But, for a while, nothing happened.

And then the lights came on.

Inside each shed, and now only visible because the hatches were open, striplights flickered into life as Jakki and Elaine flipped switches, hit buttons and then fled onto the next and the next. Even from this distance the sound of sleeping birds rudely awakened by an artificial dawn rent the air. A stuttering racket of squawks and screeches, growing into a staccato cacophony of cries and clucks - animals aware of some new sensation brought about by the provision of light: fresh air.

Like prisoners from some nightmare dungeon, a brave and disbelieving few strutted cautiously towards the open hatches, the chill night breeze ever-so-slightly ruffling their feathers, their necks poked forward, eyes scanning for threats. First a handful - a clutch - then a gathering and, finally, a mass rally of chickens clamoured into the night, sensing freedom in the distance. Soon a feathery carpet of moving animals was surging across the landscape, cawing and crying into the night like some demonic herd of baby raptors reaching out to find their prey. On and on they came, orcs being vomited from Isengard, cackling and beseeching their brethren to follow them and explore this brave new world. Thousands and then tens of thousands; an endless torrent of leathery claws and beady eyes, flowing out and covering the land with feathers and beaks.

At last, the open hatches stood silent, the sheds abandoned by all but the most institutionalised creatures, now denizens of a newly deserted habitat with space to spread their wings and nest in peace.

Thus, did two hundred thousand hens flee from the Baxter complex and seep into the surrounding woodland and moors. The moorland swallowing them, the cries and noises of their terrifying movement slowly dissipating into the night and the murmuring grass, like Zulus saluting the warriors at Rorke's Drift.

"Roland! Roland!" Sally was shaking him by the shoulder and then blinded him by turning on the bedside lamp.

"Hnnnh?"

"The girls have gone!" She was shaking him and patting him now, hard. "They're gone!"

"Hnnnh?"

"Wake up! Jemima's not in her room. Neither's Ellie. Where've they gone?"

"What?" He screwed his eyes up tight and then forced them open wide, repeating the process to wake himself up. His wife's words were just so much background static.

"And the hall light's on! Something's happened!"

Blearily he recognised the look of horror on his wife's face and it immediately snapped him to his senses. He bolted up in bed. "What?"

"The girls have gone. Somewhere!" Sally's lip was now trembling, her face scrunched up in fear and grief.

"Hey, hey. Come on, Sal." He put his arms around her. "It's okay. I'm sure there's nothing wrong. Let's go and check together, shall we?"

Roly pulled back the covers, leapt out and padded across the landing to Jemima's room, his wife at his back. The room was empty, both beds unmade and abandoned. The floor was littered with sweet wrappers and half-opened packets of biscuits. It looked for all the world like the scene of a child-snatching and he tried to force the image from his mind.

"No shoes." Sally whispered, clinging to his arm now.

Not wanting to acknowledge this accurate observation lest it confirm her, and his, fears, Roly stepped forward and flung back the covers, crouched down to check under the beds and then opened the wardrobe.

"Jemima honey!" He called, half-softly, half-manically. "Where are you, sweetheart? Can you hear me?"

They went out onto the landing and looked downstairs. Something about the lone hall light gave off a sense of emptiness - the house felt uncomfortably quiet.

"Jemima?" He repeated. "Can you hear me? Answer please, honey. Your Mum's worried about you!"

At this, Sally clutched his arm with fresh desperation. Together they stepped slowly downstairs, Roly calling out something with every tread.

"Girls? You can come out now! You're making your Mum and me very worried." Roly called into the stillness and husband and wife stood holding each other in the middle of the hall, Roly's bare feet cold on the flagstones. He looked down, wriggling his toes in discomfort, and then up at the front door. It was ever-so-slightly ajar and he stared at it, uncomprehendingly. A gust of night air blew it open and Roly's eyes grew at the sight of a strutting carpet of clucking hens suddenly changing direction and scurrying towards their hall light.

"Stop right there." Cullen froze and waited, instinctively raising his hands. The new voice echoed in the fetid air. "You're trespassing. Again."

Cullen turned slowly and came face-to-face with Malcolm. He had a shotgun carried low, near his stomach, aimed at Cullen's chest and was slowly walking towards him through the carpet of sleeping animals, kicking them casually out of his way.

Cullen gave a sweet smile. "I'm looking for you."

"In a shed?"

"In filth and squalor."

"You're persistent, I will give you that. Stupid but persistent." Malcolm sneered, shaking his head. "I could just shoot you now. Tell the police you broke in and I found you."

"I think the police will be probably looking for you by now anyway."

"It's too late for that." Malcolm blinked hard and prodded the shotgun just as Cullen blind-sided him with a flapping, enraged chicken he had grasped by its feet. The helpless animal squawked as it came into violent contact with Malcolm's chins and he collapsed like a toppled chimney stack. Dazed and lost in the blur of feathers, he was down on the ground, fighting off his mangy enraged attacker, choking on dust and mites. He put a hand to his forehead and it came away red. Shivering from shock and righteous anger, he looked up at Cullen who was kneeling over him.

"You stupid piece of-"

"Shhh." Cullen placed a hand over Malcolm's mouth and kicked the shotgun away. "Save your words for my questions."

"Questions! You think I'm going to answer your questions after this? You have a very unusual way of dealing with people. Normal behaviour would be to arrange an appointment to see me and speak to me, civilly, in my office." Malcolm was shaking and breathing hard, reaching with his left hand for a jacket pocket. Cullen stopped him and held his gaze. Malcolm was genuinely afraid.

Of what?

"These aren't normal times. And these aren't normal

questions." Cullen said but Malcolm just ran his tongue around his mouth, conducting some kind of dental audit, and spat blood.

"Operation Merlin." Cullen said.

For a second Malcolm went white but he recovered and pulled his head back, looking along his nose at Cullen. "No idea what you're talking about."

"Your father did."

"You leave my father out of this!" A flash of anger and Malcolm was shaking again.

"That… will not be possible."

"He was a noble man!"

"I doubt that."

"Doubt all you like. You're just some sort of low-life criminal, not fit to lick his boots."

"Operation Merlin." Cullen repeated. "Tell me what you know."

"I don't know anything."

"You know the name."

"I…" Malcolm's tremors were approaching convulsions and his frantic jabbing at his pocket wrestling in Cullen's iron grip. "I need… my tablets." He struggled for breath, swallowing his words.

"Tell me what you know and you can have your tablets."

"I don't know-"

"Tell me." Cullen brought a fist down hard on Malcolm's exploring hand and he howled in pain, snatching it away.

"It was nothing to do with me! I only heard about it… after."

"After what?"

"After… his death."

"What happened after his death?"

"I received his personal effects. All his writings, business affairs, correspondence. He had a flat in Pimlico. His office when he attended the House. Boxes and boxes of stuff." Malcolm was panting now, his breathing ever more ragged. He was exhaling loudly between short sentences, some kind of breathing technique to keep himself calm or, at least, conscious.

"He had a diary. Appointments and so on." Malcolm paused. "There were entries…"

"Where is it?" Cullen pulled Malcolm bodily up by his jacket and thrust his face up close.

"Burnt. All of it."

Cullen paused as if deciding whether to believe Malcolm or not. "I don't believe you."

"It's true! I burnt all of it."

"Why?"

"Why!" Malcolm snorted in derision. "To preserve his reputation. Gossip, rumour. Endless… painful… speculation."

"There's no smoke without fire."

"My father was a life peer. A peerage he earned and deserved." Malcolm's eyes narrowed. "You wouldn't understand."

"I understand." Cullen said, his voice like an empty tomb. "I understand he wasn't the only one. He was part of a system of abuse that had eyes everywhere, an ingrained establishment secret. Based on entitlement and power. The idea that they got where they are because they deserved to, and were somehow different because of it. Better because of it. Entitled to take what they wanted and get away with it." His hands were throttling Malcolm, choking the life out of him, denying him the stinking air that was all that was available in this fetid prison. "And what they wanted - what they took - were young women. Girls, most of them. Innocent girls - they liked them innocent. Each one someone's daughter, someone's child."

Malcolm was flailing in Cullen's grasp, tearing at the rigid hands on his throat, fighting for breath. But Cullen kept squeezing and talking, almost lost in his words. Words he was unaccustomed to speaking; words he had kept inside for so long they had burnt him, scarred him, buried him. And now it was he who felt he was finally coming up for air.

"One of them was my daughter. My child."

Malcolm's eyes widened in fear and horror. With these words it dawned on him that this madman was not going to let him live.

"It's nothing to do with me!"

"It's everything to do with you. You are a product of this system, a product of this sense of entitlement and corruption. Every word you say, every look you give, it drips from you like a foul poison. You give it life, exhibit it in everything you do, make it manifest by your actions and glibly continue it, inured by your certainty that the system will protect you. With its peerages and knighthoods, accolades, connections and wealth. You believe you are untouchable so you behave as if you are. It persists down the generations and the rest of us are nothing, dirt under your nails, shit under your shoes, to be used, abused, discarded and spent."

Cullen flung Malcolm away, a rag doll thrown in a heap, wiping his hands on his trousers as if he had become infected with Malcolm's attitude through the medium of touch. Malcolm scudded into a throng of feathered bodies causing another few chickens to squawk and bicker as he intruded on their sleep. Like a ripple in a stagnant pond, the rudely awoken animals stirred their neighbours and the sound of tired and disgruntled hens rose another notch. There was a noticeable stirring in the caged population and in the dim light sharp eyes seemed to glimmer, flecks of black pepper in seasoned flour.

Cullen's voice was icy. "You believe only you have value and everything else just has a price. A price you can so easily afford." He wiped sweat and dirt from his mouth with a sleeve and moved forward, menacingly. "Well that price just shot up."

Malcolm whirled to face him and spotted the shotgun lying just out of reach. Breathing with great difficulty and dripping with sweat, his face dirty and bloody, he weighed up his chances of reaching it before Cullen reached him.

And then a child's voice rang out.

Jemima had stepped into the main chicken enclosure panning her torchlight left and right and immediately her eyes grew wide and she felt herself retch. The sights were a horror she could never have imagined; a world away from the serene and gentle setting her Dad had told her all about. A tranquil and clean idyll where happily clucking hens pecked and brooded, brightly lit in a plentiful space with open air and sunlight in abundance. This was an infested midden of filth, mangy and mutilated birds and terrible stench. The air stung her eyes and she started to blink furiously.

Behind her Ellie surveyed the scene of carnage and decay in the cage, her face frozen in disbelief and dawning comprehension as her friend's spotlight cast over the dreadful array of mutilated and bedraggled hens. This was the hellhole from which her beloved Misty had been rescued but here was a multitude of unlucky creatures that never would be. She gagged and grabbed for Jemima just as her torch landed on two figures at the back of the cage, one crouching over the other.

Immediately Ellie's hopes soared, her disgust temporarily forgotten.

"Mister Cullen! Mister Cullen!" She called and waved his hat over her head like a chequered flag. "We've brought you your hat!"

TWENTY

Cullen looked up, shocked, to see Jemima and Ellie treading carefully through the cage towards him. Baxter momentarily forgotten, he noticed the spreading pool of awakened birds, movement sweeping through the flock like wind across greying barley, as the noise rose ever louder and the activity and agitation increased.

"Girls! Get back!"

The two girls had stopped and were now clinging to each other as the disturbed animals sensed their fear. Slowly they started to back out, eyes shut tight, stepping carefully backwards towards what they hoped was the doorway they'd entered from. But the chickens were roused, and Ellie's attempts to deter them by sweeping Cullen's hat in front of them like some giant fan merely served to enrage them.

Cullen straightened and turned towards them, the danger here all too clear for him to see.

Then Jemima stumbled and went down. As one, the feathered carpet spread towards her and Cullen darted forward.

Behind him, Malcolm scrabbled on the ground for his shotgun, arms flailing and flinging hens left and right as they fought to fill any space, any spare gap in the flock. It was like trying to scoop water out of a bowl in order to uncover something at the bottom - you pushed it to one side and it squeezed back immediately from the other. He lunged for the shotgun, holding his head back from the onslaught of stinking birds as he did so, grasping blindly. His right hand latched onto the stock and he brought the gun up out of the speckled-white swarming miasma of creatures and raised it to his shoulder. He felt his chest bursting and a dark pain clutched at him.

"Get away from my grand-daughter!" He yelled, the words struggling to escape from his ragged breath, the echoes lost in the compounding din from the panicking chickens. At the other end of the enclosure he could see Cullen's back as he ran towards the girls. Malcolm shakily took aim and fired.

The boom of the gun-shot ricocheted around the metal enclosure, each echo seemingly louder than the one before. Cullen's ears rang.

The air instantly filled with dust, razor-sharp claws and beaks, flapping feathers which scratched the air and the deafening shrieks of distraught animals fearing for their lives in the growing half-light. Some birds half-flew, half-jumped up into the roof rafters or top-tier shelves to escape the pandemonium that was a crush of tens of thousands of hens all screeching in the same tight space on the floor. Others fell back and sought space around the edges of the cage where there might be some respite from the claws and pecks which wounded and bled.

But the bulk of the flock sensed the source of their only escape lay in the open cage door and ran or flew towards it. A fearful cloud of birds filled the fetid air and tore at the ground - screeching, desperate animals intent only on escape from the echoing din. Anything soft in their way was going to be trampled, grabbed and flung aside, pecked to death or crushed by the weight of this aerial stampede. Anything soft.

Like two small girls.

Ellie screamed and the sound cut through Cullen's soul like cheese-wire. He blinked and lost sight of them in a fog of feathers and stirred-up dust.

It was Cullen's hat which had saved her. Eyes tightly shut and screaming at the top of her voice, Ellie had felt the flurry of feathers and wings engulf her and had instinctively put her tiny hands up to protect her face. The hat in her hands covered her head in heavy leather and the birds simply bounced off. She felt needles stabbing at her shoes, a living hell of being attacked by a rank-smelling knitting machine from all sides. Her own screams filled her ears and drowned out the sound of the clawing birds but all she could do was stand stock-still, terrified.

Jemima wasn't so lucky. With no protection other than her hands, her face was attacked by flying monsters, tearing at her, tangling up in her long hair and thudding and flapping against her as they tried to free themselves. The sound made her feel she was being eaten alive and she screamed and screamed behind her hands as the onslaught persisted, an endless rain of frantic beaks and claws, peppering her with wounds, a giant stapler puncturing her skin from left and right.

From somewhere magical, some unknown and invisible place, Jemima felt a giant hand come down and scoop her and Ellie up, fold the pair of them into a soft bundle and carry them off, immediately away from the scratching and pecking, the stench and the noise. Eyes still tightly shut, she was lifted and sped through the air until a cool stillness embraced them, the light overhead brighter and the sound of silence engulfing them like an echo of safety.

She heard the sound of heavy breathing above her and felt a rising and falling chest at her back. Jemima dared open her eyes.

Her father was standing over her, gazing at her, concern and fear splattered all over his face.

"Are you okay, sweetheart?"

Jemima numbly nodded, her eyes filled with tears.

"Are you?"

This was addressed at the owner of the heaving chest behind her and she felt the person nod silently and then the next minute her father had scooped her up into his arms and was hugging her tight, kissing her all over her face.

"What happened?" Roly addressed this at Cullen but he seemed distant and distracted, out of it, sitting on the concrete floor his back slumped against the interior wall of the egg-packing area.

Jemima found her tongue. "The chickens flew at us, Dad. They were everywhere. Mister Cullen saved us."

"What were you doing in there in the first place?"

"We wanted to see inside the sheds! For Ellie's Brownie badge."

"And give Mister Cullen his hat back." Ellie added, sniffing back her own tears.

"Girls. It is two o'clock in the morning. Your Mum and I were worried sick - we didn't know where you were. And you're not allowed in here anyway - at any time of day."

"We know, Dad. We're sorry." Jemima was still shaking, small round tears trickling down her cheeks.

"Come on. It's okay. You're safe - that's the main thing."

He held both girls tightly and shushed them this way and that, mussing their hair with his chin and taking long slow breaths, trying to calm himself down. He looked again at the man. The colour was draining from his cheeks and he was blinking stupidly in the light.

"Are you sure you're okay?" Roly asked him.

His words seemed to act as a stimulant and the stranger's glassy gaze came into focus on his face, a man just waking up. He looked around him and then down at the girls. His eyes creased ever-so-slightly at the corners and he stared back at Roly and nodded.

Slowly he pulled himself up from his sitting position, at first unsteady, a drunk man going to the bar one last time. From inside the bird enclosure, Roly suddenly heard a roar: "Cullen!"

It was his father and Roly's eyes widened. The man held his gaze and then, turning away, staggered back into the shed. Roly crouched, frozen on the spot, as the girls cried into him. Something was happening inside this shed between his father and this Cullen. What should he do?

He looked down at the top of the girls' heads and felt their warmth, their gratitude, their love. He kissed Jemima's hair and closed his eyes, trying to think. When he opened them, he was staring at the spot where Cullen had sat up against the wall.

It was stained bright red.

Sally watched, overjoyed, as she saw Roly emerge through the shed door which had been removed from its hinges. He was carrying Jemima and Ellie, each snuggled into the crook of an arm, hiding their faces in his chest. Sally sped over to them, tears of relief starting to fill her eyes.

"Sweetheart! Oh Sweetheart! Are you okay?" She reached out to take Jemima from Roly. "Is she okay? Is Ellie okay? What happened? What were they doing in there?"

Roly handed Jemima over and kept hold of Ellie. "They went in to… they wanted to see inside for a Brownie badge."

"Really?" Sally shook her head in disbelief. All this worry and fear over nothing? She stroked her daughter's hair.

"We should… go." Roly nodded in the direction of the farmhouse and pulled a strange face.

Sally frowned and then looked back at the entrance to the shed. "Why is the door off its hinges?"

Roly blinked hard. "Never mind. Come on. I think we could all use some sleep."

He carried Ellie away and Sally took a deep breath, glancing back once more at the shed. In her arms, Jemima gave her mother a sweet hug and Sally took a gentle finger and brushed some stray hairs away from her daughter's face, looking at her anew in the growing dawn.

"Oh, Jemima. You gave me such a scare. Are you okay? Look, you have scratches and blood all over you!"

Jemima gave a silent nod and then looked up at her mother with curious eyes.

"Mum, do you have a special toy?"

Shirley was giving Paul a much-needed foot massage, manipulating his toes and articulating his ankles, her strong warm hands squeezing and stroking his lotioned feet, the tightness and stiffness drifting away leaving him relaxed and breathing more easily. She was inserting her thumbs between the joints in each toe and pressing hard, a sharp crack of pain which made him cry out but she kept on all the same and he winced in a combination of pleasure and discomfort as her fingers and nails worked their way around his stiff, sore muscles.

He was knackered and his feet were killing him. He had gone from shed to shed removing the doors efficiently, until he realised he had reached the end of them and was at the farthest reaches of the compound and disinclined to walk all the way back. The doors were heavy metal jobs for a start and his toolbag wasn't exactly light. And he'd had no sleep, and it was now stupid o'clock in the morning, and what little sleep he'd had over the preceding week had been severely disrupted by the repeated nightly incursions to the Baxter premises, each preceded and followed by him chauffeuring Jakki and Elaine to and from their home in Eddleston. Like some nightshift taxi driver, Paul figured he deserved a kip in the cab - just forty winks, he reckoned. He'd slumped himself down against the rear wall of the last shed and closed his eyes. As soon as Cullen made it along the row of sheds to the end, he'd find him, wake him up and all would be well.

"Easy, Shirl." He heard himself say, biting through a breath he'd been holding. "Ow."

But she carried on massaging and pressing, and now the heat from the pain seemed to be spreading up his legs, multiple pressure points being triggered as she worked her way past his knees, along his thighs, slowly upwards. His eyes grew in a strange blend of pain and anticipation which made him wince and smile at the same time, and he briefly wondered where she'd read about this.

"Ngggg. Ow. Mmmm. Ow."

It was some weird combination of acupuncture and arousal and something stirred in his groin.

For a second.

Then a stabbing pain like no other woke him and looked down in horror at his legs and torso. He was covered by a swarming array of mangy chickens, piling on top of each other squawking and scrabbling to access each last unattacked inch of him, viciously pecking him like a thousand skewers checking to see if he was done. Paul exploded like a ball shot from a cannon. Emitting a mighty roar, he threw himself upwards, sending flapping wings and creatures in all directions. It was impossible to say who was the more startled by the sudden and dramatic movement but the end result was that the flock fell back, screeching at each other and falling over themselves to keep minimum safe distance from this human volcano.

He picked up his toolbag and wheeled it around like some ancient mace-and-chain, its heft and weight projecting feathery stragglers into the pressing, heaving crowd semi-circled around him, until the very bag's momentum grew too much for his own grasp and it flew from his hands, soaring over the heads of his startled attackers like some famed comet.

Paul watched the toolbag sink into a mottled sea, his last hope gone without trace, a minute's silence observed for its passing. The assembled hen task force blinked uncomprehendingly at this opportunity newly presented to them, unsure how to coordinate their response. Man stared at chicken and chicken gazed, blankly, right back.

For the briefest comic-book moment there was a still, eerie pause.

Then he ran.

Paul was not a fast man. He was big and powerfully built - a mighty man'o'war built from finest English oak designed for stately progress through treacherous waters and the ability to repel pirates and carry cargoes across vast distances - not some nippy little craft, zipping over white-topped waves as it zigged and zagged between marauders, its fizzing engine allowing it to effortlessly outmanoeuvre a chasing pack and avoid their guns.

But nothing in his life could have prepared him for this. He forgot all thought, presence of mind or situation, and fled. Legs pumping, heart thumping, Paul turned and ran. Wherever there was a gap he headed for it, wherever there was a thinning out of the creatures he veered towards it. Out, away from the sheds he flew, turning sharply as he found himself approaching a barbed-wire fence, arcing around as the chasing birds drew closer and then pulled away: desirous to get another taste, scared of being trampled by their huge prey. He was like some perverted, gigantic Border Collie herding sheep around a field, the pack ebbing and flowing while he hurtled around creating his own perimeter, chest bursting as he scanned ahead for some break, some escape route, some sanctuary.

And there it was. Hope.

A ditch which crossed his path, running between a fringe of trees and, beyond them, the traces of the main road. As he drew closer, he saw a burn which ran through it, the burbling black water making its merry way oblivious to his plight. The ditch was maybe eight feet across as he reached it head-on and Paul, all hesitation gone, launched himself at it - an Olympic shot-putter entered for the long jump by mistake. He pummelled the air and unconsciously emitted some echoing cry as he hung there, seemingly for ages, as time stood still and watched him smack onto the far bank and collapse in a shattered heap. There was a tremendous crunch of bone and gristle, but Paul raised his head, pulled himself up and half-ran, half-limped up the other side of the ditch, onto the road, across it and down the other side.

The vanguard of the chasing flock reached the ditch mere seconds later. The leaders flapped and flung themselves over it, ungainly, fluttering bundles unaware they were essentially flightless; the stragglers first pulling up short like refusers at Becher's Brook then, seeing some of their comrades bravely making it to the other side, hurling themselves skywards and hoping for the best. The animals in the middle of the flock kept coming, surging blindly forward, the ditch hidden by the birds in front until it was right upon them. Brute force and sheer numbers swept the carpet of birds down, over and up again until the road was running with grey-and-white hens, their claws skittering on the tarmac.

In the fields across the road from Baxter Farms, Big Paul didn't look back. With every burning breath in his body he pushed on up the slopes towards the Moorfoots.

Malcolm had managed to pull himself over to the far side of the caged enclosure but couldn't reach the door handle. He seemed unable to get to his feet and was just managing to keep the milling birds at bay with angry sweeps of his shotgun. He looked up at Cullen as he staggered in. Both men were now breathing raggedly.

Cullen waded through the feathered carpet, kicking out left and right to beat a path through. There was something wrong with Malcolm's face and he seemed to be struggling to speak.

"Help." He managed, in barely a whisper. "Get help."

"Why?"

"Stroke." Malcolm eyes were rolling back and he dropped the shotgun, one hand going to his chest.

"Merlin." Cullen insisted. "Give me something."

"Stroke." Malcolm repeated, his words slurred and barely discernible.

"Merlin."

Malcolm tried to shake his head, a task which seemed to exhaust him. His chin dropped and his head lolled to one side. Cullen grabbed hold of his face and turned it to him, his grip leaving white marks on Malcolm's jaw.

"Merlin. Tell me. Something. Anything!"

Malcolm coughed and spluttered, shaking and trying to evade Cullen's grasp but he had no strength. His eyes closed and Cullen couldn't tell if he was trying to speak or simply breathing erratically. He leant closer in and shook Malcolm's head once more.

"Mystery… scent." The faintest sounds, barely words.

"What?" Cullen shook him again.

"Pills." Malcolm managed and then tried to swallow.

"No." Cullen said. "Mystery scent? Say it again."

"Mysterial… minsterial."

"Ministerial?"

Malcolm nodded, swallowing again. "Savant."

"Ministerial savant?" Cullen's mind raced. "Ministerial servant?"

Malcolm nodded again and then his head lolled back against the cage. "Pills."

"Ministerial servant?" Cullen repeated. "What does it mean?"

But Malcolm was now a motionless shell, his breathing thin and shallow, his eyes rolled back in his head.

Cullen stood, breathing himself with some difficulty and suddenly feeling faint having risen to his feet from a crouch. All around him the dense flock of chickens bickered and fought, kicking up dust. One of them looked him in the eye and Cullen wondered what intelligence might lie there, before dismissing the thought and starting to slowly pick his way to the cage exit.

When he reached the cage door, he leant against it, panting, watching the scene. At the far end, birds were already climbing all over Baxter, pecking his legs and torso to see what this new addition to their environment was made of. At first cautious, then inquisitive, and then gradually insistent the birds gathered around him and pecked and pecked and pecked.

Cullen lurched slowly towards the exit and paused at the control panel on the wall by the door. With one final push of energy, he hit all the buttons on the display and heard the sound of gears stirring and hydraulics starting to whine. The conveyor belts started to move and the sound of chickens being provoked anew unexpectedly hammered through the cage enclosures. Cylindrical covers peeled back from the nestboxes, eggs bobbled along beneath each tier of the housing structure and disappeared from view through the wall into the anteroom.

Gradually, tentatively, and achingly slowly the hatches started to open, along the entire length of the side wall. The chill night air started to flood in and the congregation in the cage went postal.

Like escaping convicts realising there was a hole in the prison wall, from each tier a storm of birds flapped and fluttered, plummeting earthwards with all the grace of shotgunned grouse. Landing on the bodies of their compatriots, sharp claws and leathery feet grasping and knifing as each bird sensed freedom and made a beeline for the newly revealed exits. Claws, beaks and feathers filled the air and the slumped figure of Malcolm was lost in the white-grey stampede which raged across the shed floor and out to meet their brethren spreading out across the fields.

TWENTY-ONE

Elaine and Jakki stood alone on the shoulder of the Moorfoots looking down at the scene unfolding below them. Despite the cold in her bones from standing here for hours Jakki had a huge grin on her face.

"Look at it! Just look at it!"

The large sheds dotting the landscape looked like lego bricks in the growing dawn from up here, the cluster of buildings forming the main complex a toy farm, the rolling fields like so many squares on a handmade quilt. Across all of these quilt squares in their varying shades of green, was a moving carpet of grey-white, microbes spreading out across some multi-coloured petri dish. This growth ebbed and flowed, distorting and changing direction like a murmuration of starlings in an evening sky. It was chaotic and marvellous, an organic poem communing in its natural habitat.

"Poultry in motion." Jakki beamed.

The main road which sliced through this setting like a vivid wound was empty, apart from the Dinky toy vehicles gathered at the site entrance, tiny flashes of blue whipping out from them like microscopic LED lighthouses, and a growing queue of cars to their far right, kept at bay by another white car flashing blue. A huddle of police quadbikes clustered by the main gate where officers looked like they were in the process of riding out across the fields, cowboy-style, to try and gather up the escaping fowl. From away to their left came the unmistakable sound of rotor blades and a chopper appeared, buzzing across the sky, trying to get the measure of the outbreak.

"Think they'll ever be able to round them up?" Jakki asked.

Elaine was silent, checking something on her partner's phone.

"Lay?"

"Sorry, what?"

"Do you think they'll be able to round up all the birds?"

"We'd better hope they don't, really."

"Why do you say that?"

"Because these animals have to be carefully vetted-."

"Don't make me laugh!" Jakki scoffed. "You saw the conditions in there! There was nothing careful about it? Nor do I think a vet ever got anywhere near any of them. It was a scandal and the sooner the world sees it the better."

"That's not what I meant." Elaine pocketed the phone and elaborated. "The flocks are brought in en masse to each shed. Every shed contains only the hens from one flock. There is no mixing permitted. Similarly, they are kept in a controlled environment. Not exposed to disease or other biology other than what exists on the premises."

"Well there's plenty of disease on these premises!"

Elaine ignored her. "This is all necessary because food suppliers need to be able to show, and show they can maintain, traceability. No customer - and certainly not the big customers like the major supermarkets - are going to purchase any animal product without insisting on knowing exactly where it came from and that it has not been exposed to any form of disease and that it has been kept in a strictly-controlled environment throughout its life. Bio-hazard, they call it."

"So?"

"So, what we've done here is let these birds into the wild. They have mingled, cross-contaminating each other - never mind coming into contact with other animals or their droppings. They're trampling all over these fields covered in sheep, or sheep poo. They're done for."

"What!" Jakki was aghast.

"Those that don't get run over, caught by foxes, die from malnutrition or exposure or other natural causes which might affect these normally-unexposed animals - they'll be killed and disposed of. Neither they nor their eggs will make it into the food chain now."

Jakki was shaking, whether in rage or fear Elaine couldn't quite say. "Are you telling me that not only have we *not* freed these creatures into a long and happy life amongst nature but that we have in fact condemned them to an early death?"

"Yes." Elaine agreed.

Jakki was horrified, her mind racing to take aboard what her partner was saying. She cast her eyes across the scene, left and right, shaking her head trying to make sense of this new bombshell.

That was when she saw the angry figure of Eddie Helpmann jouncing over the fields towards them atop a police quadbike.

Eddie had arrived at the Baxter main gate far, far too late. The police were already there and Roland was marshalling them and the ambulance, tending to his daughter while her mother stroked her hair. Roland looked up as Eddie approached and tried to wave him back but Eddie just pushed through the few police officers standing around, brandishing his security pass.

"Go home. You're too late."

"*Too lyte fur wat?*"

"Just… look around." Roland said, shaking his head. "There's been a mass outbreak. Half of the sheds have been released."

"*Hef?*"

"Maybe more." Roland eyed him up and for the briefest moment Eddie thought he could detect his father's look in his eyes. "So much for security."

"*Hoo ded thus?*"

"Does it matter? The damage is done. All we can do now is clear up, clean up and restock." Roland turned back to one of the police officers and engaged them in conversation, Eddie apparently dismissed.

He trudged back to his car, pulled out his binoculars and started scanning the area around the farm. The hillocks and fields were alive with scattering hens, flocks of birds moving here, pausing there, many seemingly uninterested in further escape now that they were surrounded with greenery and fresh landscape to investigate. Eddie turned and scanned the fields on the other side of the road, stretching out to the Moorfoots ranged to his right. He overshot something which made him blink and then checked back to see what it was.

Near the top of the rolling hills, standing completely still, was the very distinct Laurel-and-Hardy shape of two figures silhouetted against the morning sun.

Eddie's eyes grew and he felt anger welling up in his chest, a heat rising in his throat. He put down his binoculars, gritted his teeth, and cast wildly around the main gate and driveway for some line of attack. Those damned lezzers were not going to get away with this.

"I'm getting right fed up of this place, Sarge."

"Really?" Jenkins voice was drawn and lifeless. "It's kinda growing on me."

Appleton let out a heavy sigh and took a last swig from his cold styrofoam cup of tea. The Sarge was leaning against their patrol car, his back to the main complex, legs lazily crossed, arms folded, surveying the fields ahead of them. The air was dawn fresh and you could taste the new morning with every breath. It was magnificent and something a world away from the stale un-airconditioned office back at the station. He inhaled deeply and then gagged involuntarily at the unpleasant taste that accompanied it.

"What the-?" Jenkins' unfinished question was immediately answered by the bulky, sweating figure of the Baxter security man who bustled right past his shoulder and headed down towards the main road. "Jeez. Remind me, when we're back at the station, to wash my uniform. Polyester doesn't wear well."

"Are our uniforms polyester then?" Appleton looked down at his tunic and rubbed it with an inquiring thumb.

"No. But you can't be too careful." Jenkins sniffed. "Also, remind me when I retire never to go into some related employment. Like, for example, private security."

"Is that something you're thinking of doing then, Sarge?"

"Not really." Jenkins watched, silent in thought, as the Baxter security man strode down towards the vehicles gathered by the main gate and strolled amongst them, hands in pockets, eyeing them up like a customer in a used car lot. "You know, I moan a lot about this job."

"Get away."

"Never happy, that's my problem. But you get mornings like this. Makes the early shift worthwhile don't you think?"

"Not me. I'd rather be in me bed. Snuggled up to Suzi."

"That your dog?" Jenkins ribbed.

"Girlfriend!"

Jenkins nodded absently. The security guy was now casting his eyes around the constables and officers chatting by the gate. There was something ambiguous about his manner and Jenkins watched curiously. It wasn't such a bad life was it? He had no-one else to consider, no-one to miss like this young PC here. He could mind his own business, keep his nose clean, bide his time and then retire on a full pension in a few years. He'd only be fifty. Fifty was young. He'd have his health and no commitments. If he wanted, he could travel the world, write a novel; buy a narrowboat and cruise the canals. Maybe become a farmer? Options is what he had. Hundreds and thousands of options.

With everybody's back turned at the gate, the security man was putting his hand under the handlebars of each quadbike and deftly doing something. Jenkins pursed his lips. Was he removing the keys, he wondered? Perhaps. Maybe he could become a key-cutter? Take on one of those shoe-repairer franchises they have in shopping centres? Nah, too humdrum. What about taking up painting? Move to the South of France or Tahiti to take advantage of the light?

Suddenly showing a remarkable agility for someone of his build, the security man leapt aboard the last quadbike in the line, hurled the crash helmet to the tarmac, started the engine and wheeled away before any of the chatting policemen could react. There was some immediate enactment of Keystone Cops double-takes and coffee cups being cast to the ground before the group of officers legged it to their vehicles only to find that, indeed, all their keys had been taken.

Jenkins smiled to himself as the escaping quadbike bounded over the road, through an open gate and off across the rugged field. He looked over to Appleton and jerked his head up towards the sound of the buzzing helicopter circling high above.

"You want to call it in? Tell the chopper a loonie's nicked a quadbike."

"What?" Appleton looked around in all directions wondering what was going on.

"It's all go today isn't it?" Jenkins smirked and looked out towards the Moorfoots. "Tenner says he gets away."

"Run!"

"What?"

"Run!" Jakki jerked her head towards the advancing quadbike and started running up the slope. "Your Eddie's coming for us!"

"What?" Elaine was bewildered but she saw the shape approaching and heard the buzzing engine. "He's not my Eddie."

"Well, he's not mine! Come on!"

Jakki may have started ahead in the race but she was no match for Elaine who quickly outstripped her and started hurdling up the ever-steepening gradient like a startled gazelle. She found a path through the heather and gorse and heeled right on a shallower approach up the hill. Jakki followed on, panting heavily already, but still admiring the sleek form of her partner's derriere as it flew away from her in the twinkling air.

She turned to look and saw that Eddie was incontrovertibly gaining on her and that there was no way she could escape. Jakki abandoned the path and struck out directly up the slope hoping the incline would prove too much for the bike - it was certainly too much for her. Within seconds she was stumbling and staggering, the steepness and the irregular ground making progress almost impossible.

"Over here!"

Jakki followed the sound of Elaine's voice and saw her signalling wildly with both arms, up to her right. Then she disappeared for a second only to reappear with a smile on her face. "Come on!"

Confused but spurred on by this encouragement, Jakki made one final effort to overcome her exhaustion. Sweating and panting, her thighs rubbing in her damp leggings and her boots catching in the gorse, she pumped her legs, the muscles burning and aching in her calves, her thighs, her back. God she was out of shape. Look at the difference between her and Elaine. When she got out of this she was going to get into shape, she swore.

"Ah hev yu nar, yu stewpid lizzah! It's jyle for yoo ma frhend!"

Jakki heard Eddie's shouts drifting up the hillside just as she reached Elaine and collapsed unexpectedly into a wooden pit dug into the side of the hill. She smacked her hip on the planked wall and her knees on the gravelled floor as she fell in, but Elaine helped her to her feet and she found if they both crouched, their heads were below the height of the surrounding heather.

"What the hell?" Jakki panted, gazing at this hiding place.

"It's a grouse butt." Elaine explained, eyes blazing. "It's just a dugout in the hillside where you can crouch down to hide and then stand up and shoot the grouse when they are flushed from cover. There's loads of them on these hills."

Jakki kept panting, trying to control her breathing and slow it down so she could listen for the quadbike as it scooted around below them. Together the pair crouched, quiet and anxious, like two naughty schoolgirls waiting outside the Deputy Head's office, they held their breath and waited to find out what their punishment might be. Her breathing restored to something approaching normality, Jakki listened as the sound seemed to fade to their right and die out before revving up again and appearing to their left. It grew louder and louder and, as it did, she could make out the inarticulate cursing of the halitosised warthog who had become her nemesis.

How had it come to this? What had she been thinking? She'd jeopardised Elaine, broken the law, injured herself and for what? And now Elaine was telling her that it was all for naught and, even then, she'd not been resentful or judgemental - just open and honest and supportive. She'd even found them this hidey hole which might be their only means of getting out of the mess that she, Jakki Banks, had created. What had she done to deserve someone as good as Elaine? God alone knew - not that Jakki believed in Him. But if He did exist, He would also know that she loved Elaine and would never hurt her. She'd been stupid and thoughtless and selfish -

a social media superstar? What nonsense was that? Elaine was right - what was wrong with living a quiet simple loving life, having each other and taking pleasure in the lovely everyday things that life could offer?

As the swearing and engine noise both got louder, Jakki jammed her eyes closed, her pulse racing and her mind reeling. She breathed out, counted to ten and said to herself: *Dear God, if you do exist, please save us now. I swear I will never leave Elaine, I will never seek personal fame or notoriety and I will look after her as long as we both shall live. Her needs before mine. Always. I swear.*

She stopped talking to herself and listened only to the sudden silence all around them. Opening her eyes, she saw Elaine gazing at her, her own eyes wide and moist, a strange beatific look on her face.

"Has he gone?" Jakki asked, bemused.

Elaine nodded enthusiastically and slowly rose to peek out over the top of the grouse butt. The only sound now was of the breeze rustling through the gorse and the faint bleating of sheep in the distance.

"What's happened?" Jakki poked her own head up and looked around. There was no sign of Eddie or a quadbike.

"I don't know." Elaine stepped carefully out of the grouse butt and strained to peer up and around the hillside. "Maybe he turned back?"

"I don't think so." Jakki stood, all but filling the grouse butt. "I'll go see. You stay here. This is all my doing."

"Are you sure?"

"Yes. Stay here, be safe." Jakki clenched her fists. "I won't be long."

She clambered out of the grouse butt, looked around

to get her bearings and then started up the path to her right where she had last heard the sound of the quadbike.

When Eddie opened his eyes, his face was two inches away from mud into which he had clearly been implanted. He lifted his head and spat out a few mouthfuls of it, trying to shake the worst of it from his face but it was moist and sticky and going nowhere.

As he spat, he felt a sudden sense of shooting heat in his back and then pulsing agony consumed him, darkening his vision. It felt like muscle death and he briefly distracted himself from it by trying to remember what had happened and where he was. Then the pain returned, gorging on him, and he cried out, remembering. He'd seen the razor wire far too late - too late to prevent it from tearing through his front tyres and causing the quadbike to kick up at the rear and throw him over the handlebars into this stinking bog. Had he broken his back? Was the bike on top of him? He couldn't tell.

Couldn't tell, couldn't move, couldn't care. He closed his eyes and let his face smack back into the damp mud. This facking mud and this facking country. This was the worst pain he'd felt since he'd stood on one of this country's facking stupid three-prong plugs. What had he been doing chasing those lezzers around this godforsaken hillside?

But, what did it matter? With pain came clarity; vicious clarity. Half a million chickens were roaming free so his job was as good as gone - having a mass-scale break-in resulting in the loss of your entire poultry stock was hardly something you wanted in the executive summary of your CV when you worked in corporate security. Then, not content with having to bear the responsibility for such a lapse in security, he had put the tin lid on it by stealing a quadbike. From the cops! Now, faceplanted in the black organic matter that these Celtic troglodytes called peat, paralysed it seemed and in nerve-shredding pain, he failed to see how to get himself out of this.

He heard a twig snap and jerked his head up from the mud, casting his eyes around for the source of the sound. He didn't have to cast far. The large olive-skinned giant with the goatee was treading steadily towards him, head cocked like a pleasantly surprised bird being offered some new food. Eddie's eyes widened as the brute got closer and he could see two things which made him hope like hell that this was all a hallucination:

There was a worrying gleam in the man's eyes.

And he was waving Eddie's precious knopkierie.

"You rang?"

Kate climbed out of her car where Cullen was standing. The entrance to Baxters behind him was taped off and the driveway blocked by several police cars and an ambulance, blue lights strobing silently in the morning mist ribboning out across the fields.

"Thought you'd like to be the first to know."

Kate grimaced. "If you wanted me to be the first to know you could have told me over the phone."

"Don't like phones."

She craned her neck at the lively scene behind him. "Even so. Seems like I'm amongst the last to know."

"They're here for the breakout."

"Breakout?"

Cullen shrugged. "Animal Rights protest. Nothing to do with me."

"Right." She nodded. "Nothing's ever to do with you is it?"

Cullen just stared at her blankly. Kate sighed. "So - first to know what?"

"Baxter gave me a lead."

She widened her eyes exaggeratedly. "Oh-kay. That was… very good of him."

"He didn't think so."

Her eyes narrowed instantly and she looked again over his shoulder. "Where is he?"

"In there." Cullen gave the slightest inclination of his head to the site behind him.

"Alive?"

"Last time I saw him."

Kate nodded, but she was not reassured by his statement.

"What's the lead?"

"Ministerial servant."

"Ministerial servant?"

"Yep."

She looked him in the eyes. "What does it mean?"

"No idea. Thought you might know."

Kate considered this. "Sounds like some civil servant who might have been implicated in Operation Merlin. Or some government minister's aide. Something like that. Did you get an actual name?"

Cullen shook his head.

"Cullen?"

"No name."

"Not much use without a name." She considered the

words again. “Anything else?”

“No.”

Kate sighed. “We can search through the senior appointments. Again. But if we don’t know what we’re looking for….”

“Gotta go.” He said suddenly, looking over her shoulder.

She whirled around and gazed back down the road to see two vans with satellite dishes on their roofs speeding towards the site. Between her and them was a strange white-grey mass surging across the carriageway from one field to another. She squinted as the vans slowed and the mass separated smoothly to let them pass, like waterborne algae parting for the prow of a ship.

“Are they… chickens?” she said, turning back to Cullen.

But Cullen was nowhere to be seen.

Elaine, Jakki and a somewhat dishevelled Big Paul had wandered down off the hillside only to find Paul’s van was behind a police cordon. Silent and weary the sullen trio trudged south along the A703. Behind them there was the faint intermittent whoop of sirens, the occasional sound of the chopper drifting by overhead, and the sound of normal road traffic resuming as the police removed the roadblocks they’d place at the farm entrances.

When they reached Eddleston, Paul waved them a tired farewell and trudged off alone. The women stood and watched until he was out of earshot. Jakki broke the silence with a weary moan.

“Why didn’t you tell me any of this before? About the

chickens being killed once we released them?"

Elaine looked at her partner's exhausted face: Jakki's eyes were red and unfocussed, lost in disbelief or dejection. Elaine forced a smile. "I didn't want to rock your boat. I love you. You were so energised and driven by this. You had a project and it was wonderful to see you absorbed - immersed - in it. When you're like that I love you even more."

She dropped her head in some embarrassment but Jakki didn't see it, didn't hear what she was saying.

"But it means we haven't achieved anything!"

"No, it doesn't. It really doesn't." Elaine grabbed Jakki's hands, forcing her to look her in the eye. She gazed earnestly into her lover's face. "We have caused a huge amount of disruption to Baxter's business, hurting it financially in a major way - perhaps even bankrupting it. We - you - have highlighted the treatment of these birds and done a major service to the cause of promoting and preventing animal cruelty. You have raised the profile of SLAAC on social media. Your name is going to be everywhere! I'd say that's quite some achievement." She emphasised her point by shaking Jakki's phone in her face.

"Is it?" Jakki moaned. "Is it really?"

"Yes!"

Jakki sighed, unconvinced, her downcast face speaking volumes. Elaine suddenly felt the phone vibrate in her hand and she answered the call.

"Hello?"

Her mouth fell open and she gazed, entranced, at Jakki.

"What? Who is it?" Jakki asked.

Elaine held out the phone with a smile. "It's ITV.

They want to speak to you."

The road was closed. A police sign with a patrol car behind it and an officer leaning against the bonnet on his radio to someone. Cheryl got out of the car and walked towards him.

"Excuse me?"

The policeman held up a hand to acknowledge her and then turned back to his radio. When he had finished, he clipped it back onto his lapel and walked up towards her.

"Is it possible to get through? We have an appointment at Baxter Farms."

"Sorry, madam. No vehicles allowed through for the moment."

She looked at her watch impatiently. "Well, how long will it be?"

The policeman shrugged. "'Til I get told I can open it again. Lot of chickens to be cleared away."

"I'm sorry?"

"Chickens. There's been some mass escape at Baxters. Millions of chickens everywhere."

She scanned the area behind him but all she could see was a bend in the road and a forest on one side. The Baxter facility was about half a mile further on, out of sight.

"Well, can I go through on foot?"

The constable looked confused, perhaps realising that this eventuality had not been covered by the instructions he'd been given and he might now need to apply some personal judgement. He veered towards caution.

"No, madam. No-one's allowed through until I get

the all clear. Vehicles or pedestrians." He looked behind her at more approaching vehicles. "Could you just pull up that side road there and turn around please?"

"But I have an appointment!"

"Sorry, madam. Instructions from the Deputy Chief Constable himself."

"But it's important."

"You'll have to phone through and let them know. There's chickens all over the shop. They're not going to be in any state to take visitors I don't think. Not for a while. Please. Just turn around over there."

Cheryl blew out both cheeks in protest but turned back to the car, shaking her head as she walked back to where Chris was sitting patiently in the driver's seat, the engine still running. He rolled the window down.

"We need to go up there and turn round." She pointed to the unmetalled road which bent away around the hill. "There's been some kind of incident."

She got back into the car and dialled the Baxter number which just rang out. Chris swung the car left and up onto the track which had been laid with large loose stones, no kerb on either side. He followed it for a few hundred yards looking for somewhere wide enough to do a three-point turn. Cheryl sat silently beside him, redialling.

"Hello." Chris said, and Cheryl looked up from her phone. "What have we here?"

"It's a chicken shed." Cheryl gawped. "Two chicken sheds."

"Who do these belong to?" Chris wondered out loud.

"I'll give you one guess."

The track widened into an apron which led to the two sheds. On their right, milling about in a field, was a massive flock of chickens.

"Wow." Cheryl said, shaking her head. "Bio-hazard prevention 101 - don't let your livestock roam loose."

Cheryl took one look at the scene and hung up. Her eyes narrowed.

"Shall we go and take a closer look? Conclude our due diligence?"

As Chris parked the car, his own phone trilled. He answered it, turning off the engine to hear better. The muted sound of cackling and clucking filtered through to the car interior.

"Yes… Okay… One moment." He handed his phone to Cheryl.

"It's for you." Chris said. "The Social Media team. Something about a video?"

TWENTY-TWO

"Thought I'd find you here." Kate smiled at Cullen and then extended her hand to the woman sitting with him at the garden table. "Hi, I'm Kate."

"Rosie." The woman smiled back and shook hands warily. Kate looked down at her dress uniform and realised a little explanation might be in order. "It's alright, he's not in any trouble. Neither are you. This is a personal call. Old friends. Do you mind if I have a word with him? Privately?"

"Be my guest." Rosie said.

Kate waited until Rosie had disappeared inside the house before sitting down opposite Cullen.

"A little overdressed, aren't you?" He said.

"Monthly management steering committee meeting. Up in Edinburgh." She unbuttoned the collar of her blouse and scratched her neck. "Aren't you a little under-dressed?"

"What do you mean?"

"Where's your hat?"

"Donated. To a good cause."

She followed his gaze to Rosie who had come out from the house with a full basket of laundry under her arm.

"How does it feel?"

"Not wearing a hat?" He gave a wry smile. "I haven't always worn a hat. Didn't use to wear one."

It was her turn to smile as she remembered the days

when they had worked together. "Yes. Would have looked incongruous with the uniform."

He looked again at her tunic, the buttons and insignia at her shoulders. "Suits you."

"Thanks. Although…" She checked her watch. "Shouldn't be wearing it now, technically. Off duty."

"Are you ever off duty?"

"Yes." She looked at him, pointedly. "How about you?"

He didn't respond and they sat in silence for a while, the only sound was Rosie's washing snapping on the line.

"Didn't want to leave it too long - in case you did a flit. I'd never find you then." Kate forced a smile.

"You've got my number now, haven't you?"

"Yes. But you wouldn't answer if I called, would you?"

"Probably not."

She scrutinised his face, looking at the creases around his eyes, the lines on his forehead. He seemed almost happy. "Are you okay?"

He winced ever so slightly. "Rosie pulled some small fragments of shot out of my back. I'm fine."

"You were shot?"

"Not close range. It was an accident."

"Funny. Baxter had a shotgun near him when we found the body. It had been discharged too."

She watched him for a reaction. All she got was a blink.

"His body? He's dead then."

"Very much so. Coroner says he had a stroke which temporarily paralysed him and he collapsed on the floor. The hens then took it upon themselves to peck him to death."

"Huh."

"He was conscious the entire time apparently."

Kate sat watching him for a while. He was averting his eyes, sitting stiffly in silence with her. She reached into a tunic pocket and brought out a small brown envelope, tapping it on the table between them.

"Brought you a present."

He looked down at the envelope and then met her gaze, holding it briefly before snatching up the envelope, as if worried she might change her mind. "Don't tell anyone."

"Thank you." Cullen said quietly. "Don't you need it?"

She shook her head. "Nothing on it that's not on any of the others. I guess I can trust you to keep it safe? In case I ever need it again."

He nodded and tucked it into his shirt pocket. "What now?"

"We keep looking. Keep checking. Merlin had a long list of government names. A long list." She attempted a smile. "Something'll turn up."

She watched him as he stared off into space, his profile sharp and weathered like some Scottish crag, the warm afternoon breeze ruffling his hair, softening the effect.

"What now for you?" She asked.

"I'll be on my way."

"Where?"

"I have an idea."

Kate looked at him warily. "Care to share it?"

"No."

"Listen, Cullen. You are not above the law. Leave this alone. We are on the case. I am on the case. All resources are at my disposal."

"She's my daughter."

"I know."

"I'm her father."

"That's not enough."

"It's enough for me."

"That's not what I meant." Kate eyed him sternly and then rose. She walked over to the washing line where Rosie was pegging out sheets.

"How's his wound?"

Rosie plucked pegs from her mouth as she spoke, looking over at Cullen out of earshot.

"I pulled some lead pellets out of his back and dressed it. It'll heal."

"He said. Are you a nurse?"

"Was. He didn't want to go to hospital so…" Rosie shrugged.

"He can be like that." Kate nodded. "Thank-you anyway. I'm assuming he didn't thank you?"

Rosie met her eyes. "He told me about his daughter."

"Did he? That's… not like him." She weighed Rosie up. "Did he tell you we have a lead?"

"No. A lead to what?"

"Her abduction."

Rosie's mouth formed a perfect circle before she snapped it shut.

"He didn't tell me she was abducted."

"No, he wouldn't. That's not like him either."

"How… long ago was it?"

"Twelve years."

"Oh my!" Rosie cried and then put a hand over her mouth. "That poor man."

"Yes. But, as I say, now we have a lead."

"You still think she's alive?"

Kate narrowed her eyes and paused before responding. "He does."

"The funeral is arranged for Tuesday." Roly took off his glasses and pinched the bridge of his nose. His wife looked at him with concern.

"Are you alright, love?"

"Yes." He said, not at all convincingly. Sally walked over to him and started massaging his neck and shoulders from behind. "Eddie's in hospital."

"Gosh, the good news just keeps on coming and coming!"

"Sal."

"I'm sorry, love, but there are so many silver linings here it's hard to know where to look."

She bent down and kissed his neck. He was as taut as a drum. She draped her arms over him and leant on his shoulders, embracing him. "Everything's going to be okay. Better than okay. We've got everything we want now."

"I haven't got a father."

"You never did have!" Sally cried. "He was a miserable, misanthropic, self-entitled bastard who treated you, and everyone else, like dirt or chattels or pawns in his schemes. He made our lives hell and I'm glad he's dead. There, I've said it!"

"Sal!" Roly implored, clasping her wrists to him.

"Never mind, Sal. I'm sorry for your loss. I'm sorry you're grieving. But I think you'll find it wears off pretty soon and you'll be able to look up into a bright future for all of us."

"I never wanted him dead!" Roly's body started to shake and Sally hugged him, shushing.

"Of course, you didn't."

"I just wanted him to see sense. Let me grow the business ethically and-"

"You wanted him to wake up and taste the twenty-first century and it was never going to happen."

"He pooh-poohed my ideas." Roly's voice was quiet and trembling.

"Of course, he did, sweetheart." Sally lowered her own voice and hugged him again. "He was a man of his time. And times have changed."

"He mocked my plans."

"I know. And they were great plans. Are great plans. And now you can put them into action!"

Roly nodded, silent.

"You are Baxters now." Sally urged. "You will do great things, I'm sure of it."

Roly sobbed softly while his wife continued to hold him. The pair held each other in silence as the light started to slowly fade, gloom gathering in the cosy kitchen.

"It's all my fault." He whispered, swallowing hard and trying to push away the tears.

"No. It's not. It really isn't. Please don't blame yourself, sweetheart."

"It is."

"How can it be? You didn't release the hens! You didn't convince Tesco to abandon the deal! You didn't give your father high blood pressure!"

"No." He paused. "But I did upload the video."

"No, you-. Wait, what?"

"It was my video that went viral.

@RestoreThePeckingOrder. That was me."

"But I thought it was the protesters?" Sally blinked, confused. "They took the video. I've seen the big woman on TV being interviewed. She's everywhere."

"Now she is. The breakout - yes, that's them. But that video? Exposing the conditions in the sheds the week before? That was mine. I took it and I uploaded it."

"No, hun. I heard her saying that they'd taken a video exposing the conditions."

"Oh, they took a video alright, but it was awful. No-one saw it. Got about 50 hits. Mine got 350,000."

Sally considered this news for a moment, in silence. Roly resumed shaking, his sobs louder this time, coming in great gulps and waves. She hugged him tightly to her, trying to squeeze the pain away, but on and on he went.

"And that night in the shed… when we found the girls." His voice was ragged now, ripped and raw. "There was a man called Cullen in some altercation with my father. In the cages. It was him who saved the girls, not me."

"Shush now. It's okay. It's okay."

"He went back in. And I let him!"

"Hey, hey! The girls were your top priority. Of course, they were."

"And now he's gone!"

Sally blew out a long, slow breath. "Yes, Roly. He's gone. He was going to go some day, and that day came. And we - and you - must move on. Think of Jemima! She's our future. She's what's important. And I think maybe Malcolm would have agreed with that."

"But he was my father!" Roly wailed, his cry echoing off the flagstone floor.

"Yes." Sally confirmed. "He was your father. But you

know what? He was never your Dad."

Rosie was washing dishes, gazing out at the rainclouds rolling in from the hills. On hearing a sound behind her she turned to see Cullen standing sheepishly, fully geared up with backpack on, ready to depart.

"You off then?"

"Yes." His voice was quiet and sad and Rosie put down her washing-up brush and wiped her hands on a tea towel.

"Without your hat?"

His eyes were puffy and a little red and he bowed his head as if to hide them from her. "I think she's earned it."

Rosie eyes widened in surprise. "Oh no. I wouldn't want Ellie to have something you need that is so personal - especially in this weather."

"It's been with me a long time. Seen a few things." He sighed. "Let it see some more - through a child's eyes."

"Are you sure?"

Cullen hesitated and then lifted his face to look at her. "Can I just say goodbye?"

"To Ellie? I think she's out."

"To my hat."

Rosie barely contained her smile and nodded. "Of course. You know where it is."

He turned and padded down the hall towards Ellie's room and Rosie heard him as his pack scraped through the door and he disappeared inside. She stood staring at empty space until he reappeared looking vaguely apologetic. Or maybe embarrassed. He was holding a small cardboard box in his hand.

"This if for you."

"Whatever for?" Rosie said, making no move to accept it.

Cullen proffered it again. "Please. I'd like you to have it." He gave her a strange look. "You might need it."

"Why would I-?" He thrust it into her hands and she looked down to see the word FRAGILE handwritten on the box lid. "What is it?"

"I'm sorry." He said, as if that was some sort of answer to her question. "Please say goodbye to Ellie for me."

"Are you sure you won't stay until she comes back? You can say goodbye yourself."

He looked so sad and weary, as if the simple act of remaining would wear him out.

"No." And then as an afterthought he said: "You have a wonderful daughter."

"Well… yes, I know. Thank-you." She looked down again at the present. "May I open it?"

He winced with his eyes and a shadow fell across his face. "I'd rather you waited until I've gone. I'm not… good at this sort of thing."

Rosie looked into his eyes and tilted her head slightly to one side. She spoke softly but wanted him to know she was in earnest. "Please take care, Cullen. You might have recuperated but you're not fully recovered as far as I'm concerned. It's cold and damp up on those hills, any time of year."

She gestured towards them with her head and his eyes followed and then flicked back to hers.

"I'll be fine. It's where I belong, out there. It feels… right."

Rosie smiled. "Well, we each have to do what we feel

is right. Don't we?"

He returned the smile, warmly this time. "I do."

And with that, he turned and let himself out of her kitchen door. Rosie turned back to the window and watched as he walked down the farm track between the fields, down to the footbridge across the burn. She put the cardboard box down on the windowsill and resumed her washing up, thinking. When she looked up again, he had crossed the bridge and was trudging up the hill, head-down, the rain starting to drive into him. She stood watching until he disappeared behind a copse and was gone from her sight.

"Oh shit." Elaine looked up and saw Jakki striding into the diner, heading straight for them. Shirley was right behind her. Elaine elbowed Paul next to her, his face buried deep in his fry-up.

"Quick!" Paul spluttered, looking up. "Eat the evidence!"

"Lover!" Shirley demanded when she reached the table, wide-eyed.

Paul swallowed a last mouthful, his plate still rich with grease and brown sauce. "It was a veggie sausage, vegan bacon and an organic, free-range egg."

"Was it?" Shirley asked.

"No." Paul relented. "Just a normal egg."

"You bloody liar!" Shirley turned on Elaine. "And you! He's weak, God knows. But you? I thought better of you."

"Lay, how could you?" Jakki added, her eyes wet with tears. Elaine cast her eyes down and said nothing, her own plate betraying her.

"What are you doing here?" Paul asked his partner, looking around the diner at friends who were now all suddenly intent on studying their own plates with renewed, silent interest.

"I could ask you the same question." Shirley mocked. "But what would be the point of that when I already know the answer?"

"It's not what it looks like."

"It bloody is! Do you think I'm puddled?"

"No, my sweet." Paul gave a weak smile but the wattage from Shirley's glare made it shrivel and die.

"Well, the course of action is now clear is it not?"

"Is it?" Paul glanced at Elaine for possible clarification but she was still sitting, ashamed, with her head down.

"It should be. Do you want your life to be governed and limited by episodes of gout?"

"No."

"Do you want to remain in a relationship with me?"

"Yes."

"So, can you perhaps guess what a suitable course of action would be?"

Paul pursed his lips. "I could apologise?"

"That would be a good start." Shirley agreed. "Followed by?"

"Um." Paul now realised he was on some kind of ascending barchart where each bar was higher than the next. He was going to have to keep going until Shirley considered he'd reached high enough and would permit him to stop. This thought made him carefully sequence his suggestions so that the order went up, not down, if only up by a tiny amount each time. Baby steps.

"A promise to not come here again?"

Shirley folded her arms. Okay, bigger steps were required.

"And agree to avoiding meat?" He proffered.

"Go on."

"Whilst limiting my alcohol intake to five-"

Shirley glared.

"Four?" Still glaring. "Two… days a week?"

"Pathetic." Shirley bristled. "Come on, we're leaving."

"Wha-?"

"You've finished, haven't you?" She looked over at Tricia. "Or have you ordered seconds?"

"No." Paul thought, instantly wondering why he'd never thought of that idea in all the previous visits here he'd made. "Although-"

"Right! Forget it."

"My sweet?"

"No. My sweet isn't going to cut it anymore." Shirley said through clenched teeth. "I never thought I'd say this, but my mother was right. I can't trust you. How could I ever trust you? You're so… weak!"

Shirley turned on her heels to go before shooting Elaine a stern glance and checking up at the clock on the wall. It showed 10.30am. "And I'll expect to see you at work in thirty minutes."

Elaine swallowed and gave a tiny nod and Shirley strode out of the now silent diner. As soon as the door closed behind her, the hubbub started up again, the atmosphere reshaping itself in the diner as if denying she had ever been there.

Paul looked sadly down at his empty plate, head bowed in reverence for what he now knew had been his last supper. Elaine put a gentle hand on his knee.

"Go after her."

"I can't."

"Do you love her?"

Paul nodded, dumbly.

"Then go after her."

"I can't". He repeated.

"Why not?"

Paul hesitated and then looked at her, his eyes wet. "Because she's right."

Elaine looked up reluctantly at Jakki who was wiping her own tears away. This act seemed to galvanise her.

"Paul, don't be a stupid bastard." Jakki said. "It's really very simple. Let me put it in terms even a man can understand. Look at me!"

Paul raised his eyes to meet hers and Jakki put her hands out, palms upwards, and weighed them like an empty scale in front of him. "Which do you love more? Meat? Or Shirley?"

Paul's gaze lingered on the empty scales as if hypnotised.

"Paul?"

"Shirley." His voice was small and lost, barely audible amid the diners' chatter.

"Right." Jakki snapped. "So go after her."

Paul looked up at her but didn't move. Jakki sighed. "Forget about… everything she said. She's angry. She's upset. All of that can be sorted out. If. You. Go. After. Her." Jakki admonished. "So… GO AFTER HER!"

Paul jumped at Jakki's bark and blinked.

"Good luck." Elaine whispered, patting his knee.

Paul silently nodded, slid himself out from the booth and trudged, stooping, out of the diner.

Satisfied, Jakki snuck in to the space left by Paul and sat next to her partner in silence. Eventually Elaine lifted her head and looked at her lover.

"I'm so sorry, Jaks. I should've told you."

"Yes. You should."

"I… I…" Elaine faltered. "The truth is… I just don't think I'm cut out to be a vegan."

"I can see that." Jakki looked down at her partner's plate and then back up to her face and held her gaze for several seconds. "I've been a fool and I'm sorry."

Elaine furrowed her brow. "*You're* sorry?"

"Yes." Jakki reached for Elaine's hand and held it between her own, stroking it. "I'm the vegan fangirl. I'm the one with a mission, the zealot. I've got what I wanted - it wasn't what you wanted. And why should it be?"

"I don't-"

"Lay. I've got what I wanted and now I don't think it's what I want at all. You should see our house. It's besieged. After you left this morning, vans and TV crews appeared out of nowhere, reporters jostling to shout through the letterbox, flashbulbs going off everywhere, stepladders by the gate. Someone called the police and they're cordoning the road off. The street is jammed. I had to close the curtains and sneak out the back."

Elaine watched as Jakki's face softened and emptied, her eyes roving up and out into empty space as she contemplated her own mental picture. "Phone keeps pinging and ringing. My Facebook page's gone mental and I'm trending on Twitter." Jakki's focus returned to her partner's face. "It feels like I'm in a war zone."

Elaine squeezed Jakki's hand but her partner was still shaking her head in disbelief and shame. "And, worse than that, in wanting it so much I put you in harm's way. Twice. You needed a bodyguard for Pete's sake! I've been an idiot."

"It's okay."

"Is it? You didn't want a part of it and I browbeat you. Like I browbeat you to be a vegan with me! And you tried - you really tried. I know that. But it's not you and you know what? That's okay! In fact, it's more than okay - it's actually preferable. Why should you be the same as me? Everyone's different and differences can be amazing! Fantastic things can come from being different. And you and me - we're fantastic! And that's what I had and what I lost sight of. What's the point of me going in search of internet fame believing it'll make me happy when what makes me happy is right under my nose. We were happy and I insisted on changing things - changing things so much. And you, because you love me, went along with it. Didn't want to hurt me. So I kept pushing and pushing, leaving less and less space for you until you had to run and hide in the shadows where I couldn't see you."

She lifted Elaine's hand to her mouth and kissed it.

"And that's where I found you." Jakki looked up and around at the busy diner.

Elaine gazed into her lover's eyes and lifted her other hand to stroke Jakki's face. "How did you find me, here?"

"Shirley saw Paul's van." Jakki gave a wry smile. "I had a hunch."

Elaine smiled back. "Well. I'll forgive you if you forgive me?"

Jakki sniffed back tears. "Sensible Elaine, you have a deal."

Elaine held out both hands - weighing an empty scale. "Which do you love more: fame or Elaine?"

"Elaine."

Elaine kissed Jakki and let out an enormous sigh. "I love you, Jakki Banks."

"And I love you, Sensible Elaine."

"Mum! Come see!" Ellie had raced into the kitchen breathless with excitement. She grabbed her mother by her skirt and start dragging her towards the door.

"What sweetheart?" Rosie said, laughing. "What is it?"

"It's a surprise! Come see!"

Rosie took hold of her hand, her daughter's fingers wriggling in her grasp like an excited eel, and let herself be led down the hall to Ellie's bedroom. "Shall I close my eyes?"

"Ooh, yes. Good idea."

They stopped at the threshold and Rosie made a show of holding her apron over her face and letting Ellie lead her slowly into the room. It was warm and dark, the sound of soft clucking adding to the intimacy of the space.

"Okay. You can open them now."

Rosie unpeeled the apron from her face and looked down at her daughter. Ellie was pointing proudly to Misty's cage where the bird was strutting around like a gold-medal winner, flicking straw up in the air as if trying to create the effect of a confetti cannon celebrating a royal birth. Rosie couldn't quite work out what the surprise must be - a strangely exultant Misty strutting in her cage was some cause for celebration she supposed; at least it must mean she was on the mend. But it wasn't sufficient to create this level of excitement in her daughter.

And then she saw it.

In the far corner of the cage was Cullen's upturned hat half-filled with straw sitting on its blanket - a throne more than a nest, at least in this triumphant little scene before here. Nestling delightfully in the centre of this nest was a perfectly-shaped egg, speckled and a beautiful pale blue, a rare gem winking in the dust.

"Misty laid an egg!" Ellie shrieked and jumped on the spot. "She's laid an egg and it's so beautiful!" Her daughter clasped her hands together under her chin and hugged herself in delight.

Rosie couldn't stop herself from smiling and shaking her head in wonder. "What a clever girl she is, darling. And you too - for bringing her back to health so she would lay again. Well done you! Shall we take a photo so that you can put it in your Badge book?"

Ellie shot out of the room and went in search of her mother's phone. While she was gone, Rosie scrutinised the hen and the egg in its nest, looked at Misty as she peacocked around its cage. She moved over to the window and pulled back the curtains, flooding the room with Sunday morning light. Ellie dashed back in and Rosie unlocked her phone and handed it back to her daughter so she could take a picture with it.

"I'll get that printed out later, sweetheart." Rosie said. "Gosh - wait until we tell Dad."

"And Mister Cullen!" Ellie's eyes grew even wider.

"I'm afraid Mister Cullen had to go, sweetheart. He said for me to say Goodbye to you." Rosie bit her lip as she watched Ellie's face crumple.

"But Misty's laid an egg! In Mister Cullen's hat!" Her daughter had dashed from delight to despair in a moment and, despite having seen this a hundred times in her daughter's young life, Rosie still felt her own heart break a little every time it happened. She tried a kindly smile but Ellie's lips trembled just the same. "He has to see it, Mum."

"I can send him the photo, darling." Rosie suggested, wondering to herself how in hell she would ever be able to do that to a man whose number she didn't know and who probably didn't even own a phone.

Ellie sighed. "It won't be the same."

"I know, sweetheart. I'm sorry." She searched for some words of consolation. "But look - he has left you his hat. And that is a very special gift because I know how much that hat meant to Mister Cullen. So, think how pleased he'll be to know that Misty laid an egg in it. When I send him the photo."

"I suppose so." Ellie's imagination was already starting the speedy process of transitioning her back into happiness and hope. "Maybe we can send him a photo every time she lays an egg?"

"Every time?" Rosie said, hesitantly.

"Yes! Now she's laid an egg, she'll lay one every day, won't she? That's what you said, isn't it?" Ellie looked up at her mother, expectation in her eyes.

"Um. Yes. I did, didn't I?" Rosie looked again at the unhealthy scrawny bird, still with scraggy sections of plumage and flaking patches on its legs, and this perfect blue egg. How on earth had it even managed to lay this one?

Ellie was skipping around in a small circle, clapping, scuffing up her rug. "I'm going to show Jemima."

"Yes, sweetheart. That's a good idea." Rosie watched absently as her daughter skipped out of the room and out of the house in search of her friend. A sudden thought occurred to her and she wandered back into the kitchen and reached for the cardboard box still sitting on the window ledge where she had left it.

The box wasn't sealed shut, just the flaps tucked underneath each other to keep it closed. Gently she pulled back the top flap and revealed a folded piece of A4 sitting atop a pile of straw. Picking up the sheet of paper revealed a blue carton of eggs underneath, the label *Blue Maran Superior Organic Free Range Eggs* emblazoned across the lid. She flipped the carton open and found five identical beautiful blue speckled eggs and one empty space.

Rosie looked up and out of the window, the sun shining brightly over the fields and her daughter dashing happily down the farm track, pushing on her scooter with all her might, her hair streaming behind her as she flew. Rosie raised her eyes up to the Moorfoot hills as if expecting to see Cullen standing there, arm raised in one final salute before disappearing out of sight.

But, of course, he wasn't there. All that was left of him was his hat in her daughter's room, this carton of eggs and two words on the sheet of paper: DUTY CALLS.

"Why Misty?" Paul was struggling with a Pepperami which was getting stuck in his teeth as he chewed on it.

"Hmm?"

"Why did the little girl call her hen Misty?"

Paul was sitting with the sun behind him as he waited patiently for the fish to bite on Gladhouse Reservoir. Cullen squinted at him and blew out his cheeks. "Is that the full extent of your interest in the whole story? Really?"

"Well, it's a missed opportunity isn't it?"

"Is it?"

"Well, it's not every day you get to name a chicken. You could do so much better than Misty."

"Like?"

"Well, what about… Eggy Pop!"

"Who?"

"Or David Peck'em! That's a good one."

"You do know chickens are female?"

"Oh yeah. Alright then, what about…. Shelly Bassey!"

Cullen rolled his eyes.

"Laidy Luck! No, wait - Laidy Cluck!"

"Look-"

"Yolko Ono!"

"Will you shut up about the hen?"

"Just sayin'."

"Please don't. Misty is a perfectly fine name for a hen if you're nearly seven."

"Margaret Hatcher!"

"Shut up!"

Paul heaved his shoulders and sulked. Cullen treasured the silence for a long time.

"So, how's the Shirley-enforced diet going." He eyed the pork product wrapper Paul was stuffing into his pocket.

Paul dimmed. "We've fallen out."

"Oh."

"I have to choose meat or her."

"So, you've chosen meat?"

"No!"

"Um, exhibit A?" Cullen nodded to Paul's pocket.

"I'm just… thinking about it. While I eat."

"A last supper sort of thing, you mean?"

Paul sighed. "I said I can change, she says I can't."

"You haven't."

"I could! I'm just... fond of bacon."

"And pies. And pork and ham and sausages and-"

"Oh, sausages." Paul sniffed the air as if in expectation of a freshly-cooked delivery. When one failed to appear, his mood darkened once more. "All this non-meat stuff. It's hard! Have you ever had blackened tuna with cabbage?"

"No."

"Don't. It tastes like cremated mermaid. But in a bad way."

"Anything worth doing is usually hard."

"That's helpful." Paul pulled a face and looked to the horizon. "If I'm ever to have a chance with Shirl again, I have to deny the existence of bacon. Forever."

"Why?"

"There was... let's just call it *an incident*."

Cullen raised an eyebrow. "Are you sure?"

"That I have to renounce bacon?" Paul considered. "Okay, no. I'm guessing. Have to because she won't bloomin' talk to me."

"Maybe it's not the meat that's the problem." Cullen volunteered.

"Eh?"

"Maybe it's the deceit."

Paul considered this for a moment. "Pretty sure it's the meat."

The two men sat in silence for a while, each alone with their own thoughts.

"So, what are you going to do?" Cullen asked.

"I don't know." Paul said, glumly.

"Maybe there's a halfway house. A compromise. You

don't need to completely forgo meat but you do need to show her you can change and that she can trust you again."

"Or?"

"Or that's the end."

"But I don't want it to be the end."

Cullen shrugged. "Everything has an end."

"Aye." Paul said forlornly. "But sausages have two."

"I'm going to dedicate my badge to my Grandpa." Jemima said, looking more mature than her years when she nodded her head with a determined pout.

"What does *decidate* mean?" asked Ellie.

"To remember him by."

"Is he in heaven now?" Ellie looked up at the sky as she stroked Misty on her lap.

"Yes. I said a prayer to him last night. I asked him to ask God to give me my Brownie Badge."

"Can he do that?"

"Of course." Jemima confirmed. "When you're in heaven God is there too. You can go and chat to him if you like. Although you probably need to make an appointment."

"I don't think I need God's help." Ellie gave a firm little shake of her head, her eyes bright with wonder. "I've got blue eggs!"

"That is very unusual." Jemima's poultry knowledge was extensive and Ellie knew it. She smiled at this acknowledgement of Misty's special gift.

"I think…" Ellie confided, her voice dropping to a hush. "…they might be magic eggs."

"What sort of magic eggs?"

"I don't know. I would have liked to ask Mister Cullen but he's gone away."

"Is he coming back?"

"I don't know. Mum says he probably won't." Ellie looked sad, then brightened. "I could decidate my badge to Mister Cullen!"

"Yes." Jemima agreed. "But he left his hat!"

"He said I could have it." Ellie nodded to herself, validating the statement. "For ever and ever."

"Amen."

"Why do you say *Amen*?"

"Because that's the law. Whenever you say *for ever and ever* you have to end it with *Amen*."

Ellie closed her eyes tightly. "For ever and ever, Amen." She paused. "What does *Amen* mean?"

"It means *thank you very much and good-day to you*." Declared Jemima. "It's how you end a phonecall with God. Or baby Jesus."

Truly, there was no end to her friend's amazing knowledge. This is what her Mum must mean when she talked about public school education.

"What do blue eggs taste like?" Jemima asked.

"They taste just like normal eggs." Ellie admitted, the disappointment clear in her voice. She had been expecting something special when her Mum had boiled one for her breakfast that first time. Her dejection had been palpable. They hadn't even been blue on the inside.

"Well, it doesn't sound like they're magic eggs, then. That's a pity."

"They could still be magic!"

"How?"

"Because Misty never laid any eggs before and now she has Mister Cullen's hat as a nest she has laid blue eggs!"

"But that means Mister Cullen's hat is magic, not the eggs!"

"Oh!" Ellie was astounded at her friend's intelligence. "Yes, it's a magic hat!" She jumped up, startling Misty who clucked unhappily away, and started skipping in a circle, clapping her hands as she went. "I've got a magic ha-at! I've got a magic ha-at!"

"Well, it may be magic." Jemima sniffed. "But if all it does is make eggs laid in it look blue, then it's not *very* magical is it?"

But Ellie didn't care. She had a magic hat, a rejuvenated pet that laid special blue eggs and both of them would help her win her first Brownie Badge. As far as Ellie was concerned, you really couldn't get much more magical than that.

POSTSCRIPT

Roland Baxter inherited his father's estate in its entirety and is currently successfully steering the business along the organic/animal welfare strategy outlined in his business plan, *Baxter:The Future?* As part of this strategy he purchased a flock of Blue Maran hens and delivers two cartons of their eggs each week to the Critchley household, free of charge.

Jakki Banks deleted all of her SLAAC social media accounts and married **Elaine Dunwoody** in Eddleston Parish Church. Every Sunday they go together to Tricia's Diner where Jakki buys Elaine a cooked breakfast.

"Sensible" Elaine Dunwoody accepted an offer from Roland to take her old job back and apologised to Shirley for doing so. The pair remain good friends. In a bid to lose her *sensible* moniker she took a pair of edible knickers on honeymoon.

In accordance with The Land Reform (Scotland) Act 2016, **Ewan & Rosemary Critchley** were able to purchase their farm and land from Baxter Farms, for the sum of £1, after Roland rescinded the eviction order. Ewan and Roland spent a weekend together up on the Moorfoots removing all traces of razor wire from the grouse shoots. Every morning, before Ellie is awake, Rosie creeps into her room and plants an egg in Misty's nest.

Ellie Critchley was enrolled in Brownies after her seventh birthday and awarded her *Keeping A Pet* badge. She is currently working towards her *Grow Your Own* badge whilst doing everything she can to avoid eating her own vegdibbles. Every night she says a prayer for Mister Cullen and then says *thank you very much and good day to you* to the Baby Jesus.

Eddie Helpmann was treated in hospital for anal-penetrative wounds consistent with those caused by a large blunt instrument. He has difficulty sitting. He was dismissed from Baxter Farms and deported to South Africa after it came to light that he had never been granted a full working visa. He took with him his only personal possessions: his knopkierie, and a water-damaged, badly burnt diary.

Cheryl Kilshaw signed a Key Supplier Agreement with Baxter Farms Limited to supply all of Tesco's Free Range Organic eggs in Scotland. She now only eats medium eggs.

Detective Chief Superintendent Kate Lorimer continues to pursue all leads in the reopened investigation into Operation Merlin. She keeps Cullen's number at the top of her Contacts list.

Detective Sergeant Dean Jenkins completed the remainder of his uniformed stint and is now back in plain clothes doing the job he hates. He is very much looking forward to his retirement.

Shirley Harriet Stevenson still manages the Greggs branch in Peebles. She disappears into the back office whenever Paul comes into her shop, only to peek at him wistfully through the one-way glass.

Paul McInnes has made it known, via his network of contacts at the Lamb & Flag, that he is available for bodyguard services at reasonable rates. So far, he has had no takers. Meanwhile, can he win Shirley back? Find out in the free follow-on short story *Teetering On The Veg* by signing up to the Cullen & Big Paul Fan Club at *https://download.markfarrer.com/misty.*

Mungo James Cullen resumed sleeping rough after his physical injuries healed. He continues to roam the Scottish Borders in search of clues to his daughter's fate and has developed a new habit of keeping his mobile phone on him and charged at all times.

AUTHOR'S NOTE

I am indebted to Charles Scott and his mother Corinne, at Howden Farm in East Lothian, for giving me a tour of their premises. I can wholeheartedly recommend them as suppliers of Free Range & Organic eggs produced to the highest animal welfare practices - not just because they gave me a free tray of double-yolkers. They very kindly spent time with me and listened to my questions about egg production and poultry welfare whilst gamely batting away ideas as to how someone might meet a sticky end in the bowels of a chicken shed. In the end, though, they gave me the idea I actually used here with Malcolm, so that was handy. Their own farm is spotless and in no way resembles the horrendous descriptions I have used in this book. But where's the fun in describing lovely facilities when you can write about a fictitious monster and the appalling conditions he condones?

I'd also like to point out that Baxter Farms are in no way based on, connected with or in any way related to, any other egg production facility that may, or may not, sit at the base of the Moorfoots on the A703. I know no-one who has ever worked at such a hypothetical facility, have never spoken to anyone involved (past or present) or seen inside it and have only used its theoretical location as the embryo (sorry) of this book. I imagine the business practices and production facilities of such a company would in no way resemble the ones I have described here. And anyway, they are already a major supplier of eggs to Tesco. Probably.

There is, alas, no Pet badge in the Brownies My Badge Book - at least not in the UK (although there is in the US). This is a damn shame, quite frankly, and I'd like to think that if any of the powers that be read this book they will introduce one pronto. I actually bought a copy of the Brownies My Badge Book as part of my research and was gutted to find this omission. At least I can claim it back on expenses.

Tricia's Diner is based on a former establishment called the Scots Pine Tea Rooms, a single storey building just outside Eddleston. I never went in but I imagine it was never, ever, anything the like the one I depict here. The original building now stands empty, although I recently saw some work going on there so perhaps it will be reborn as something approaching Tricia's one day.

The more observant amongst you might notice that the subordinate policeman in this book is called Jenkins. Again. I have to admit that I didn't realise until I checked back to find that, in *Where Seagulls Dare* and *The Good The Bad & The Rugby,* there are two other policemen also called Jenkins. I must stress that all three of these police officers are different, fictitious people and unrelated to each other - it just seems to me that Jenkins is a damn good name for a policeman, so I left it in as a bit of fun to mess with the pseuds. Maybe I'll make a little in-joke of calling all my policemen Jenkins. We'll see.

The letter of recommendation that Malcolm wrote for

Sensible Elaine is based on personal references from my own line managers down the years. Only joking. Or am I? Yes, I am. They were taken from the *Lexicon of Intentionally Ambiguous Recommendations (L.I.A.R)* by *Robert Thornton*, a bestselling book which is packed with them.

Thanks to JT for another superb cover design and for putting up with my unconstructive yet insistent demands for "a greener green" or "more 3D straw" or any of the other myriad changes he so patiently and skilfully rendered until I was happy with it. And, while I'm on about the cover: No, it's not a cockerel, it is a Lohmann Silver hen - a widespread and popular egg-layer which looks remarkably like the hen on the front cover. These things don't just happen by chance you know. Google it if you don't believe me. And No, they don't lay blue eggs - but I have explained the blue eggs in the story, so there. I know it looks like someone is taking the egg away rather than putting it there, but you know better now, don't you? It can be our little secret.

My usual shout out to Big Paul, for allowing me to draw a completely fictitious representation of him and his life. He would though, I imagine, be similarly unimpressed with the diet Shirley imposed on him. I would be. I'll double-check next time I see him - if he's still talking to me, now that Shirley's not talking to him.

Penultimately, I'd like to thank my Beta readers: Deidre M, John K, Madeleine N, Pete B and Mike M. They were incredibly helpful in pointing out issues, errors, inconsistencies and identifying where I'd completely misunderstood my own character creations. They were nearly always right and I hope the finished book is worth the effort they spent helping me with it. It means a huge amount to me to know that I have a team of Beta readers prepared - even eager - to read my stuff and help make it better. Thank you all.

And last, but by no means least, my partner and Alpha reader, Claire. She is without doubt the most helpful, valuable, patient and constructive critic I could have and this book would not be the same without her.
Thanks, Sweetie.

As usual, I take full blame and responsibility for any inaccuracies or omissions. I've had to say it many times in my life, but I'll say it again: *it's all my fault.*

Finally, to those of you crying "Oh No! What about Paul and Shirley? Will they ever get back together again?"
My answer is: *Trust the soup.*

mjf
20.11.2020

Tell others what you thought…

As an indie author I am highly reliant on user reviews to help other readers decide whether my books might be for them. If you enjoyed this book, please tell your friends and leave a review on Amazon at ***http://a-fwd.to/4GYrMH4***

CULLEN & BIG PAUL will return in …

TROUBLE WITH THE PERV

COMING SPRING 2021

Until then, you can read more **Cullen and Big Paul** adventures by going to

https://bit.ly/3fT9klR

About the Author

You can learn more about Mark Farrer at www.markfarrer.com, like him on Facebook here or follow him on Twitter @mark_farrer

Printed in Great Britain
by Amazon

62070068R00219